Rebecca Muddiman

Rebecca Muddiman is from Redcar and has lived there all her life except for time working in Holland, where she lived on a canal boat, and in London, where she lived six feet away from Brixton prison. She has a degree in Film and Media and an MA in Creative Writing. She won a Northern Writers' Time to Write Award in 2010 and the Northern Crime Competition in 2012. Her first novel, *Stolen*, was published in 2013, and her second, *Gone*, in 2015. She lives with her boyfriend, Stephen, and dog, Cotton, in a semi-detached house which they have christened 'Murder Cottage'.

Also by Rebecca Muddiman

Stolen
Gone

REBECCA MUDDIMAN

Tell Me Lies

MULHOLLAND
BOOKS
HODDER

First published in Great Britain in 2016 by Mulholland Books
An imprint of Hodder & Stoughton
An Hachette UK company

First published in paperback in 2016

1

A CIP catalogue record for this title is available from the British Library

Paperback ISBN 978 1 444 79164 8
eBook ISBN 978 1 444 79166 2

Printed and bound by Clays Ltd, St Ives plc

Hodder & Stoughton policy is to use papers that are natural, renewable
and recyclable products and made from wood grown in sustainable
forests. The logging and manufacturing processes are expected to
conform to the environmental regulations of the country of origin.

Hodder & Stoughton Ltd
Carmelite House
50 Victoria Embankment
London EC4Y 0DZ

www.hodder.co.uk

To Jonathan and Donna

PART I

PART I

I
Tuesday, 28 December

'Pick up, pick up, pick up. Please.'

She fumbled with her phone, dialling another number, praying to God that he'd answer her. 'Please, please, please . . .'

The ringing cut off. She was through to voicemail. But what should she say?

'Daddy. You've got to come over. It's . . . Just come. Please.'

She hung up. Her heart was hammering in her chest and she could feel dampness seeping through her jeans onto her knees. She wondered if it was the frost or the blood.

She tried calling again. Tried another number. Why wouldn't he answer her? Why wouldn't *anyone* answer?

She closed her eyes. She could hear a bird chirping somewhere. She tried to focus on that. Tried to get out of her own body, her own thoughts. *Think about the bird.*

Still no answer. Who else? Who else could help her?

She tried another number, listened to the ringing, drowning out the bird.

'Where are you? I need you. I don't know what to do. Please call me back.' She dropped her hand to her side. Clutched her phone. 'Please, tell me what to do,' she whispered.

She stood up. Her legs were soaked, frozen. She wanted to go back into the house but she couldn't. What if someone saw her? What would that look like? Just leaving him there?

She squeezed the phone in her hand. Anger started to creep in through the gaps in her fear. Why had they just left her to deal with this alone? Again. They all claimed to love her. Claimed they'd protect her until the ends of the earth and yet they'd all disappeared. All hiding somewhere, away from the mess. Away from her.

She threw her phone to the ground and it landed beside him. Almost touching him. He could've reached out and taken it, easily, if he wanted to. He'd always wanted to before. Always checking her phone. Always asking where she'd been. Who she was with. What she'd done.

And what had she done?

She stepped closer. She was standing over him now. He looked smaller than usual – feeble, somehow. She kind of liked it.

Her feet were almost touching him. She wondered if she kicked him whether it would leave a mark. If they'd know she'd done it.

She blinked and stepped away. What was she doing? She picked up the phone, rubbing it against her thigh to dry it off. She knew what she had to do; knew that no one else was going to help her now.

She made another call. This one was answered straight away.

She listened to the words the woman said. She'd heard them before so many times but only on TV. It seemed strange that they were the same words in real life.

'Hello?'

She realised that the TV words had stopped and she didn't know what to say. What was the next line? Maybe if she'd stuck with drama school she'd have been able to do this better. Do something right for a change.

'He's dead,' she said. It wasn't the best opening line but it'd do. It was the truth at least.

'Who's dead?'

'Ritchie.'

'Who's Ritchie?'

'My boyfriend. Ex-boyfriend.' She wondered if the woman thought she meant ex in the sense that he was dead. But that's not what she meant. 'We broke up weeks ago,' she explained. 'I broke up with him. He didn't want to.'

'Okay, love, what's your name?'

'Lauren. Lauren James.'

'Okay, Lauren. Where are you?'

'At my house. In the back garden.'

'Okay. And where's your house? What's your address?'

Lauren reeled off her address as she stood looking down at him. She could still hear the bird singing somewhere above her head. She wanted to focus on the bird but the woman on the phone interrupted.

'Okay, Lauren. An ambulance is on the way. Can you—'

'It's no good. He's dead already.'

'Okay. Can you tell me what happened?'

'I don't know.'

'Did you find him?'

'Yes.'

'When?'

'Not long ago. I saw him in the garden. I looked out the window and saw him. On the ground.'

'Did he have an accident?'

'I don't think so.'

'Is he ill? Heart problems?'

'No.'

'Tell me what you see, Lauren.'

'Ritchie. He's dead.'

'Did you check his pulse?'

'No,' Lauren said.

'Okay, do you think you could try that?'

'No,' she said. 'I can't. There's too much blood. Too much . . .'

'Okay, Lauren. It's okay. The ambulance will be there soon.'

'It's too late,' Lauren said. 'He's dead. Send the police.'

Lauren hung up the phone. She could hear the bird again but this time it was louder, not so sweet. Not a bird, a siren.

2

Lauren sat on the garden bench watching the paramedics pack up their things. She'd seen the disappointment on their faces when they saw the state of Ritchie. There was nothing they could do. But she'd told them that. Told the lady on the phone. Ritchie didn't need an ambulance. He didn't need anything any more.

But they'd looked at her like she was to blame. That she'd wasted their time. The one with the moustache glared at her. The other one, the skinny one, asked her if she was okay. But she could tell he didn't care too much. She nodded and so he turned back to his partner and they both looked past her as more people showed up. Police, this time. And then she didn't remember much. She watched them as they walked up to Ritchie as if they didn't quite believe her when she'd told them he was dead. But why would she lie about it? Why would someone say their boyfriend – ex-boyfriend – was dead in their back garden when he wasn't?

She could hear them talking, hear their radios. Hear them moving around her. But nothing made sense. It was like just another scene from *The Bill*. If only she'd watched to the end instead of falling asleep in front of the TV. Maybe she'd know what to do.

Lauren closed her eyes. Her head was banging. She shouldn't have drunk so much last night, but it was too late for regrets now. She had bigger things to deal with: the police, the body, her dad. What would her dad say when he found out?

She wondered if Peter would be the one to tell him. If he'd go straight to her dad or if he'd do what she'd asked first. She'd called him again after hanging up on the police. She'd done what she had to. Done the right thing. Now she needed to protect herself.

Lauren opened her eyes to the commotion around her, the police, the paramedics, on their way out now. More people showed up. Men in suits, mostly. Some carried cases, bags of tricks. One started to pull on a plastic suit and she turned away. Someone was holding a reel of blue and white tape, someone else pointed towards the alley. This was a crime scene. That's what it was.

She looked at the small crowd gathering by her back door. Another new face had arrived. This time people collected around him, talked at him. She heard someone address him as DI Gardner. He seemed to take it all in before speaking. And then he looked past them all to where Ritchie was. His eyes narrowed. Maybe he should've been wearing glasses.

Lauren stared at him and a shiver went through her as Gardner looked in her direction. Their eyes met and she felt like she was being judged.

3

DI Michael Gardner stood on the patio, stamping his feet in an attempt to warm them up, and listened to each person relate in turn what they knew. He glanced down the garden, seeing the body at the end, sprawled, face down. The house owner, Lauren James, had called it in. He scanned the small crowd for her, stopping when he saw a young woman, late twenties at most, standing a few yards away, her jeans soaked with blood and mud. She saw him looking at her, held his gaze. Didn't look too distraught for someone who'd found her ex-boyfriend dead in her garden.

He focused his attention back to those around him. The deceased, Richard Donoghue, had several injuries, mostly to the head. Time of death was approximately six to ten hours ago.

Gardner checked his watch. Nine fifteen a.m.

He stepped out of the huddle and assessed his surroundings. Lauren James couldn't have been short of money. Her house was large, detached, in one of the nicer parts of Middlesbrough, a part they rarely talked about on the news. The garden was bordered by tall hedges on both sides. She liked her privacy.

He stepped onto the lawn, facing the house. Lauren had apparently seen the body from the kitchen window when she came down this morning. He looked up at the neighbouring houses and then back down the garden towards the body. The garden was long. It was likely a neighbour could see the end of it from an upstairs window. He'd check with them later, but for now he headed for Lauren.

'Ms James?' She nodded. 'I'm DI Gardner.'

Lauren barely made eye contact, instead looking beyond him. She didn't look like she'd been crying at all but maybe she was in shock.

'Sir?'

Gardner turned to find one of the uniforms nodding towards the gate they'd all come through. DCI Atherton walked in, catching Gardner's eye immediately.

'Excuse me,' Gardner said to Lauren, and walked slowly towards Atherton. He wondered why his boss was there. He rarely got his hands dirty, only when it was a high-profile case. As far as Gardner could tell this was not a high-profile case. The name Richard Donoghue rang a distant bell but Gardner got the feeling it was because he was some low-level criminal who'd made a small impression rather than that he was some kind of kingpin. So what was Atherton's interest?

Gardner was about to ask Atherton when someone else came through the gate. Detective Superintendent Hadley. What the fuck was Hadley doing here? Gardner wondered what he was missing. The bloody Queen would turn up in a minute.

He glanced back at Lauren for a reaction. Maybe Hadley was a relative. That'd explain Atherton's arrival, too. Ready to kiss arse at any given moment. But Lauren didn't show any sign of recognition.

'Atherton,' Hadley called out, and he jumped round like a trained poodle. Hadley took Atherton aside and had a quiet word.

Laindon [laikiosk2]
Please keep your receipt
Renewals/Enquiries: 03456037628

Borrowed Items 13/02/2018 16:21
XXXXXXXXXX6011

Item Title	Due Date
* Tell me lies	06/03/2018
* It started with a tweet	06/03/2018

* Indicates items borrowed today
Thank you for using Essex Libraries

www.essex.gov.uk/libraries
or visit www.essexcc.gov.uk/libraries

Gardner waited for the confab to finish so he could g
orders but Atherton and Hadley kept talking, glanci
Lauren every so often until their eyes settled on Gardner.
Hadley patted Atherton on the shoulder before walking away.

'What was that about?' Gardner asked Atherton as he came
towards him.

'What was that about, *sir*?' Atherton said and Gardner
wanted to punch him in the face. He refused to repeat his
question but he knew that wasn't the point anyway. 'Is there
something I should know about the case?' Gardner asked.

'Superintendent Hadley wants me to be SIO on this,' Atherton said.

'Why? I'm quite capable of—'

'I know your capabilities, Inspector, but Hadley wants me
on it. You will act as deputy SIO.'

Gardner knew there was no point arguing. If Hadley wanted
Atherton, there had to be a reason. Whether Gardner was ever
let in on that reason was another matter. All he knew was that
he was the better detective. Atherton was a politician.

'He's someone important, then?' Gardner said, nodding
towards the body of Ritchie Donoghue.

'Not so far as I'm aware. But she is,' Atherton said, his eyes
settling on Lauren James.

'Make sure none of them get past the cordons in the alley,'
Hadley said to no one in particular, addressing those gathered
by the house as one before wandering back over, interrupting
Gardner and Atherton. 'Media's here already,' he said.

Gardner studied Hadley's face, trying to work out how
concerned he was, whether this was going to be an enormous, or merely a large, pain in the arse. He still didn't know
who the hell Lauren James was but she was clearly someone
worth something for Hadley to be there. Gardner hadn't had
much to do with Hadley personally, didn't know a great deal

about the man. He knew he was capable; he hadn't got where he was through politics alone, though it helped. But there'd always been rumours that Hadley was someone willing to turn a blind eye to certain things. Gardner didn't know if those rumours had any truth to them, but he wasn't willing to discount them altogether. Hadley was a climber, just as much as Atherton, and just because someone is good at their job, doesn't mean they're not also immoral. Gardner would take orders from the man but it didn't mean he'd grant him his trust.

'Should I talk to them?' Atherton said, nodding over his shoulder towards the gathering reporters they could hear beyond the fence.

'No. I'll handle it. I don't want any names out there yet but no doubt it won't be long before the rumour mill starts to turn.' Hadley glanced down the garden, his eyes resting on the prone body of Donoghue. 'I really hope something horrible happens today. Make this look about as interesting as littering.' He sighed and then walked away.

'So?' Gardner asked. 'Who is she?'

'Lauren James,' Atherton said and Gardner shrugged. 'Daughter of Walter James.'

Gardner felt his stomach drop. At least now he knew why Atherton was there. Why Hadley was there. But knowing didn't make it any more palatable.

Walter James. A man with fingers in so many pies Gardner was amazed he hadn't burnt them all off. Self-made millionaire. Owner of various businesses. On more committees and boards than it was really necessary for one man to be. A man with connections to anywhere that could give him a little boost of power, the local police department included. Also, a man who was currently campaigning to be elected as MP for Middlesbrough.

Gardner doubted that Walter James would win the seat. Despite playing up to both sides – his humble beginnings were flaunted in some areas, his status as Rich Important Man highlighted elsewhere – Gardner got the impression not many people liked him. Or maybe that was just him. Either way, James had little experience; a few years as a councillor at best. Surely no one was going to vote for him, even if the other options were limited. As far as Gardner could tell, the campaign was nothing more than another way to boost his ego and his profile, another grasp at the power he desperately wanted.

But win or lose, the man *did* have power, if only because of his available cash flow and his association with those in real positions of power. One of James's campaign slogans was 'Family First', a ridiculous proposal from a man on his third marriage. But it seemed those marriages had been another stepping stone to his power grab. His former brother-in-law, from marriage number two, was a high-ranking officer, currently the head of the Professional Standards department. His current brother-in-law, a man who was apparently easily swayed by gifts, was a member of the police authority. Having the ear of both men meant Walter James was someone to be careful around. Basically, the man was a major pain in the arse.

Gardner had never liked him; he had the smarm and smugness of the politician turned up to eleven. But more than that he interfered in things that weren't his business. Gardner was aware of several cases that had been prevented from going to court due to Walter James's intervention. Often it was due to some business association rather than him trying to help out a mate. As long as his money was protected, James didn't seem to give a damn whether his associates were sent down. But if it was going to affect him in any way, then clearly something had to be done. Favours had to be called in. Gardner himself had never had any major investigation disrupted by James but about a year earlier, Gardner had arrested James's son, Guy. If things had gone smoothly, Guy would've been looking at a prison sentence for possession with intent to supply, but the case never got past the first hurdle. Somehow all the evidence seemed to disappear in a puff of smoke. It was hardly the crime of the century. Guy James was a stupid little rich kid rather than anyone they should really be concerned with. But it bothered him nonetheless.

Since then, any mention of James's name – and with his campaign in full swing it seemed to be mentioned a dozen times a day – made him bristle. So no, he didn't want to be working on a case in any way related to the man.

This investigation wasn't going to be allowed to proceed as normal. Walter James would see to that. He had friends in high places and clearly wasn't afraid to call in favours. Gardner looked around for Hadley and found him beside Lauren James.

Atherton leaned in towards Gardner, his voice low. 'I don't think I need to tell you that this is a sensitive matter.'

'A murder, you mean?' Gardner said. 'I always treat murders with sensitivity. It's part of the training.'

Atherton did his almost-laugh thing and then scowled at Gardner. 'This needs to be dealt with quickly and quietly. If you can't help me with that, I'll find someone who can.'

Gardner wanted to tell him he'd treat this case the same as any other case, but Atherton had already walked away.

Gardner watched the three of them – Atherton, Hadley and Lauren. Apart from the blood on her knees, they looked for all the world like they were gossiping at a fundraiser, not standing yards away from a dead body. Hadley's hand rested on Lauren's shoulder. Protective. Reassuring.

Hadley looked up at Gardner, nodding, before breaking away from the party. Gardner steeled himself. 'I just want to say you and DCI Atherton have all of my confidence. I'm sure you'll clear this up for us.'

Gardner smiled. 'That's what I'm here for.'

Hadley gave him a tight smile and straightened his tie. 'I'll leave you to it,' he said and walked back to Lauren and Atherton. Gardner watched as Hadley said something into Atherton's ear before disappearing to spin some stories to the press.

Gardner knew that Hadley was tight with Walter James. Had seen the photographs of them together at charity events, had read all the sickening sycophantic shows of support in the papers. There was no way Hadley was going to let this investigation proceed as normal either. At least not until Lauren was cleared of any suspicion.

Walter James was going to make sure his daughter didn't go down for this. But Gardner wasn't about to let someone guilty get away with anything. He didn't give a shit whose daughter she was. If Lauren James had killed Ritchie Donoghue, he was going to prove it.

4

One hour later, Gardner was fuming. Not only had Atherton been acting as if he were organising a wedding rather than a murder investigation, fluttering around making sure everything was just right, making sure Lauren was comfortable, that Walter was going to be happy, he had also assigned DC Craig Cartwright to the case. Gardner couldn't stand Cartwright any more than he could Walter James. Cartwright made mistakes. He was more interested in working his way up the ladder than actually doing police work. And he was an arrogant little shit, too. But he was Atherton's little shit, so there he was.

At least Cartwright had been put on house to house. He could manage to fuck that up as well, but anything as long as he was out of Gardner's way. But no sooner had Gardner arrived back at the station than Cartwright was there, handing out orders and requesting information from support staff.

'What are you doing?' Gardner asked and Cartwright turned with a smug little grin. 'You're supposed to be knocking on doors.'

'DCI Atherton thought I'd be better utilised here,' Cartwright said.

'And the door to doors?'

'Covered,' he said and turned his back on Gardner, who wanted to throw the little shit across the room. But what would be the point? Atherton probably *had* authorised the change, but not because Cartwright's talents were being wasted out there, because Cartwright thought knocking on doors was below him and would've had a tantrum.

This might not have been Gardner's case but he sure as hell wasn't going to let Cartwright rub his stink all over it. If he had to work alongside him, fine. He'd worked with people he didn't like before, he could do it again. But he was here for one reason only and that was to find out who killed Ritchie Donoghue. That was if Lauren James's solicitor ever showed up so they could get started.

Unable to watch Cartwright lording it over him any longer, Gardner headed outside for some fresh air. He leaned against the wall around the corner from the main entrance to the station, glad he'd had the foresight to put his coat on. It was times like this that he wished he still smoked. Not that he was overly stressed yet, not that he was craving one, it was just something to do. Truth was, he hadn't smoked since he was in his early twenties and even then it had been more about something to do with his hands than a real addiction. But it was a good reason to be standing outside in the drizzling rain by himself. The weather hadn't even had the good grace to snow for Christmas, just brought ice and freezing rain. As his mum used to say, it was too cold for snow. Someone walked past in a hat with reindeer antlers on the sides, possibly a pre-Christmas insanity purchase or an unfortunate gift. Either way he didn't look thrilled to be wearing it.

Gardner watched people come and go as he stood there and wondered if he should call Freeman. He'd met DS Nicola Freeman a couple of weeks earlier on a case that he really should've stayed out of. But she'd dragged him into it and maybe it'd done him some good. He might not have completely exorcised all his demons but he'd at least given them a bit of a kicking, and that was pretty much down to Freeman. There was something about her. She was easy to talk to; didn't seem to care much about what anyone thought of her. He hadn't stopped thinking about her since that day in the pub. He'd even turned down a second date with a woman he'd met on the internet because of her. Or maybe that had been because the idea of internet dating made him feel a bit queasy. But anyway, if it hadn't been for a drunken phone call – hers, not his – on Christmas Eve they might not have stayed in touch. It was likely he'd have bottled it and never called her again. She'd been through her own shit lately and was obviously feeling down – alone and needing someone to talk to. Gardner knew the feeling and was more than happy to listen. What else was he going to do? It wasn't like he was inundated with festive visitors either. The next day he'd invited her down for New Year and instantly regretted it in the face of her uncharacteristic silence. At least she'd had the good grace to say she'd think about it.

So now New Year's Eve was closing in and it didn't look like he'd be doing any partying, never mind having an awkward encounter with a colleague he barely knew. But did he really need to call her to cancel? Was it likely she'd show?

'Oi.'

Gardner looked up and saw Harrington standing in the doorway, freezing in his short-sleeved shirt.

'Her solicitor's ready,' Harrington said.

Gardner nodded and followed him inside. 'Let's do it.'

5

DS Nicola Freeman did another circuit of the TV channels, barely pausing long enough on each one to figure out what it was, never mind if it was worth watching. In the end she let it stop on some animated film that was bound to start annoying her eventually.

Out of the corner of her eye she could see the Christmas tree lights blinking away and wished she hadn't bothered with decorations. Not that a single foot-high tree with two baubles and a few lights constituted decorations. It was worse than not bothering at all. At least having *no* decorations was a statement. This was just lazy. She shuffled around on the settee until she could no longer see the thing and pretended it wasn't there. Maybe she should just take it down anyway. It wasn't Christmas any more. It was that stupid, depressing time between Christmas and New Year when all the goodwill people had been feeling for weeks had worn out and now everyone was just counting down the days until life got back to normal. There was New Year's Eve, of course, but only idiots thought that was something worth looking forward to.

She switched the TV off and sat there in the half-light of the grey morning wondering how long it would take to drive to Merthyr Tydfil. Not that she particularly wanted to go to Merthyr but at least her brother, Mark, and his numerous offspring would be making noise, distracting her from her own thoughts. And there'd be food, lots of food. They'd have had a proper turkey dinner for Christmas instead of an overdone baked potato.

Freeman turned her back on the room, pulling the blanket around herself, and tried not to think about how shitty she was feeling. Why had she thought putting in some annual leave over Christmas would be a good idea? It wasn't like she had anything to celebrate, and with the rest of the Family Freeman gone to Wales she didn't even have anyone to pretend she was having fun with. She'd spent Christmas Eve moping around, wondering if she'd done the right thing in not telling her ex, Brian, about the abortion. And then she'd got drunk and almost called him. Thankfully a knock on the door had saved her from that fate. But after a couple of hours and half a dozen sherries at her neighbour's, she'd ended up making a stupid, drunk call anyway. Fortunately she'd been beyond calling Brian at that point and instead chose to call the one person who knew what she'd done, the one person she felt she could talk to at 11.30 p.m. on Christmas Eve – Michael Gardner. And why wouldn't she? She'd met him barely a fortnight ago. He was an acquaintance. Why wouldn't she drunk dial him at Christmas?

Freeman pressed her face against the blanket, cringing at the memory. He'd answered her call, somewhat bewildered, but to give him credit he'd listened to her ramble on and even called her back the next day to wish her a more sober happy Christmas as well as to check she was okay. Despite the unbelievably bad hangover, she'd enjoyed talking to him, but after half an hour or so it had become awkward and she'd said she had to go and sort the dinner. She didn't tell him that meant her Christmas potato was burning. So he'd wrapped things up, wished her happy Christmas again, and then asked her if she'd be interested in coming down to Middlesbrough for New Year. And then there'd been that buzz on the line where no one speaks for just a second or so but it seems like forever. She'd eventually said she'd think about it but that pause had made it awkward and she bet he wished he'd never asked. And to be honest she wished he hadn't either. Not that she didn't enjoy his company or that he wasn't attractive, it was just that she didn't know what kind of offer it was. He knew about the abortion, about Brian, so was it a pity invite or was he just as lonely and desperate as she was?

Anyway, they hadn't spoken since but the thirty-first was quickly approaching. She couldn't just not bother. She needed to speak to him either way but she didn't know what to say.

She pulled the blanket further over her head and wondered why she was making things complicated. She liked him. He was easy to talk to. They'd spent hours in the pub just before Christmas but that had been dissecting the case they'd just worked together. But what if that was all they could talk about? Maybe she'd just call and say she had a cold or something.

She was just drifting off beneath the blanket when she heard the knock. No doubt it was her neighbour armed with more sherry. It was never too early for sherry, apparently. Freeman wondered if it was mean to ignore her but a second knock before she could decide shifted her from the settee. She shuffled towards the door with the blanket wrapped around her, feeling the cold air from the hallway hit her as she pulled the door open.

And then she saw him standing there and the whole world seemed to stop.

6

Lauren sat in the interview room, waiting for something to happen. She knew they were watching her but she didn't know how she should respond to that. What were they expecting her to do? Cry? Beg for mercy? Scream that she didn't do it?

Her solicitor, or rather her dad's solicitor, Harry Warren, sleazebag extraordinaire, had told her to say as little as possible. Answer their questions but don't offer anything up voluntarily. This guy was obviously used to dealing with guilty people. Everyone else was pussyfooting around her. She guessed that was down to her dad. She knew he could pull strings. But could he really make this go away?

Ritchie was in her garden. He was *dead* in her garden. Nothing could change that. Not even her dad. Lauren closed her eyes, tried to focus on something, anything but her own thoughts, but there were no birds singing in here. Just the sound of the solicitor scribbling on a notepad. She'd asked him where her dad was, if he was on his way, but he'd said no. Apparently Daddy Dearest had things to do.

She wanted to know what they were all thinking, what was going to happen. So far no one had said very much at all. Everything was whispered, muttered as they turned away from her. One detective had spoken to her, said she'd have to go with him. She'd have to answer some questions, make a statement. And then someone had taken her clothes, put them in a bag. Another started scraping under her nails. She noticed one of her nails was broken, the polish chipped. She looked a state.

Another officer asked if she minded if he took her phone. She didn't know what she was supposed to say. This was before Harry showed up and told her to keep her mouth shut. She guessed now that she should also have refused to hand anything over. But how was she to have known? Why wasn't her dad there to tell her what to do? They'd said she was under caution, that's all. She could go whenever she wanted. They just wanted a statement. Nothing difficult.

Lauren looked up at the door again. Where was everybody? She tried to remember what she'd said on the phone. She couldn't remember. Harry sighed at her. But she couldn't remember what she'd said when she called her dad, when she called Peter. The longer she sat there the less she recalled about anything. It was all becoming a blur.

7

Freeman didn't know how long she'd been standing there without speaking but as he wasn't saying anything either, she was starting to wonder if she was actually asleep, if this was a weird dream. But he looked different. Surely if she was dreaming she'd see him how he'd looked back then. Before he was gone.

She could feel her heart pounding in her chest and realised she hadn't taken a breath in a while. But what if she started and he disappeared? What if she woke up? She wanted to say something to him, wanted to reach out and see if he was real, but that might make him disappear too. So she just stood there, suspended in time, her brain that had been thinking so many things now stuck on one thought: *I thought you were dead*.

'Hey, Nicky,' he said.

Freeman blinked and felt the blanket drop from around her shoulders. She lurched forwards and her arms flung themselves around him, smothering him. He was real. He was really there.

'What the fuck?' she whispered, not sure if it was a question for him or for herself. She stepped back and looked at him, her hands still on his shoulders. He looked different, older. Of course he did. It'd been five years. Five years since he'd disappeared. Five years since the police had found his car, had told their parents that the body hadn't been recovered. Five years. And even longer since she'd seen him. Since he'd told her he never wanted to see her again. That she'd betrayed him, ruined his life. And yet here he was.

'Can I come in?' Darren asked, his eyes never meeting hers.

Freeman stepped back to let him in and he walked past, into the living room, looking around, taking it in. For a moment she wondered if he was there to case the place. She closed the front door and felt like a dick for thinking that way. When had Darren ever taken anything of hers? Even at his lowest, he had never stolen from his family.

She followed him in and tried to think of something to say. She wondered if she should call her parents, wondered if they already knew. If her mam, in some act of spite, had deliberately not informed her that Darren was back.

'Have you—?' Freeman started but Darren turned, finally looking at her.

'I need your help,' he said. 'I need you to do something for me.'

Freeman felt her stomach drop. So that was it. Her brother had come back from the dead because he wanted something. Not because he missed her, not because it was time to make amends. But because he wanted something from her. Of course he did. He was in trouble and he needed his cop sister to get him out of it. The cop sister he swore he'd never speak to again. Who he'd called a fucking pig. But that was then. When he was strung out on drugs, when he'd been locked up because of a call she'd made.

She looked him over, tried to decide if he was high. He was nervous, she could see that much. Tense. But that was to be expected. She was nervous too. She tried to look for the telltale signs but couldn't see any. Maybe he was clean. Or maybe it'd just been too long since she'd had to look for them.

'Are you going to help me or what?' Darren said, pulling his sleeves down over his hands.

'Is that the only reason you came here? Because you want help?'

'Why else would I come?' he said, shrugging his skinny shoulders, which were buried under his baggy clothes.

Freeman shook her head. 'Do Mam and Dad know?' Darren looked away from her, his eyes on the sad little Christmas tree. 'Do they? Have you all had a happy little reunion without me?'

'No,' he said. 'I haven't seen them. I don't want . . .' He walked towards the window, staring out across the car park as if he were looking for someone.

Freeman stared at the back of her brother's head, a million thoughts running through her head, not least: How am I going to tell Mam and Dad? How was that conversation going to begin? She closed her eyes and tried to focus. Mam and Dad were miles away. She had time to work things out.

'How did you even find me?' Freeman asked. Darren didn't say anything; continued looking outside. 'Darren?'

'I went to Mam and Dad's. You know she still keeps a key under that stupid frog thing? I figured they'd gone away. The curtains were shut all the time. I was going to stay there a while but I found your address, thought maybe you could help me out.'

Freeman thought of Darren sneaking into their parents' house while they were gone. Eating their food and sleeping in their bed like Goldilocks and not even letting them know he was alive.

'What do you need? What's happened?' She waited but he didn't reply. 'Darren?'

'Something bad's happened.'

Freeman felt her stomach drop a little further. Something bad? That was usually an understatement. 'For fuck's sake,' she muttered.

'I just need your help. If you don't want to help me, I'll go.' He waited a few seconds and when she didn't answer he started to leave.

Freeman put her hand out, grabbing his sleeve. 'Don't,' she said.

'Are you going to help me?'

'I don't know. I don't know what you want.' Darren rolled his eyes and shrugged away from her. 'How can I say yes if I don't know what it is?'

'It shouldn't matter! You owe me, Nicky,' he said, his eyes hard now. Freeman looked away. She could feel the tears burning the back of her own eyes. She didn't want to admit it but he was right. She did owe him.

8

Gardner waited for Lauren to say something. It was an easy enough request – tell me what happened – but she seemed to be struggling. Perhaps she hadn't had enough time to get her story straight. Or maybe she was just in shock. He was trying not to let his feelings for Walter James cloud his opinion of the woman in front of him but so far he was losing that battle.

He was surprised that he and Harrington had been allowed to conduct the initial interview with Lauren. He'd expected Atherton to do it himself so that there could be no accusations of upsetting Walter's daughter. But Atherton was busy rallying the troops. He wanted his best people on this. So he'd given Gardner the go-ahead to speak to Lauren but made it clear that she was in no way to be treated like a suspect at this point. *No way*. Gardner was expecting to be kicked off the case at any moment for not toeing the line, and to be honest he wouldn't lose sleep if he was. He knew there was going to be interference but it was Atherton's problem now. He just hoped Atherton had the balls to stand up to Walter James if necessary. He knew Atherton was more interested in politics than police work, but he wondered if he would cross the line and let someone get away with murder if it served his ambitions.

Gardner caught himself. He was as bad as they were. He was letting who she was steer his opinion of her – in the opposite direction to the rest of them but steering it nonetheless. Unlike Harrington, who was grinning at her like a schoolboy.

'I saw him when I got up,' Lauren said and Gardner looked up. Finally. She speaks.

'I got up, went downstairs to get some coffee. I was waiting for the coffee machine and looked down the garden. And I saw him.' Lauren looked Gardner in the eye before shifting her attention to Harrington, who shuffled in his seat when she met his gaze. 'I didn't know it was him at first. I mean, I didn't know *what* it was. I thought . . . I don't know what I thought it was. That's why I went out. I thought someone had dumped something. I went out and as I got closer I saw it. Him.'

She stopped and looked from Harrington back to Gardner and that was it. Was that the whole story? All she had to say?

'So what happened next?' Gardner said. 'You went out, found Ritchie's body. Then what?'

Lauren blinked; glanced at her solicitor, Harry Warren, another pain in Gardner's arse. Not that Gardner saw a great deal of him. For most cases Warren sent one of his minions. Clearly Walter James paid well enough for Warren to actually leave his office and do some work.

'I called the police,' she said.

Gardner nodded. 'Was that the first thing you did?'

Lauren frowned. 'What do you mean?'

'I mean, did you touch the body? Move him? Check to see if he was alive?'

'No,' she said. 'I bent down. He was facing the ground but I knew it was him.'

'How?'

'His clothes. His hair.'

'Okay. So you didn't touch him?'

'No. I mean, yes. I reached out to him.'

'Did you check to see if he was alive?' Gardner asked.

'No. He looked dead. There was blood. I think he'd been there for a while.'

'Why did you think that?'

'He was cold,' Lauren said.

'It's a cold day. I'd be cold if I was lying in a garden. Doesn't mean I'm dead,' Gardner said.

'Detective, I don't think this is the time or place for being facetious,' Harry said, looking over his half-moon glasses at Gardner.

Gardner noticed Harrington look at him from the corner of his eye. Maybe that *had* been out of line. Forget who she is, Gardner reminded himself. He cleared his throat. 'So you didn't check for a pulse.'

'I'm sorry,' Lauren said.

'That's okay. It must've been hard, finding him like that. And you're right, there was nothing you could've done. So you found him. Could see he was dead. And then what?'

'I called the police,' Lauren said.

'Straight away?'

'Pretty much.'

'Pretty much? So, what – a few minutes later?'

'I think we've established she made the call to the police,' Harry said.

'I'm just trying to establish when exactly that was. Did you have to go back into the house to make the call?'

Lauren shook her head. 'No. I had my phone in my pocket,' she said.

'You didn't call anyone else first?'

Lauren shook her head again. 'No.'

'Detective, can we move on? My client called the police. What is so difficult to understand about that?'

Gardner turned to Harrington and could see the same thoughts were passing through his colleague's mind. Either Lauren James was completely stupid – she'd handed over her phone straight away – or she was a compulsive liar who knew that it didn't matter what she said. That Daddy was going to bail her out no matter what. Or maybe she was in shock and confused. He supposed there was still that option.

'You didn't make any other calls this morning before you rang 999?'

'Detective—'

Lauren swallowed and the tears finally made their debut, settling around her eyes but not quite ready to fall. 'I tried to call my dad but he didn't answer.' Her solicitor sat up straight, suddenly looking more engaged.

'All right,' Gardner said. 'Why did you try to call your dad first?'

'I don't think any of this is relevant here. My client called the police, as was her duty. Who else she called is her own business,' Harry said.

'I didn't know what to do,' Lauren said, the tears now running down her cheeks.

'Lauren,' Harry said, glaring at her like *he* was her father.

'That's understandable. You were in shock. You'd just found your ex-boyfriend's body in your back garden. I think I'd panic too,' Gardner said. He looked at Harrington and he nodded. 'So you tried to call your dad but he didn't answer. Then what? You called the police?'

Lauren shook her head. 'Not straight away.'

'Lauren—'

'Why not?' Gardner asked, ignoring Harry, his fingers brushing the sheet of paper in front of him. He already knew what Lauren had done next. He knew she'd made a few calls before calling the police. Harry's eyes focused on the piece of paper.

'I don't know. I was scared.'

'Of what?'

'I don't know,' Lauren said again. 'I thought my dad would know what to do.'

'What did you think your dad would tell you to do?'

'I don't know.' She stopped and wiped her face, took a breath. 'He would've told me to call the police.'

Gardner nodded. 'Seems likely, doesn't it?' Lauren didn't respond. Gardner glanced at the sheet of paper with the details of the calls and slipped his glasses on. Harrington had asked him, when he'd worn them for the first time a week back, whether it was an affectation. If he was trying to make suspects think he was cleverer than them by putting on some specs. He hadn't dignified it with an answer. Also, he didn't like to admit that he was having trouble reading without them. Getting old was no fun. 'We checked your phone, Lauren. You made *several* calls this morning before you called 999.'

Something flashed in Lauren's eyes for a moment and then it was gone. Anger? Was she pissed off that someone dared cross her? Did she think they'd just remove the body from her garden and let her get back to her day of shopping and manicures?

Harry started to speak but Gardner cut him off. 'Ms James handed her phone to us voluntarily.' The man looked at Lauren but she wouldn't meet his eye.

'I want a moment with my client,' Harry said. Gardner sighed and stood up. Harrington stopped the tape and they left the room. He could see where this was going.

Gardner and Harrington stood against the wall outside the interview room. Gardner knew he should've held off on the phone stuff. Atherton was going to be pissed off about it and no doubt Harry Warren was in there trying to come up with a way to make it go away. But if there was nothing to hide, why not answer the questions? Why not tell him why she'd felt the need to call her dad, her brother and someone called Big P numerous times that morning, before she finally called the police?

'Wonder who Big P is,' Harrington said, a smirk on his face.

'I don't know,' Gardner said. 'But at this rate we'll never find out.' He checked his watch just as Harry appeared at the door, nodding for them to re-enter. As they settled back into their seats, Harry grinned at Gardner.

'How long have you been a detective, Mr Gardner?' Harry asked. Gardner didn't respond. That was a rhetorical question if ever he heard one. Now all he had to do was wait for Harry's solution to the little problem of the phone. 'My client wasn't under caution when her phone was taken—' Gardner tried to interrupt but Harry kept talking. 'Nor was she advised to speak to her solicitor first.'

'This is bullshit,' Gardner muttered, hoping it wouldn't be picked up on the tape.

'Lauren? Did this gentleman or any of his colleagues formally caution you before taking your phone or your clothes? Did they allow you to speak to me before demanding them?'

Lauren frowned and shook her head. 'No,' she said and then, catching Gardner's eye, said, 'I don't remember. I was in shock.'

Gardner tried not to laugh. This was ridiculous. Of course Lauren had been cautioned. She'd been given the opportunity to wait for her solicitor before anything had happened and she'd declined it. Maybe it had been stupid not to wait, especially considering the interference bound to materialise from Walter James's end, but if Lauren had nothing to hide, what did it matter?

'Now, I suggest you move on and ask some pertinent questions or else my client is leaving,' Harry said.

Gardner glared at Harry. The man was known for blocking as much as possible, for shutting things down at the drop of a hat, but in this case it was Walter James making the moves. He could practically see James's hand up Harry's arse.

He dragged his eyes away from Harry's smug face and looked at Lauren. 'All right. Why don't you just tell us what happened last night?'

9

'I'll help you,' Freeman said. 'I'll help. Just tell me what's going on.'

'Some guy thinks I took his money,' Darren said.

Freeman sighed. 'Okay. But I meant what's going on, as in where the fuck have you been for the last five years?'

Darren rubbed at the woolly hat on his head, pulling it down further over his eyes. 'It doesn't matter,' he said.

'Doesn't matter?' Freeman thought her eyes might pop out of her head. 'It doesn't matter? What the fuck is wrong with you?'

'I don't know, Nicky. You tell me. You're the one who thinks you know best, so you tell me.'

'You've been gone five years, Darren. Five *years*. I thought you were dead. Mam and Dad thought you were dead. How could that not matter?'

'This is bullshit,' Darren said and pushed past her towards the door.

'Where're you going?' she said and grabbed hold of him. He tried to shake her off but she clung on. He didn't get to just vanish again. 'Darren. Stop.'

'Why can't you just act like my sister instead of a fucking copper all the time? All I want is for you to help me.'

'And I *want* to help you,' Freeman said. 'I do. But you need to tell me what happened.'

35

'Why? I was gone and now I'm here. That's what happened. And you said you'd help me. So are you going to or not?'

Freeman let go of him. 'Yes,' she said. 'I will. I do owe you. But you owe me too. You owe me an explanation.'

Darren leaned back against the wall and knocked his head off it a couple of times. Freeman waited. He was softening. Whatever he needed was worth telling her the truth for and that made her nervous. What had he got himself into now?

'I just need you to do this one thing for me and then I'll tell you whatever you like.'

Freeman made a face. She'd heard that before. Just let me have your chocolate bar and then I'll give you two tomorrow when I get my pocket money. Just don't tell Mam I've gone out and I'll give you my ticket to see The Breeders. She never got those chocolate bars, still hadn't seen The Breeders.

'I swear,' he said. 'I just need you to do this first. It's kind of time sensitive.'

Time sensitive? That made it sound even worse. Whatever it was had to be serious. Why else would he have come to her? And no matter what he'd said about her just being his sister instead of a cop, what he really needed was his cop sister. That much was obvious.

She moved beside him, resting her head against the wall too. She looked up at him. He had a good few inches on her and yet he was still short. It had bothered him his whole life. She watched him as he stared off through the window of the spare room. Wished she could read his mind. But if she could do that then maybe none of this would've happened. Maybe he'd still be the happy-go-lucky kid he'd been up until his twelfth birthday. Not that it was all bad after that. He was still a funny kid, still a sweet kid. He lashed out at himself more than at those around him. He just didn't seem to realise that hurting himself *did* hurt those around him.

'Tell me,' she said, eventually. 'What do you need?'

10

'Nothing happened last night,' Lauren said. 'I found him this morning.'

'Okay. But just so we can get things clear in our minds – what did you do last night?'

'You mean like an alibi?'

'I mean, I just want to know what you did yesterday, right up until this morning when you found Ritchie.'

'Nothing,' Lauren said.

'You didn't see Ritchie at all yesterday?'

'No,' she said and then glanced down again. 'I mean, he came round but I didn't want to see him.'

'So you didn't *want* to see him, but you did *actually* see him?'

'Only for a minute,' Lauren said.

'And what happened in that minute?'

'He turned up at my house. He wanted to talk to me but I didn't want to. He got angry but then he left.'

'Why was he angry?' Harrington asked.

'She already informed you that she didn't speak to him. How would she know what he was angry about?' Harry said. 'Move on.'

'You said you and Ritchie had broken up. Do you think he wanted to get back together with you?' Gardner said.

'Detective, you're trying to put words in her mouth.'

'I think so,' Lauren said. 'But I wouldn't talk so he left.'

Gardner caught an eye-roll from Harry. 'That was it? He didn't hang around? Didn't try to push it?'

'No. He got the hint and left.'

'And what time was that?'

'I don't know. About ten. Ten thirty maybe.'

'And what did you do after he left?'

'Nothing. I went to bed.'

'That was it?'

'Yes.'

'You did nothing else?' Gardner watched as Lauren dug a fingernail into her skin.

'Nothing,' she said. 'I went to bed. I was wound up a bit because of Ritchie so I took some sleeping pills. That's it.'

'Nothing else at all?' Gardner said. Was she really that stupid?

'We've established she did nothing else. Move on,' Harry said.

'And you think it was about ten when Ritchie showed up, correct?' Gardner asked.

'I don't know. I can't remember.'

'And he stayed how long?'

'I don't know,' Lauren said, her voice a whine now.

'But not long, right? Not if you wouldn't talk to him,' Gardner said and Lauren nodded. 'He came round, you wouldn't talk to him and he left. But then you made some calls.' He put his glasses on again although he knew who she'd called. Maybe Harrington was right about it being an affectation.

'Detective Gardner, you don't seem to be grasping the fact that Lauren's phone was taken without her being under caution. Anything gleaned from it will be inadmissible. I suggest you move on. The calls Lauren made this morning are no longer relevant.'

'I'm talking about the calls she made last night,' Gardner said. 'Would you mind answering a few questions about those, Lauren?'

Lauren looked to Harry for guidance.

'Lauren made calls to four people last night. One of those people could help us locate the killer of Ritchie Donoghue. It's in Lauren's interests to answer my questions,' Gardner said.

Harry nodded.

'Thank you. You made four calls last night, all within fifteen minutes. The first at ten forty-five. Had Ritchie left by then?' he asked, looking up at Lauren.

'Yes,' she said.

'The first call was to your dad but he didn't answer. He's a difficult man to get hold of, isn't he?' Gardner looked at the sheet again. 'You left him a message and then you called someone called Big P and left a message for him too. What did you say to them?'

'I don't know,' Lauren said. 'I can't remember.'

'All right, can you tell us who Big P is?'

'Peter Hinde. He works for my dad. I thought he might know where he was.'

Gardner noted Peter's name and wondered if Big P was a nickname used by everyone or just Lauren.

'In what capacity does Mr Hinde work for your dad?'

Lauren sighed. 'He runs the campaign and stuff.'

'Have you known him long?'

'How is this relevant?' Harry asked.

'Just establishing the facts. Ms James obviously knows him well enough to call him late at night,' Gardner said and indicated for Lauren to talk.

'Ages. Since I was a kid. My dad knew his mum. Helped her out.'

'In what way?' Gardner asked.

Lauren shrugged. 'I don't know. Her husband died so Dad helped her.'

'Financially?'

'Maybe,' Lauren said. 'I don't know, really.'

'So you've known him since you were a kid. He's a friend as well as someone who works for your dad?'

'Not really.'

'But you called him last night. Called him this morning. You have him in your phone as Big P. That sounds like a nickname for a friend to me. At the very least,' Harrington said.

'That was Guy,' Lauren said. 'He started calling Peter "Big P" ages ago to wind him up. It was a joke. I thought it was funny so I put it in my phone.'

'So you only called Peter Hinde to find your dad,' Gardner said. 'But you've made a lot of calls to Peter recently. Some lasting a little longer than it'd take to ask him where your dad was.'

'This is completely irrelevant,' Harry said.

'Look, I was scared. I just needed to talk to someone,' Lauren said and Harry put his hand on her arm but she shook him off.

'Of what? Ritchie'd gone, hadn't he?'

'I thought he might come back,' Lauren said. 'You don't know what he was like. I've seen the things he's done to people. I didn't think it would bother him to do the same to me. I didn't want to be by myself.'

'So you called your dad. What for? Did you ask him to come round? Did you tell him Ritchie was bothering you?'

'I can't remember. I just wanted to scare Ritchie so he'd go away.'

'I thought Ritchie had left before you made the call,' Gardner said.

'He had. But I thought he might come back and if someone was there he'd leave me alone.'

'So you asked your dad and Peter to come round to chase Ritchie off?'

'No. I just wanted him to think that someone might come.'

'How would he know you were calling someone if he'd gone, Lauren?'

'I don't know,' she said.

Gardner let the silence grow for a while before he went back to his sheet. 'So you left messages for your dad and Peter. Then you called your brother, Guy. He picked up and you talked for about two minutes. What did you say to him?'

'I just said that Ritchie had been round and I wanted to talk to someone. But Guy was out.'

'Out where?'

'He was in Newcastle with some friends,' Lauren said.

'So he couldn't come and scare Ritchie away.'

'Enough, Detective,' Harry said.

'What about Jen Worrall? Who's she?'

'She's an intern for my dad,' said Lauren and Gardner caught the look of repulsion as she spoke. 'I thought she might know where my dad was.'

'At almost eleven o'clock at night?' Gardner said, wondering if that explained the look of disgust when he'd mentioned Worrall's name. There were always rumours about Walter James's love life, despite his campaign built on family values. 'Did she know where he was? You spoke to her for about thirty seconds.'

'She said that my dad and Peter were in an important meeting,' Lauren said.

'At eleven at night?' Harrington said.

'She meant they were in the pub. That's what my dad always says when he's going for a night out – he's going for an important meeting.'

'Did she say where?'

'I don't see how that's relevant here,' Harry said.

Gardner checked his notes again. 'Your dad tried to call you back. Just after eleven thirty. You didn't answer.'

'I must've been in bed by then,' she said.

'Were you?' Gardner said.

'For goodness' sake, she just told you she was,' Harry said.

'I took some pills. I went to bed after I spoke to Jen; I figured Dad would be out for the night.'

'So you went to bed. And the tablets worked? Knocked you out?'

'Yes.'

Gardner could swear he could see a film of sweat on Lauren's face. 'You didn't get up again after an hour or so?'

'No,' she said.

Gardner and Harrington waited. She had to know what was coming. Had to know they'd have found it.

'You say you were in bed, out of it, by what, eleven thirty?'

'Detective, this is going to end if you don't start asking some *actual* questions,' Harry said.

Gardner and Harrington looked at each other. 'So how did you send Ritchie a text at twelve-thirty in the morning telling him to meet you at your house in ten minutes?' Lauren's face lost all colour. 'Now, why don't we start again?' Gardner said.

'No,' Harry said. 'This is where this ends.'

11

'This guy, Healy, he thinks I took his money,' Darren said.

'Okay. So, what? You need money?' Freeman asked.

'No,' he said, frowning. 'Why? You got some?'

'No. I don't have any money. Why does this guy think you took his money?'

'I don't know,' Darren said, his voice defensive. 'I didn't take it, Nicky.'

'I never said you did,' she replied and wondered if her expression had betrayed her thoughts. Maybe Darren had never stolen from family, but that was about as far as his moral code went. He'd had no problems stealing from other people.

'I don't *know* why he thinks I took it. I guess it's just easier to blame me.' He stood up straight. 'I need you to prove it wasn't me.'

'And how am I supposed to do that?'

'I think there're some tapes.'

'What sort of tapes?'

'Like, security tapes. Whoever took it must be on the tapes.'

'So, why don't you tell this Healy guy to look at the tapes? What do you need me for?'

'You don't get it,' Darren said, walking away, back into the living room where he flopped down on the settee.

44

'No, I don't get it. Because you've told me nothing. I can't help you if you don't tell me what's going on. Who is this guy? Why does he think you took his money? Do you know him?'

Darren rubbed his head under his hat again, groaning in frustration. He was always like this. Couldn't be bothered talking. If their parents asked him anything and he couldn't be bothered to explain he'd just say, 'I don't know', even if it meant getting into more trouble than telling the truth.

'I thought it was time sensitive,' Freeman said.

'It is.'

'So start talking.'

Darren heaved a sigh and sat forward. 'This guy, Healy. Mark Healy. I sort of work for him.'

'What kind of work?' Darren just looked up at her as if she were stupid. 'Okay. So the kind of work I'd rather not know about. Go on.'

'I basically do all his running around and whatnot. So he asks me to take some money to Gary, this guy he owes. He gives me the bag. Tells me there's like fifty grand in there. Says it like I should be grateful I get to carry around that much money. So I take it to the club Gary owns, and I give it to this other guy, Tommy. He takes it, puts it in the office and that's it. I've done my job. But then Healy shows up all crazy, telling me I'm a thief, that I'd better give it back or he's gonna break my legs. I don't know what he's talking about. He says Gary is claiming there was only thirty grand in the bag.

'But I didn't take the money. How can I pay it back if I don't have it? I said maybe Tommy took it. He's like, I don't know, Gary's right-hand man but maybe he thought he'd take it, maybe his boss treats him like shit too. But Healy won't have it. These guys are threatening Healy too. He was, like, panicking and shit. Swears this guy is on the up and up. Like, how stupid is he?'

45

Freeman raised an eyebrow but said nothing. She truly believed her brother was a good person at heart but he wasn't the brightest spark. 'So Healy gave you the money, you handed it over and then some of it magically disappeared.'

'Right.'

'And this guy, Tommy, put the bag in the office at the club?' Darren nodded. 'You saw him put it in there?'

'Yeah.'

'Did he count it?'

Darren frowned, thinking. 'No. He threw the bag in a locker and then started telling me some bullshit about this new dancer or something. Kept jabbering on like I wanted to stand there listening to him all night.'

'And who else has access to the office? Is it locked?'

'Yeah, it's locked. I guess Gary and Tommy. I don't think anyone else is allowed in, not unless Gary's in there. That's what Rachel says.'

'Who's Rachel?'

'My girlfriend. She works at the club.'

'Okay. What does she do?'

'She works on the bar. She's not a stripper.'

'All right. So Rachel works there and you need to see the security tapes. Why don't you just get her to do it?'

'I asked her but she can't get into the office. No one else has keys and no one's allowed in without the say-so of the boss or Tommy. And if they're the ones who took the money, they're not gonna let me in, are they?'

'Have you told Healy about the tapes? Why doesn't he demand to see them, to prove those guys didn't take the money themselves?'

'Duh,' Darren said. 'They're not gonna let anyone see them. Are you listening?'

'Yeah, I'm listening. But I don't understand what you want from me.'

'If those guys didn't take the money themselves, they'd have looked at the tapes and seen who did it, right?'

'No, they'd probably think that you or Healy were ripping them off and never brought fifty grand in the first place.'

'But I know *I* didn't take it. Someone from the club must've taken it and set me up. That's why I need you to get those tapes. Prove it wasn't me.'

Freeman sat down beside Darren. 'Okay. Say someone from the club *did* take the money out and then told Healy it wasn't all there. What makes you think they'd do it at the club? Especially in front of the cameras?' Darren frowned but Freeman continued. 'They could've easily taken the bag home and then called Healy to tell him some money was missing. And even if they *did* keep the money at the club, if he took it into the office, is there a camera in there? Would there be any evidence of what went on in there?'

Darren looked at the floor. She could almost see the cogs in his brain whirring.

'And do you even know if Healy sent fifty grand to start with? Did you see him put the money in the bag? Did you count it?'

'I'm not stupid, Nicky,' Darren said. 'The money was all there when I got it, it was all there when I handed it over.'

'And I believe you. But I don't think there's going to be anything on those tapes to prove who really took it. Who'd be stupid enough to steal money in front of the CCTV cameras?'

Darren stared at the floor for a while and Freeman thought maybe she'd won. 'What if someone else at the club took it?' Darren said.

'Like who? I thought no one else was allowed into the office.'

'Yeah, but what if it wasn't in the office? What if it was before then? I remember I put the bag down by the bar while I went to the toilet. When I came back, Tommy was there. There was some guy at the other end of the bar. One of them could've done it while I was gone.'

'You left fifty grand sitting by itself while you went to the toilet?'

'No, Rachel was there. She was watching it for me but she could've got distracted if someone wanted a drink or something.'

'Have you asked her? Did anyone go near the bag?'

'She said she doesn't remember.' Darren shrugged. 'I don't know, Nicky. There's got to be something on the tapes somewhere. I just need to prove it to Healy. Show him it was one of them, not me.'

Freeman sighed. 'My advice would be to just stay away from them all. Let it blow over.'

'Blow over? He threatened to break my legs. And I'm pretty sure he was playing it down. He knows where I live.'

'So come and stay with me for a while.'

'I can't. He knows Rachel too.'

Freeman sighed. 'So bring her as well. Look, I can't help you prove anything but I can keep you safe here. And I'm guessing you know a fair bit about this Healy guy. Maybe you could give me something that I can use and then—'

'I'm not a grass, Nicky.'

'Jesus, Darren. This isn't primary school. This guy has threatened you. He's more than likely set you up, too. If you want him off your back just give me something and I can do this properly.'

Darren stood up. 'Forget it. I'll sort it out myself.'

'How?'

'I don't know. I'll break into the club or whatever.'

Freeman stood up, running to the door, blocking his exit. 'Wait,' she said. 'Just wait.' She closed her eyes for a moment, knowing this was pointless but if it was the only way to keep him there then so be it. 'I'll go to the club. I'll take a look at the tapes. But if there's nothing on them, you have to promise me you'll stay. Right?'

'Whatever,' he said.

'Okay. Tell me where it is.'

12

Gardner watched DCI Atherton shepherd Lauren and her solicitor back into the interview room. He was practically bowing at the feet of Harry Warren and Harry gave Gardner a smirk to show he realised it too. Harry had ended the interview and was intent on taking his client home until Atherton had scuttled up, apologising for Gardner's behaviour and dressing him down in front of Harry, proving who was in charge.

Harry accepted the apology and agreed to a few further questions as long as Gardner was not the one who'd be asking them. Instead Atherton would conduct the rest of the interview and Harry could happily report back to Walter James that only the questions he saw fit to be answered were asked, but they could still make out that Lauren had cooperated fully. It was bullshit.

As Atherton closed the door behind him, he glared at Gardner once more, just to make sure he knew he was being sent to the naughty step.

Gardner went into the room down the hall where the monitors showed what was happening in each interview room. He watched Atherton pull out the chair for Lauren as if he were the maître d' at a fancy restaurant. Gardner rolled his eyes. They might as well all go home now.

He'd begged Atherton to press Lauren on the text message sent after she claimed to have been asleep in bed but he knew it wouldn't happen. He listened as Atherton apologised once more and then formally re-started the interview.

'I know it's hard, Lauren,' Atherton said. 'But I'd like to ask you a little about Ritchie.'

Gardner watched as Lauren took a long drink from the plastic cup of water. He watched her hand shake as she put the cup down on the table. He'd yet to work her out. Was she a spoilt brat, waiting for Daddy to come and rescue her? A scared woman, perhaps guilty, perhaps not? She seemed to swing from one extreme to the other. One minute she was blasé, the next on the verge of tears. There'd been moments when she'd seemed to want to talk and if it hadn't been for Harry Warren's interference, they might've got something useful. That was never going to happen now.

She pushed her hair behind her ear and let out a long, slow breath. 'Ready?' Atherton asked. She nodded. 'So, how long had you known Ritchie?'

She blew out her cheeks. 'About a year,' she said. 'Maybe a little less. I can't remember.'

'And how long was he your boyfriend?'

'About ten months, I think.'

'Okay. How did you meet?' Atherton said.

'In a club. One in town; I couldn't tell you which one.'

'Did someone introduce you?'

'No,' Lauren said. 'He just came over, started talking to me. Thought he was something special. And I guess I fell for it.'

'And then what?'

'What do you think?' Lauren stared at him, challenging him to say it.

'You went home with him?' Gardner could almost see Atherton blushing as he said it.

'Yeah,' she said. 'Then he didn't call me for a while but I saw him again when I was out one night.'

'And then you started seeing him,' Atherton said.

'Yeah. And then he turned into an arsehole. He was always chatting other lasses up. I'd be right there and he'd still do it. Or he'd try and make me look stupid in front of his friends, tell them stuff about me, about what we did . . . together.'

Gardner watched as Lauren's face changed. For a moment she looked younger, almost childlike. Gardner felt a twinge of sympathy for her. It didn't matter who she was, how much money she had, there was always some arsehole that could treat her like shit. 'So I dumped him.' And like that, the defiant Lauren was back.

'And when was that?'

'A few weeks ago,' Lauren said.

'And how did he take it?'

'He was pissed off. I guess he just didn't want to get dumped. Bruised his ego. He thought he could get stuff from me. Money, a taste of power, I guess.' Harry put his hand on Lauren's arm and she stopped talking.

'So what happened when you told him?'

Lauren looked down at the table, the attitude dropped again. 'I made sure we were out when I told him. In the pub, lots of people.'

'You were scared of him?'

Lauren shrugged again. 'I guess,' she said. 'He had a temper. I knew he'd start kicking off.'

'And did he?' Atherton asked.

'He tried to drag me out of the pub. I got him off me and ran into the toilets. I was in there for ages and when I came out he'd gone. The barman had threatened to call the police.' Lauren ran her finger along the edge of the desk. 'I got a taxi home but when I got there he was at my house. He knew where the spare key was; he'd let himself in. So I just told the taxi driver to take me to my brother's house.

'I stayed at Guy's for a couple of days. Ritchie kept calling me over and over but I didn't answer. Then he went quiet for a few days so I went home. I got a text the next day. He said he was sorry, wanted to come over and talk. I agreed to meet him in town, in a bar. He was all apologies at first, brought me flowers, brought me a bracelet. But I said it wasn't going to happen and he went mad again. He hit me,' she said, quietly. 'I called my dad and Ritchie backed off, made some stupid threat.'

'About what?' Atherton asked.

Gardner thought that if he'd still been in there, if he were the one asking these questions, Harry would've been walking out by now, telling them it was irrelevant. It wasn't, of course. It was completely relevant. If Lauren and Ritchie broke up recently and there was animosity between them; if Ritchie had a temper and turned up at Lauren's wanting to get back together; it was entirely possible that this was what got Ritchie killed, whether it was by Lauren herself or someone else defending her.

'He said he had ways to hurt me,' Lauren replied.

'What did he mean by that? You said he'd physically hurt you already.'

Lauren swallowed and looked past Atherton to the door. 'I don't know,' she said. 'I didn't hear from him for about a week. I thought he'd got over it. And then he showed up last night.'

'And what happened last night?'

'I already told the other one,' Lauren said, the whine in her voice back.

'Tell me,' Atherton said and Gardner wondered if Atherton had more balls than he was letting on. Either that or he was allowing her to adapt her story now she'd had a little coaching.

53

'He came round, wanted to come in but I said no. He hung around for a while and then left.'

'Did Ritchie threaten you again last night?'

Lauren paused. 'No,' she said eventually.

'Okay, Lauren, that's great,' Atherton said. 'Thank you.'

'I just wanted it to stop.'

'Wanted what to stop, Lauren?' Atherton asked, looking up at her.

'This interview's over,' Harry said. 'My client has answered all your questions.'

For a moment Atherton looked like he was going to push it, ask her again what she meant, but instead he just nodded and ended the interview. Gardner leaned forward, both hands on the desk below the monitors. It'd been a complete waste of time. No one was going to touch Lauren James.

13

Freeman followed the satnav's directions and pulled up outside Slinky's Gentlemen's Club in Newcastle's city centre. Driving through Newcastle was low on her list of things she enjoyed at the best of times, but between the beginning of December and mid-January it was especially painful. Despite the temperature, the streets were clogged with bargain hunters taking advantage of the sales, buying junk they didn't even want. Freeman disliked a lot of things about the modern world, but internet shopping wasn't one of them. The fewer people she had to interact with, the better.

She got out of the car and looked up at the building. From the exterior, Slinky's looked quite grand, like many of the buildings in the city. But she doubted it would extend to the interior. In the end, gentlemen's club and strip joint meant the same thing. It was just that one charged a bit more.

She walked up to the door, trying to decide what she was going to say. She knew she had no right to be there, that Gary wasn't obligated to show her the tapes, but maybe a flash of her ID would ease things along. If he had nothing to hide then helping out a friendly copper might be a possibility.

As she walked in she got a sense of overwhelming depression. A strip club at night was ugly, but in the day? It was just

55

pitiful. One old guy sat in front of the podium, his hands resting on the platform, his head resting on his hands. He might well have been asleep. Above him a young woman half-heartedly gyrated, repeating the same movements over and over. Freeman realised the woman was fully clothed. Maybe she was practising.

At the bar another woman, slightly older but no less attractive, was cleaning glasses. She looked miserable and winced each time the bass thumped through the speaker above her head. Freeman wasn't sure why they needed the music so loud when there was no one there, but maybe it helped keep more depressing thoughts at bay.

'Can I get you something?' the woman asked and Freeman wandered over to the bar, which was intermittently covered in half-bald bits of tinsel. It didn't look like they'd splashed out on decorations.

'Is Gary here?' she asked and the woman narrowed her eyes.

'No,' she said. 'Can I help?'

'You know where he is?'

'He's not here.'

Freeman let out a breath. She couldn't decide if this woman was just naturally unfriendly or if Gary had taught his staff to say as little as possible at all times. She decided it was time to bring out the ID.

The woman stared at it and her face changed. She bent over and turned down the volume. Freeman's internal organs stopped throbbing and she smiled at the woman. 'Do you know when he'll be back?'

'He's away for a few days. Is there a problem?'

'No,' Freeman said. 'What was your name?'

'Vicky.'

'Vicky. Do you recall a fight in here a couple of nights ago?'

Vicky grinned. 'Are you kidding? There're fights in here virtually every night. They never get out of hand, though. We've got canny security.'

'Sure,' Freeman said. 'I'm just looking to find out about an incident a couple of nights ago. Boxing Day. It seems these guys took their dispute outside but the victim claims it all kicked off in here. Don't worry, the club's got nothing to do with it, I'm just hoping there might be something on your CCTV that identifies the attacker a little more clearly than the camera in the street. He did a pretty good job of rearranging this guy's face, so . . .'

Vicky looked away, towards a corridor. Freeman took it the office was down there. 'I'm not really supposed to go into the office,' she said. 'Unless it's an emergency.'

Freeman nodded, all understanding. But at least now she knew that Vicky *had* access. Did that mean all the staff did?

'Is there anyone else here who could let me take a look?'

'Not right now,' Vicky said. 'Tommy won't be back until tonight, I think. We're never busy until then so they leave me to it.'

Freeman made a show of looking at her watch and blew out a breath. 'I have a thing tonight. You couldn't just let me in, could you? We don't even need to let Gary know, unless I need a copy of anything. And I'm not holding my breath on that. I just need a quick look. It'd really help me out.'

Vicky sighed and glanced up at the camera above the bar. Freeman wondered if Gary kept a watchful eye over his staff at all times, if he scoured the footage each night, making sure his staff behaved themselves. She'd clocked three cameras since she came in. God knew how many were actually in the place.

Vicky came around from behind the bar and indicated for

Freeman to follow her. As they passed through the club the dancer eyed them up but if she was particularly interested in what was going on she wasn't showing it.

When they got to the end of the corridor, Vicky pulled a set of keys from her pocket and flicked through to find the right one. She opened the door and went in, standing in front of a small desk with two monitors on. One was split between four smaller screens showing various parts of the club. One showed the dancer twirling around a pole, her heels almost touching the old guy as he rested his head. So that was the live feed. She scanned the desktop, looking for clues on how to work it, wondering where the tapes went.

'Digital?' she asked Vicky, pleased such a dive was so well equipped. It would make her life easier if there was anything worth copying.

'Don't ask me how it works,' Vicky said. 'I can barely use my DVD player.'

Freeman looked back at the monitor and noticed someone coming into the club. She hoped it wasn't Tommy; she didn't need him demanding a warrant now she was in.

'Wonders never cease,' Vicky said. 'A customer.' She eyed Freeman up. 'You mind if I get back to the bar?'

'No, of course not. I'll figure this out.' She sat down in front of the monitors. Not having an audience would make this much easier. 'Thanks, Vicky.'

Once the woman was gone, Freeman looked around the room. There was no camera in here, so seeing someone swipe the money seemed unlikely unless, of course, someone at the bar had taken it.

Once she'd figured out how to view old files she went back to the night Darren had taken the money to the club. He said he'd got there around seven so she found the right place and watched as the image of her little brother walking in played out in front of her. He carried a bag that was too heavy for him, making him look like a hunchback. Once he reached the bar he plonked it down on the floor and a young, pretty woman leaned over the bar and kissed him. Kissed him for a little too long. Rachel, she guessed. Once she'd put him down they talked for a few minutes, Darren gesturing as if he was mad about something. After a few moments Darren stood up and started to walk away before seemingly remembering that he'd just left fifty grand in the middle of a strip club. He went back and dragged the bag around behind the bar before kissing Rachel again and then disappearing towards the toilets.

For a few seconds Rachel stood there, leaning against the bar, before she bent over. Freeman couldn't see what she was doing but it didn't take a genius to figure it out.

'Little bitch,' she said.

She sat back and watched the rest of the scene play out. Just before Darren appeared on screen again, Rachel popped up from behind the bar and another man appeared from the corridor. He nodded at Darren, who lifted up the bag and followed the man out of frame. Rachel looked around but didn't leave the bar. Had she just left the money under it?

Freeman pressed fast-forward. After a little while another woman appeared behind the bar. Vicky. As the club filled up, Vicky and Rachel moved quickly, trying to stay out of each other's way as they served the slavering men. About twenty minutes after Darren had left the bar he reappeared. He tried to get Rachel's attention but she just waved him off, too busy for another snog as what looked like a stag party crowded the bar. Darren took the hint and left. About half an hour later, Rachel dropped a glass behind the bar. She bent over again, out of sight, apparently sweeping up the mess. When she re-emerged she held her hand up to Vicky and then walked away from the bar towards the toilets, her arm across her waist, clutching her hand.

When Rachel finally left for the night she was carrying a large handbag. No one checked the staff's bags; all they got from the security staff was a grin and a slap on the arse.

Freeman sighed. So Rachel took the money. And she obviously knew that Healy was blaming Darren and yet hadn't spoken up. Some girlfriend. It was always the same with Darren. For someone who hung around the scum of the earth he was incredibly trusting. Especially with women. Every girlfriend he'd had had screwed him over in some way or another.

She sat back and wondered what to do. Fortunately Vicky hadn't been back yet, but no doubt she'd return if Freeman stayed much longer. She put the pen drive she'd brought with her into the computer and started copying the footage of Rachel. Darren probably wouldn't believe her if she didn't show him the proof. Plus, if he wanted to he could show it to Healy.

When it'd copied she put the drive in her bag and stood up. And then she thought about Rachel. Darren was clearly besotted with her, even though she obviously didn't deserve his affection. She didn't look very old, didn't look that bright. She shouldn't have taken the money, shouldn't have screwed Darren over. But maybe she was scared. She'd done something stupid and now didn't know how to get out of it. And if Gary or Healy found out? Maybe they wouldn't be averse to breaking her legs too. Or something worse. And would these guys really believe that Darren was unaware of what she'd done?

Maybe if Darren talked to Rachel, got her to give the money back to Healy, maybe he'd let it go. Tell the club guys it'd been a mistake. And so long as she had the proof there on the pen drive as backup . . .

Freeman sat down again and wondered about the best way to proceed. If she was going to do this then no one could know she had been here. Vicky had seen her ID but if there was nothing else . . .

She stopped the recording and went back to the start of the night Darren had been here, deleting everything from then on, including her arrival this morning. Now there was nothing on Darren, on Rachel, or on her. She hoped this girl was worth it.

She closed her eyes as a message came up on screen telling her the files had been deleted and felt sick, regretting it immediately. That was stupid. What if someone found out? She tried to find a way to restore it.

'Find anything?'

Freeman jumped as Vicky came back in to the office. She stood up, taking her phone out. 'I think there's something wrong with the system.'

'What do you mean?' Vicky asked.

'Well, there's nothing there,' Freeman said and watched Vicky's face drop. 'I went back over the tapes but there's nothing from the last few days. I don't think it's recording. Is it supposed to be on all the time?'

Vicky stepped towards the desk but appeared to have less idea than Freeman. 'It should be,' she said. 'There's nothing?'

'Nothing at all. I thought I should mention it. You might need to get someone in to look at it unless it's just been turned off by accident.'

'Shit,' Vicky said.

'Sorry, I need to go,' said Freeman, waving her phone. 'Thanks for your help, anyway.' She walked out of the office, past the podium where the old man who'd been asleep was now propped up. His rheumy eyes followed her. She felt bad in case she'd got Vicky into trouble. But more than that she felt ill at the thought of what she'd risked because of one, stupid, fleeting moment of madness. Hopefully the club's owner, Gary, would accept it was just one of those things, and let it go, and no one would be any the wiser.

14

Gardner watched as Lauren James walked across the car park and got into a waiting taxi. He wondered why Harry hadn't given her a lift, why no one else had come to get her, maybe one of the people she'd been relying on the night before for help. Why the mighty Walter James hadn't come to get his daughter – why he hadn't shown his face at all, in fact. Lauren seemed to rely on her father, had called him for help before calling the police. So why wasn't he there for her? Unless the calls hadn't been about needing help at all.

Gardner sighed. There was nothing else he could do about her now anyway. She'd given a statement, confused as it was. She'd answered their questions. She'd cooperated. And now they'd let her go. Gardner got the feeling he'd never get another chance to ask her anything else. Even if they did find reason to bring her in again, they weren't going to let him near her. Atherton would handle any further contact with Lauren, which, as far as Gardner could make out, meant that unless Lauren confessed, he could safely say she was off the hook.

He'd risked another bollocking by going to Atherton and Hadley and requesting more time with Lauren. It didn't even have to be him who spoke to her, just as long as someone pressed her a little harder on what had happened the night before Ritchie's body was found.

'Her nails were broken,' Gardner said. As he left the interview room he'd noticed Lauren dig her nails into her scalp. One nail was shorter than the others. Her nail varnish was chipped.

'Hardly damning evidence of murder,' Hadley said.

'No. But Donoghue had scratches on his arms and face which I bet we'll find traces of her nail varnish in.'

'And if that happens, we'll speak to her again.'

'But she claimed she barely even spoke to him, never mind fought with him. She's lying,' Gardner said.

'DI Gardner, Lauren James came here voluntarily. She answered all your questions, all of Atherton's questions. If any more evidence presents itself linking Lauren to the murder, she will be brought back in. Until then, I suggest you do your job and look for the evidence,' Hadley said. 'Where are we with that side of things?' he said to Atherton, dismissing Gardner.

'Waiting on the autopsy. It's scheduled for the morning but I've tried to hustle them for something sooner.'

'Try harder,' Hadley said.

Atherton cleared his throat and nodded. 'We're chasing up CCTV footage too but there's a lot of ground to cover.'

'Sir, if I may, I really think we have enough to hold Lauren James. She's admitted he came round last night wanting to talk. She's admitted things were difficult with their relationship, that Donoghue had a temper. The scratch marks have to be from Lauren. She sent him a text to lure him back – which she lied about. She called several people for backup. I can't see how that isn't enough to keep pressing her.'

'Enough, Gardner,' Hadley said. 'Let it go. We need to do this right.'

'Meaning what? That every other time we do it wrong?'

'Let it go,' Hadley repeated and picked up his phone, waving his fingers towards the door, dismissing them both. Gardner walked out behind Atherton and continued trying to argue his case but Atherton just said, 'Briefing. Ten minutes,' and walked away.

Before the briefing started, Gardner wandered over to Harrington's desk. He could see Walter James's face on his computer screen and wondered what he was up to.

'Check this out,' Harrington said and pressed play on a campaign ad seemingly made by schoolchildren on Walter James's behalf. There was lots of grinning and waving and the camera panned across Middlesbrough's most beautiful vistas. Gardner resisted the urge to vomit and watched as the picture changed to black and white and the man himself appeared on screen spouting some gibberish about making Middlesbrough better despite the hardships we were all facing. 'Listen for it,' Harrington said as Walter spoke the words, 'Making the best of a bad situation.'

'That's his slogan?' Gardner asked.

'That's one of them,' Harrington said. 'Just think of the field day the papers will have with it once this gets out.' Harrington stood up as the team started making its way out to the briefing.

'So how do you think Mr James will make the best of this bad situation?' Gardner asked.

'I don't know. Outreach for criminal daughters, maybe?'

'No,' Gardner said. 'That doesn't fit with his party line. Maybe "one more dealer off the streets" would do it, though.'

Harrington laughed and they made their way along to the incident room. Gardner watched as PC Dawn Lawton walked up the corridor towards him, running her hand across her hair. She'd had it cut short a few days earlier and was clearly self-conscious about it. He thought it suited her. Maybe he should've mentioned it.

'Anything useful?' he said as she approached him.

'Maybe,' she said and he opened the door for her. He hadn't been expecting much; if anyone had seen what happened they would've called the police last night. He'd tested out his theory of the neighbours being able to see the end of Lauren's garden from an upstairs window before leaving Lawton to it. Turns out the tall hedges were enough to keep anyone from seeing anything. It was possible to catch sight of a corner of her garden if you were really trying, but it was doubtful anyone was looking out at that time of night.

As the room filled up, everyone seemed to gravitate towards the tray of doughnuts someone had brought in. Gardner tried to see if there were any chocolate ones left without making it look like he cared. Truth was, he was trying to keep away from them or was at least planning to. New Year's resolution. It wasn't that he needed to lose any weight, but he had what he liked to think of as pre-middle-aged spread. No overhanging gut yet but a definite softening around the middle. He stepped away from the doughnuts and glanced around the room. Harrington must've put away at least three of them but it never seemed to show on his wiry frame. DC Marcus Berman was broader but that was from weightlifting rather than cake-lifting. Of course there was Don Murphy, currently on the sick with another case of gout, who made anyone look slim in comparison. And at the other end of the scale, Cartwright – a skinny streak of piss. But who was keeping tabs?

Once everyone was assembled, Atherton took his place at the front of the room, hands behind his back, swaying back and forth until the noise died down. 'Thank you,' he said. 'I'm going to keep this as brief as possible. There's still a lot to be done but I thought it necessary to get us all on the same page.' He turned and pointed at the image of Ritchie Donoghue on the board. It wasn't the most flattering photograph: a mug shot that appeared to have been taken when Donoghue was drunk. His mouth was open, saliva collecting in the corner.

'Richard Donoghue, aged thirty-seven. Known drug dealer, also has previous for ABH and burglary. Found this morning at approximately eight a.m. by Lauren James in the back garden of her home. Ms James admits to a previous relationship with the victim but claims that ended several weeks ago. Approximate time of death has been narrowed to between twelve and three a.m. this morning.'

'But as Lauren sent a text to Ritchie at twelve thirty a.m., it's likely he was still alive at that time,' Gardner said.

'Only if we're assuming Lauren killed him. Which we're not,' Atherton said, trying to stare Gardner down to make his point. He cleared his throat and continued. 'Victim appears to have been assaulted, possibly with two weapons, possibly gardening tools. A spade was found at the scene but appears to have been wiped, so no prints. There were still traces of blood on the spade, though, which is currently being compared with the victim's. Second weapon was likely a blunt instrument but so far nothing's been recovered. There were several rocks at the scene, which are possibilities, but we'll see. Preliminary cause of death is head trauma. Both DI Gardner and I have spoken to Ms James.' Atherton looked to Gardner who stood and took over.

Gardner summarised Lauren's statement but bit his tongue before he said, *I think she's full of shit.* 'The people she called last night and this morning – her father Walter James, her father's employees Peter Hinde and Jen Worrall, and Lauren's half-brother Guy James – we need to speak to them all. Lauren's solicitor's claiming she hadn't been cautioned when her phone was taken as evidence so whatever we get from that might not help us, including any prints etc. But we'll get a warrant for the phone records anyway, if necessary, and see where they lead.'

'If necessary,' Atherton said, which Gardner took to mean that wouldn't be happening.

'Speaking to the aforementioned people is still vital, though. Even if it's just to get background on the victim. We've already got some witness statements from the house to house. Lawton?'

Lawton stood and her face flushed so she put her head down and consulted her notebook. 'Neighbour to the right of Lauren, Elizabeth Mortimer, says she saw Ritchie turn up about ten-ish but couldn't say one way or another if he went into the house. Says she saw him going up the drive as she was drawing the curtains. Had seen him there before, didn't like the look of him. Went to bed soon after and didn't hear anything later on. It's unlikely she would've heard anything unless they were outside and making lots of noise. Those houses are pretty far apart.'

'Perfect for a bit of privacy when you're murdering an ex-boyfriend,' Harrington said.

'What was that, Detective?' Atherton said and Harrington looked at the floor, muttering an apology. Gardner nodded to Lawton to continue.

'The house on the other side is empty. Has been for three weeks,' Lawton said. 'But the woman who lives opposite Lauren James, Ann Earnshaw, said she saw Ritchie leaving. Didn't see him arrive so she doesn't know how long he was there but she heard shouting at about ten forty-five. Looked out the window and saw Ritchie walking away from the house, making gestures, she said.'

'So if they're right, Ritchie was there for around forty-five minutes. A lot longer than Lauren claimed,' Gardner pointed out.

'But that's assuming the witnesses are correct. I think we all know the odds on that,' Atherton said.

'Did she see anything else? Did he come back?' Gardner

asked, ignoring Atherton, although he knew he was right. Eyewitnesses were frequently mistaken, especially when it came to details like time.

'She said she went up to bed about half an hour later. Woke up when she heard a door slam sometime around twelve twenty. She was waiting for her daughter, Kirsty, to come home from a night out, so she was anxious. Heard a car, thought it might've been her daughter in a taxi. Looked out and saw a car parked outside Lauren's house. Wasn't her daughter so she went back to bed. Heard her daughter come in about two a.m., possibly slightly earlier.'

'Did she recognise the car?'

'She said she'd seen similar cars parked there before. One was Lauren's dad's. She knows who Walter James is, obviously. But she said there was another one that came. Didn't know who it belonged to. A man, but she doesn't know him. Anyway, she didn't get a licence plate but said it was a black car, possibly a BMW but she wouldn't swear to it.'

'Does Lauren have a BMW?' someone asked.

'Doesn't drive,' Atherton said. 'No licence, no cars registered to her.'

'Okay, are we trying to find out if anyone Lauren knows has a black BMW?' Someone nodded and Gardner turned to Lawton. 'Did you speak to the daughter? She could've seen something if she came back at two.'

'Not yet,' Lawton said. 'Her mum said she went out to work at seven this morning.'

'After getting in at two? Must be a teenager,' Gardner said.

'Seventeen.'

'Okay, see if you can get hold of her. Anything else from the neighbours?'

'Nothing much. Lauren's neighbour, Mrs Mortimer, said Lauren had only been there about a year. Didn't know her really. Wasn't the kind of person she'd socialise with. Said she was fairly quiet most of the time, kept to herself. But occasionally she had parties that could go on all night. Didn't seem too upset by it, though. I think she was more concerned that a dead body might lower the house prices.'

'Right,' Gardner said. 'Speak to the daughter. See if she saw anything when she came home.'

Atherton stepped up again. 'Currently we have three possibilities. One, that this was related to Ritchie Donoghue's business. He's a known dealer. We need to find out who his associates are and if there have been any disputes of late. Secondly,' he said and his eyes flashed towards Hadley who was lurking at the back, 'it *could* be a domestic dispute. We have no reason to believe Lauren James had anything to do with it so far but we need to rule it out. And thirdly, it's possible someone else known to Donoghue or Lauren was involved.'

'One of those people Lauren called,' Gardner said.

Atherton sighed. 'Yes, Inspector. It's possible the calls were related to the murder so we need to look at the recipients of these calls. And *if necessary* we'll get billings for all the recipients' accounts to see if they had any contact with Donoghue. As Donoghue's phone is missing, we're also waiting for billing information for that. Hopefully it will shed some more light on the events of last night.'

'If I may,' a voice from the back piped up and everyone turned as Superintendent Hadley stepped forward. 'There is also the possibility that neither Lauren James nor anyone she knows was responsible.'

The room was quiet for a moment so Gardner decided to fill the air. 'I think DCI Atherton covered that possibility.'

Hadley barely glanced in Gardner's direction as he responded. 'What DCI Atherton posited was that one of Ritchie Donoghue's associates, someone else involved in the drug business, could be responsible. What I'm saying is that it could be someone else completely.'

'A random attack, you mean?' Atherton asked.

'Why not?' Hadley said but no one answered. Gardner assumed no one wanted to be the one to say, 'Duh' to the superintendent. 'Let's just keep our minds open, shall we?' He nodded for Atherton to continue, his two cents offered.

A few more members of the team spoke up, mostly with information about the scene. They'd found tyre marks in the alley behind Lauren's house, which they'd try to match to any cars that fitted the witnesses description or those known to Ritchie and Lauren. It was possible Ritchie had been attacked in the alley and then made his way into his ex-girl-friend's garden where the attack continued. They'd found a small amount of blood leading from the alley into Lauren's back garden, and a larger amount of blood had been found where the body was with spatter a few feet around it. That could be a good thing for Lauren. Why would she attack him in the alley where someone could see her? And why would he then crawl *towards* her house? But if someone else had attacked him, maybe he thought she'd help him and call an ambulance.

Gardner sighed. It wasn't worth speculating on such things at this point. He looked around for Cartwright. He hadn't seen him for a while. So much for being more useful here.

'And one last thing,' Atherton said. 'Despite certain rumours circulating online already, no one related to this investigation will be named until otherwise notified. All interviews will go through myself or through Detective Superintendent Hadley. And anyone mentioning the name Walter James anywhere outside of this office will find themselves looking at a discipli-nary.' Atherton's eyes met with Hadley's, who just nodded, and Atherton continued.

Once all the tasks were doled out, the room started to empty. Gardner kept an eye on Hadley who made his way to Atherton and had another quiet word while Atherton nodded in agreement. Gardner was trying to listen in when he heard Harrington shout at him.

'This'll butter your muffins,' Harrington said and Gardner resisted the urge to ask what he was on about. 'Walter James has a black Audi S4 Saloon.'

'That could be mistaken for a BMW in the dark by someone who doesn't know cars, couldn't it?' Gardner said and felt a surge go through him.

'Possibly. *But*,' Harrington continued, 'it was written off last week.'

'Don't toy with my emotions, Harrington.'

'I'd rather not. Anyway, as I was saying, good old Walt has, or *had*, a black BMW-like car, but unless he's driving a wreck it wasn't his car parked outside Lauren's.'

'So who was it? What happened to my muffins being buttered?'

'Peter Hinde, or Big P as I'd prefer to call him, has a black BMW.'

'So, Peter Hinde was there last night?' Gardner said and Harrington shrugged.

'Let's find out,' he said.

15

Freeman pulled up outside the block of flats and stared up at her living-room window, wondering if Darren would still be there. She imagined he would be. He was desperate enough for her to go and look at the tapes, so surely he'd wait for some answers. She just wasn't sure how long he'd stick around once he knew who had really taken the money.

She leaned forward, resting her head on the steering wheel. She couldn't believe he was back. It hadn't sunk in yet; she couldn't quite get her brain around it. For five long years she'd thought her younger brother was dead, likely by his own hand or at least from an accident that'd happened while he was high. She'd sat beside her mam after the police had informed them they'd found his car in the river. But where she'd been silent and numb, her mam had been hysterical, lashing out at everyone, especially Freeman. After all, it was her fault Darren had gone to prison. Grassing up her own brother. How did she sleep at night?

Not very well, truth be told. She'd put herself through hell trying to decide whether to go to the police in the first place. She'd only just signed up herself, not even started the training, and was constantly torturing herself about whether she was giving him up because she thought she *should* if she was going to be one of them, or whether she

73

was wanting to *be* one of them so she could help people like her brother.

Darren had been on a downward spiral for a long time. It was mostly petty crimes he was into – shoplifting, stealing wallets in pubs. But he'd got in with an older crowd and she was worried he was getting himself into worse things. He suddenly had large amounts of money, at least large for him, and even though he was spending it on drugs like there was no tomorrow, he still managed to find more. When the police came looking for him in connection with an armed robbery, Freeman knew he was in too deep and would only get deeper. The police mentioned some names that she'd heard before, that most people in the area had heard before. The kind of people you wouldn't want anyone, let alone your little brother, getting involved with. In the end she decided that maybe prison was the best place for him. That it might shake some sense into him. Strings were pulled to make sure Darren would be sent to a different prison and kept away from the rest of them. The plan was to get him out of that world, away from those people he'd started associating with, get him clean. Only Darren wouldn't talk, so he was the only one who went down anyway. So she'd been naive. She was young.

But Darren *was* clean for a while. Even started making plans for when he got out. He'd go to college. Take some of those exams he'd skipped at school. Maybe get a flat of his own. One that didn't have bars on the windows. Not that he'd told Freeman any of this. She'd only managed to visit him a few times before he told her he didn't want to see her any more. Things were looking up for him, but he would never forgive her for what she'd done. Everything she knew about Darren after that day came from her dad or older brother Mark. Her mam was with Darren on the forgiveness front.

Another car pulled into the car park and Freeman sat up

straight. The douchebag that lived above her was obviously starting the New Year celebrations early. She watched as he lifted two cases of lager and a couple of bottles of vodka from the boot and tried to carry them whilst fumbling in his pocket for his keys.

Freeman got out of the car, knowing she couldn't put it off any longer. She had to face Darren. Had to tell him what she'd found. The bad feeling in the pit of her stomach was increasing and it wasn't all to do with her brother's predicament. She'd made a mistake erasing the footage from Slinky's. She'd scanned through it and hadn't seen anything criminal going down, other than Rachel's theft. There didn't seem to be any reason why anyone would need what was on those tapes. And yet . . . She knew it was wrong. Knew if anyone found out or if Gary disputed her version of events that she could be in some serious shit. Maybe she should've just stayed there until she'd worked out how to restore the footage. How likely was it that Vicky would know what she was doing? What she'd done? But it was too late now. She'd made her bed. She just hoped that nothing would come of it.

As she opened the door to the flat she could hear the TV playing. She stuck her head into the living room and saw an old *Tom and Jerry* cartoon was on, playing to itself.

'Shit,' she muttered, turning to check the bathroom but the door was wide open. She walked into the living room, reaching for the remote and turning the TV off.

'I was watching that.'

Freeman jumped, spinning around to find Darren standing in the dark kitchen, helping himself to the meagre contents of her fridge. He was attempting to make a sandwich although she doubted there were enough ingredients there to make anything resembling one.

She was about to switch the TV back on but instead flipped open her laptop and turned it on. 'I checked the tapes,' she said and Darren put down the knife he was holding, licking the butter from it first. He came back into the living room and sat down at the table in front of the laptop.

'Was it that arsehole? The one I gave the money to?'

'Just watch it.' Freeman pushed the pen drive into the laptop and waited for it to be recognised. 'But now I've done what you wanted, you have to tell me what happened, Darren. You owe me that.'

'I *owe* you? What, like we're even now?'

'That's not what I meant,' she said, although part of her did feel it. Tit for tat. Just like when they were kids. I get you thrown in prison; you get me to risk my job for you. Even-stevens.

The computer found the drive. 'There's no camera in the office,' she said, tapping keys over Darren's shoulder. 'And apparently Gary is away for a few days. Hasn't been there since you left the money. So anything him and his buddy got up to isn't on the tapes.'

'So you got nothing?'

'No,' Freeman said, annoyed at his tone. She was about to press play but stopped and pulled up a chair beside him. 'How long have you known Rachel?'

'What's that got to do with anything?' Darren asked and Freeman just looked at him. 'Long enough,' he said, still not getting it.

Freeman sighed and pressed play. She watched Darren watching the footage, his expression blank. She glanced at the screen just as Rachel was bending down, out of view. She looked back at Darren but there was still nothing. When the footage had finished she waited for him to say something. Instead he just shrugged. 'That's it? There's nothing happening.'

'You need to see it again.'

'What for? That doesn't show shit. Those arseholes from

the club must've took it later and then called Healy telling him it wasn't all there.'

'Are you kidding me?' Freeman said.

'What?'

'*Rachel* took the money. That is Rachel, right? The one who stuck her tongue down your throat?'

'Yeah, that's her, but she didn't take anything.'

Freeman started the footage again. 'Look at it,' she said. 'You left the bag with her. No one else touched it except you, her and Tommy. And if *you* didn't do it and *he* didn't do it . . .'

'But he *did* take it.'

'Darren, you left the money with her. What do you think she was doing on the floor all that time? She takes some of the money, she hides it under the bar and then later on she sneaks it to the toilets.'

'That's bullshit. You can't even see anything. The camera doesn't show anything behind the bar.'

'Exactly. And you think she doesn't know that?'

'No,' Darren said, standing up. 'She wouldn't do that. And if she had she would've told me.'

'How long did you say you'd known her?'

'It doesn't matter. I know her. I trust her.'

'How long?'

'It doesn't matter how long. That's not how it works. I've known *you* my whole life and I don't trust you.'

She felt like she'd been punched in the gut. He could call her all the names under the sun, frequently had, and she didn't care. But he didn't trust her? She turned away from him, not wanting him to see her eyes fill up.

'Why did you come here, if you don't trust me?' she said, quietly.

'Because I needed help and I couldn't think of anyone else to go to.'

Freeman sat there, not speaking, afraid of saying something else she'd regret. She should've known that this wouldn't make things better. It didn't make them even. Not even close.

'Okay,' she said. 'You've got what you came for. I'm sorry it's not what you wanted but . . .' She extracted the pen drive and held it out for him. 'Do what you want with it.'

Darren took the drive, pushing it into his jeans pocket, before grabbing his jacket, shrugging it on and walking away without another word.

16

Gardner stuffed the remains of the sandwich into his mouth as DC Marcus Berman approached his desk.

'Peter Hinde's here,' Berman said and grinned. He knew that Gardner had been hauled out of the interview with Lauren but he was being allowed to speak with Walter James's employee.

'Thanks,' Gardner said and sat back and thought about what they had so far. Lauren James was clearly lying through her teeth. He was waiting for word from forensics about the nail varnish, but he could take a wild guess at the results.

Lauren claimed that Ritchie had never entered the house last night, that he'd just wanted to talk and when she refused he left. But witnesses claimed he was there much longer and the fact that he had scratches on his face and arm suggested they'd done a little more than exchanged a few words on the doorstep. But the time of death was apparently hours later. Mrs Earnshaw claimed to have seen Ritchie leaving, so he must've come back later, presumably after Lauren had sent him a text. So had she planned to kill him? If she *had* she could've picked a slightly more inconspicuous place to do it. Or had she just rallied some backup by then and what she'd planned to be a warning to Ritchie got out of hand?

Then there were all the phone calls. If the time of death was correct she'd made the calls before the murder, before she'd even lured Ritchie back, suggesting she didn't act alone. This would make sense. Ritchie Donoghue was a big guy, with a history of violence. It was doubtful Lauren could have killed him by herself. They had one witness so far, Ann Earnshaw, who claimed to have seen a car – possibly Hinde's – outside the house late at night. Had they done it together? There were two weapons, according to the pathologist. Peter Hinde was clearly something more than just an employee of Walter James and was, so far, the one with the biggest link to the case. Gardner was itching to talk to him. Find out what Big P had to say for himself.

Gardner stood as Harrington came in carrying two coffees. He took one from him. 'Is Lawton back yet?' he asked and Harrington indicated behind him. 'Give me two minutes,' he said and walked over to Lawton. 'Any luck with the neighbour's daughter?'

Lawton nodded. 'Kirsty. Said there was a car in the alley when she came home. Fairly positive it was a BMW, dark. Couldn't recall much else about it. Judging from the state of her this morning, I'd guess she had a big night out last night.'

'Does she remember which taxi firm she used? Maybe the driver will remember something.'

Lawton shook her head. 'She didn't get a taxi. Walked home.'

Gardner let out a breath. He bet the girl had promised her mother she'd get a taxi home. 'Was she with anyone else?'

'Yes. Another girl, named Samantha Reilly. Haven't tracked her down yet but Kirsty said they saw someone in the alley. A tall, skinny man. Said they were messing about, walked past the end of the alley and saw someone come out of Lauren's gate. He looked at them and then got into the car and drove off.'

'And I suppose it'd be wishful thinking to ask if she could identify him.'

Lawton gave him a smile. 'Tall and skinny is all she could say. Old, young. She has no idea.'

'Could she describe anything else about the car?'

'Just big. Dark.' Lawton shrugged.

'Does she remember the time?'

'No. Just late, she said. Her mum thinks around two a.m.'

'Peter Hinde's in room two,' Berman shouted from the doorway and Gardner nodded at him.

'Okay, good work,' he said to Lawton. 'See if you can get anything else from the friend.' He grabbed Harrington before heading down to meet the mysterious Big P.

As they entered the room the man they'd come to meet stood up. He was not what Gardner had been expecting for a man nicknamed Big P. He had the air and dress sense of someone with a lot of money. From what Lauren had told him, that Walter James had helped out Peter's mother, he'd been expecting something different, some kind of street waif dragged from the slums to be Walter James's minder. The man in front of him looked more like a public schoolboy. He was also tall, about Gardner's height, and what some might describe as skinny.

'Peter Hinde,' he said and extended his hand. From his voice it appeared Gardner was right. It reeked of private education.

'Please, take a seat,' Gardner said and waited as Peter removed his suit jacket, folding it carefully and then draping it over the back of his chair.

'Is Lauren all right?' Peter asked, his face pinched with concern.

'She's okay. A bit shaken up,' Gardner said and then reminded Hinde he was under caution but free to leave any time he liked. Hinde nodded but suddenly looked slightly nervous. 'Lauren

James left a couple of messages for you, correct? One last night, one this morning. What did her messages say?'

'Umm . . .' Peter shook his head. 'She asked where I was, where her dad was. Said she needed help. Asked me to call her back.'

'But you didn't?' Gardner asked but he already knew the answer.

'No, not last night.'

'Why?' Harrington asked. 'She said she needed help.'

Peter looked confused. 'I didn't get the messages until later this morning. I spoke to her later.'

'You work for her dad, right? You're not friends with Lauren,' Gardner said.

Peter's face flushed. 'I wouldn't say that,' he said.

'So you *are* friends?'

'Of course. I've known her a long time.'

'Are you more than friends?' Gardner said.

Peter paused; seemed to be weighing things up. 'No. If I wasn't working for her dad we probably wouldn't be in touch any more.'

'Okay. So she called you looking for her dad last night and then again this morning. Correct?'

'Yes.'

'But you didn't respond?'

'No.'

'What about the call later this morning?'

Peter swallowed and shuffled in his seat.

'You answered that call, didn't you?' Gardner asked.

'Yes.'

'What did Lauren say?'

Gardner knew that this call had been made *after* Lauren had reported Ritchie's murder to the police.

'She . . . she told me what'd happened. To Ritchie.'

'And?'

'And that was it. She was upset.'

'Of course,' Gardner said. 'So why did she call you?'

'I don't know. I guess she couldn't get hold of Walter. She needed someone.'

'But you didn't come round to the house.'

'No,' Peter said.

'Why not? You said she needed someone.'

'I didn't think showing up at a crime scene would be appreciated. I didn't want to get in the way.'

'You could've come to the station.'

'Yes. I didn't think.'

'Can we talk about last night? Where were you?'

'At the pub with Walter, Walter James.'

'Do you remember what time that was?'

'From around nine thirty p.m. to just after eleven p.m., I think.'

'And after that?'

'Home. I left Walter, walked home, went to bed.'

'Can anyone confirm that?'

'I live alone.'

'Okay,' Gardner said. 'You said you walked home. You didn't drive?'

'I'd been drinking.'

'Is that a no?'

'Of course it is,' Peter said.

'So your car was at home all night?'

'No. I left it at the office last night. We were going for a drink after work.'

'What time was that?'

'Like I said, about nine thirty, give or take a few minutes.'

'And it's still there?'

Peter looked puzzled. 'No. It's here. I took a cab to the office this morning and then drove here when you called.'

'So you didn't drive the car at all last night?'

'No.'

'You said you left it at the office. Did you leave the keys?'

'No,' Peter said and reached into his jacket pocket, holding up the keys to show them. 'My house key is on there too.'

'So, you had the keys with you at all times. No one borrowed them. No one could've taken them from your pocket while you were drinking?'

'Not these keys,' Peter said.

'It's a BMW, yes?' Harrington said. 'I'm guessing they'd be pretty hard to steal. One of the reasons to buy it, right?'

'I suppose,' Peter said.

'So, you're sure no one else could've taken your keys?'

Peter was still for a moment, and his eyes moved quickly from left to right. 'I have a spare key,' he said.

'All right,' Gardner said. 'And where's that kept?'

'Usually at home.'

'Usually?' Gardner asked.

'It was at the office.'

'Why did you move it to the office if you usually keep it at home?'

'Walter's car was involved in an accident last week. It was undriveable. He needed to be at a meeting yesterday so he borrowed my car.'

'So Walter James had a key too,' Gardner said. 'Was it possible he took your car last night?'

'No, of course not.'

'How can you be sure?'

'Because we'd been drinking. He wouldn't have driven the car. He got a taxi home.'

'But you don't know where he went once he left you.'

'Who else had access to your car?' Harrington asked. 'Had anyone else driven it? Who knew the keys were at the office?'

Peter shrugged. 'No one else has driven it, to the best of my knowledge. But people knew the keys were there. It wasn't a secret. I trust the people I work with.'

'Who? Who knew the keys were there? Who had access?'

Peter sighed. 'Walter. Jen. I don't know. Maybe everyone knew.'

'So what you're saying is anybody who works in that office could've taken your car last night?'

Peter sat forward, letting out a breath. 'I suppose they could.'

They were going around in circles and Peter Hinde was as full of shit as Lauren James. There was something going on between them but neither was budging. Both stuck to their story that he was her dad's campaign manager, that was it, and that she'd only gone to him because Walter was MIA.

And his alibi, like Lauren's, was flimsy at best. The whole thing stunk but they'd let Hinde go. For now. They'd check CCTV around the office and Lauren's house, and check ANPR – Automatic Number Plate Recognition – for any movements last night.

'Where are we with the others?' Gardner asked, meaning the other recipients of Lauren's late-night calls.

'We're still unable to reach Guy James, by phone or at his address. I'll keep trying,' Berman said. 'Same with Jen Worrall.'

Gardner looked at his watch. 'Would the office be open today? After Christmas? Has anyone tried her there?' He looked around the room but no one else spoke up so Gardner kept talking. 'And why the hell isn't Walter James here yet?'

Berman raised his hand as if it were a maths lesson and he'd figured out the answer. 'I spoke to him earlier. He said he'd be here as soon as he could. He said he was organising things so he could give us his full attention.'

'What?' Gardner said. 'Why hasn't someone *dragged* his arse in?'

He got a wall of looks that said: *Not me.*

'I guess when you're golf buddies with the DCC, you get to choose when you cooperate with a murder investigation,' Berman said.

'This is bullshit,' Gardner muttered and grabbed his coat. 'Harrington.'

Harrington followed and they took the stairs down to the car park. 'So what, you're just going to storm his office? Demand he comes with you?' Harrington said. 'You *do* still want to work here, don't you?'

Gardner stopped. 'His daughter could be up for a murder charge and he's at the office doing paperwork?'

'So that makes him guilty?'

'It's a power play,' Gardner said. 'This is his *daughter.* Why isn't he here, wringing his hands, making demands? Why is he sat on his fat arse in his office, telling my people when he'll deign to speak to us?'

Gardner walked away. He didn't care who Walter James was. How much money he had. Who his golf buddies were. This was a murder investigation. And things would be on *his* terms. Not James's.

17

Gardner pulled up outside the office registered to the Walter James campaign. It wasn't quite the grand building he'd been expecting but a modern, soulless place with a printer shop on one side and an unused space on the other.

Campaign posters covered most of the windows so he could see little of the activity going on inside. He'd seen the image from the poster before – numerous times. He'd lost count of the number of campaign flyers that had been posted through his door and then put straight in the bin. James clearly wasn't campaigning on any environmental promises.

He looked around the area. It wasn't a busy street, not much traffic; a few pedestrians passing by. The only thing that looked out of place was the throng of reporters across the street. So much for keeping schtum. They all looked up as Gardner approached the office but they probably knew no one was going to speak to them. But if they happened to see him going inside and then escorting Mr James out, well, that didn't mean he was suggesting anything, did it? Maybe they were just friends.

He looked up for any sign of CCTV, noticing just one camera on the building across the street. Hopefully it'd cover traffic in and out of Walter's office.

He'd pulled up onto the pavement, parking directly in front of the office, but there were no other cars there. He wondered where Peter Hinde had left his car the day before.

'Shall we?' he said to Harrington and led them inside.

The office was something of a shambles. Two desks were covered in papers. The floor was piled high with boxes, no doubt filled with more junk mail to inflict on people. A phone was ringing on one of the desks but there was no one in the room to answer it.

'Hello?' Harrington said as they walked further inside. Gardner noticed a small kitchen to the right with another door leading off it, possibly a toilet. There was a third door at the back of the main office, opening on to a corridor. Gardner walked through it and found two smaller offices, one on each side of the corridor. One was like the main room, bursting with paperwork but lacking in people. In the second he found what he was looking for.

Walter James, Peter Hinde and a young woman with blond hair, tightly pulled back from her face, all turned to look at him. She was taking notes. Jen Worrall, he assumed.

'Can I help you?' she said and started walking towards him.

'DI Gardner. This is DC Harrington.'

Jen turned to Walter for a reaction.

'Walter James,' he said, extending his hand, grinning like it was a meet and greet. 'And this is Jen Worrall, our star intern.' Walter put a hand on Jen's shoulder, which she looked like she wanted to shrug away from. 'And you've met Peter, I believe. So, what can I do for you, Inspector?'

'I'm sure you're aware of what's happened. I'd like you to come down to the station with me. Just to answer a few questions. Make a statement.'

'Of course. But you needn't have come all this way,' Walter said. 'Young Craig's come to escort me to the station.'

'Craig?' Gardner said and saw DC Craig Cartwright step out from behind the door, unable to keep the smug grin from his face.

'Sir,' he said to Gardner.

'What're you doing here?' Gardner asked.

'DCI Atherton requested I come and escort Mr James to the station, sir. At his convenience.'

Gardner looked over his shoulder at Harrington, who rolled his eyes. Craig Cartwright was Atherton's lap dog. He was no more a detective than Gardner was a flamenco dancer. There was no way on earth he was going to conduct the interview with Walter James.

'Sorry you had to come down here for nothing, DI Gardner,' Walter said. 'I assumed your boss would be keeping you in the loop. But I'm all yours now. So,' he said, 'shall we?'

Gardner's blood was boiling. James was trying to play him. Trying to make it known who was in charge. And maybe he was. Gardner didn't have Hadley in his pocket. But he wasn't going to play along.

'Why don't you go along with Cartwright? I'll be there in a while. There're a few things I'd like to do here first.'

Walter's smarm decreased by a degree and he looked to his staff. 'I hope you're not going to cause my people any grief, Mr Gardner. My campaign staff have nothing to do with what's happened with my daughter.'

'I just want a quick look around.'

Walter stared at Gardner a little too long before smiling and saying, 'Of course.' He took his coat from the stand in the corner of the room and followed Cartwright out.

Gardner waited until they'd gone before speaking. 'Ms Worrall, would you mind taking a seat?'

'What for?' Jen said, looking to Peter for answers.

'Just a few questions. Harrington,' he said and nodded to his colleague to stay and keep the intern company. 'Do you mind showing me where you left your car last night?' he said to Peter and followed him outside, leaving Harrington to no doubt try and chat up the other witness.

Peter led him to the end of the corridor, through the back door, into an alley. They walked a few yards until the alley opened up into a small, makeshift car park, just big enough for the three cars currently occupying the space.

'Just here,' he said.

'And is this where you usually park when you come to work?' Gardner asked as he looked around. There was no CCTV in sight, no windows overlooking the car park. It was hardly secure.

'Usually. There's not much room, as you can see. Often it's used by me and Walter and someone from the printers next door.'

'It's not allocated parking?'

'No. First come, first served. If I'm not here early enough to snag a spot I'll park in the car park down the road. That's where I've left it now.'

'You wouldn't be happier leaving it in a real car park, with security?'

Peter shrugged. 'This is more convenient. Besides, how often does car park security really work?'

Gardner nodded. He had a point. 'Okay, thanks,' he said and started to follow Hinde back inside when he heard raised voices coming from the front of the building. Gardner glanced at Hinde and then walked round to the front to find Walter James holding court and the gathered reporters firing questions. Cartwright stood beside James, his hands crossed in front of him, eyes scanning the small crowd, no doubt just like he'd seen in a dozen films about protecting the president.

'As I said, all I know is that a friend of my daughter was attacked last night and she's helping police with their inquiries. That's all I can say except that I'm sure you'll understand that my daughter is very upset at this turn of events, so it would be appreciated if she could be left to grieve in private. Thank you.'

Gardner watched as Cartwright led James to his car and settled him into the front seat like the good little chauffeur he was. Beside him, Peter Hinde let out a sigh and headed back down the alley to go inside. He clearly had as much desire to speak to the reporters as Gardner did and for a moment Gardner felt sorry for the man who was responsible for Walter James.

He followed Hinde inside and picked up where they left off. 'So, where did you leave your keys? Your spare keys?'

Peter pointed to the office opposite Walter's. 'In here, my office,' he said. Gardner followed him in and Peter pointed to the top drawer of his desk.

'You keep it locked?'

'Not usually,' Peter said. 'There's not usually anything worth taking.'

'And I gather you've checked to see if the keys are in there?'

Peter nodded. 'Yes.'

'And?'

'Still here,' he said, opening the drawer and showing him the keys.

'You mind if I take them?' Gardner asked and Peter frowned. 'We'll check for prints, see who else might've had hold of the keys.'

'Sure,' Peter said.

'We might also need to take a look at your car.'

Peter rubbed the back of his neck but said, 'Fine.'

Gardner gave him his thanks and left him to whatever it was he had to do for the Walter James sideshow. He could hear Harrington talking to Jen Worrall as he crossed the corridor back to Walter's office. If he was trying to chat her up he wasn't doing a very good job. The woman had a face like thunder as Gardner went back in.

'Sorry to keep you,' Gardner said and Jen just nodded. 'I assume you know what's happened.'

'Yes,' Jen said. 'Mr James told me when he got in this morning.'

'And what time was that?' Gardner asked.

'About nine, I think.'

'And what about you? What time did you get in?'

'About eight. Maybe just before.'

'First in?'

'Yes.'

'Is that usual?'

'Most of the time.'

'But you don't park out the back?'

Jen huffed what might've been a laugh. 'No,' she said. 'I park down the street.'

'Even though you're first in,' Gardner said, and she shrugged. 'Not important enough?'

'Something like that,' she said and crossed her arms in front of her.

'Is it just you, Peter and Mr James?' Gardner asked, looking around the office, wondering how many people it took to get someone elected.

'No. There're a couple more, part-timers. And then the canvassers,' Jen said. 'I can give you a list.'

'Thank you, that'd be very helpful. But first, tell me about the call you received from Lauren James last night,' Gardner said and Jen rolled her eyes and sighed.

'She rang up, asked where her dad was, where Peter was. I said they were in a meeting. She hung up.'

'That's it?'

'That's it,' Jen said.

'She didn't ask you to go and find them, try and contact them?'

'No. I'm not *her* intern. I draw the line at favours for family members.'

'She called you quite late.'

'She knows I work long hours. Longer than Mr James.'

'So you were here, at the office? Do you always work that late?'

'Sometimes, not always.'

'Was anyone else here?'

'No,' Jen said. 'They'd gone for their meeting.'

'And when you say meeting, you mean . . .'

'I mean they were in the pub. Most of their meetings are held in the pub.'

'But you weren't invited?' Harrington said and got a withering look.

'Like I'd want to spend my evenings with them. I don't spend enough time with them already?'

'You were here though, working. Wouldn't it be more fun to go to the pub with your colleagues than stay here alone?'

'I'm not here to have fun. I'm here to get experience so I can get a proper job.'

'Fair enough,' Gardner said. 'So, no one was here with you. What time did they leave?'

'Just after nine, I think.'

'And what time did you leave?'

'About eleven.'

Gardner whistled. 'That's a late night. Do you actually get paid for this?'

'Barely,' she said.

'But you still stay until eleven at night? And at Christmas, too. That's some commitment.' Jen just shrugged. 'So, Lauren called you, asked where her dad was, asked where Peter Hinde was. Did she say anything else?'

'I don't think so,' Jen said. 'It'd be unlikely.'

'Why's that?'

'We're not exactly friends.'

'You don't get along?'

'I don't really know her. But I know her enough to tell we wouldn't get along.'

'Why not?'

'Have you *met* her?' Jen said, leaning forward, suddenly animated. 'She's never worked a day in her life. She gets her daddy to pay for everything. That house she's in? Gift from Daddy. Whatever she wants. She wraps men around her little finger. Thinks fluttering her eyelashes is her only job in life. She sometimes hangs around the office, getting in the way, getting . . .' Jen's eyes flicked towards Peter's office and then back again. 'She's just not the kind of person I'd want to be friends with.'

'All right,' Gardner said. 'So she didn't say anything else. How did she sound?'

'I don't know. Like she usually sounds. Whiny.'

'Whiny? Not distressed?'

'No. I don't think so. She sounded wound up, maybe, but she always does. She's a drama queen.'

'So after she hung up, what did you do?'

'I went home. I'd been packing up my things when she called. I almost didn't answer. It's a work phone. Technically it wasn't office hours and I wondered why anyone would be trying to call us that late. I thought it might've been Peter.'

'Why would Peter call you that late? Did he know you were staying?'

'No,' Jen said. 'I just thought, they were out, maybe he needed something.'

'Lauren tried to call Peter a couple of times. You said she asked you where he was too. Not just her dad. Do you know if she calls him a lot?'

This time Jen did laugh. 'You know she's fucking him, right?' Gardner didn't say anything, he just let her vent. She laughed again. 'She didn't tell you, did she?' She leaned forward, conspiratorially. 'They've been at it for months. Her dad doesn't know but it's *so* obvious.'

'So you're just guessing?' Harrington said.

'No. I saw them. All over each other,' she said, spitting out the words.

'It didn't cross your mind to tell your boss? You've said you're not a fan of Lauren's. You weren't tempted to snitch.'

'No,' she said. 'It'd be Peter who took the blame. Not her.'

'You think Walter would fire him over it?'

'Maybe,' Jen said and glanced over to Peter's office again. 'Anyway, I don't snitch on people.'

'So Lauren was seeing Peter. While she was still seeing Richard Donoghue?' Gardner asked.

'Yeah,' Jen said. 'He came here one day, looking for her. She was in Peter's office. I heard her giggling,' she said, her lip curling at the word. 'I told him she wasn't here.'

'Why?'

'Have you seen Ritchie?'

'Not alive, no,' Gardner said.

'He's like a gorilla in Nike. He'd have killed Peter with one hand.'

'So you were protecting Peter, not Lauren.'

Jen shuffled in her seat. 'I just didn't want any trouble in the office. What he did to her outside – who cares?'

'Okay. So you were first in the office this morning.'

'I'm always first in,' Jen said. 'I open up. Put the coffee on.'

'Which way do you come in? Front or back?'

'Back,' she said.

'Did you happen to notice if Peter's car was there this morning when you arrived?'

'Yes, I put the keys back in his office when I got here.'

Gardner looked at Harrington. 'You had the keys last night?' he said to Jen.

'No,' she said. 'I picked them up. Someone had put them through the letterbox at the back.'

18

Lauren sat with her knees pulled up to her chest. She was alone for the first time all day. All she'd wanted when they said she could leave the station was to go home and get into bed. But how could she go home? She thought about Ritchie's body, lying there on her lawn where she used to sunbathe, where she'd lain on the ground looking at the stars while she was getting high. How could she go back there again? Would they even *let* her go back? She'd asked the taxi driver to take her to her dad's house, hoping he'd be there, but instead Susan had answered the door and almost recoiled when she'd seen her stepdaughter.

'Your dad isn't here,' Susan said, leaning against the door, making sure there was no gap for Lauren to sneak in.

'Okay.' Lauren turned to leave but she didn't know where else to go. She couldn't go to Peter's. Not after she'd lied to the police about him. How would that look? 'Can I come in?' she asked.

Susan sighed and then moved back. Lauren gave her half a smile but Susan didn't reciprocate and Lauren wished she had somewhere else to go, wished her mum was still alive. Wished she had some real friends, people she could rely on. People who wouldn't start posting stuff on the internet as soon as she turned her back. As far as she was concerned,

Susan was the living embodiment of the evil stepmother. She wouldn't get any sympathy here.

'Make yourself at home,' Susan said. 'But don't go in the dining room. I've had the carpet cleaned.'

Lauren nodded and sat down on the uncomfortable sofa. She looked at the Christmas tree in the window. The fancy lights that Susan had spent a fortune on weren't switched on and the place just looked sad.

'I'll try and get hold of your dad.'

Susan disappeared and Lauren sat back, closing her eyes. She could hear someone's voice, which sounded like it was coming from next door. She hoped it wasn't a reporter. She'd seen them gathering as the police took her away from her house, down to the station. She didn't know if people were aware yet, that it was her house, her ex-boyfriend. She wanted to check Facebook but the police had kept her phone. She'd told them it was fine but she missed it already and they'd already caught her out on stuff because of it. And now she'd probably dug herself in deep because she was too stupid to think on her feet. Too stupid to realise they had everything they needed on her phone. The thing about the text had thrown her. She couldn't under-stand it. She couldn't clearly remember coming home. Maybe it was the shit she took, messing with her head.

'Your dad's not answering his phone. As usual,' Susan said, shaking Lauren from her thoughts. 'I've left him a message. Said you're here.' Lauren didn't respond. She just sat staring out of the window hoping Susan would go away. 'Right then,' Susan said after a moment of standing there like a spare wheel. 'I need to go out. I'm sure your dad won't be long. Help your-self to a drink and what have you. But not the lime cordial. I need that.'

Lauren ignored her again and eventually Susan got the message and buggered off. She wondered how long her dad would actually be. At least she now knew it wasn't just *her* he didn't answer his phone to. But after a few minutes she started to feel angry with him. Where'd he been all morning? What was so important that he had to do that he couldn't answer her calls, that he couldn't come down to the station and be there for her, to get his mates to leave her alone. Why hadn't he used his connections to make it all go away? He only ever used them to get what *he* wanted. He'd tell her she had to make her own way in life and then the next day he'd show up with some present to apologise.

But this time it was different. There'd be no house, no luxury holiday, nothing that could make this better. All she could hope for was her dad's support and he wouldn't even give her that.

Gardner and Harrington drove back to the station having
instructed someone to go and check Walter's office for prints,
particularly the letterbox the spare keys had been posted
through. Gardner thought about the charming Jen Worrall.
Her alibi was as flimsy as the others'. She claimed she had
driven home after the call from Lauren but her flatmate was
away for the Christmas holidays so there was no one to verify
her story. He found it hard to believe that Jen had anything to
do with the murder – she was hardly going to stand up for
Lauren James. If it'd been Lauren's body, on the other hand,
Ms Worrall would be climbing to the top of the list of suspects
fairly rapidly.

She claimed she'd only met Ritchie a couple of times: once
at the office when he came looking for Lauren and the other
time at a fundraiser where he'd come as Lauren's date and
intimidated the rest of the guests. Other than that she had
nothing much to offer. Except the little nugget about putting
Peter's car keys back this morning. Gardner thought it was
unlikely Worrall had actually taken the car the night before.
Why volunteer the information about the keys if she had?
Unless she was trying to cover herself when they inevitably
found her prints. But it didn't feel right. Why would Jen kill
Ritchie? But the fact that *someone* had returned the keys,

presumably overnight, was interesting. It was possible it'd been Peter Hinde, trying to cover his tracks. But it was also possible it was someone else completely. Someone they had yet to speak to. For now Worrall wasn't a suspect and had little else in the way of information to offer, so he focused his attention on someone else.

He thought about Walter James and whether he could be involved. He was a politician, one in the middle of a campaign. He wouldn't want to get his hands dirty. So what was with staying away from the police for as long as he could all about? Purely a dick-swinging exercise. Had to be. James knew he had his back covered by his friends in high places. Murder investigation or not, the man could do pretty much what he liked and he was going to make sure Gardner knew that too.

'You remember that arson case a few years back?' Harrington said. 'The factory in Stockton?'

'Vaguely. What about it?'

'Didn't James have something to do with that?'

Gardner tried to remember the case, though it'd had nothing to do with him. 'Insurance job, right? On one of his businesses.'

'Right, except the investigation suddenly came to a stop and was declared an accident,' Harrington said. 'You think he can get this written off as an accident?'

Gardner wanted to laugh but he knew that where Walter James was concerned, nothing was impossible.

He found a parking space and headed inside without a word to Harrington. They both knew an interview with Walter James was going to be a major production. He wasn't going to answer anything he didn't want to and their superiors would make sure no one pushed the man too far. He was there voluntarily. His daughter was under suspicion, not him. Have a little respect. Gardner doubted he would be allowed to conduct the interview but even Atherton couldn't be stupid enough to let Cartwright do it. Even if they were trying to let Walter James and his daughter get away with murder, Cartwright would find a way to fuck it up.

Gardner stood watching the monitors as Walter James walked into the interview room down the hall. Harrington came in, closing the door behind him.

'Have I missed anything?' he asked.

'No, Atherton's still preparing the finger sandwiches,' Gardner said and Harrington sniggered. 'He didn't want a solicitor in there? Not even the great Harry Warren?'

'Said he didn't need one,' Harrington said.

'He's an arrogant shit,' Gardner replied and watched as Walter moved his chair from in front of the desk, sliding it to the side, forcing Atherton to move too if he wanted to look at him. He sat down and stretched his legs out in front of him.

'Thanks for your time,' Atherton said. 'We shouldn't keep you too long. I know you're a busy man.'

Gardner kept his eyes on Walter as Atherton spoke. He looked bored; hardly the response you'd imagine from a man whose daughter was caught up in a murder investigation.

'Could you tell me where you were between nine thirty last night and eight a.m. this morning, Mr James?' Atherton asked.

'Am I a suspect, Atherton?' Walter said, a smile plastered to his face.

Atherton let out a strangled laugh and shook his head. 'Of course not. I wasn't implying—'

'Calm down, Atherton, it was a joke. I was in the pub from around nine thirty until just after eleven, I think.'

Gardner watched Atherton make a note; he was barely able to make eye contact with James. What the hell was wrong with the man?

'Can I ask who you were with?'

'Peter Hinde.'

'Okay, so you were in the pub until about eleven. And then?'

'And then I called a cab,' Walter said.

'Did you get a cab with Mr Hinde?'

'No. We went our separate ways. He doesn't live far from the pub so he said he'd walk.'

'Do you know which taxi firm you used?'

'Yes, the number of the taxi firm is in my phone, and I'm sure if you check with them they'll confirm things.' Walter tapped his fingers on the edge of the desk as if he were killing time waiting for his coffee order rather than speaking to the police about a murder.

'And you went straight home?' Atherton asked.

'No,' Walter said. 'I stopped off at the office first. I'd left some paperwork I wanted to have a look at before a meeting today. I asked the driver to wait and then I decided to do some work while I was there so I went out and told him to go.'

'Can I ask how long you stayed at the office?'

'Jesus,' Gardner said. '*Can* I ask? Is he even going to mention the calls from Lauren? Ritchie? Anything relevant at all?'

Walter looked up as though he was thinking. 'A couple of hours, I think. Possibly slightly longer. Time got away from me somewhat.'

'So it was about one, one thirty by the time you left?' Atherton said.

Gardner made a mental note to check the CCTV footage from opposite the office.

'I'd say so,' Walter replied.

'And how did you get home?'

'I got another cab.'

'Same firm?'

'Yes.'

'All right. What time did you finally get home?'

'Around quarter to two, I think.'

'And was anyone else at home who could verify that?'

'My wife was home but I didn't wake her.'

Gardner lit up a little at the thought of James having no alibi but then he spoke again.

'I do have a security camera outside my house. That would confirm what time I came home.'

'Thanks,' Atherton said. 'That's very helpful.' He cleared his throat. 'We know that Lauren made a couple of phone calls to you last night and this morning. Could you tell us about them?'

'Not much to tell,' Walter said. 'She called last night but I didn't hear my phone in the pub. I tried calling her back later. She sounded a little concerned in her message so I rang back while I was at the office, to check if things were okay. But there was no answer.'

'Didn't that worry you?' Atherton asked.

Walter shrugged. 'I assumed if there was a real problem Lauren would've kept calling. That's her usual MO.' He let out a long breath. 'To be honest, my daughter, as much as I love her, can be something of a drama queen. She has a tendency to call me for the littlest thing. When I couldn't get hold of her later on I assumed that whatever the problem was, it had gone away. This pains me to say,' he went on, 'but my daughter is not the most stable person. Lauren is highly strung. She's had problems, drugs – things I'd prefer were kept quiet.'

'Of course, of course,' Atherton said.

'Not that that makes her guilty of anything. I don't believe she killed him, not at all. She's not a stupid girl. She knows she's in trouble, she knows how it looks. And I don't *know* what happened last night. I don't know what evidence you have or haven't got. But I do know that if a body is found in someone's back garden, a body that belongs to an ex-boyfriend, then the police are going to be looking at that person quite closely. They'd be fools not to. She has to know that. But whatever happens, I'll stand by her.'

Gardner wondered if Walter had spent the morning preparing that statement. He waited for Atherton to speak but he paused, perhaps waiting a moment to be sure the speech had finished. 'Did you know Ritchie Donoghue?' he asked eventually.

'Barely,' Walter said. 'We met on a few occasions but he was hardly the sort of person I'd have a long conversation with. She knew my feelings about him.'

'So you didn't approve of their relationship?'

'Come on, Atherton, don't be stupid. I know what sort of man Richard Donoghue was. I'd be very surprised if he wasn't known to police, so I assume you're aware of the things he was into. Hardly the kind of man you hope your daughter will end up with.'

'Of course,' Atherton said and Gardner wanted to run in there and shake him. Was he really that gutless? James had even called him stupid and he was still fawning over him.

'You said Lauren had problems with drugs,' Atherton said. 'Did Ritchie get her involved in all that?'

'No, I can't blame Lauren's issues on him. She'd been using various drugs for a number of years before she ever met him. That particular problem I blame on another ex-boyfriend of hers. She's fairly weak willed when it comes to things like that.'

'When Lauren left you a message last night, did she mention Ritchie? Did she say he was there? That she was scared?'

'No,' Walter said. 'I don't think so.'

'Can I just go back to what you said about being at the office?' Atherton said. 'Did you notice if Peter Hinde's car was there when you got there or when you left?'

Finally, Gardner thought. He'd mentioned the car and the keys to Atherton before the interview began. Begged him to mention them to James. Atherton had brushed him off, telling him he'd ask whatever he thought relevant, and to remember that Walter James wasn't a suspect, but Gardner could tell his interest was piqued.

'I'm not sure,' Walter said, shaking his head. 'I know I looked out the window; I was pacing when I called Lauren back. Come to think of it, I don't remember seeing it there.'

'But you're not sure,' Atherton said.

'I wouldn't swear to it, no, but I don't remember seeing it when I looked out.'

'Peter Hinde said you borrowed his car yesterday. Can I ask what you did with the keys when you were done?' Atherton said.

'I returned them to his drawer.'

'Jen Worrall said she picked up Peter's car keys this morning,' Atherton said. 'That someone must've posted them through the letterbox overnight. Do you recall seeing them? Or hearing anything while you were at the office?'

'Can't say that I did,' Walter said, flashing another smile.

20

Freeman pulled herself up from the settee where she'd been sitting for the past twenty minutes, wallowing in the fact that she'd let Darren go. While she'd been out at the club she'd been wondering, again, how she was going to break the news to her parents but now it looked like maybe she wouldn't have to. Or maybe she would. But how could she tell them that not only was Darren alive but she'd let him disappear again? She might as well just cut herself off from the family now, save her mam a job.

She rubbed her eyes and sighed. She needed to do something. Needed to find him again. He'd obviously been in Newcastle. Maybe he would go back to the club, maybe to confront Rachel. Or maybe he'd just disappear again now she'd ruined things for him once more. Even if Darren didn't show at Slinky's, presumably Rachel would, and maybe she could tell Freeman where her brother was.

It was risky going back there. She didn't really want to show her face again, having messed with the CCTV footage. But if it meant finding Darren she had to try. She grabbed her bag and coat and headed for the door. As she ran out she almost fell over him as he sat, hunched over in the hallway.

He looked up at her with his stupid, sad eyes and said, 'Hey.'

'Hi,' she said and held out her hand. 'You want to come back inside?'

Darren grabbed her hand and she pulled him up, taking him back into the relative warmth of the flat. Without speaking, Darren made himself at home on the settee and Freeman made them some drinks and finished off the sandwich he'd started making earlier, wishing she had something better to offer him than crisps in a bun.

She took it through, sat down next to him and waited. And waited. She could hear music thumping upstairs. Darren didn't seem to notice, instead just focused on his sandwich. When it was gone he put the plate down and finally looked at her.

'So, you want to tell me what happened?' she asked.

An hour later Freeman felt as if her heart had been ripped out and chewed up by wolves. How could her little brother have been through all this shit? Have felt so alone and worthless that he thought being dead would be a better option?

After he'd left prison he'd returned to their parents' house, where things had been fine for a while. She'd known this; her mam had been willing to share that much information at least. But it hadn't taken long for Darren to realise that things don't always happen the way you want, that it takes time to make things work, and he'd fallen back into old habits. He was soon hanging out with all the scumbags that'd got him into trouble in the first place, spending too much time in the pub or the bookies. He was back on the smack and doing whatever it took to get it. Even in his fucked-up state he knew how painful it was for Mam and Dad to see so he decided to leave. First to Leeds, and then to Hull where he managed to crash his car into the river. He knew he'd be fucked if the police found him, driving under the influence and all that. So he just walked away, hid for a while. And then he saw the news. Witnesses never saw the driver escape. Divers had searched the river but no body was recovered. No one had seen Darren Freeman since. It didn't look good.

But Darren saw it as an opportunity. Being Darren Freeman was shit. It didn't matter what else he did in his life, there was always going to be all the crap that had come before. He'd ruined his parents' lives. He'd hurt everyone he knew. Darren Freeman was better off dead. So he just walked away. Got the next bus to Liverpool and stayed there for a while. Found somewhere to crash. Worked cash in hand. Moved on when anyone started asking questions he didn't want to answer.

Eventually he'd ended up in Manchester and met Rachel in a squat. He knew as soon as he saw her that she was the one. So when she suggested they move to Newcastle, he followed. She had connections, could make some real money for a change. They could get a place together. They could have a proper life. Sure, he was hesitant at first. Newcastle was a little close to Blyth, to home. What if someone he'd known in his old life saw him? What if his family found him? Didn't matter. He loved Rachel. He'd do anything to be with her.

He'd been off the drugs for a while. Was starting to sort himself out. No, he wasn't living like normal people. Didn't have a bank account or a mortgage or any of that shit. But he was trying. Rachel got herself a job at Slinky's and between them they were doing all right. And then Rachel introduced him to Healy and he started doing bad things again.

And now the one person he trusted, that he believed had helped him get his life back together, had fucked him over.

History repeating itself.

21

'Guy James is here,' Harrington said and Gardner followed him towards the interview room. As with Peter Hinde, he'd been given permission to speak with Walter James's youngest son. There was a clear hierarchy at work dictating who Gardner could talk to – Walter James, no way; Lauren James, not after last time; James's employees, knock yourself out; his son, go nuts. Gardner didn't remember Guy James that well but this turn of events spoke volumes. Guy James was not important to his dad.

As they turned the corner Gardner was surprised to see Walter James still there after he'd abruptly ended the 'interview' with Atherton, telling the DCI he had things to get back to. But there he was, him and his son displaying the kind of beautiful family reunion usually engineered by Jeremy Kyle. Beside them was Harry Warren, looking like he didn't get paid enough for what he was dealing with.

Guy James appeared to be trying as hard as he could to be nothing like his father. He looked like he'd slept in a hedge and was talking loudly in the kind of fake gangsta style that was popular with both morons and rich kids wanting to rebel. Walter tried to talk to his son in a ridiculous stage whisper, clearly embarrassed. When he spotted Gardner and Harrington approaching, Walter stopped talking, turning on the charm instead.

'DI Gardner,' Walter said. 'This is my son, Guy.'

'I remember,' Gardner said.

Guy just nodded at Gardner. If he remembered him he didn't show it. 'Where's Loz?' he said. 'She all right?'

'Lauren's fine. She's at my house,' Walter said. 'Don't worry, we'll have this sorted in no time.'

'Yeah?' Guy said, eyeing up his father. 'What you gonna do? Bribe 'em?'

'Just talk to them,' Walter said and turned his back on his son as his phone started ringing. He nodded to Harry and walked away.

'If you want to follow me . . .' Harrington said and Guy sloped off after him while Gardner lingered in the corridor, his eye on Walter James. He wondered why he cared so little for his son that he was allowing Gardner to talk to him and yet had called in the services of Harry Warren. Especially when he'd declined the help for himself. Did he think Guy needed a solicitor because he'd *done* something stupid or just that, guilty or not, his son was likely to *say* something stupid?

Gardner watched him disappear and then caught up with Harrington and Guy, who was sitting slumped in his chair, arm across the desk, head resting on one hand. He had the sheen of someone with a hangover.

'Can I get you a drink of anything?' Gardner asked.

'Have you got any Red Bull?' Guy said.

'No. We have water or tea.'

Guy waved Gardner's suggestions away and continued staring at the wall, probably wishing he was still in bed. Gardner knew that Guy James was twenty-two, four years younger than his sister, but he had the air of a sulky teenager. Guy didn't have a job – had never had one – but had his own flat, probably paid for by Daddy Dearest despite the animosity between them. Apparently the reason Walter James was without a car at the moment was because Junior had taken it for a spin without asking and totalled it. Of course, Walter hadn't wanted to press charges or make any fuss. That would've done no one any favours. A son with a criminal record wasn't what an MP wanted. But Guy seemed hell bent on making his dad's life as difficult as possible. Gardner was almost warming to him.

He noticed Guy had a black eye and wondered if it could've been given by Ritchie Donoghue, but on closer inspection it looked like it'd been done days earlier, the bruise yellowing around the edges. He wondered if that was from the incident with Walter's car or just another gift from Daddy *because* of the incident with the car.

'So,' Gardner said. 'You're aware of what's happened?'

'Yeah,' Guy said, still not sitting up straight. 'Someone offed that knobhead Ritchie.'

Harry cleared his throat and Guy made a face.

Gardner tried not to smile. 'So you didn't like him, then?'

'Why would I? He was a knobhead.'

Harry coughed and Guy rolled his eyes at him. Harrington couldn't suppress his grin. 'You know it's pretty stupid to tell the police you think that someone who's just been murdered is a knobhead?'

Guy shrugged. 'I'm not gonna lie. And he was a knobhead.'

'Good,' Gardner said. 'I'm glad you're not going to lie to us. So can you tell us where you were last night?'

'Newcastle,' Guy said. 'Mate's stag do.'

'Name?'

'Ozzy,' he said and then seeing Gardner's expression said, 'Daniel Osborne.'

'Who else was there?'

'Dunno. Didn't know most of 'em. Ozzy'll tell you.'

'Okay, so where did you and Ozzy go?'

'All over. Pub crawl.'

'You remember the names of any of the pubs?' Gardner asked.

'Not really.'

'Your sister called you last night. What did you talk about?'

'She said the knobhead had been round, giving her grief,' Guy said.

'Anything else?'

'Not really. I think she wanted someone to come round and see him off.'

Harry let out a heavy sigh and Guy spun around to him. 'What? I'm just being honest.' And that, Gardner thought, was probably what Harry was afraid of. But Gardner couldn't imagine that Ritchie Donoghue would be seen off by Guy James. Ritchie could've picked Guy up with one hand. He couldn't weigh more than eight stone, wet through.

'Is that what she said?' Gardner asked. 'That she wanted you to come round and get rid of him?'

'No,' Guy said. 'She just said he was there, but I was in Newcastle so I couldn't do nowt.'

'So did she say he was still there or that he *had* been there?'

'I dunno,' Guy replied. 'I was pretty wrecked by then.'

'I think if my client was so inebriated, anything he recalls from that conversation would be unlikely to be accurate,' Harry said.

'All right,' said Gardner. 'What time did you come home?'

'I can't remember. A bit after she rang me,' Guy said.

'So you *did* come back to help her?'

Guy sat up properly. 'She sounded wound up so I felt guilty and came back.'

'Straight away?'

'No. I dunno. We was in a strip club. I went back in after I talked to Loz. Told Ozzy I had to go but he was all pissed off about it so I finished my drink, bought him another round. Had a dance.'

'It was around eleven p.m. when you spoke to her, correct?'

'Dunno, maybe.'

'And you left, what? An hour, two hours later?'

'I can't remember.'

'How did you get home?'

'Taxi.'

'What did you do when you got back to Middlesbrough?'

'Went to Loz's.'

'Can I have a moment with my client?' Harry said and Gardner started to get up but Guy said, 'I don't need a moment, thanks, mate.' Harry sighed again and Gardner sat back down.

'And what happened at Lauren's?'

'I knocked on the door but she never answered,' Guy said. 'So I let myself in.'

'You have a key to her house?' Gardner asked.

'She has a spare. I know where she keeps it.'

'So you went in. And?'

'I shouted to her but didn't hear owt so I went upstairs and she was in bed.'

'Alone?'

'Yeah,' Guy said, lip curled. 'She was fast on so I left.'

'And you didn't see Ritchie?'

'No.'

'What time was that?'

'I dunno,' Guy said, stretching out the word to a moan, just like his sister. 'I was pissed.'

'You do realise that this is a murder investigation and we need an alibi from you?' Harrington said.

'I never killed him,' Guy said as if it was the first time he'd considered they might suspect him.

'What happened after you left Lauren's? Did you go home? You weren't at home this morning when officers came round.'

'I just wanted some kip, I was knackered. I couldn't be arsed to walk home so I went to my mate's house. Kipped there.'

'Who?'

'Ozzy's.'

'Ozzy who you left in Newcastle? Was he there?'

'No.'

'So you know where he keeps his spare key too?'

Guy looked down at the floor. 'I went in the window.'

'So you broke in?'

'No. It was unlocked. He wouldn't have been bothered. He kips at mine all the time.'

'So no one can verify what time you got in?'

'Not unless his cat's learned how to tell the time,' Guy said.

'This isn't the first time you've talked to the police, is it?' Gardner said and Guy rolled his eyes. 'You've been in a few times for fighting, carrying a knife. Drugs.'

'The charges were dropped,' Guy said, a flicker of recognition on his face.

'Wonder why?'

''Cause it was bullshit,' Guy said, squirming in his seat. Gardner had found his weak spot. Guy James was prepared to accept Daddy's help when it mattered, he just didn't like being reminded of it.

'None of this is relevant,' Harry said, rolling his hand, indicating they should move on.

'So, apart from thinking Ritchie Donoghue was a knobhead, what was your relationship with him? Did you know him well?'

'Not really.'

'But well enough to think he was a knobhead.' Gardner looked up at Harry as he said it but the solicitor didn't bother to respond this time.

Guy shrugged. 'I met him a few times. Me and Loz'd go to the pub together sometimes, he'd tag along. I never talked to him much; he was hardly a good conversationalist.'

Whereas you're a regular Oscar Wilde, Gardner thought. 'So, you went out with him but didn't really talk. How was he with Lauren? What was their relationship like?'

'She could've done better. I told her that.'

'And how did she react?'

'She knew I was right. I think she wanted to break up with him ages ago but she was scared.'

'Of what? That he'd hurt her?'

'Probably,' Guy said.

'Did you ever see him act violently towards her?'

'Not really. But then he wouldn't do it in front of me, would he?'

'Why's that?' Gardner asked.

''Cause I'd 'ave him,' Guy said, leaning forward, mustering the scariest look he could manage.

'Guy,' Harry said and Guy leaned back in his chair again as if that would take back what he'd said.

'Tell us about Peter Hinde,' Gardner said and saw Guy's expression change from posturing to disgust.

'Posh wanker,' he said. 'If he's not kissing my dad's arse, he's staring at Loz's tits.'

'You think he's interested in your sister?'

'I know he is. Drools all over her. Always been the same.'

'He's known the family for a long time, right?'

'Yeah. And now he's working for Dad he thinks he's the heir to Walt's throne.'

'You sound pissed off about that. I didn't imagine you'd have much interest in your dad's world.'

'I don't,' Guy said. 'But he's got nothing to do with it. He's not family.'

'What does Lauren think of Peter?'

Guy shrugged. 'She doesn't fancy him, if that's what you mean.'

'You think she'd go to him for help?'

'No,' Guy said. 'Why would she?'

'She called Peter a couple of times last night, and then this morning as well. She called him before she called you.'

Gardner watched the muscles in Guy's jaw work. He'd found another weak spot.

'Whatever,' Guy said. 'She'd have been looking for Dad.'

'Yeah, that's what she said too,' Gardner replied and Guy sat back, content that his sister wasn't going to a posh wanker for help instead of him. 'All right, Guy. That'll do for now. If you remember the name of the club you were in, let us know, won't you?'

Guy stood up and clicked his fingers. 'It was something like Slappers. Or Slinkers. Or something stupid like that.'

22

Lauren heard the door and stood up when her dad came in. She started crying immediately, despite wanting to be angry with him. Walter stood looking at her, and she tried to work out if he was pissed off. He smiled and she went over, wrapping her arms around him.

'I'm sorry, Daddy,' she said and she laid her head on his shoulder. Eventually, Walter pulled back from Lauren and indicated she should sit. He took a seat beside her and leaned forward, brushing her hair back from her face. 'It was horrible,' she said. 'They treated me like shit.'

'Who did, princess?'

'Those policemen. They kept pushing me, saying awful things.'

'I know it's not nice, Lauren, but it's their job to ask hard questions. This is serious.'

Lauren sat back from her dad. Why was he being like this? 'So I guess they weren't your *friends*, then. Where were all those guys? The ones you get me to suck up to at parties?'

'Careful, Lauren,' Walter said, staring at her until she looked down at the floor. After a moment he sighed and brushed her hair from her face again. 'Tell me who they were, sweetheart?'

Lauren tried to remember their names. There was the one with the hair gel and the gold chain around his wrist that reminded her of Ritchie. Except he'd worn his chain around his neck. When they had sex he never took it off and it used to dangle over her face, as if he were trying to hypnotise her. And then there was the one with the glasses. 'Gardner,' she said and Walter nodded. 'What's going to happen, Dad?' Lauren asked and he blew out a breath.

'I don't know, sweetheart. But we'll get it fixed.' Walter put his hand on her cheek. 'I'm sorry I didn't answer your calls. Wasn't there for you,' he said. He hung his head and went silent for a moment. 'He didn't hurt you, did he? Ritchie?' Lauren shook her head. 'So what happened? You can tell me.' She started to cry again. 'Shhh,' Walter said. 'There's no need for that.'

'But—'

'Whatever happens, I'll be here for you. Just remember that. I'm always here for you.' Walter smiled at her and she grasped his hand. 'Everything will work out. They just need to talk to us to make sure they cover all their bases. Don't worry. They're talking to your brother at the moment. Although if the idiot manages to get through it without implicating himself in some way, I'll eat my hat.'

Lauren smiled. She felt bad about the way their dad talked about Guy but sometimes he *could* be an idiot. And her dad was probably just trying to cheer her up.

'Listen, princess, I need to get back to the office for a while. You'll be all right, won't you,' he said, already heading for the door. 'Just call if you need anything.'

Lauren watched him leave and felt a knot in her stomach as she sat alone again.

23

They'd released Guy James back into the world and he'd probably gone home to sleep off the rest of his hangover. Gardner wasn't convinced he could've killed Ritchie Donoghue – surely no one would be so thick that they'd admit to everything he had if he was guilty. But then Guy James obviously wasn't the sharpest tool in the box. Plus he clearly had the idea that his father would provide get-out-of-jail-free cards whenever they were required. And that probably wasn't too far from the truth. Maybe they shouldn't dismiss the idea altogether.

Gardner sat back in his chair wishing he'd never come in that morning. He could've called in sick. He thought he could feel a cold coming on. He looked out of the window but all he could see was the grey sky meeting the grey river with only a few grey buildings to separate them. It was depressing. He swivelled his chair around and looked at the Christmas tree by the kettle. He wasn't sure who'd decorated it but the tree was too small for the number of baubles thrown on, making it look like a tired Christmas shopper weighed down by too many bags. If he was looking for something to cheer himself up, he was in the wrong place.

He watched as Lawton came over to his desk, frowning. 'What's up?' he asked.

'I found the club Guy James was referring to,' she said. 'It's called Slinky's. A *gentlemen's* club in Newcastle. I spoke to

Daniel Osborne who confirms that he was there with Guy but has no idea what time he, or Guy, left. So I called the club to see if they have security cameras. The owner wasn't there but the man I spoke to, the manager, Tommy Newburn, was pretty angry. Apparently they do have CCTV cameras but they're not working. Or they weren't working.'

'That's convenient,' Gardner said. 'So there's nothing showing what time Guy left the club?'

'No.'

'But you said they're working now?'

'That's the thing,' Lawton said. 'He said someone had been there this morning. Claimed to be a police officer and asked to see the tapes. She had a look but said there was nothing on the tapes for the last few nights.'

'Someone wiped them?' Gardner said, wondering if this was linked to Guy James's visit.

'Well, this guy from the club is pretty pissed off. He wasn't there when this woman came but he seems to think she did something to the system.'

Gardner frowned. What possible motive could someone have for deleting Guy's alibi? Unless someone was trying to set him up. 'You got the number for the club?' he asked and Lawton nodded, handing him her notebook.

He dialled the number. 'Slinky's,' a bored-sounding woman said by way of a greeting.

'Can I speak to Tommy Newburn, please?'

'Hang on,' the woman said and then shouted, 'Tommy!' far louder than necessary. Gardner waited, listening to the sounds of glass clinking and loud music in the background.

'Yeah,' a man's voice said.

'Tommy Newburn? This is DI Michael Gardner from Cleveland police. I believe you spoke to a colleague of mine not long ago about your CCTV.'

'Yeah,' Tommy grunted.

'Can you tell me what happened?'

Tommy huffed and then explained the situation, finishing by saying, 'She probably pressed the delete button, the dozy cow.'

'So you don't have it backed up?'

'I don't know. I'm not a fucking computer nerd,' Tommy said.

'Do you know how much footage is missing?'

'Everything after late afternoon Sunday is gone. Boxing Day.'

'Do you remember the name of the officer?'

'I wasn't here. Hang on.' Tommy put the phone down and shouted, 'Vicky.' Gardner listened as Tommy asked the woman if she remembered a name.

'She said she was called Freeman,' Tommy said. 'Nicola Freeman.'

24

After the third ring Freeman picked her phone up off the table, checking the display. Gardner. *Shit*, she thought. She didn't want to have to deal with that right now too. She declined the call and looked at Darren.

'Just work,' she said.

'You don't need to get it?'

She shook her head. 'So what're you going to do? Are you going to tell Healy who took the money?'

'No,' Darren said, as if she were stupid. He'd already told her how much he was in love with this Rachel so she shouldn't have been surprised.

'Are you going to at least ask her about it?' Darren shrugged. 'She is *aware* that Healy is threatening to break your legs, right?' Freeman said. 'So, tell her you know it was her and tell her to at least give it back even if she's not going to own up.'

'But if I say anything to her she's gonna think I don't trust her.'

Freeman bit her tongue and counted to five. She wanted to say, *You* shouldn't *trust her, she's a lying skank*, but she doubted Darren would take it well. 'Darren. She took the money. We know that. We also know she didn't tell you about it, even when you were being threatened. Now, I don't know why she did it. Maybe she's planning to buy you something nice and didn't want to ruin the surprise. But either way, she's going to get you maimed or killed if she doesn't hand it over. So, do you think you could maybe call her?'

Darren frowned and then pulled out his phone. Freeman waited, listening to the quiet ringing and then watched Darren pull the phone away from his ear as Rachel answered in a loud, shrill voice.

'Hey, baby,' she said. 'Where are you?'

'Hey, monkey,' Darren answered and Freeman thought she saw his cheeks flush. She didn't really want to listen to the conversation but without her sitting next to him Darren would probably chicken out of asking his girlfriend about the money. She could hear Rachel jabbering in the background and gave Darren a prod. 'That's great, Rach,' he said, to whatever bit of news she'd just relayed. 'Listen, you know that money. Healy's money.' For once, Rachel didn't speak. 'Well, thing is . . . It's just . . . And I'm not . . .'

Freeman rolled her eyes and snatched the phone from her brother. 'Hi, Rachel. This is Darren's sister. I know you took the money and I'd really appreciate it if you handed it over so my brother doesn't get his legs broken. Okay?'

There was no reply for a moment and Freeman wondered if Rachel had hung up. Darren stared at her like she was insane and maybe she was. She didn't know anything about this girl, how she'd react to such a direct request.

'Who is this?' Rachel said eventually, her voice all attitude.

'Nicola Freeman. Darren's sister.'

'Bullshit. Darren doesn't have a sister.'

Freeman felt another stab in her guts, even though she should've expected he wouldn't have told his new friends about her. Maybe this Rachel didn't even know his name was Freeman.

'Unfortunately he does. And it's me. And did I mention I'm a detective?'

Darren's eyes widened and he tried to get the phone back from her but she pulled away, walking to the kitchen to finish her conversation.

'Look, I know you took the money, I've seen the CCTV tapes from the club. And I don't really care that you took it. I'm not planning on arresting you for theft. I just don't like the fact that you're willing to let my brother take the fall for it. So I'm asking you nicely to give the money back to Healy, give him your best apology and leave Darren out of it.'

Rachel didn't answer again but this time Freeman could hear her breathing down the phone. 'I want to speak to Darren,' she said after a few seconds. Freeman held the phone out to her brother and he grabbed it from her.

'Rach?' he said. 'Listen, don't pay attention to—'

Freeman tried to hear what Rachel was saying. She was obviously pissed off – whatever was being said was being shouted – but Darren moved away from her so she couldn't hear the actual words. He walked towards the bedroom, glancing back at her with a scowl, before slamming the bedroom door. Five minutes later, he emerged.

'What did she say?' Freeman asked.

'What do you think she said? She's pissed off at me for getting the cops involved. For calling her a liar.'

'You didn't call her a liar.'

'No, but for saying she took the money.'

'She *did* take the money.'

'I know that!' he said, really acknowledging it for the first time.

'Is she denying it? Did you tell her we've got proof?'

Darren looked down at his shoes.

'What?' Freeman said.

'I got rid of it. The pen drive.'

'What? Why?'

'I didn't want Healy to find out.'

'But that's all we had to prove it wasn't you. Where is it?'

'In your bin, outside. I stood on it.'

Freeman sighed. 'Why are you sticking up for that little skank?'

'She's not a skank.'

'She took the money and lied to you about it.'

'She isn't lying,' Darren said. 'She admitted it. She admitted she took the money but it was for *us*. She took it for us.'

Freeman was dumbfounded. 'For you? She took it for you but didn't tell you?'

'You don't get it.'

'No, I don't.'

'She took it for us, so we could get out of all that shit. So we could start over. She didn't think they'd notice for a while. She thought we'd be gone.'

'And when was she planning on going? How long did she think these guys would go without noticing twenty grand was missing?' She watched her brother, his face betraying his feelings. She wasn't making it better by shouting at him like this. 'Whatever. Just tell her she needs to give it back.'

'I did,' he said. 'She doesn't have it any more. She spent it.'

'On what?' Freeman asked, her blood boiling once more.

'Coke,' he said.

25

Gardner said thanks and hung up. When Lawton had first mentioned the club's CCTV being wiped he'd assumed someone was trying to cover something up, and that someone was unlikely to be an actual police officer. Whether it had anything to do with Guy James and the Ritchie Donoghue murder was another matter. It didn't seem to make sense. Why would anyone bother destroying Guy's alibi when he'd *already* admitted to coming back to Middlesbrough anyway? Maybe the bloke from the club was right and whoever had been looking at the tapes had accidentally wiped them. He wasn't sure it was that simple but was willing to keep an open mind.

Then the bloke had said it was Freeman. Gardner doubted that accidentally wiping the tapes was something she would do. But why had she even been there? He was pretty sure that when they'd talked a few nights earlier she'd said she was on holiday. He'd tried calling her at work only to be told he was right – she was on annual leave. So why had she been at the club?

He tried calling her mobile several times but got no reply. And as things weren't getting anywhere with the Ritchie Donoghue case and there was nothing more he could do that night, he decided to drive up to Blyth and see what was going on. He was pretty sure she would have a reasonable explanation and asking her in person wasn't really necessary. But he wanted to see her. He wanted to talk to someone who had nothing to do with the Donoghue case, who had no knowledge of Walter James, someone to tell him he was right to be pissed off at the way things were being handled.

Gardner put his foot on the brake as he realised he was going way over the speed limit. He tried to tell himself there was nothing he could do if the higher-ups decided it was going to go down like this. But that just made him feel worse.

He swung the wheel, turning onto the road he believed led to Freeman's flat. He'd dropped her off there a week ago after their cokes had turned into vodka and cokes – for her, anyway – and she'd had to leave her car at the pub. As he'd pulled up outside her flat he'd wondered if she'd ask him in, but she was clearly at the point of being melancholy-I-want-to-be-alone drunk instead of tipsy-I-might-regret-this-in-the-morning drunk, and had got out of the car without so much as a goodnight, stumbling towards the building and disappearing inside; what he thought would likely be the last time he'd see her. But then she made that call.

He wished he could be there under different circumstances. As he pulled up outside the flats, he wondered if he should just turn around and go home. Who gave a shit about the club's CCTV? No one else cared about investigating this case properly. Maybe he should just let sleeping dogs lie.

He noticed he was parked beside her car, which meant she was probably at home. He sat looking up at the nondescript building. It was a new build, one of those that looks the same as every other put up in the last few years. He wondered if it was as depressing inside. It looked like something from the Eastern bloc.

As he stared up at the windows he realised he didn't know which number she lived at. He tried her phone again but it cut off to voicemail straight away. Maybe she was busy. Maybe she really didn't want to see him again, that's why she wasn't answering. Maybe he should just go home.

He got out of the car and headed towards the door. Outside was a wall of post boxes. No names on them, just the numbers of the flats. Twelve in all. He could start pressing buzzers, hope for the best. As he was about to press number one, someone opened the front door, holding it ajar for him. He nodded his thanks and wondered what the point of the locked door was when they let anyone in. He waited for the door to close then found the first flat and started knocking.

26

Darren jumped up at the sound of the door, looking around as if searching for another way out. Freeman stood up and grabbed his arm.

'Calm down,' she said. 'It's probably my neighbour. It's sherry o'clock.'

She ignored the look Darren gave her and went to the door, expecting to find an old lady waving a bottle at her but instead it was Gardner standing there, looking vaguely surprised.

'Fifth time lucky,' he said.

'What're you doing here?' she asked, trying to replay the drunken conversation in her head. Had she asked him over today? Had she even told him where she lived? What the fuck was he doing here? She wasn't even sure she wanted to see him again. New Year's was still undecided on, so why was he just showing up at her door?

'We need to talk,' he said. 'I've been trying to call you.'

Oh shit, she thought. He's a psycho. A bloody stalker who thinks we're going to get married after having one drink together.

'Look,' she said. 'It's not really a good time. And I think maybe we should just forget about New Year and—'

'No,' he said. 'That's not why I'm here.'

'Oh. Okay,' she said, pausing for a moment to reconsider. She stepped aside to let him in. 'What's up?' Gardner closed the door behind him and started to walk towards the living room, stopping when she didn't move from the hall.

'All right,' he said. 'Your name came up today, as part of an investigation.'

'Mine did?'

'Yeah. Regarding Slinky's gentlemen's club.'

Freeman felt the bile rise in her throat. She'd bloody known this wouldn't go unnoticed. Just didn't think it would be Gardner that did the noticing.

'Apparently someone went to the club earlier to check the CCTV footage, only there was something wrong with it. Woman from the club claimed it was a Nicola Freeman.'

'Fuck,' she said. There was no point denying it. 'What's the case?'

'Murder.'

'Fuck,' she said again, squeezing her eyes shut.

'Not in the club. A potential suspect was allegedly there earlier last night.'

Freeman turned away from Gardner, pressing her forehead to the wall. What had she done?

'Look, this guy says he was at the club but still admitted to coming back to the scene later on. We're just trying to work out a timeline. It might not matter. But if it does, I don't think I can keep your name out of it.'

Freeman turned back to him. He didn't seem pissed off; it was more like he was just warning her the shit could hit the fan. She supposed she should be grateful.

'You want to tell me what happened? Why you were there when you're supposed to be on leave?'

Freeman sighed and then noticed Darren standing in the doorway. Gardner followed her stare and turned to him too.

He looked at Darren for a moment before turning back to Freeman.

'This is my brother, Darren,' she said. 'Darren, this is Gardner.' Darren nodded at Gardner but didn't say anything. 'Darren's in a bit of trouble.'

27

Gardner listened to the highlights of Freeman's story and wondered if she'd lost her mind. He could understand her wanting to help her brother but surely she could've done it in a better, more legal, way.

He watched Darren. He was sitting on the settee, knees up to his chest, not saying a word but looking like he might bolt at any second. He wasn't sure how old Darren was – late twenties, maybe – but he looked like a kid. A lost kid. A closer look at his face gave him away but his clothes, his mannerisms, all made him seem like a child. Freeman had told him about her younger brother during their night together in the pub. Not everything, but enough that he could understand how hard it must've been for her to see him at her door this morning. It was obvious she would've done anything to get him to stay but she wasn't thinking clearly; wasn't thinking, full stop.

'So what's going to happen?' Freeman asked.

'Well, I'll try my best to keep you out of it. Hopefully we'll track down the taxi firm Guy used and that'll give us what we need. But I suggest you start thinking of a good reason for being at that club this morning.'

'Can't I just say, like, I stole your ID? Got someone to pretend to be you to get in there?' Darren said.

'No. You need to keep out of it,' Freeman said. Darren looked like he might argue but Freeman cut him off, saying, 'Can you give us a minute?'

Darren unfolded himself from the settee and walked out of the room. When Gardner heard a door shut elsewhere in the flat she spoke again.

'Thanks,' she said.

Gardner waited for her to say more but she was quiet, staring out of the window.

'Has he said much?' Gardner asked. 'About where he's been?'

'A little,' she said. 'It's my fault, you know. If I hadn't done what I did, maybe none of this would've happened.'

'Or maybe he would've been dead for real. You can't blame yourself.'

'What am I going to tell my parents? Happy New Year, Darren's not dead?'

'Well, it'll be a shock, sure. But they'll have him back.' He could hear a phone ringing in another room but Freeman didn't make a move to answer it so he kept talking. 'That's all that matters, right?'

'I swear to fucking God, man, I didn't do it.'

Freeman jumped up when she heard her brother's voice, and ran into the bedroom. Gardner followed, hearing a tinny voice on the other end of the line that was straining with anger. Freeman held out her hand for the phone but Darren pulled away.

'I swear it, man. Why would I take your money?'

''Cause you're a piece of shit,' came the reply from the other end. Healy, Gardner guessed. 'And when I get hold of you, you're fucking dead. Get me? I've been patient, I've given you a chance and you've fucked up. No more chances. You're fucking dead.'

'Tell him,' Freeman hissed but it was too late. Healy was gone. 'What the fuck is wrong with you?'

'Just keep out of it,' Darren said, pushing past her. She grabbed hold of his hoodie.

'I *can't* keep out of it. *You* got me into it,' she said.

'And I'm sorry, but there's nothing else to do.'

'Tell him Rachel took the money.'

'No. I can't do that. He'll kill her.'

'He'll kill *you.*'

'So what?' Darren said, shrugging. 'Maybe that'll solve everyone's problems.'

Gardner flinched when Freeman began to hit Darren, who just stood there, taking it. Eventually he intervened, pulling Freeman away from her brother.

'When the fuck will you get it? You have people who care about you. *I* care about you.'

'I know,' Darren muttered.

'So stop acting like you don't and start behaving like someone with something to live for.' She walked to the window, eyes darting about. 'Does Healy know your real name?'

'What?'

'Does he know you're Darren Freeman? Have you been using your real name?'

'Yeah. I guess.'

'So it's possible he could find you.' She paced up and down the small room. 'You need to go somewhere else.'

Gardner felt his stomach tighten. He knew what was coming next and it wasn't going to happen. Freeman looked up at him and he shook his head.

'If he's out of the way, somewhere Healy can't find him, I can sort this,' she said.

'How?' Darren asked.

'I'll find Rachel, get her to tell Healy what really happened.'

'No way,' Darren said.

'I'll go with her. I'll make a deal. Either he keeps the coke or he gives her time to sell it. He gets his money back either way.'

'And then he kills her. Or us.'

'No,' Freeman said. 'I'll make it clear. He leaves you alone or else I find trouble for him elsewhere. He's a businessman, right? He won't want me watching him for the rest of his life. He'll take the deal.'

'And Rachel will be okay?'

'Sure.'

Gardner knew it was all bluster. By offering Healy anything she was only digging herself deeper. Hopefully this Healy was as naive as Darren was.

'So where am I gonna go?' Darren asked and Freeman turned back to Gardner. 'With this guy?'

'Look, I've got a lot on. I can't babysit for you,' Gardner said.

'I'm not asking you to babysit. I just need him away from here until it's sorted.' She turned back to Darren. 'You can look after yourself, right?'

'Yeah,' Darren said.

'Look, I'm sorry but I can't,' Gardner said. 'I've got too much going on at the moment.' He put a hand on her shoulder. 'Let me know what happens.'

Gardner left the flat and headed back to his car. As he unlocked it he heard Freeman shout at him. He turned and watched her jog over to the car, the sleeves of her jumper pulled down over her hands.

'I know I've fucked up with the CCTV thing but I'll fix it,' she said.

'It's not about that. I just can't be doing with babysitting your brother.'

'Please,' she said, her eyes pleading. 'I swear he'll be no trouble.' Gardner looked at her as if she thought he'd just been born. 'He'll behave himself. Honestly. He knows we're only trying to help him out. It'll just make things easier for me if I know he's out of the way somewhere.'

'Can't he stay with a relative? Or a friend?'

'No one else knows he's back. And I don't want to just dump him on someone without warning.'

'Whereas I've been expecting his visit for weeks, you mean?'

'Please,' she said, shivering. 'I can't sort it with him hanging around me. I'll owe you big time.'

'Fuck's sake,' he muttered. 'A few days. That's it.'

28

Wednesday, 29 December

Gardner watched as the troops gathered in the incident room for the briefing and he tried not to yawn. After Freeman promised that he wouldn't be babysitting, the last thing she said as he got into his car was to keep an eye on Darren and make sure he didn't do a runner.

So he spent a large portion of the night listening to Darren's incredibly annoying ringtone as this Healy guy kept calling and Darren kept ignoring him. Gardner eventually suggested switching the phone off but Darren was concerned he'd miss a call from his girlfriend. She never called. But Healy left a few messages that made Darren look ill. So Gardner had spent most of the night awake expecting to hear movement in the spare room. He hadn't needed to worry; when he got up Darren was awake, wrapped in a duvet on the settee, watching cartoons and eating the rest of his bacon and what appeared to be three sausages in one bun. He'd managed a 'Morning', but that was it. Darren wasn't much of a talker. He'd barely said a word on the drive home the night before, just stared out of the window and idly flicked through Gardner's CDs.

It seemed likely that Darren would spend the day in front of the TV, eating whatever he could lay his hands on. But Gardner decided to swing by at lunchtime just to make sure he was still around.

'All right, everyone,' Atherton said over the racket, and the conversations died down one by one. 'Let's go over what we've got. DI Gardner?'

Gardner stood. 'So far the only alibi that's standing up is that of Walter James. His wife and neighbour both verified what time he arrived home, as did the CCTV at his residence. He also doesn't match the description given by our witnesses. *But* he's not ruled out completely as far as I'm concerned, as the approximate time of death of Ritchie Donoghue and James's arrival home could still have given him plenty of time to kill someone and get back.' He glanced up and saw DCI Atherton staring at him, his jaw clenched. Clearly Atherton wasn't pleased with Gardner's lack of faith in Walter James. But so what? If it were anyone else they'd still be looking at him. What made James so special?

'Guy James's alibi is still being checked. He has admitted to returning to Middlesbrough from Newcastle and that he went to Lauren's house, but he has no idea what time that was and no one saw him. We're trying to find out which taxi firm he used, and also look at any CCTV in the local area that might've picked him up. How's that going?' he asked Harrington.

'We're about halfway through the list of taxi firms from Newcastle. None of them so far had a fare to Middlesbrough.'

'Okay, keep at it,' Gardner said. 'What about the CCTV?'

'Still working on it,' someone else piped up.

'Okay. Jen Worrall, not really a suspect at this point but as no one can verify her whereabouts that night and she had access to the car, she's still worth keeping in mind. Cartwright, how's it going with Ritchie's known associates?'

Cartwright stood up and cleared his throat as if he were about to perform a soliloquy from *Hamlet*. 'I've managed to dig up five people so far who've had issues with Donoghue in the past, mostly to do with drugs. Two are in prison, two have solid alibis, the last one I'm still chasing up. I'll keep digging, though. Looks like this guy had a lot of enemies.'

'Fine,' Gardner said. 'So, that leaves us with Lauren James and Peter Hinde. So far what Lauren has told us seems to be . . .' He wanted to say bullshit but instead went for, 'confused. We're still waiting on results to see whether she actually did have an altercation with Donoghue that night. And then there's Peter Hinde. As we know, witnesses claimed to have seen a car matching the description of Hinde's at Lauren's on the night of the murder. ANPR picked up the car being driven in the general direction of her house but there're no cameras close enough to confirm that's where it ended up. Plus, the car has tinted windows so seeing who was in it is impossible. Where are we with the warrant to search the car or the results from the tyre tracks in the alley?'

'Tracks look like a match. Warrant was sorted first thing. Should be being given the once-over as we speak,' Harrington said.

'What about the prints from the spare keys and the letter-box at the campaign office?'

'Only prints on the keys were Peter Hinde's and Jen Worrall's.'

'But Walter James had used them the day before, right? So where are his prints?'

'Ever heard of gloves?' Cartwright said. 'It is the middle of winter.'

'Or maybe someone wiped the keys before putting them through the door and only Jen and Peter picked them up that morning.'

Harrington coughed and waited to see if the little pissing match was over before saying, 'Found a few prints on the letterbox but none matching our suspects. I'd assume we'd be looking at several hundred potential postmen and delivery people to narrow things down. And if whoever took the keys was clever enough to wipe their prints off them, it's unlikely they'd leave them in the letterbox.'

'Fine,' Gardner said, still glaring at Cartwright. 'What about the teenage witnesses? Have we got any more from them?'

'No. Just that Kirsty saw a tall, skinny man leaving the scene in the car. She couldn't be more specific but her friend verified this independently,' Lawton said.

'Had they been drinking?' Gardner asked.

Lawton shook her head. 'They claim not but as they're both seventeen they're probably lying so they don't get into trouble.'

Gardner nodded. It'd make his life easier if the girls hadn't been drunk but as they'd been coming home at two in the morning, it seemed unlikely. 'What about Ritchie's flat? Anything come up from that?'

Berman nodded. 'Got a few prints. Ritchie's and Lauren's, obviously.'

'Guy James or Peter Hinde?'

Berman shook his head. 'But someone had been there before us. It's a ground-floor flat, and a window had been smashed at the back. Prints were taken from the window and inside the property but again, nothing matching our guys. Inside, the place looked like it belonged to a neat freak. Not a speck of dust, no skid marks in the toilet,' he said to a few chuckles. 'But things were pulled out. Someone had been looking for something. And I don't know if they found it but we got something. Photographs and sex tapes.' Someone at the back wolf-whistled to another round of giggles.

'Have you watched them?' Gardner asked.

'Course he has,' someone shouted.

'They show Lauren James. We haven't logged all of them yet but the photographs suggest they were taken on several different occasions, mostly in his flat but some elsewhere. But if that's what our burglar was after he didn't do a very good job. Unless these were copies. It's possible whoever broke in was disturbed and left, though.'

'Blackmail?' Gardner said.

'Someone was blackmailing Ritchie?' someone said.

'No,' Gardner said. 'Not if someone else was looking for the photos in his flat. I'd say it's more likely Ritchie was blackmailing Lauren.' He turned to Atherton. 'That sounds like a motive to me. Let's bring her in again.'

'Let's not jump to conclusions. What about the car? The man witnesses saw?' Atherton asked.

'So I was right and she called someone for help that night. Either to kill Ritchie or to help afterwards.'

'There were two kinds of injuries,' Harrington said. 'Pathologist confirmed that the garden spade was the weapon but we've got no prints on it whatsoever. There was also blunt force trauma to the back of the head, possibly from a large stone. Why would she use two weapons?'

'There could've been a struggle. Ritchie was way bigger than her. She hits him, he struggles, she drops the spade and picks up a rock or whatever, finishes him off,' Gardner said.

'Or there were two killers.'

'So who was it?'

'Witnesses say a tall, skinny man. Peter Hinde matches that description,' Lawton said.

'So does the brother,' Harrington pointed out.

'But whose car was there?'

'Plus Jen Worrall claims Lauren and Peter were seeing each other, something I'm inclined to believe. And who would be most likely pissed off about Ritchie blackmailing Lauren over sex tapes?' Gardner said and turned to Atherton, who looked like a man aboard a runaway train. 'Let's bring Peter Hinde back in too.'

29

Gardner made a quick getaway after the briefing to avoid getting involved with the press conference. Not that there was much chance of being asked, but he hated those things so much that disappearing, just to be on the safe side, seemed necessary. But before he'd fled the room Gardner overheard Hadley coaching Atherton.

'Just keep it brief. And for God's sake, whatever you do, don't mention Walter James. If any of the little vultures mention him just brush over it. It's the last thing we need,' Hadley said and Atherton nodded like a good little soldier. Gardner left them to it to get on with some actual work while they waited for Lauren to be brought in.

What they'd discovered during the search of Ritchie's flat had made things much more interesting, as had the test results and CCTV images that had arrived just after the briefing that proved, among other things, that Ms James was a liar. Not even Hadley could come up with a good reason to not arrest her this time.

'Gardner.'

He looked up and thought, *Speak of the devil*. Hadley marched over to his desk and stood over him. 'Lauren James is here.'

For a moment Gardner thought he was back in, but Hadley's eyes scanned the room. 'DC Harrington, where's he?' Gardner made a show of looking around the room and then shrugged. 'Well, find him,' Hadley continued. 'I want him to conduct the interview. Atherton and Cartwright are with the press.'

Gardner wasn't sure what he was most surprised at. That Hadley wanted Harrington to do the interview, or that they'd let Cartwright loose with the media.

'Think he's capable?' Hadley asked and Gardner had to assume he was referring to Harrington.

'Yes, he's more than capable.'

'Good,' Hadley said and walked away.

Gardner watched as Harrington went into the interview room and Lauren barely glanced at him. She looked tired, dark circles under bloodshot eyes. Harry Warren, on the other hand, looked like he'd spent the morning on a sun bed.

'Sorry to keep you,' Harrington said and took a seat. 'Lauren, you told us yesterday that after Ritchie had left you went to bed. That you didn't go anywhere that night.'

Lauren looked to Harry for help and Gardner nodded. Harrington was doing as he'd said, holding off on the photos for now, kicking off with the stuff she couldn't dispute, the things that proved she was a liar. It would all be on record before Hadley could shut it down again.

Harrington pushed a photograph, taken from a CCTV camera in the town centre, towards Lauren. 'This was at one a.m. That's you, isn't it?' She nodded, barely. 'So you went to a club that night when you told us you were in bed.'

Lauren looked to Harry again and he picked up the photo. 'It's not very clear,' he said.

'It's clear enough,' said Harrington. 'Besides, Lauren's just admitted it's her. So why did you lie?'

'Because I didn't want you to find out I'd taken coke.'

'Lauren,' Harry said but she waved him off.

'That was all. I didn't want to get into trouble for that. I thought if I said I was out, you'd talk to people at the club and they'd tell you about the coke.'

'All right,' Harrington said. 'I can understand that. So let's go over what happened. You left the club just before one a.m. How did you get home?'

'I walked,' she said.

'And that took how long?'

'About half an hour, maybe. Maybe less.'

'So you got in around one twenty, one thirty. Was Ritchie there when you got back? You sent him that text at twelve thirty. Did you change your mind about meeting him? Was he still waiting?'

'No,' Lauren said. 'He wasn't there. I didn't— I don't remember texting him. I didn't see him again after he'd left earlier. Not until . . . not until he was dead.' Her face crumpled and she pressed her sleeve into her eyes.

'So what happened, Lauren?'

'I'm sorry,' she said, sobbing. 'But I didn't kill him.'

Gardner watched her closely. Something wasn't right; she still wasn't telling them the truth.

'Tell us what happened when you got home,' Harrington asked.

'I went in. I was still buzzing but I was getting wound up about him. I just wanted to go to sleep. I'd thought going out would make me forget about him but it didn't. So I took a few pills and went to bed.'

'And then what?'

'And then nothing. I got up in the morning and found him.'

'So when did you fight with him?'

'I didn't fight with him,' she said.

'Come on, Lauren,' Harrington said. 'You fought with him. Things got physical.'

This time she didn't answer, just hung her head, weeping quietly.

'I think that's enough,' Harry said and started gathering his things.

'Ritchie had scratch marks on his face and arms. Quite deep scratches, too. Not accidental. There were traces of nail polish in the scratches. Nail polish that matches yours.' Harrington pulled out a report and handed it to Harry. 'Plus we found traces of his skin under your nails. How do you explain all that, Lauren?'

Lauren looked at her hands, tears dropping onto them. 'I'll ask you again. What happened with Ritchie Donoghue?'

30

Freeman drove towards Newcastle again, this time to the address Darren had given her for Rachel. He'd also given her Healy's address and she wondered if she should cut out the middleman and go straight to him. But it seemed unlikely Healy would just back off with an idle threat from her. He'd want something in return – his money, for example. Plus, Freeman wanted to meet this Rachel, get her to take some responsibility and discover what happened when she fucked with Freeman's brother.

She pulled up on a wide road lined with takeaways and bookies and independent shops that looked like they'd been in a state of disrepair for decades. Most of the businesses seemed to have flats above them and it was in one of these that she'd apparently find Rachel. Freeman found the right number, noticing it was above a nail and beauty bar that had its shutters down. In fact most of the shops on the block had their shutters down.

Freeman pressed the buzzer for the flat and waited, moving back to see if anyone was looking out. As far as she could tell, the flat was as deserted as the street. She buzzed again and then used the key Darren had given her. Freeman went inside and thought it was more like a squat than a flat. She had a look around, hoping she'd find Rachel, but the place was empty.

She went into each room and checked for any large amounts of cash or drugs but there was nothing. She tried the phone number Darren had given her for Rachel and it rang and rang without diverting and Freeman hung up. After a few minutes she decided it was too cold to hang around in there – it was almost as cold as it was outside – and went down and got back in the car. She wondered if she should try the club, although Darren claimed Rachel only worked the night shift.

Inside the car, she warmed her hands on the heater's vents and wondered how Darren and Gardner would be getting on. Gardner hadn't been keen to take Darren with him but he was too good a guy to refuse. She owed him big time.

Her phone started to ring and she pulled it out, about to answer it automatically. And then she saw the caller ID. Mam. Freeman stared at the phone. She frequently paused before answering her mam's calls anyway but usually gave in out of guilt. But this time she let it go to voicemail. She couldn't speak to her parents without mentioning Darren and she hadn't figured out what to say yet.

When the voicemail icon appeared on her phone's screen she listened to it straight away.

'Nicola, it's Mam. We've decided to come back early. Mark and one of the bairns have got flu so we're leaving them to it. We'll be back in the morning. I'll be doing a dinner for New Year if you'd like to come. *If* you can spare some time. Bye.'

Freeman rolled her eyes. Her mam was incapable of leaving a message without getting a little barb in there somewhere. She sighed. If she didn't speak to her in the next day or so then there'd be hell to pay. She'd need to know in advance if she was going for dinner. How else would she know how many potatoes to make? Or what size joint of meat to get? Like it was the end of the world if they had some leftovers.

Hopefully things would be sorted out by tomorrow and she could not only call her mam back and tell her she'd be there for dinner but also let her know her youngest son was home. Maybe Gardner was right and it wouldn't matter how she broke the news. All her mam and dad had ever wanted was for Darren to come home. Maybe they'd even be grateful to Freeman for being the one who got him back.

From the corner of her eye she saw someone moving across the street and turned for a better look. The woman was short, not quite as short as Freeman but still small, and her long blond hair looked like it hadn't seen a brush in days. Freeman almost turned away and then the image from the club CCTV sprang to mind.

That was Rachel.

She pushed the car door open, stumbling on the kerb. 'Rachel!'

The woman turned, curious at first and then panicked. Her eyes were smudged with last night's make-up. She stared at Freeman for a second and then turned and ran.

'Wait,' Freeman shouted after her, trying to catch up, which should've been easy considering the heels Rachel was wearing, but as Freeman turned the corner she could no longer see her.

Freeman slowed, checking the side streets, peering through the few shop windows that didn't have shutters down. No sign. She tried the phone number again but got no answer. 'Shit,' she muttered. Had Darren warned her? Or was she running from a lot of people? Had she made a habit of ripping people off?

Making her way back to the car, Freeman decided to wait it out. Rachel would have to come back eventually. And then she'd have some explaining to do.

31

'He was going to hurt me,' Lauren said, wiping her face. 'He threatened me.'

'All right,' Harrington said. 'So you fought back. Self-defence. I can understand that. Why was he threatening you?'

'Because I'd broken up with him. He was angry. He wanted to get back with me but I refused.'

'So he threatened to hurt you?'

'Yes.'

'Did he actually hurt you? Did he physically assault you that night?'

'You don't have to answer these questions, Lauren, you're not under arrest – we can leave right now,' Harry said but Lauren shook her head and kept talking.

'No. Not really. But he would've. I know he would. He had . . .'

'He had what, Lauren?'

'He wanted to hurt me,' she said. 'He said he could make things really bad for me.'

'How?'

Gardner leaned in to the monitor, hoping this was it. That she'd snap and give them what they wanted.

'I can't say,' she said and started to cry. 'I just can't.'

Gardner sighed and stood up straight again. He wondered about going ahead and asking about the photos and tapes but if someone had been to Ritchie's to look for them but had been unsuccessful, maybe they'd risk going back again, when things had died down a little. It was a long shot, but worth a try.

Harrington changed tack. 'Tell us about your relationship with Peter Hinde.'

'That's irrelevant,' Harry said.

'No, it's not,' Harrington said and focused on Lauren.

'I already told you,' Lauren said, picking at her broken fingernail. 'He works for my dad.'

'Sure,' Harrington said. 'But I mean your personal relationship with him.' Lauren looked up this time. 'He's not *just* one of your dad's employees, is he? I mean, you wouldn't call someone who just worked for your dad if you needed help. If you'd just found a body. Would you?' Lauren stared at him and if looks could kill Gardner thought Harrington would be as dead as Ritchie Donoghue. 'So he's more than just someone who works for your dad, right? You've known him a long time.'

'So we're friends,' Lauren said.

'Good friends, I'd guess,' Harrington said. 'Someone willing to do a lot for you?'

'Where's this leading, Detective?' Harry said.

'I was just trying to get hold of my dad,' Lauren said, ignoring her counsel.

'We have witnesses who say that they saw a car that looked like Peter's parked outside your house late that night.'

Lauren frowned. 'They're lying.'

'Both of them?'

'Peter wasn't there that night.'

'Was someone else there?'

'No.'

'They also said they'd seen the car there before. Frequently.'

'So?' Lauren said, crossing her arms. 'Was it that nosy cow across the road? She should try getting her own life, stop messing in mine.'

'So Peter does come to your house? Frequently?'

'No. He's been there before, but not loads. He drops my dad off sometimes.'

'And stays overnight?'

Lauren started to cry again. 'I don't want my dad finding out,' she said, looking at Harry from the corner of her eye.

'Why don't you want your dad to find out about you and Peter?' Harrington asked.

'Because he'd kill us,' Lauren said.

Gardner felt a nudge of sympathy for her as she spoke. Why would a grown woman be so afraid of what her father thought that she felt she had to lie to the police rather than let on about a relationship her dad might disapprove of? He didn't even understand why Walter would oppose it. If it was a choice between Peter or Ritchie, surely it was a no-brainer. Even Gardner had to admit that Peter Hinde was likeable. Of all of them involved in this mess, Hinde was the only one who hadn't displayed a lack of respect, who had, despite the mounting evidence against him, been helpful.

'Why would your dad object so much to you and Peter seeing each other?' Harrington asked. 'He's obviously fond of him. He's known him from when he was a kid. Gave him a job on the campaign.'

'Exactly,' Lauren said.

'Exactly what? I don't get it,' Harrington said.

'He thinks of Peter like a son,' Lauren said.

'So . . .' Harrington said, dragging out the word. 'What? He thinks it'd be like incest? But it's not, right? You're not actually related?' He looked from Lauren to Harry as if he was missing something and Gardner rolled his eyes. Accusing her of incest wasn't going to help their case.

'No, we're not related,' Lauren said. 'But when we were kids, or I was a kid anyway, I fancied him like mad. Couldn't wait for him to come over. Sometimes Dad would be out late but Peter would stay anyway, said he was just waiting for him. We'd sit and talk or listen to music or whatever. And there was one night, a few months after I turned sixteen. He came over, there was just me and him in the house . . .

'It was all me,' she said. 'I came on to *him*. He wasn't taking advantage of me. But obviously he felt the same way. Dad came in and caught us. He went mental,' she said. 'He hit Peter, over and over. I'd never seen him like that. Ever. Peter left, I was in tears. He was threatening to go after Peter but I convinced him it was all me. I don't think he saw me in the same way ever again.'

'So what changed? Him and Peter are like two peas in a pod these days, aren't they?' Harrington said.

'Not really. They didn't talk for like, years. And then Peter's mum died a couple of years ago so Dad got in touch. After the funeral Dad just started acting like nothing had happened. And when he decided to run in the election he offered him a job.'

'And Peter didn't mind? After what'd happened?' Harrington said.

Lauren shrugged. 'I guess not. I think I always thought that maybe Peter liked my dad more than he liked me. He was just happy to be back in the fold. But I could tell he was on his guard, always seemed a bit nervous of Dad.'

'And you really think your dad would be as angry now? If he found out?'

'Like I said, I don't know why but he just can't stand the idea of me and Peter being together.' She turned to Harry now, looking like a kid. 'You aren't going to tell my dad all this, are you?'

'He's not allowed to,' Harrington said but Lauren didn't seem convinced.

Gardner heard a noise behind him and realised Atherton had come into the room. He nodded at him and turned back to the screen.

'So how long have you been together?' Harrington asked.

'About three months,' Lauren said. 'Not long.'

'But you were seeing him while you were still with Ritchie?'

She nodded. 'I broke it off with him soon after, but yes. They overlapped.'

'And did they know about each other?'

'Peter knew about Ritchie. He wanted me to break up with him so I did. Ritchie didn't know about Peter, though. Or at least I thought he didn't.'

'But?'

'But that night he said something. He knew, somehow.'

'And that's what you fought about?'

'You are trying to lead my client, Detective, and I think we've had enough,' Harry said.

Gardner turned to say something to Atherton and saw the door closing behind his boss as he left the room. Next thing, the door to the interview room opened and Atherton informed Harrington he was to end the interview. Gardner left the room and caught up with him, wanting to know what was going on.

32

'Fine. We don't have enough to charge her yet,' Gardner said, 'but at least arrest her, allow us to keep pressing her without Warren threatening to leave every two minutes.'

'There isn't sufficient evidence to warrant that course of action,' Hadley said and Gardner looked at him in amazement but Hadley remained impassive. He turned to Atherton for backup – surely he could see the grounds to continue? – but Atherton just stared out of the window, completely under Hadley's thumb.

'She was about to tell us what happened. So far she's done nothing but lie,' Gardner said.

'She was in shock. She's explained her actions, her reason for not disclosing her whereabouts that night,' Hadley said.

Gardner laughed. 'You really believe she'd rather lie during a murder investigation than own up to buying a little coke? What about the scratches on Donoghue? What about the text she sent him, asking him to come back?'

'There were other prints on her phone, were there not? We don't know Lauren sent that text.'

'No, you're right. There were other prints. Not that that knowledge is of any use to us as Warren's claiming she wasn't under caution when we took the phone. But Peter Hinde's prints were on there. Ritchie's. Walter James's, too. You want me to ask him if he sent the text?'

'You're being ridiculous.'

'Am I? What I think is ridiculous is the way everyone is bowing down to Walter James because of who he is and who he knows.'

Hadley glared at Gardner but didn't respond. Atherton interrupted the awkward silence.

'The results came back from Peter Hinde's car. Small amounts of blood were found inside, above the passenger door. We're still waiting to confirm it's Ritchie's but as they found his fingerprints in there too it seems obvious what the result will be.'

'Good. I think that's grounds to arrest Hinde,' Hadley said, looking at Gardner with something approaching smugness.

'And you don't think that if Hinde's responsible then Lauren must be connected too?'

'One doesn't follow the other.'

'But she called Hinde after Ritchie was there, after she'd had an altercation with him.'

'Yes, I'm aware of your thoughts,' Hadley said and sighed, turning to his desk and flicking through paperwork. 'As far as I'm concerned, we're done with Lauren James for now.' He looked at Gardner briefly and said, 'Dismissed.'

Gardner walked out and told himself not to slam the door as he left Hadley's office but he couldn't help himself. He stormed downstairs towards his office, almost running into Lawton. 'Where's Peter Hinde?' he asked. 'Is he here yet?'

'No, sir,' Lawton said. 'We've checked his home and work, tried his phone. No response so far.'

'Keep on it,' he said to Lawton. 'Get someone to the office and his home address.'

'Okay. But Mrs Donoghue's here,' Lawton said and Gardner stopped and sighed.

'All right,' he nodded, 'let's go.' He followed her down the corridor to where Ritchie's mum was waiting. He wasn't looking forward to speaking with her. Speaking to relatives was always difficult, especially when he had no answers; nothing to offer them.

'Mrs Donoghue,' Lawton said as she opened the door. 'This is DI Gardner.'

Gardner walked in and found a small, thin woman, struggling to get up from her seat. She couldn't have been more than ten years older than him, mid-fifties at most, but she seemed frail. Finally on her feet she put out her hand to his, giving him the best smile she could muster, and he realised this woman was not what he was expecting. Firstly, how a woman this small had ever given birth to Ritchie Donoghue was one of nature's mysteries. And secondly, she was not the Mrs Kray-like battleaxe that he'd imagined. She was a small woman made smaller by grief, looking for answers about her son.

'Please,' he said, 'sit down.' Mrs Donoghue sat and tore at the tissue she clutched in her hand. 'I'm very sorry for your loss,' Gardner said and the woman swallowed a sob. Lawton handed her a glass of water and Gardner waited. He realised, not for the first time, that he actually was sorry about the death of a scumbag dealer. He tried not to go down that road too often, the one that questioned whether the world was better off without some people. But it didn't really matter who the victim was – a kid or a mother of three, or some bastard who'd made people's lives miserable. At the end of the day they all had someone who loved them, who was grieving for them.

'I'm sorry to bother you,' Mrs Donoghue said. 'I know you have a lot to do but I just needed to come and . . . I know my Ritchie wasn't an angel but he didn't deserve this.'

'No,' Gardner said, 'he didn't.'

'Did she do it?' She looked him in the eye for the first time. 'Lauren.'

'I don't know. That's what we're trying to find out. We're looking at Ms James as Ritchie was found in her garden, and because of their history. But we're looking at other possibilities too.'

Mrs Donoghue nodded. 'But it's possible? That she did it? She hurt my Ritchie?'

'We can't say anything for sure yet.'

Mrs Donoghue let out what might have been a laugh but her face was deadly serious.

'Did you know Lauren?' Gardner asked.

'Not really. He brought her to the house once. I made them tea but she turned her nose up at it. Said she was a vegetarian but I knew that wasn't true. She was just a snob. She just sat there and played with her phone while me and Ritchie ate. I didn't know what to make of her but she never came back, so . . .' She shrugged.

'Did Ritchie talk to you about her? About their relationship?'

'Not really. He seemed very keen on her, though. Had pictures of her on his phone, showed her off a bit when he first met her. She is a very pretty girl. But I got the feeling she didn't feel the same. She'd say she'd come over but always changed her mind at the last minute. When Ritchie came for his tea he'd sit staring at his phone. I think she was playing him for a fool.'

'Why do you think she stayed with him for so long if she didn't really like him?'

'I don't know. Maybe she liked the attention he gave her. There've been others, before her, who only liked him for his money, for what they could get from him. But I don't know if that was the case with her. She could get that from her father, couldn't she?'

'You knew who her dad was?'

'Oh yes, it was the first thing out of her mouth,' said Mrs Donoghue, her lip curling slightly. 'And I'm not stupid, Mr Gardner. I read the papers. I know that Walter James has a lot of influence in how things work around here. I just want to know that this will be done right. It breaks my heart when I think of some of the things my son's done,' she said, trying to hold back the tears. 'But he at least deserves this to be done right. To find who killed him and make them pay for it. He deserves that. *I* deserve it.'

As Gardner watched Lawton escort Mrs Donoghue out he noticed Walter James lurking at the other end of the corridor. He knew Walter had used his connections to make sure Lauren was treated differently. He just didn't know how far his connections went. If Walter had his claws in that deep, it seemed unlikely that anyone Gardner went to on this would be willing to do things by the book.

He started walking towards Walter, noticing the grin on the old prick's face. This wasn't a man concerned about his daughter. This was a man pleased he was winning the game.

As Gardner got closer he noticed Lauren was sitting by the door, waiting to leave, while Walter chatted to Craig Cartwright. Cartwright looked like he did when Atherton gave him a gold star. He was sucking up to Walter James almost as hard. Did he think that by doing whatever Walter wanted it'd help his career? Probably. And maybe he was right. The little shit had made it to detective without having the first clue about the job.

Walter slapped Cartwright on the arm and turned to leave, stopping short when he saw Gardner watching. Cartwright looked embarrassed and scuttled away.

'I didn't realise anyone had requested you come back in. Yet,' Gardner said.

'I'm here for my daughter,' Walter told him and reached for Lauren's hand. He pulled her up and she looked like a child beside him, staring at the floor.

Gardner grunted and walked away, knowing it was pointless making any threats because Walter would know as well as he did that they were empty. Maybe Hadley was right. Gardner did need something more solid on Lauren because without something airtight, Walter James was never going to let his daughter take the blame – guilty or not.

When Gardner was a few yards away, Walter spoke again. His voice was low and Gardner had to go back to hear him.

'I know you're just doing your job, Mr Gardner. But I won't stand for you bullying my little girl.'

'Bullying?'

'I have a very good memory,' Walter continued. 'I never forget when someone does me or my family wrong.'

'Is that a threat?' Gardner asked.

Walter ignored Gardner, grabbed Lauren, and disappeared through the doors without looking back. As Gardner watched the door swing shut he wondered just how idle Walter James's threats were.

33

Gardner walked into the office, which was buzzing with activity. Even if Hadley and the rest of Walter James's mates weren't taking the case seriously, at least the rest of the team were. He sat down and thought about what they'd gleaned from Peter Hinde's car. There was blood, only a small amount but it was something, especially when you considered they'd matched the tyre marks from the alley, too. So what had happened in the car? Ritchie clearly hadn't been murdered in there. There wasn't enough blood. So had things just started in there? An argument that got out of hand?

Gardner picked up the phone and called the pathologist, Kerry O'Hara. Five minutes later he had his answer. As he hung up, Lawton approached his desk.

'I took Mrs Donoghue home,' she said. 'Her sister's with her.' She sat down and looked at the desk, playing with a stray paperclip. Sometimes he wondered about Lawton, whether she was cut out for this job. In a lot of ways she was one of the best he'd ever worked with and he was convinced she'd make a fantastic detective, even if she wasn't so sure. But sometimes things seemed to get to her too much. Perhaps it was just inexperience, or her personality, but she seemed to feel for the victims and their families more than most. Maybe that was a good thing. Maybe he'd lost that part of himself a long time ago.

'I just spoke to O'Hara,' Gardner said and Lawton looked up. 'The blood in Peter Hinde's car? O'Hara says Ritchie has a cut and bruising on his left temple that she'd bet anything came from him having his head smacked into the car door frame.' He reached out to Lawton's head. 'If someone in the driver's seat slammed Ritchie's head against the door . . .' he said, pushing her head gently. Lawton pulled away from him and he dropped his hand. 'The head injury matches exactly where the blood was found.'

'So they were arguing in the car and things got physical,' Lawton said. 'But who was it?'

Gardner shrugged. 'O'Hara says it would've had to have been pretty forceful so I wouldn't rule Lauren out but I'd be more inclined to say it was a man. What happened after that, though, is anyone's guess.'

'Also, Lauren doesn't drive, so why would she be in the driver's seat?'

'Exactly,' Gardner said. 'We need to get hold of Peter Hinde as soon as possible.'

Harrington rushed over with a pile of papers. 'Got Ritchie Donoghue's phone records,' he said. 'Most of it's fairly innocuous, calls to and from his mother. Little other activity. Who knew Ritchie Donoghue was such a mummy's boy? *But* you'll never guess who he'd been calling a lot recently.'

'Who?'

'Jen Worrall. Nine calls to or from her in the last two weeks.'

Gardner took the records from Harrington, scanning through the data. Harrington had highlighted the calls to and from Jen Worrall's number. Most of them had lasted between twenty and forty seconds. Not long conversations, then, but it seemed the pair were more chatty than Worrall had made out.

'Let's pay her another visit,' Gardner said, grabbing his coat. 'Lawton? Call me as soon as Hinde shows up.'

* * *

Gardner pulled up outside the campaign office, noticing there were no lights on. Usually, under these sorts of circumstances he'd think that was pretty normal – that operations would stop while the investigation continued – but Walter James wasn't normal. As far as he was concerned the small matter of a murder wasn't going to derail his campaign. So where was everybody? Apart from a small gaggle of reporters, the street was empty. A far cry from the scene the day before. Maybe they knew James wasn't there, and without the star act there was no show.

He got out of the car and peered through the window, seeing no movement. Gardner tried the door and finding it unlocked, walked into the office. He could hear Jen Worrall's voice coming from the back and followed the sound. She was pacing up and down, one phone pressed to her ear, another in her free hand.

'And I'm sure you'll understand that I can't comment. This is a police investigation and any queries should be directed to them.' She hung up, throwing the phone onto the desk before raising the other to her ear. 'Are you still there? Well I'd appreciate it if you could get back over here and help me out . . . I know that, but it's worse over here, I prom-ise you, Peter. Fine. Whatever.' She hung up the second phone and threw that on the desk too. The first phone had already started to ring again. Jen looked at it and was about to answer but Gardner interrupted.

'Looks like you could do with a break,' he said and Jen turned around, noticing him for the first time.

Gardner led her out to the front office where there were fewer ringing phones. He and Jen took a seat and Harrington loitered by the window.

'Was that Peter Hinde on the phone?' Gardner asked.

'Yes,' she said.

'Did he say where he was?'

She shook her head. Usually people in these circumstances asked what they could do for the police or what the visit was about but Jen sat there, arms folded across her chest, scowl on her face, so Gardner just jumped right in.

'You said you barely knew Ritchie Donoghue,' he said.

'I don't.'

'But you made several calls to him recently. Received a few calls too. That's quite a bit of contact from someone you barely know.'

Jen's face dropped slightly but she didn't move at all. 'He was looking for Lauren,' she said.

'And when you called *him*? Were you telling him where she was?' Jen shrugged. 'How did Ritchie get your mobile number?'

'I don't know,' she said. 'It's a work phone. Maybe Lauren gave it to him?'

'Why would she do that? What reason would Lauren have to give your phone number to a man she was trying to avoid?'

'I don't know,' Jen snapped. 'Maybe he found it in her phone.'

Gardner looked over his shoulder at Harrington who moved closer to the desk, taking over the questions.

'Come on, Jen,' Harrington said. 'You and Donoghue didn't have nine chats about Lauren James's whereabouts. So what was going on?'

Jen sucked her cheeks in and looked like she was considering her options. In the end she sighed and looked at Gardner. 'I'd started seeing him,' she said.

'You and Ritchie? The man you described as a gorilla in Nike?'

She shrugged. 'I know Lauren had split up with him but I didn't want anyone to find out. I thought it'd be weird. And we hadn't done anything. We were just flirting really. Nothing serious.'

Gardner looked at Harrington. It was total bullshit and they both knew it.

'So you were flirting with Ritchie over these nine calls? No texts though.'

'So?' Jen said.

'So, when I'm flirting with someone, I tend to do it by text. I think most people do,' Harrington said.

'So I'm not most people.'

'Okay,' Gardner said. 'So you were flirting with Ritchie. He was flirting back. So why was he still going round to Lauren's house, trying to get back with her?'

'I don't know. Maybe because men are all arseholes?'

Gardner couldn't help but notice that Jen looked at Harrington when she said this and he wondered if Ms Worrall was more perceptive than he'd realised. 'So you liked Ritchie, you were flirting with him and then he was murdered. I have to say, you don't seem too upset by what's happened.'

'Well, like you said, he went to Lauren's to try and get back with her after flirting with me. Why should I be upset?'

They left Jen to it and Gardner turned to Harrington as soon as they'd walked out of the office. 'You think one of these people might actually tell us the truth at some point?' He slammed the door behind him.

'Wouldn't count on it,' Harrington said.

34

Freeman had given up on waiting outside Rachel's flat. It was too cold, and if the girl was trying to hide then it was unlikely she was going to come back any time soon. She'd thought about going back to the club but didn't really want to show her face there in case there was any blowback from the CCTV issue. Gardner had told her that Tommy was pretty pissed off about it but had been under the impression that the deletion had been down to female user error rather than any deliberate illegal activity. For once, it looked like a little misogyny had been useful.

If only her boss would see it that way then maybe she'd be okay. She'd prepared a story about her ID being stolen along with her purse. It was weak but she'd figured a pre-emptive strike could work in her favour. But when she'd showed up to the station, DCI Routledge was out and she wondered at the logic of her story. Vicky, the woman from the club, would be able to ID her if necessary, and there was always the possibility that the CCTV footage could be restored anyway, in which case she'd be screwed. She decided it was best to wait for the problem to come to her. And as long as Gardner could keep her little visit to the club under his hat, and as long as Tommy didn't make a complaint, maybe she'd be okay. Maybe she wouldn't be up in front of Professional Standards.

While she'd been in the building she'd had a sneaky look at Mark Healy's history. It appeared he'd been arrested on several occasions but not much had ever stuck. He was slippery, and somehow had the money for a very good solicitor, Leon Webber. Unfortunately Leon Webber was now in prison for fraud. Freeman had enjoyed that piece of news when it came. Webber was as corrupt as the clients he represented.

But Healy's history worried Freeman. A few of the arrests had been in relation to serious assaults and his profile showed that Healy was, at 6 foot 5, almost a foot taller than Darren, and even though he was slim, he could still crush her brother like a grape.

Freeman checked the time and called Darren. He had to be out of bed by now. On the fourth ring he picked up.

'Yeah,' he said.

'Hey, it's me. How's it going?'

'Fine,' he said.

'What're you up to?' she asked.

'Nothing. TV.'

'Is Gardner there?'

'No.'

Freeman wondered why she'd bothered. Darren was hard to talk to at the best of times. 'I went to the flat,' she said.

'Did you see her? Is she okay?'

'I saw her. Unfortunately she saw me and ran. Does she always do that? Run away from people who come to see her?'

'No. She probably just thought you were, like, after her or something.'

'So do you know where she's likely to go? You said she works nights, right? So where else would she go in the day?'

'I don't know. We mostly sleep during the day.'

Freeman rolled her eyes. 'You must go somewhere, sometimes.'

'I don't know. The pub?'

'Which pub?'

'The one on the corner. The Clarry.'

'Okay. Anywhere else?'

'You're not going to do anything that's gonna get her hurt, are you?'

'No. I told you. I'm going to get her to work things out with Healy and get Healy to back off. That's it.'

Darren sighed. 'She could be at Mickey's.'

'Who's Mickey?'

'He's like a bookie, sort of. Rach likes to hang out there sometimes. Mickey has a hard-on for her. She likes it.'

Freeman bit her tongue again. She sounded lovely. She wondered why Darren couldn't see it. 'So where's this Mickey live?'

Darren gave her the address and Freeman hung up after promising him again that she wouldn't do anything to hurt his Rachel. As she headed towards Mickey's, she wondered how long she'd still have a job and whether Darren was worth it.

35

Gardner sat down opposite Peter Hinde. Lawton had called him while he was talking to Jen, saying Hinde had finally shown up, claiming he'd been at a dental appointment, that's why he hadn't answered his calls. He was very sorry for the inconvenience, less so once he learned he was under arrest. Gardner noticed that Harry Warren was missing from the scene; instead the duty solicitor was called in. Clearly Walter James wasn't too concerned about his employee.

'Lauren told us about your relationship,' Gardner said. 'She told us it caused quite a stir between you and Walter James back in the day.'

'He had every right to be upset,' Peter said. 'I was older than Lauren. Walter trusted me.'

'So you think he was right to hit you? Cut you out of his life?'

'He was upset.'

'So you felt guilty about it?' Gardner said. 'But not enough to not repeat your mistake?'

'Things are different now,' Peter said.

'But you're still keeping it a secret. Do you think Walter would still be as upset?'

'I don't know,' Peter said. 'I'm not sure he'd approve.'

'Why not? You're both grown-ups. And you'd think he'd prefer his daughter to be with someone he regards as highly as you instead of some reprobate like Ritchie Donoghue.'

Peter shrugged. 'Perhaps. But we weren't willing to risk him finding out. Not yet anyway. Not until after the election.'

'Lauren said she thought her dad would kill you if he found out. Both of you.'

'I think Lauren's being a bit dramatic,' Peter said.

'You weren't exactly discreet, either,' Gardner said. 'A witness said she'd seen your car outside Lauren's on numerous occasions. You weren't afraid Walter would show up?'

'Well, it's not often Walter shows up at his daughter's house at night,' Peter said.

'There were a lot of phone calls too,' Gardner said.

'Again, I don't think he'd have been checking her phone.'

'What about yours? Does he ever have access to your phone?'

'No. Why would he?'

'He had access to your car,' Gardner said.

'While his was off the road.'

'We have witnesses who saw the car outside Lauren's the night of the murder. The tyre tracks from the alley match your car.'

'Well, I wasn't in it,' Peter said.

'The tinted windows won't help us confirm that,' Gardner said.

'Are you suggesting that I'm lying?' Peter said, looking to the solicitor for help but he just sat there, mute.

'I'm not suggesting anything. I'm *saying* that *someone* was in your car that night, outside Lauren's house. You've just told me that her dad doesn't frequent her house at night whereas you're a regular visitor.'

'Not that night,' Peter said. 'You know the keys were left at the office, that anyone could've taken them.'

'We also found something in your car this morning. Can you hazard a guess as to what it is?'

'I've no idea.'

'How often was Ritchie Donoghue in your car?' Gardner asked.

Peter's face reddened, his fingers curled into fists. 'That man has never been in my car.'

'Hmm,' Gardner said. 'So, to the best of your knowledge Ritchie Donoghue was never in your car.'

'That's right.'

'So why did we find his fingerprints on the passenger side door? Inside and out?'

Peter paled a little. 'No idea.'

'There was also a trace of blood in the interior.'

Peter's face dropped completely and the duty solicitor perked up a little. 'It must be a mistake.' Gardner just waited; let Peter keep talking. 'He's never been in my car! Why would I have that piece of shit in my car?'

'You tell me.'

'I wasn't there!'

'I imagine you'd be pretty pissed off that someone was harassing your girlfriend. So I think you went there to try and stop Ritchie.'

'No,' Peter said.

'You just wanted him to leave her alone but things got out of hand.'

'No. I wasn't there.'

'Ritchie refused. He was a big guy, probably thought you didn't pose much of a threat. But you caught him off guard—'

'Detective, please,' the solicitor said.

'I wasn't there. For God's sake! Someone else must've taken my car. You have nothing on me at all apart from my car being seen.'

'We have two witnesses who saw a man in the alley outside Lauren's garden. A tall and skinny man.'

Peter paused and then let out a desperate laugh. 'So that's your evidence? A tall, skinny man.'

'I think that's a pretty good description of you, Peter,' Gardner said.

'And a lot of other people. Him, for instance,' Peter said, looking at Harrington. 'Maybe *you* were there.'

Gardner had to admit that that was true. The description was vague at best. But there was the car, the phone calls, his relationship with Lauren *and* the potential blackmail. He didn't mention that last part yet, waiting to see how things played out.

'So if you weren't in your car that night, who was?'

'I don't know. Like I said, anyone could've taken the keys.'

'And who do you think would've done that?'

'I don't know. I just know it wasn't me.'

'Jen Worrall said she put the spare keys back the morning after the murder. Said they'd been posted back through the door.'

Peter looked puzzled, as if they were trying to trick him. 'What are you saying? That Jen took the car?'

'Just that someone had the spare keys overnight. Or at least someone wanted it to look that way. Who else would've driven your car, Peter?'

'Walter had used the car that day,' Peter said.

'Did he keep hold of the keys?'

'How would I know?'

'Walter James said he went back to the office after he left you that night. If he had the keys, why didn't he just put them back in your office instead of posting them through the door?'

'I don't know. Maybe he forgot until he was leaving, had already locked up.'

'Jen Worrall claimed the keys were posted through the back door. Walter left by the front.'

Peter let out a breath, clearly getting anxious. 'Then I don't know. Maybe he didn't have the keys. Have you asked him?'

'We have. He claimed to have returned them straight away.'

'Well there you have it then,' Peter said.

'So, if Walter didn't have the keys, in theory anyone could've used the car, is that right?'

'I suppose. Anyone from the office.'

'But if he *did* have them, then that would limit things a little. To you or him.'

'Or maybe someone took the keys after Walter left. Or he never had the keys and someone took them earlier. I don't know. All I know is I wasn't there.'

'What time did Walter come back from his meeting that day, in your car?'

'I'm not sure. Late, I think. Around six.'

'And was anyone else still there, working?'

'Just me and Jen.'

'Who else has keys to the office?' Gardner asked.

'Me, Walter and Jen.'

'So no one else from the office could've taken the keys after hours?'

Peter sighed. 'I guess not.'

Gardner let that hang in the air for a few moments. They'd received the CCTV footage from the building across the street from the campaign office. Walter had indeed been dropped off by a taxi around 11.20 p.m. that night. And he left again just after 1.30 a.m. What went on in the meantime was still a mystery, though, as there was no CCTV at the back. Could James have gone out of the back door, committed murder, and then come back in? As much as Gardner wanted this to be the case, firstly it seemed unlikely, and secondly, he couldn't prove it.

'Let me ask you about Jen Worrall. Was she in a relationship with Ritchie Donoghue?'

Peter laughed. 'Is that a joke?'

Gardner looked at Harrington. 'Why would that be a joke?'

'Because as far as I'm aware, Jen's a lesbian.'

36

Freeman parked at the end of the road and walked along it, past the groups of kids loitering on the corner, finding the address Darren had given her for Mickey at the top of the street. Darren's description of Mickey as a 'sort of bookie' led her to believe that Mickey was in the business of taking money from the poor, hopeful and/or the not too bright. He probably had a lot of cash but he wasn't putting it into property, that was for sure.

As she reached the front door she noticed several dog turds in the small patch of garden at the front and spotted, after she'd knocked, a 'Beware of the dogs' sign in the window. She wondered if it was purely to keep prospective thieves at bay but before she'd dropped her hand back to her side she heard the sound of furious barking and then a man's voice shouting at the dogs to shut up.

The door opened and a chubby, middle-aged man stood before her in his dressing gown, a bowl of cereal in one hand. It was hardly the threatening impression of a major criminal. The man continued eating his cereal as he stared at Freeman. The dogs, two enormous Rottweilers, stood behind him, uninterested in her, instead staring at the bowl in their master's hand.

'Are you Mickey?' Freeman asked.

'Yeah?'

'I'm looking for Rachel.'

Mickey finished his Coco Pops and wiped a dribble of brown milk from his chin before leaning over and putting the bowl on the floor. The dogs pushed each other out of the way, scrambling to get the dregs.

'I'm Darren's sister,' Freeman said. She'd almost instinctively reached for her ID but she didn't want to play it that way, not yet at least.

Mickey squinted at her. 'I didn't know Spazzy had a sister,' he said and stood aside, gesturing for her to go in. Freeman tried to squeeze past the dogs and hoped Mickey was wearing something beneath his gown as she brushed against him. She didn't comment on the nickname he'd given Darren, afraid she might end up punching him and ruining any chances of speaking to Rachel.

Mickey led her into the living room, which comprised two filthy settees, a coffee table, and the biggest TV she had ever seen.

'Take a seat,' Mickey said. 'Can I get you anything? Cup of tea? Lager?'

Freeman looked at the crusty mugs on the table beside her and shook her head. Mickey shrugged and disappeared, hopefully to get Rachel. As she sat waiting, the dogs came in and stared at her, blocking the exit with their massive frames. She tried smiling at them, hoping a friendly face would make them less likely to rip her face off.

Beside the filthy mugs, Freeman noticed a mobile phone – pink with a diamante trim. Rachel's. Surely. She glanced towards the door before picking up the phone. She checked texts first and found plenty to Darren, sickening in their lovey-doveyness. She ignored them and scrolled through until she found a conversation with Healy. Freeman opened it up and found dozens and dozens of messages to and from the man threatening to kill her brother, most of them verging on the pornographic. The little bitch was cheating on Darren.

Freeman searched through, trying to find anything proving that Rachel and Healy were in this together, that they were setting Darren up. But there was nothing but flirting and full-on sexting. So what was her game? Was she playing them both?

She could hear movement upstairs and wondered what was going on, if Rachel was cheating on Darren with Mickey too, if she'd interrupted something. She was about to stand up and go and see for herself when one of the dogs jumped up onto the settee beside her. For a few seconds it stared at her, eye to eye, before lunging forward and licking her face. Freeman pulled away, wiping the saliva from her cheek. She tried to stand but the dog collapsed onto her, half its bodyweight on her knees. The stupid thing thought it was a lap dog. It rolled over, kicking its legs in the air and Freeman groaned under the weight. The other dog lay down in front of her, whimpering.

'Get out of it,' Mickey shouted at the dogs as he came back into the room and they scarpered. 'Sorry about them. Pair of wusses. Rachel's just getting dressed.'

Freeman nodded and noticed Mickey's smug expression. He had to know she'd understand the implication – I'm sleeping with your brother's girlfriend – but he didn't seem concerned.

Mickey turned as Rachel came in and Freeman stood up as it looked like she was going to run.

'This is Spazzy's sister,' Mickey said.

'Don't call him that,' Rachel said before looking at Freeman more closely. 'You're the copper.'

'What?' Mickey said, jumping up and flashing a little bit more than Freeman cared to see. 'You're a copper?'

'I'm not here as a copper. I'm here about Darren,' she said. 'I need to talk to you.'

'What about?' Rachel said.

'In private,' Freeman said and led Rachel towards the kitchen. She closed the door, to the dismay of the dogs, and stood against it so Rachel couldn't flee. 'I want you to come with me to Healy's and tell him you took the money.'

'Whatever,' Rachel said. 'You think I'm stupid, or something?'

'I have proof you took the money. So you can either do this my way, where everyone's happy, or I just go to Healy with the CCTV footage and you can work it out between yourselves.'

'Darren told me he got rid of it. You don't have shit.'

Freeman squeezed her hands into fists. Maybe Healy wouldn't need to kill Darren. Maybe she'd just do it herself. Why the hell had he told Rachel he'd destroyed the evidence?

'Look, Rachel. You're obviously a smart girl, so just think about it. If you don't own up, Healy is going to hurt my brother. Do you want that to happen? Because even if you don't give a shit about him, which I'm starting to think is the case, if anything happens to him I will personally make sure your life is hell.' She watched as Rachel squirmed. 'If you come with me and tell Healy you took the money, on the other hand, I will make sure no one touches you.'

'He'll kill me,' she said.

'I doubt that,' she said, thinking about the texts. 'You offer him either the coke or all the money you make from selling the coke and he backs off. That's the deal. He doesn't want me sniffing around him any more than you do. He'll take the deal and everyone's happy.'

Rachel pouted. 'So I have to give him all the money I get? Even if it's more than I took? That's not fair.'

'You stole his money, Rachel, what's fair isn't an issue right now. So, do we have a deal?'

'Fine,' Rachel said. 'Whatever.'

'Good. Let's go.' Freeman opened the door and the Rottweilers clambered up from the floor, shaking their whole bodies in excitement. She patted them on the head as she made her way to the door.

'You're leaving?' Mickey said from the settee.

'I'll be back soon, honey bear,' Rachel said and Freeman fought the urge to vomit. She pointed Rachel in the direction of her car while Rachel dug around in her handbag. She pulled out a lipstick and applied it as they walked. When Freeman realised she couldn't hear the clip-clop of Rachel's heels behind her any more, she turned to tell her to move.

She only saw the can of hairspray once it was too late, once it was pointed at her eyes. She heard the sound of the aerosol and then her eyes were on fire. Freeman bent over, unable to see a thing. But now she could hear the clip-clop again, receding as Rachel disappeared into the distance.

37

They didn't get much more from Peter Hinde and eventually Gardner gave in and Hinde was taken down to a cell until they decided how to proceed. The autopsy report had concluded that Donoghue had been attacked with two weapons – the spade and, most likely, a large rock or stone. In O'Hara's opinion the stone had been the weapon that had killed Donoghue. No one could say whether the two weapons had been wielded by two different people and as far as Hadley was concerned, Peter Hinde was looking like their man. He wanted to wait until the results came back on the blood from the car – make sure it was Donoghue's before they charged Peter. But it looked like Peter Hinde was going to take the fall for it. Gardner wasn't concerned by this in theory. In all likelihood Peter *was* involved, but he was sure Lauren was guilty too.

But then, as they took Peter away, some new facts came to light. Guy James's taxi driver had been located, and had confirmed dropping him off at Lauren's address just after 2 a.m. That, at least, placed him somewhere on the timeline, which would be good news for Freeman; the CCTV footage from the club wouldn't be necessary. It wasn't such good news for Guy James, though, who was now moving his way back up the list of suspects.

Guy had already admitted to going to his sister's house that night, even if he couldn't remember what time it had been. Unfortunately for him he had neglected to mention he'd also paid a visit to Ritchie's flat forty minutes later.

Guy was dragged in and shown footage of himself at the top of Ritchie's street, heading towards the deceased's home. The camera wasn't positioned well enough to see Guy actually go to the flat but it seemed like an awfully big coincidence that he just happened to be on that street, that night. There'd been another man caught on camera too, spotted both fifteen minutes before and ten minutes after Guy. It was probably unconnected and the man had a hat pulled down low and a scarf over his face, so identifying him was impossible. They'd appealed for him to come forward, though, just in case he'd seen Guy enter Ritchie's flat.

'Did you go into the flat?' Gardner asked.

'There's no evidence Mr James went to the deceased's flat,' Harry said.

'That's why I'm asking,' Gardner said and wished the duty solicitor would come back.

'How would I of got in?'

'The same way you admitted getting into your mate's house, I assume.'

'Nah, this is bullshit.'

'Someone broke into Ritchie's flat. They were looking for something, made a bit of a mess.'

'What would I be looking for?'

'You tell me,' Gardner said.

'I can't, 'cause I never went in there.'

'So what were you doing, Guy? Why did you go to his flat at almost three in the morning?'

'Again, there's no evidence he went to the flat,' Harry said.

'I was still pissed. I just wanted to have a word with him. Tell him to leave Loz alone,' Guy said and Gardner tried not to smile at Harry. He had his work cut out with this member of the James family.

'So you walked all that way to Ritchie's flat, just to have a word?'

'Yeah. I went over, knocked on the door. He never answered. I left. End of.'

Gardner was doubtful that Guy went there just to talk. But the real question was did he kill Ritchie and then go to his flat to search for the photos of his sister? Or was he under the impression that Ritchie was still a danger to her? He wasn't a bright spark but you'd think he would've been more careful if he'd just killed someone, been a bit more covert in his visit to Ritchie's flat.

In the end, Harry made sure that Guy was released, just like his sister. And Gardner had had enough. He was going home for the night. He just hoped Darren hadn't suddenly developed a taste for conversation.

When he arrived home he was surprised to hear voices from the living room. Unless Darren was talking to himself, which was a possibility, he had a guest.

Gardner stuck his head around the door and the conversation stopped. Freeman stood up and Darren shook his head, walking out of the room without a word to Gardner.

'Am I interrupting something?' he asked.

Freeman just shook her head and sat down again, head in hands. 'Don't worry about it.'

Gardner took his coat off, draping it over the back of the armchair. He wasn't really in the mood for talking but, he supposed, at least it would be about someone else's problems for a change.

'You find the girlfriend?' he asked and Freeman looked up at him.

'Yes. But then I lost her again. She's a fucking delight, that one.'

Gardner almost smiled. 'Not going to own up, then?'

'No,' she sighed. 'I don't know what to do. The only evidence we had, Darren destroyed. And he won't hear a bad word about her. She sprayed hairspray in my eyes and he still thinks she's a fucking angel. Plus she's cheating on him with Healy *and* this other arsehole Mickey and God knows who else.'

'She's involved with Healy? Have you told Darren?'

'Not yet,' she said. 'He's completely besotted.'

'So what're you going to do?'

'I don't know. I guess I'll try and find somewhere safe for him to stay for a while, wait for it to blow over.'

'What about you?' He thought she looked exhausted. Fragile, even. 'Why don't you stay here tonight?'

'I don't think he wants me here,' she said, looking back at the bedroom door.

'It's not his call.'

Freeman exhaled loudly and flopped back onto the settee. 'My parents are coming home tomorrow and I can't face them. I don't even know if he's going to stick around, if he'll see them.' She dropped her head into her hands again.

Gardner didn't know what to say. They sat in silence for a while and he watched the light from cars on the road outside climb the walls, making shadows. After a few minutes he rose. 'I'm going to take a shower if you want to order something to eat. It's unlikely there's anything left in the cupboards after your brother got to it.'

Freeman sat up, smiling. 'Thanks,' she said.

As Gardner passed the spare room he could hear Darren's voice again, this time in a one-sided conversation. Gardner stopped and listened, wondering who Darren could be talking to. He felt slightly embarrassed when he noticed Freeman beside him but she seemed as intent on listening as he did.

'C'mon, Rach,' Darren said. 'I don't care about the money. I just want to see you. Come down here – I'm sure this Gardner dude won't mind you staying too.'

Gardner felt like pushing the door open and telling Darren that actually yes this dude did mind. He wasn't running a doss house. But he wasn't quick enough and before he could react Freeman was in the room, snatching the phone from her brother.

'What the fuck, Nicky?' Darren said.

'You told her where you are?' Freeman said. 'Are you stupid?'

'What're you talking about?'

'You really think you can trust her? She's fucking—' Freeman stopped herself. 'She sprayed hairspray into my eyes. You think that's the behaviour of a normal, balanced person?'

'Maybe you deserved it. You *can* be really annoying, Nic.'

'I'm trying to help you,' she said. 'I didn't sign up for all this bullshit.'

'So don't help then,' he said and pushed past her.

'Where're you going?'

'I don't know. Anywhere.'

Freeman grabbed hold of Darren. He tried to pull away but she wouldn't let go so he pushed back until Freeman put him in a headlock. Gardner rolled his eyes, feeling like he'd suddenly become a primary school teacher without noticing.

He pulled them apart and told Freeman to back off and Darren to sit down. Surprisingly they both did what he asked.

'She's right,' he said to Darren. 'I don't know this girl but she's clearly not trying to help you. So for now, telling her where you are is a very stupid idea.'

'But—'

Gardner put his hand up and Darren stopped talking. 'How much did you tell her?'

'Not much. Just that I was in Middlesbrough.'

'All right. You tell her my name?'

'No.'

Gardner raised his eyebrows.

'Just, like, your second name. That's it.'

'Fine,' Gardner sighed. 'Give me your phone.'

'What? Why?'

Gardner held his hand out and Darren passed over his crappy, brick-like phone. He prised the back off and took the SIM card and battery out. 'Don't speak to her again until I say so.'

'Whatever,' Darren muttered and Gardner nodded for Freeman to follow him. Once they were back in the living room he spoke.

'You really think this girl can't be trusted?'

'Did I mention the hairspray?' she said, pointing to her still-red eyes. 'I don't know if she's *trying* to get Darren hurt or if she's just trying to look after herself. But either way, I don't trust her as far as I can kick her.'

38

Gardner had ordered in a takeaway and opened a bottle of wine and Freeman felt some of the stress melting away. Spending New Year's Eve with him would've been nice but it seemed unlikely that would happen now. But maybe this was better. They could talk, just be in each other's company without any pressure. Without it being a *thing*. And then the food arrived and, rather predictably, Darren emerged from his sulk to hoover up as much of it as possible.

Any attempts at conversation were stilted at best, but once Darren became hypnotised by his endless changing of channels, Gardner opened up a little, telling her about the case he was working on, how much it was frustrating him. She sat beside him and listened intently.

'So what is it about this guy that bothers you so much?' she asked when she could get a word in edgeways. He'd been ranting about this politician for ten minutes straight.

'He's dirty,' Gardner said.

'Aren't they all?'

'True. But this guy just really grates on me. His whole campaign is based on family values and making Middlesbrough a safer place. Install more CCTV cameras, crack down on drug dealers. But he's out there making deals with all sorts of lowlifes. There've been rumours about him for donkey's years but nothing ever sticks. He buys people off. He thinks if he gives them what they want, they won't touch him.' He gulped down the rest of the wine from the bottom of his glass. 'And I suppose it's working. The whole investigation is a farce.'

'You think this girl did it?'

'Lauren? Maybe. She keeps lying through her teeth but just like her dad, nothing sticks. I almost feel sorry for her, having him as a father. But whatever's going on, her dad's making damn sure we can't dig too deep.'

'What about him? You think he could be involved?'

'All the evidence so far suggests not.'

'But?'

'But I don't trust him as far as I can throw him. And he's a tubby little git.'

Freeman grinned at him. 'So are you just gunning for him because you don't like him, then?'

Gardner leaned his head back on the settee and stared at the ceiling. 'Maybe. I'd do anything to wipe that smug look off his face.'

Freeman watched as Gardner closed his eyes. She lifted the wine bottle, holding it up to the light, but it was empty. She glanced over at her brother. His eyes were closed too so she picked up his glass and finished it off.

Gardner nudged her then, saying, 'I can always open another bottle.'

Freeman realised how close she was sitting beside him; she could feel his body heat, his eyes on her face.

'I'll have some more.' They both looked up as Darren stirred in the armchair across from them, completely oblivious.

Freeman sighed and stood up, the moment had passed. 'You boys do what you like. I'm going to bed.'

39

Thursday, 30 December

Gardner woke up and felt like he'd aged fifteen years. Sleeping on the settee was not a good option for the over-forties. It was times like this he wished he wasn't so bloody chivalrous. He pulled himself upright and stretched his back. With Darren holed up in the spare room, he'd insisted that Freeman take his room. He'd sort of hoped that they would've shared the bed but when it became clear that wasn't happening, he'd done the honourable thing. Seemed a good idea at the time but now he was wondering why he hadn't made one of the short-arses take the couch.

He was about to move when he turned his attention to the news. It was her voice that caught his attention. Gardner turned up the TV and saw Mrs Donoghue's face, red from the cold or the grief, speaking to someone off camera. 'And just because of who her father is, I don't see why she should be treated differently, special. The police haven't said one word about my son's death. Not really. They're trying to brush it under the carpet. They think because of who he was it doesn't matter. Or because of who she is. They're not doing their jobs properly. And I'm not having it. I want justice for my son and I don't care about Walter James or his campaign or who his friends are. I just want justice.' Mrs Donoghue dissolved into tears and someone led her away from the camera.

Gardner almost smiled to see that someone was standing up to Walter James. It was just a shame that it was a grieving mother and not his colleagues. He switched off the TV and, making the decision to add a couple of ibuprofen to his breakfast, he headed for the bathroom. At least he'd had some sleep this time. He'd imagined Freeman would be listening out for her brother so he'd happily given in to fatigue.

The briefing that morning started off with the usual updates and overviews, delivered with voices trying to disguise yawns. Not much new had happened, or at least nothing that was of much use. They were still waiting for a positive match on the blood found in Peter's car.

'I've also decided to stop the surveillance on Donoghue's flat,' Atherton said, catching Gardner's attention. 'We haven't got the resources to have someone sitting there all day, and besides, I doubt anyone's stupid enough to go back to the flat when they're under suspicion. Plus, I think the most likely candidate is Hinde and he's not going anywhere. Not for a few hours at least.'

'But they could send someone else,' Gardner said. 'As long as they're not aware that we've found the tapes and photographs, they'll still be looking for them.'

'Or maybe this has nothing to do with blackmailing Lauren James and we're wasting resources,' Atherton said.

'But—'

'If you'd like to spend your free time sitting outside the flat, by all means do so, Inspector. But in the meantime I suggest we speak to Lauren, Peter and Guy again, mention the tapes, and see how they react. If this is about blackmail, the only way to find out is to ask.'

Gardner knew there was no point arguing any more. But he was convinced that someone was going to go back to that flat. Maybe he *would* spend his free time there. Had to be better than sitting at home with Darren Freeman watching children's TV.

'We've got the billing information from all the phones – Lauren, Peter, Guy, Jen and Walter. They were all willing to cooperate,' Berman said.

'Walter James kicked up a fuss,' Gardner said and when everyone turned to him he realised he was being petty. None of them had been keen to let their phone records be analysed in detail. Walter James had made a stink about his civil liberties but in the end had agreed, wanting to do whatever was best for the investigation.

'Not much we didn't already know,' Berman said. 'The calls between Donoghue and Jen Worrall we know about. No texts unfortunately because it'd be interesting to see if they were actually flirting or if there was something else going on.'

'Peter Hinde reckoned there's no way Worrall was seeing Ritchie Donoghue. Said she played for the other team,' Harrington said.

'Is that true?' Atherton asked.

'I spoke to Worrall again and she denied it. Said someone at the office started the rumour but says it's not true.'

'So it's possible she *was* involved with Donoghue?'

'We'll keep an eye on her,' Harrington said.

'There *was* one flag on Walter James's records from the night of the murder,' Berman continued and as Gardner's ears pricked up at this he noticed Atherton looking a little uneasy. 'He made a call at one o-five a.m. to an unregistered number. Call lasted thirty-two seconds. Might be worth a look.'

Atherton nodded. 'What about the interviews from the pub?'

'Spoke to the landlord and two bar staff, also a couple of regulars who were there that night,' Harrington said. 'All of them confirm Walter James and Peter Hinde were present when they said they were. No one recalls anything out of the ordinary, no angry phone calls, nothing like that.'

'All right,' Atherton said. 'Next briefing at five p.m.'

Everyone shuffled out and Gardner pulled his phone from his pocket. He sincerely wanted to be the one to ask Walter James about his late-night phone call. But first he wanted to do something else. He had wondered how Freeman was going to cope with being cooped up in the flat with her brother if they weren't on speaking terms. It might not have been a great idea but it was worth offering.

'Morning,' Freeman said. 'I found a toothbrush in the cupboard, hope that's all right.'

'No problem,' he said. 'Listen, I don't know what you had planned for today but I was wondering if you could do me a favour.'

'Sure,' she said. 'What is it?'

'Well, it might be a long shot, but I'm wondering whether one of these idiots involved in the Donoghue case might go back to his flat. Someone was looking for something in there.'

'You think they'd be stupid enough to go back?'

'They know the flat was searched but not that we found the stuff on Lauren. Not yet, anyway. Atherton wants us to start asking them about it, but until then . . .'

'You want me to watch the place?' Freeman said.

'If you don't mind. I thought you might want to get out of the house for a while.'

'Sure,' she said. 'What's the address? I'll watch the place as long as you want.'

Gardner was about to speak when he heard Darren's voice in the background. 'You don't have to leave on my account.'

Freeman sighed. 'I didn't think you'd want me hanging around all day. Bothering you.'

'Whatever,' Darren said and Gardner heard a door slam.

'Sorry,' she said and Gardner gave her the address. 'Give me a few minutes and I'll head over there.'

40

Freeman came out of Gardner's bedroom, dressed in yesterday's clothes and ready to go, to find Darren had emerged again and was now sprawled across the settee, elbow-deep in a bag of Doritos. He didn't look away from the TV and she considered ignoring him, just slipping out without a word. Instead she approached the settee, picking up the bit of paper with the address on.

She paused, wondering if she should invite Darren along. Maybe they could talk. But that would defeat the object. Gardner was giving her a way out, an escape. Neither she nor Darren was ready to talk yet and sitting cooped up in her car would be worse than staying in the flat. She'd give him some space and maybe they could work it all out later.

'So, what're you going to do all day? Watch TV?' she asked, her way of apologising.

Darren chucked the almost empty bag of crisps onto the table and threw back the duvet he'd cocooned himself in. 'What do you expect me to do, *Mam*? It's not like I have a lot of options.'

'I was just asking,' Freeman said.

'Whatever. I'm going out for a bit,' he said and pulled his shoes on, heading for the door without tying the laces.

'For God's sake,' Freeman muttered, following him. 'Where're you going?'

'Out.'

'Out where?' she said, and realised that she did sound just like their mam.

'Anywhere. I need to get out of here for a while.'

Freeman followed him down the stairs. 'Just go back inside. I won't ask you any more questions.'

Darren stopped, spinning around to face her. 'It's not about you. I just want to get some air. I'm not going to call Rachel if that's what you think. Your boyfriend took my phone, remember.'

'That's not what I'm worried about.'

'Well, you don't need to worry about me, Nicky. I'm fine. Just leave me alone for a while.'

Darren walked away and she let him go, watching the door close behind him. It was pointless going after him. And maybe he was right. He needed some space too. She waited a few minutes so it didn't look like she was following him and then got in her car and headed for a dead man's flat.

Freeman had done it enough times to know how boring a stakeout could be but after two hours she was losing the will to live and starting to curse Gardner. She wasn't sure if he really thought one of his suspects might show up or whether he was just trying to do her a favour by getting her out of the flat. But if it was the latter, he could've pointed her to the nearest cinema or something.

No one had been anywhere near the flat since she'd been there. The closest thing to action had been a cat running across the road in front of her car and a parcel being delivered to a house across the street. Her legs were seizing up and she was starving. Plus she couldn't stop thinking about Darren.

What if he hadn't gone back to Gardner's? What if he'd done something stupid? Maybe she needed to go and check on him instead of sitting here watching nothing happen.

Freeman started counting the houses with tacky Christmas lights outside, mostly flashing out of time with each other. A few minutes later, another car pulled up behind hers and she straightened up, wondering if something was finally going to happen. She watched as the woman turned off the engine but didn't get out. Freeman squinted into the mirror, trying to see the woman's face and realised she vaguely recognised her. Gardner must've sent over some relief.

Freeman got out of the car, checking the street to make sure no one was watching. As she approached the other car the woman rolled her window down, looking slightly confused.

'PC Lawton, right?' Lawton nodded. 'Nicola Freeman. We met before. Very briefly.'

'Right,' Lawton said.

'Are you taking over?' She glanced towards the flat. Lawton nodded again but looked concerned. Had Gardner not told her that Freeman'd be there? 'Well, nothing's happened so far, so . . . Good luck.' She turned and went back to her own car. It had been clear at their previous brief encounter that Lawton had a crush on Gardner and maybe she saw Freeman as a threat. Or maybe she just didn't like anyone. Either way, Freeman was happy Lawton was there to take over so she could go back to Gardner's place to try and talk to her brother once again.

41

As Gardner took his place in front of the monitors again he wondered why he bothered coming in any more. He could stay at home and watch drivel on the TV. And that was bound to be what he was about to witness. Atherton had decided to ask Lauren about the photographs they'd found in Ritchie's flat but Gardner couldn't imagine him pushing her. It was more likely he'd just apologise to her.

'I wanted to ask you about some photographs and videos,' Atherton said and Gardner watched as Lauren's face flushed. That answered his question, then. She already knew about them.

'What kind of photos?' Lauren said, her voice no more than a whisper. When Atherton didn't answer immediately she reached up and scratched at her face.

'Personal ones,' he said. 'They were found in Ritchie's flat.'

Lauren's chin wobbled and her eyes filled with tears. Gardner wondered whether she knew she was screwed, that they'd found their motive and now there was no use lying any more, or if she was just embarrassed about the fact that the man sitting opposite her had seen her in some extremely compromising positions. He did feel sorry for her. And if Ritchie was planning on blackmailing her then she had every right to be pissed off. Threatening to show the world her most private moments was a pretty shitty thing to do to anyone. He could understand Lauren's anger. But maybe that anger had gone too far.

'I know this is hard, Lauren,' Atherton said. 'And I don't want to embarrass you. But you realise that I have to ask you about them.'

Lauren pressed her lips together until they turned white, but the tears she couldn't stop from coming.

'Did you know about the pictures, Lauren?' She shook her head. Gardner hadn't seen them all but from what he'd been told, the majority appeared to have been filmed or taken without her knowledge. There was no looking at the camera, no playing up to it. As he watched Lauren shake with tears Gardner felt his sympathy for her grow. No matter how difficult her relationship with Ritchie had been, she'd at least trusted him in her most intimate moments, a trust clearly misplaced. Lauren held her sleeve to her eyes, wiping the stream of tears.

'I didn't know,' she said. 'I didn't know he took them. I wouldn't do something like that.'

'Okay,' Atherton said, softly. 'But did you find out about them later?'

She nodded and then looked at her solicitor. 'Yes,' she said. 'He told me.'

'When did he tell you?' She shrugged. 'Was it that night, Lauren? The night Ritchie died?'

Lauren sniffed and dug her nails into her palms. 'He showed me a picture. On his phone. He said he had more but I didn't know if that was true.'

Okay, Gardner thought, now we're getting somewhere.

'I got mad at him and I tried to get the phone, but he held it over his head and laughed at me. He was being so horrible to me, just laughing at me. So I hit him,' she said, her voice louder now.

'Lauren,' Harry said, his hand on her arm. She turned to him but kept talking.

'I slapped him and he kept laughing so I kept hitting him. You saw him, how big he is. He wasn't bothered by it. So I scratched him, on his face,' she said, her hand on her own cheek. 'Then he got angry with me and pushed me over. Told me to shut the fuck up. I got up and ran at him. I was so angry with him. I was just hitting him and he kept laughing at me like it was nothing but he put his arms up to stop me.'

'That's how he got the scratches on his arms?' Atherton asked.

Lauren nodded. 'I guess. In the end I just gave up. He wasn't bothered. I told him to leave. Tried shoving him towards the door but he was such a fat fuck.' She stopped and caught her breath. 'I picked up the phone and said I'd call the police or my dad or someone. He just shrugged but I pretended to dial nine-nine-nine and he left. I could hear him shouting outside and I started thinking he might come back. I wanted someone to come and stay with me. I was scared.'

'So you called your dad and Peter and your brother,' Atherton said.

'Yes.'

'Okay. So what happened next?'

'I couldn't get hold of anyone. Only Guy, but he was in Newcastle. So I decided to go out. I didn't want to be in the house by myself.'

'So you went to a club, right? So why did you send Ritchie the text telling him to meet you at your house? You said you were scared; you'd got rid of him once. Why ask him to come back, Lauren?'

'I don't know. I don't remember that. I didn't think I'd even taken my phone with me. I was going to call a friend on my way to the club but I couldn't find my phone in my bag.'

'This is the first time you've mentioned leaving your phone. Why didn't you tell us this before?'

'I don't know,' she said. 'I didn't think it was important. I don't even know . . . Maybe I *did* have it, but . . .' She looked to her solicitor for help but he was making notes. 'I couldn't find it when I wanted to call my friend, I remember that. But maybe, at the club, later . . . I don't know.'

Gardner sighed. The text had been sent while Lauren was out. If she hadn't had her phone then someone else must've sent it, someone else must have lured Ritchie to the house. Maybe someone whose prints were on the phone – Peter or her father. But as Lauren wasn't sure, it didn't really help her. He made a note to check if they could find out where the phone had been when the text was sent.

'Who else has a key to your house, Lauren?' Atherton asked.

'My dad. Peter. I keep a spare key outside, too. But I don't know who else knows it's there. Guy, I guess.'

'Okay, Lauren, thank you,' Atherton said and nodded to Harry.

Gardner sighed. On the one hand they had her admitting to knowing about the photos, about being angry enough to fight with Ritchie about them. But then they had the phone. If that was true, that she hadn't had it with her, that she hadn't sent the text luring Ritchie back, were they really any further forward?

42

The interview with Lauren had only clouded things further. They'd speak to Peter Hinde again, ask him about the photos, and to Guy and, maybe, Walter. If any of them could've sent the text to Ritchie they needed to be looked at more closely. They only had a few more hours to hold Peter without charging him but Hadley was holding off until the blood results were back. Usually it was the bosses pressing him to make something happen but with the shadow of Walter James looming over proceedings, they were trying their hardest to let nothing stick. They should have been working for Tefal.

Unfortunately Atherton had been canny enough to see that Gardner would've enjoyed pulling Walter James up on his late-night call so instead he had given Berman the task. Walter had apparently been expecting the question and claimed he'd met a woman in the pub that night. Had taken her number and drunkenly decided to call her. He hadn't mentioned it earlier because he was ashamed. He was a married man. A family man. It was a silly mistake, and one he hoped would be kept under wraps. Oh, and he couldn't remember the woman's name either. It could've been Rosie. Gardner had pointed out that this didn't tally with witness statements from the pub. No one had mentioned James talking to a woman. But, according to Hadley, just because someone didn't see it, didn't make it untrue.

On his way to work that morning Gardner had passed a poster promoting James's election campaign. Another slogan advertising him as the new Messiah, promising everything from restoring Middlesbrough to its glory days to ridding the town of poverty and crime and, the old classic, bringing family values back to life. What a load of horseshit. Walter James wouldn't recognise family values if they bit him on the arse. And as for ridding the town of crime? It didn't matter how many CCTV cameras he installed or how many more coppers he put in communities: when the problem was him and his own associates, crime was going nowhere.

At this point he had no reason to suspect James was involved with the murder at all, just with interfering with the investigation. There was the mystery woman, of course, and the fact that James's prints were on Lauren's phone. That could be something if she had in fact left the phone at home that night. He'd already asked someone to check where the text to Ritchie was sent from. Maybe he should've found out where James made his call from too. Whether he did call from his office like he claimed.

Gardner answered his phone as he leafed through some more reports that gave him nothing but a headache.

'Sir, it's Lawton.'

'How's it going?' he asked.

'Fine,' she said. 'I'm outside Ritchie Donoghue's flat. I thought maybe you were right about someone showing up so I decided to swing by, stay for a bit. But I just wanted to know what DS Freeman had to do with the case. Why's she even here?'

Gardner put down the report and focused on Lawton. He was glad someone still had faith in him, was on his side, but why had she chosen *now* to disobey Atherton's orders? 'She was just doing me a favour.'

'But why? She doesn't work here.'

There was an edge to Lawton's voice, one that rarely presented itself. Freeman had suggested that Lawton might have feelings for him, something that had crossed his mind before but he didn't like to think about. Was that what the tone was about? Jealousy? Gardner cleared his throat. 'She had some spare time on her hands and offered to help after Atherton called off the surveillance. We're just—'

'She was at that club in Newcastle,' Lawton said and Gardner felt his face flush. He'd got the wrong end of the stick so completely that he was barely holding onto the stick any more. At least she'd stopped him before he'd made a total tit of himself. 'She might've deleted evidence that could've been important to this case and now she's helping out? I just want to know what she has to do with it. Is there some connection to the club?'

Gardner felt his stomach tighten. He hadn't really thought about the possible consequences of involving Freeman in the case any further, didn't think anyone would find out. The CCTV footage from the club shouldn't have been an issue now they could trace Guy's movements without it. But maybe bringing Freeman down here was a mistake. What if someone, someone other than Lawton, put two and two together?

'DS Freeman was at the club on an unrelated matter. I called her to find out what'd happened with the tapes. She swears there was a problem with the system and that was it.'

'So why's she here?'

'Because we're friends, Lawton. I invited her down for New Year. She was at a loose end before that so she came down and I asked her to do me a favour and watch the flat. All right? *That's* her involvement.' He listened to the buzz on the line and realised that he'd developed a tone of his own, one Lawton hadn't deserved. 'I'm sorry,' he said. 'Don't worry about Freeman. Just keep your eyes peeled over there.'

'Sure,' she said.

'I've got to go. Let me know if anything happens.'

'Fine,' she said and hung up.

Gardner spent the next hour searching through mounds of paperwork, going over every statement again and again, looking for something to break the case, until he thought his eyes might bleed. He was about to start over when Harrington came rushing in.

'We've got someone,' he said. 'Lawton's bringing him in now.'

'What? Who?'

Harrington shrugged. 'Some guy turned up at Donoghue's flat. Was trying very hard to get inside. Lawton approached him, he got a bit mouthy, she arrested him.'

Gardner stood up. 'Is she all right?'

Harrington shrugged again. 'I don't know but Atherton and Hadley look like they're going to shit themselves with excitement.'

'Who is he?'

'No idea. All we have is a name so far. Healy. Mark Healy.'

43

Freeman was pacing the floor when she heard the door. She expected it to be Gardner but stopped short when she saw Darren. She didn't know whether to hug him or punch him. She'd returned to Gardner's hoping to find him stretched out on the settee again and maybe, if they could both behave like adults, they could have a real conversation and work things out.

Sitting in the car for hours had given her a lot of time to think and she knew she should be the one to apologise. No matter how hard things had been for her, they had been worse for Darren. And at the end of the day, she was partly responsible for how things had turned out. She had to face up to that. So she'd decided to go back and make things right. Hopefully it'd all be over soon and they could go home. Maybe Darren would even stay with her for a while and they could repair their relationship. Maybe things would even be okay with their mam and dad.

But then she'd got back to the flat and Darren wasn't there. Where could he have gone for so long in a town he didn't know? She didn't imagine he had much money. But how much did you need to get into trouble?

She'd started with the pubs. But if there's one thing Middlesbrough wasn't lacking in, it was pubs. She couldn't have covered a quarter of them before she'd given in. She wished they hadn't taken his phone from him. And what use was taking it anyway? He could always find another phone to call Rachel. Maybe he'd contacted her again and invited her to stay. Or worse, hopped on the next train to Newcastle to see her.

After running out of options she'd come back to the flat to wait. It didn't seem right to ask Gardner for more help, especially as Darren wasn't really missing. He just wasn't there. So she'd waited and waited. Wearing down the soles of her DMs as she paced back and forth.

And now here he was. Standing there like nothing had happened.

'Where've you been?' she said, all the apologies disappearing before they even arrived.

'Are we really going to do this again?' Darren said and walked past her to the kitchen. 'I told you I was going out.'

'That was hours ago.'

'So?'

Freeman was about to launch into another tirade when her phone interrupted her. She picked it up, seeing Gardner's name on the screen. 'This isn't over,' she said and answered the phone. 'Yeah.'

'What the fuck is going on?' he said.

'Woah. What're you talking about?'

'Healy.'

'What about him?' she asked, feeling her pulse quicken.

'He's here. At the station. Under arrest.'

'What?'

'What is going on?' Gardner said again, his voice lowering. 'I don't know what's going on. What's he been arrested for?'

'At the moment it's attempted B&E. But it wouldn't surprise me if it's the murder of Ritchie Donoghue.'

'What? How is that possible?' Freeman said.

'I don't know. You tell me. Healy claims someone told him to meet them there. That he'd get his money if he went to that address.'

Freeman watched her brother searching the fridge for more food, oblivious to her and the conversation she was having.

'It's got nothing to do with me, I swear.'

'So how has this guy suddenly turned up in my murder investigation? How has he turned up at the flat *you* were watching? Because I seriously doubt this is all one big coincidence.'

'This has nothing to do with me,' Freeman repeated. She could hear voices in the background and Gardner promising he'd be there in one minute.

'I've got to go. But there'd better be a good explanation for this.'

'But—' Freeman put down the phone, realising Gardner had hung up. Darren came out of the kitchen, sandwich in hand.

'What's going on?'

44

Gardner watched as Harrington started the interview, studiously ignoring Mark Healy's protests that this was all bullshit. Gardner had chosen not to go into the room, instead watching the interview from outside, because he knew he was going to agree with Healy. This *was* bullshit.

He had no idea how the man had ended up at Donoghue's flat, but he had a creeping feeling that Freeman must've been responsible. How else could it have happened? Maybe he'd been wrong to help her, to trust her. She'd already messed with evidence. What else was she capable of?

And Lawton was already suspicious about Freeman being there. What if Healy started talking about Darren? The shit would well and truly hit the fan. The best he could hope for was that Harrington saw this for what it was – a mistake. Someone trying to break into a house for money or whatever, and unfortunately choosing the wrong house. They had nothing on Healy other than him showing up at Donoghue's place. With any luck he'd be out in half an hour. And what he did after that, Gardner didn't care any more. Freeman and Darren were on their own.

'What's the story?'

Gardner turned and saw Cartwright enter the room, eyes fixed on Healy. Gardner shrugged. 'No idea,' he said and bristled as Cartwright moved beside him, arms crossed in front of him, waiting for the show to begin.

Harrington had made all the necessary introductions and was waiting for Healy to explain what he was doing at Donoghue's flat. Healy's hands curled into fists and he leaned forwards.

'I already told that stupid bint. I was meant to meet someone there.'

'Who were you meeting?'

'Darren Freeman.'

Gardner felt his stomach churn. It didn't look like Harrington had noticed the name yet but Lawton was bound to.

'So why were you meeting him at Ritchie Donoghue's flat? How do you know Donoghue?' Harrington asked.

'I don't know anyone called Donoghue. Freeman told me to meet him there. Said he had my money.'

'What money?'

Healy leaned back again, realising that maybe talking about money wasn't a great idea. 'Just money I'd lent him. He told me to go to the flat. He didn't say whose place it was. I didn't ask.'

'So how does this Darren Freeman know Ritchie?'

'I don't know. You could try asking him.'

'I will,' Harrington said. 'How can I get hold of him?'

Healy shrugged. 'I've got no idea where the little shit is. Stood me up. His number's in my phone.'

Gardner tensed again, hoping to God that Darren's phone was still in bits and that they wouldn't be able to trace him.

'You live in Newcastle. Why were you meeting in Middlesbrough? Seems a long way to come for a bit of cash.'

Healy shrugged again.

'PC Lawton said you seemed anxious to get into the flat. Looked like you were trying to break in.'

'Bullshit.'

'She said you tried the door instead of ringing the bell and then you approached the back of the property where you appeared to be trying to force entry. That doesn't sound like you were there to meet a mate.'

'Who said he was my mate? All I wanted was my money.'

'From the flat?'

'From that little shit.'

'So you *weren't* trying to gain access to the flat?'

'Only to get my money. I don't know whose place it is. I thought Freeman was in there. I thought he was going to try something stupid.'

'Like what?'

'I don't fucking know.'

'Where were you on Monday night? Between eleven p.m. and three a.m.?'

'What?' Healy said. 'What the fuck's that got to do with anything?'

'Just answer the question.'

'I don't know. Home, probably.'

'That's not much of an alibi.'

'An alibi for what? I thought this was about breaking into some bloke's flat,' he said, turning to the duty solicitor, a man who looked barely old enough to drive.

'It is,' Harrington said. 'But that bloke was murdered three days ago, so it makes things a little more serious.'

Healy paled; his eyes flickered from side to side. 'Little fucker. He's set me up,' he said.

'Who?'

'Darren Freeman.'

Harrington sighed. 'So you think this Darren Freeman

killed Ritchie Donoghue and then led you to the flat to try and set you up? Why would he do that?'

'I don't know. Because he's a little shit who knows he's in trouble.'

'With who? You?'

'This is bullshit,' Healy said again.

Gardner noticed Cartwright checking his phone, tapping it against his leg. Glad to see he was so interested in the interview.

'Where were you on Monday night?' Harrington asked.

'Home,' he said. 'In Newcastle.'

'Can you prove that?'

'I was with Rachel, my girlfriend, left hers about midnight.'

'Shame. That still gives you time to get to Middlesbrough. How did you get to Middlesbrough today?'

'A mate gave me a lift.'

'Who?'

'Weasel. Sam Weasly.'

'And where's Weasel now?'

'Fucked off when that copper showed up.'

'Does Weasel have issues with police officers? Where's your car? You do have one, right? A dark blue BMW.'

'It's at home.'

Harrington nodded and stood up. 'I'll be back in a few minutes.'

As Harrington left the interview room, Cartwright left Gardner alone, disappearing down the corridor. Harrington took up his place beside Gardner, followed by Lawton.

'So?' Harrington said. 'What do you think?'

'Nothing to think. Yet. We have no idea who this guy is, how he's connected to Donoghue, if he even is at all.'

'You think he's telling the truth about this other guy, Darren Freeman?' Gardner's chest tightened. He couldn't look at Lawton. "Cause I was thinking maybe that ties in with the tapes from that club somehow,' Harrington continued. 'That was DS Freeman who looked at the tapes, right?' Gardner chewed his lip. Maybe Harrington wasn't as dense as he looked.

'Well, Freeman's a common enough name, plus this guy could be lying, so let's not jump to any conclusions just yet. Start looking at Healy, see what you can find on him. If there's any connection to Donoghue,' Gardner said and Lawton held out some sheets of paper.

'I made a start,' she said. 'Has a record, lots of arrests, but only one conviction, six years ago – drug related.'

'That could be a link,' Harrington said.

'Maybe,' Gardner said and took the reports from Lawton without looking her in the eye. 'Keep digging, see if there's anything solid to link them. Also, check out this alleged girlfriend. See if she can place him at home that night. Other than that we don't have a lot to go on.'

'What about the car? Dark blue BMW.'

'One of many,' Gardner said. 'Half the dealers in the country drive BMWs. Besides, we've got Peter Hinde's car. There's the blood and fingerprints. I think we're agreed that was the car spotted at the scene.'

'Not necessarily,' Harrington said. 'Witnesses never got a licence plate.'

Gardner gave him a look. 'So the blood and prints are just a coincidence?'

'All right, what about this Darren Freeman? You want me to find him?' Harrington asked.

'I'll look into it,' Gardner said. 'You make a start on Healy.'

Harrington nodded and walked away. Gardner started to follow when Lawton spoke. 'Can I have a word, sir?'

Gardner finally looked her in the eye and he could see the questions, the doubts. He didn't want to lie to her, to anyone really, but he couldn't tell her the truth either. They all just needed to do their jobs and sort this out. Healy would be gone in a few hours and they could concentrate on finding the real killer.

'What's going on?' she asked.

'Just keep looking at Healy,' he said and walked away.

45

Freeman had bundled Darren into the car and was heading up the A19 towards home. She'd wanted to stay and explain to Gardner what'd happened but he'd called to tell her the shit was about to hit the fan and when it did he didn't want them holed up at his flat.

Darren hadn't spoken since they'd got in the car but she kept noticing him glancing in her direction, probably wondering if it was safe to speak. She was angry, sure, but more than anything she wanted to pull over, curl up into a ball and cry. Darren had been back in her life for two days and look what'd happened. This wasn't what she'd hoped for all those years. And she hated herself for thinking it but she wished she hadn't answered the door. Wished she hadn't agreed to go to the club. Wished Gardner hadn't found out.

She didn't know how this was going to end but it wasn't going to be pretty. If there'd been a chance of her keeping her job after the CCTV incident, that was now out of the window. She'd be lucky to escape prosecution, never mind keep her career intact. And Darren wasn't going to get away with it. If they couldn't find anything to charge him with, Healy was going to be released shortly and would be even more pissed off than he was already. Maybe she wouldn't have to worry about telling their mam and dad because there was no way Darren could stay now.

But more than anything she feared that Gardner would be under fire. He'd done nothing wrong but this would all end up on him unless he told his bosses what she'd done. Part of her wished he would, that he'd look out for himself. But the other half? There's nothing like self-preservation.

She looked in the rear-view mirror, noticing the car behind – some douchebag in a sports car, coming up fast. Reluctantly, she moved to the inside lane to let it pass and noticed the car behind the sports car pulling into her lane too, keeping a steady pace. She wondered if they were already on to her.

'I'm sorry,' Darren said and she took her eyes away from the mirror.

'Don't,' she said.

'I didn't think it'd matter.'

'How could it not matter?'

'I don't know. I heard you talking to Gardner. He said the case was bullshit. I figured what's the difference?'

'The difference is Healy has nothing to do with it.'

'So? It's not like he's a good guy. He's got away with all kinds of stuff before. Maybe he deserves it.'

'That's not the point and you know it. I don't care what he's done before or whether he deserves to be locked up. None of that matters because nothing's going to happen to him. In a few hours they'll let him go because they won't have anything on him and the only people who are going to be fucked over are us.'

'I'm sorry, I didn't think—'

'No. You never think. What the fuck did you really think was going to happen? That Gardner would just go "Oh look, here's someone now. Let's lock him up." That Healy would go down for this without saying a word about you, and you'd just tootle off with your imbecile of a girlfriend and live happily ever after?'

'I had to do something. He was going to hurt her.'

'How do you know that?'

'Because when I called her, he was there. I heard him and I panicked and said I had the money and he could come and get it if he left her alone.'

'Jesus. She was fine, Darren. He hadn't done anything to her. And you know how I know that? Because she's fucking him. I saw her phone. She's fucking Healy and that ratface Mickey too. She'll have been there with Healy, laughing at you. Or telling him that you took the money. She's screwing you over, Darren.'

'No, she isn't.'

'What did she say when you called? Did she beg for help? Did she say Healy was going to hurt her?'

Darren went quiet, staring out of the window.

'Well?'

'No. She just talked for a while and then said Healy wanted to speak to me. But for all you know he had a gun to her head.'

'And what did he say to you? Did he say, "I'm going to kill her if you don't bring me my money?"'

'No. He said he was going to find me. That he knew I was hiding in Middlesbrough and he'd find me.'

'And how did he know that? A fucking premonition?'

'*She* didn't tell him. She wouldn't have.'

Freeman shook her head. 'You've fucked us all over for a girl who doesn't give a shit about you. I hope you know that.'

Darren turned away, looking more and more like the stupid, scared kid he'd been that day in court. Nothing had changed since, and that hurt. But not as much as the thought that kept coming back to her – that she wished he'd never come back at all.

46

'In September 2005 Darren Freeman's car is pulled out of a
river, no body recovered, presumed dead.' Gardner handed
the information he'd pulled on Darren to Harrington, who
read through the highlights.

'In September 2005 Darren Freeman's car is pulled out of a
river, no body recovered, presumed dead.' Gardner handed
the information he'd pulled on Darren to Harrington, who
read through the highlights.

'Quite a history, though,' he said. 'Several arrests, prison in
2002, known associate of several dealers. Could have links to
Donoghue.'

'Could also be dead,' Gardner said. He looked over his
shoulder but Lawton was nowhere to be seen.

'But what if this guy is related to Nicola Freeman? Seems
likely, right? Have you checked that?' he said. Gardner ignored
the question, his eyes fixed on the paperwork. 'What if she
deleted those tapes on purpose because there's something on
them linking Darren to Guy James?'

Gardner wondered if he should just come clean – about his
link to Freeman if nothing else. But until he could speak to
her, find out what had happened, he didn't want to say
anything. He was furious with her but wasn't ready to give her
up just yet. It had to be her who'd got Healy there – that much
he knew. She was the only one who knew the address and had
made sure she left the scene before Healy showed up. She'd
wiped the tapes to help her brother supposedly only because
she thought there'd be no repercussions. Maybe she *was* just

trying to help Darren. But how could she not see the consequences of leading Healy to the flat?

'Go in and speak to Healy again. See what he has to say about Darren Freeman.'

Gardner went into the viewing room to watch Healy's reaction. He wondered if Cartwright would be there, lurking again, rather than doing any real work. He hadn't seen him since the last interview ended. No doubt he was making friends somewhere.

Healy looked up as Harrington entered the room, sitting back as if to say, 'Can I go now?' but Harrington just pulled up a chair in front of him and slid the photo of Darren towards him.

'You recognise him?'

'Yeah. Darren Freeman.'

Harrington pulled the picture back across the table. 'You known him long?'

'Not really. Why?'

'Because Darren Freeman has been missing for five years. Presumed dead.'

'Well, he's not dead. I can tell you that much. I spoke to him a few hours ago.'

'Yeah. That phone number you gave us. Pay as you go. Not registered. So . . .'

'So what? Ninety per cent of the people I know probably have unregistered phones.'

'Why doesn't that surprise me?' Harrington said and Healy shuffled, maybe trying to decide what he should and shouldn't be saying. 'But it doesn't help the fact that there's nothing to prove you know Darren Freeman or that he sent you to that flat. The call you claim was from him was made from a public pay phone. Anyone could've made that call.'

'And how's that my problem?'

'Well, it's a problem because for all I know you're lying and you were actually there to find something in the flat of the man you murdered.'

'Bullshit,' Healy shouted, coming to life again. 'Go to my flat. Freeman's been there, you'll find proof there, fingerprints or whatever. Ask his girlfriend. Unless she's been shagging a ghost she'll tell you he's alive and kicking.'

'Are you giving us permission to search your flat?'

Healy stopped and swallowed, no doubt trying to work out what kinds of incriminating things were littered about his place.

'Rachel, his girlfriend, works in a strip club. Slinky's.'

'This the same Rachel as your girlfriend? Wow, you must be good friends.'

Healy ignored the comment. 'Go to the club. Freeman's always in there. Check the CCTV.'

Harrington turned to the camera, looking at Gardner, and said, 'You'll be lucky.'

47

Lauren sat with a blanket wrapped around her, staring into the TV. She'd been watching the same show for the last hour and had no idea what was going on.

She'd thought she was going to die when they asked her about the photos and tapes. They'd found them at Ritchie's flat, so he wasn't lying after all. And knowing all those policemen had seen them made her sick. They were out there now. She knew how it worked. There was always someone willing to sell, always willing to cross a line if the price was right. Even if it meant crossing the mighty Walter James. Everyone had a price.

The knock at the door startled her and she let the blanket drop from her shoulders. She lingered, halfway between standing and sitting, wondering if she should answer it. So far the police, maybe her father, had managed to keep a lot of things out of the media but then Ritchie's mum had gone on the news. She'd never liked her. She could tell as soon as Ritchie took her home that first time that his mum thought she wasn't good enough for her precious son. As if.

There was another knock and she stood, walking slowly to the window to see who it was. She closed her eyes when she saw him. He had a key but rarely used it, respecting her privacy too much to just barge in. She walked to the front door and let him in.

'How're you feeling, princess?' he asked.

'Okay,' she said, leading him to the living room. 'I thought maybe it was the police.'

He smiled again and sat down, patting the leather seat beside him. 'That's why I came to see you.'

Lauren felt sick. Was this it? 'They told you they know about the photos?'

Walter looked up quickly, something flashing in his eyes. 'What photos?'

Lauren paused. Hadn't they mentioned them to him? Were they at least giving her that? 'What photos, Lauren?' her dad asked again.

'I didn't know about them, I swear. He took them without me knowing.'

Walter sat back a little. 'He took pictures of you?' He let out a breath. She could practically see his brain whirring. Probably working out how much damage it'd do to his campaign. 'Well, this might make you feel better,' he said. 'Things are looking up.'

'What do you mean?'

'They've arrested someone. Some scumbag dealer. Found him trying to break into Ritchie's flat.'

Lauren frowned. 'I don't understand. Who is he?'

'His name's Mark Healy. Ring any bells?'

'No.'

Walter shrugged. 'He's not local. Lives in Newcastle. But he has links to the drug world so I assume they're thinking Ritchie's murder could be drug related.'

'Do they have any proof? What about Peter's car? What about—?'

'Listen, Lauren, I don't know a great deal about it, but . . . I shouldn't have this. I was given it by a friend.' He pulled a sheet of paper from his pocket, straightening it out on his knee. Lauren looked at it – a photograph of a man. 'Do you recognise him?'

'No,' she said. 'I've never seen him before.'

'Look carefully. This is important.'

'I *have* looked. I don't know him.'

Walter sighed. 'Lauren, you know that I'm trying to do my best for you. But you need to meet me halfway.'

'I don't understand.'

'You're in a lot of trouble. You understand that, don't you?'

'I'm not stupid.'

'And no one is saying you are. But you need to think carefully. The police have a lot of evidence against you. You've made some bad decisions. You've lied.'

'I know. And I'm sorry.'

'And now these photographs too. So you need to think about what's going to happen. This could go one of two ways. But unless they have something damning on this man, you're still going to be the one they'll look at hardest. So, have you seen this man before? With Ritchie?'

'I can't lie to them, Dad.'

'I'm trying to *help* you, Lauren, but I can't do everything myself. The police have obviously picked this man up for a reason so there's every chance that he *did* have something to do with Ritchie's murder. All I'm suggesting is you could say you've seen them together. Maybe they had a business dispute. It's perfectly plausible. All you're doing is giving them a little push. They'll work out the rest.'

Lauren looked at the picture of the man – this Mark Healy. He was a dealer, a bad guy. And he *had* been at Ritchie's flat, so maybe he did know him. Maybe they did have a dispute. Why else would he be there? Maybe it wouldn't be totally implausible.

'What about Peter?' she asked. 'Will they let him go?'

'They haven't charged him yet. Now I guess they won't have to.'

Lauren thought about Peter in jail because of her, because of Ritchie.

'Just think about it,' Walter said, kissing her on her forehead and standing up. 'I only want what's best for you.'

Lauren listened to the front door close and her dad's words rang around her head. She looked at the picture of Mark Healy again. If it was a choice between him and those she loved, this stranger or herself, she knew who she had to choose.

48

Gardner put the phone down but waited before joining the rest of the team. He'd known it was going to be impossible to keep Freeman out of it but now Healy had placed her brother at the club, it was going to be difficult to keep Darren out of it too. Someone was going to identify him and he was going to be resurrected and dragged into a murder investigation.

So he'd called Freeman and made it clear that she was going to have to come clean about the club and about Darren – or at least about him being alive. They weren't going to stop looking for him now and between Healy, Rachel, the club and God only knew where else he'd been, someone was going to find him. But for now, Gardner could still plead ignorance. No one knew that Darren had been crashing at his flat and he intended to keep it that way.

Gardner walked over to where his team was gathered and cleared his throat. The chatter died down and all eyes turned to him.

'I've spoken to DS Freeman again. Darren Freeman is her brother and he is alive.' He watched Harrington and Lawton's faces change. Suddenly it was all getting very interesting. 'She's sticking to what she said before – she did go to Slinky's and she did look at the tapes. She denies deleting anything, though.'

'And you believe her?' Harrington asked. 'Why was she even there? What case was it related to?'

'It wasn't. She said someone claimed to have seen her brother Darren there about a week ago. She didn't really believe it but curiosity got the better of her and she went down there to see for herself. She doubted anyone would just tell her if he was there given the nature of the establishment, and also doubted he'd be using his real name, so she chose to look at the security footage instead, only the last few days weren't there.'

'So how did she find her long-lost brother?' Harrington said.

'He was crashing at their parents' house. They'd gone away over Christmas,' Gardner said. 'But Darren Freeman being alive doesn't mean that either Darren Freeman or Healy killed Ritchie Donoghue. So far we have nothing other than Healy trying to break into the flat. He has no other links to Donoghue, not even any links to Middlesbrough so far.'

'So maybe we need to focus on Darren Freeman instead,' Lawton said. 'If we could talk to him, maybe we'd get some answers. Like why Healy was here at all.'

'Right. But DS Freeman says he's disappeared again. She's working on trying to find him,' Gardner said, the pain in his stomach worsening by the minute.

'What about his parents?' Lawton asked. 'Should I contact them? See if he's been in touch?'

'No,' Gardner said. 'DS Freeman told me that her parents still believe he's dead. I don't want them involved unless it's absolutely necessary. If Darren had been in touch with them, Freeman would know about it.'

Lawton sighed and gave a slight shake of her head. Gardner ignored her and turned to Berman. 'What's happening with Healy?'

'His solicitor's in with him. He's arguing we've got no reason to hold him. We should either charge him for attempted B&E or let him go.'

'Well, he's probably right,' Gardner said. 'If we don't find something else shortly we're going to have to release him. I'll be with Atherton if anyone needs me.'

The group dispersed and Gardner made for the door but Lawton cornered him. She waited until the room had cleared before she spoke.

'This isn't right,' she said. 'What aren't you telling us?'

'You know everything I do.'

'Don't lie to me,' she said and then looked to the floor, her face flushing. 'DS Freeman was at Ritchie Donoghue's flat.'

'And I explained that to you. She was doing me a favour.'

'Is that why you haven't told anyone else about it?' Lawton said.

'It's not important.'

'Bullshit. She was there and then the guy I arrested starts pointing fingers at her brother. That's not a coincidence. I might be green but I'm not stupid. You're covering something up for her. At the very least.'

'At the very least? What is it you think is happening, Lawton?'

He watched her jaw tighten. 'I don't know. But whatever it is, it's not good and I don't want you to get involved in it.'

'I think I can look after myself, don't you?'

Someone passed by the door and they both went quiet until they were alone again. Lawton looked him in the eye with something he'd never seen in her before, not directed at him, anyway. He hated that Lawton was doubting him, that she didn't trust him. But maybe she had every right.

'Did Darren Freeman kill Ritchie Donoghue? Is that what you're covering?'

'No, of course not.'

'So how is he involved? Why is *she* here?'

Gardner sighed. 'Look, I don't know exactly what's going on yet. I'm trying to find that out. But I do know that neither Darren Freeman nor Mark Healy killed Donoghue. Things have just got complicated. And I need time to work it out.' He put his hand on her shoulder. 'Do you trust me?'

She gave a non-committal shrug. 'Should I? Why are you covering for her? You're better than this.'

'And I'm going to sort it. Trust me. Just give me some time. Okay?'

'Fine,' she said and stepped away.

Gardner let out a breath and headed for Atherton's office. He wondered if Lawton was right. Should she trust him? And why *was* he covering for Freeman? Loyalty to a friend? Or because he wanted it to be something more? If so, there had to be better ways to impress a woman.

He watched Lawton disappear down the corridor and hoped that she had as much loyalty to him. Because if she didn't, they could all go down for this.

49

Lauren got out of the taxi in front of the office and wondered if she was doing the right thing. She knew her dad was right – she was in deep trouble – and he'd never steered her wrong before. But something was nagging at her. What if the police found out she was lying? She didn't have anything to prove she'd seen Mark Healy with Ritchie. Surely the police would want some evidence. They weren't just going to take her word for it. Not after the other lies she'd told. She needed to talk to someone.

She pulled her collar up against the wind and could feel the first flurry of snow. She almost smiled until she heard someone shout her name and turned to find a reporter jogging towards her. She almost spoke, almost shouted at him to leave her alone, but remembered what her dad had said – say nothing. She walked quickly to the office door, panicking that it'd be locked, surprised to find it open. The room at the front was empty so she made her way to the offices at the back. Lauren poked her head around the door to Peter's office. His chair was empty so she went across the hall and found Jen Worrall behind her dad's desk, reading something from a file.

'Hi,' Lauren said and Jen's eyes flicked up to her but her head didn't move. 'Is Peter here?'

Jen looked up now, closing the folder. 'He's been released?'

'I don't know,' Lauren said. 'My dad thought they might let him go. They arrested someone else.'

'Who?'

'Mark Healy. I think he knew Ritchie,' she said, testing the waters. 'He was at Ritchie's flat. They think he was looking for something.'

Jen stood up, moving the file across the desk, on top of a package. 'Like what?'

Lauren shrugged. 'I don't know. The police already searched the flat. They found photos.' She stopped. She didn't want Jen to know about the images. One more thing for her to judge her on. 'I don't think I'm supposed to know about it but my dad told me. He—'

'He what?'

'Nothing,' Lauren said. She shouldn't have gone to the office, definitely shouldn't have spoken to Jen.

'What sort of photos did they find?' Jen asked.

Lauren felt her face burning. Why had she been so stupid? Why couldn't she ever keep her mouth shut? She wished Peter were there. He was the only one she could trust, the only one she could really talk to. 'I don't know. It doesn't matter. Just tell Peter I was looking for him.' She started to walk away but Jen stopped her.

'So Peter's going to be all right?' Jen asked.

Lauren turned to Jen, wondering why she was so concerned with Peter, why she'd claimed to be seeing Ritchie when she was actually gay.

'What?' Jen said, catching Lauren staring.

'How come you told the police you were seeing Ritchie?' Lauren asked. Jen's face reddened and she moved away from Lauren again. 'I'm not bothered,' Lauren said. 'I just . . . Peter told me you were . . .'

'What?' Jen said.

'That you were gay.'

Jen rolled her eyes.

'You're not?' Lauren said.

'No. Not that it's any of your business. Or Peter's. Or the police's.'

'So you *were* seeing him?'

Jen looked away. 'The police misunderstood. Ritchie asked me out a few times. That was it. We never actually did anything. I had no interest in him. At all.'

Lauren nodded, but she didn't really believe her. Ritchie wouldn't have asked her out. He'd said horrible stuff about her – that she was stuck-up, that she was sneaky. Lauren had never seen Jen as a threat, not like that anyway. Lauren had even tried to make friends with her when Jen'd first started working with her dad. And even though Jen must've been at least five years younger than her, she looked down on her, as if she were so much better. And maybe she *was* better. She was certainly cleverer than her.

There was a knock at the front door and Jen huffed out a sigh and said, 'Hang on,' before storming off to answer it. Lauren heard her mutter, 'Fucking reporters,' as she walked away.

As soon as she heard Jen talking at the door, Lauren went to the desk and lifted the file Jen had been looking at, wondering why she'd moved it when Lauren got too close to the desk. She saw a small package and craned her neck to see what it was.

Her heart was in her mouth. The address label was made out to DI Gardner, Cleveland Police. Why was Jen sending stuff to the police?

Lauren listened for Jen coming back and picked up the envelope. She felt it; something small, thin.

She heard Jen slam the front door and panicked, pocketing

the envelope. She started to walk out, didn't want to see Jen but as she got to the back door she heard her.

'Bye, then,' Jen said.

Lauren turned and tried to smile. 'I'm going to go out this way. Don't want that lot seeing me.'

'Whatever,' Jen said and went back into her office.

Lauren started running as soon as the door closed behind her. She didn't know what Jen was playing at, but she was going to find out.

50

Freeman sat staring at the floor, tears burning the back of her eyes. It had got shitty so quickly. Gardner had called and said she was going to have to come clean. Or at least partly clean. Admit being at the club. Admit Darren was alive. But do that without making it seem like either of them had really done anything wrong.

And then there was Gardner himself. He was still pissed off with her, still thinking she'd set Healy up. He hadn't given her a chance to explain anything. Maybe he never would. Things weren't going to be the same between them any more, no matter what happened. It was over before it had even begun, whatever *it* was.

As for her parents . . . She'd been worried about telling them Darren was alive, that he was back. That little conversation suddenly seemed like a dream compared to the nightmare she'd have to let them into now: that their youngest son had somehow managed to implicate himself in a murder inquiry, dragging her along with him. She almost laughed. As if that last bit would matter. They'd never been proud of her achievements. Never cared about how she lived her life. Not her mam, anyway. She'd probably blame Freeman for getting Darren into trouble instead of the other way around.

She could hear the TV playing in the bedroom. She'd barely spoken to Darren since they got home and in the end he'd retreated to the other room so she could sulk by herself. She didn't even know if they should be here. Surely it'd be the first place the police came looking for them.

The car she'd spotted on the A19 had followed them all the way home, only passing them once she pulled into the car park behind the flats. She'd watched it drive past, on to the main road, and then she'd lost sight of it. Maybe it was nothing. But she kept checking the window just in case.

She'd thought about asking her neighbour to babysit Darren for a while. She doubted she'd mind. She loved a bit of excitement. But in the end, what good would it do? They'd find him. Someone would, whether it was the police or Healy, and maybe it didn't matter which.

Freeman looked at the clock. She was tired. Wanted to sleep but knew it would be impossible. Besides, Darren was sprawled out on her bed. Maybe she could just leave. Walk out the door, down the stairs, and just keep going. Someone would find her in a day or two, freezing and hungry, and she could blame it all on a mental breakdown. She thought maybe she was due one.

The phone interrupted her fantasies of leaving it all behind and she checked the screen. Same as before – Gardner, calling from his office. She watched the screen for a while, considered not answering but then snatched it up. Maybe this time she could explain.

'Freeman,' she said.

'Healy's been released,' he said.

She sat up straight. 'Is that good or bad?'

'You tell me,' Gardner said. 'He's still a suspect.'

'Shit.' The line buzzed quietly. 'I'm sorry,' she said. 'I never wanted this to happen.'

'What *did* you want? What did you think would happen by sending him there?'

'It wasn't me,' she said. 'Darren saw the address. He knew everything *I* did about your case. He heard us talking last night. He thought he could get Healy out of the way for a while and that he could disappear. He's an idiot.' Gardner was quiet. 'I swear to you,' she said. 'I had nothing to do with it. I wouldn't do that.'

'You wiped the tapes.'

She closed her eyes. 'That was different.'

'How?'

'Because I didn't think it would affect anyone else. This did. And I wouldn't do that to you. To anyone.' She waited for Gardner to speak but he didn't. 'If you need to tell them everything, I understand. I'm just sorry I dragged you into this.'

'I don't know how much longer I can keep things under control. If I can find something solid on Lauren or Peter or whoever the fuck actually did this, then maybe this will go away. They've released Healy for now but they're looking for Darren. And they'll find him eventually. I think you need to talk to your boss, explain why you were at the club, give yourself a head start. Even if there's nothing connecting Darren to the murder, it's not going to go away. If they keep looking at him, they're going to find something. It's going to hurt you. And maybe me too. The best we can hope for is they drop the Healy angle before it gets too far along. After that, you're on your own.'

Freeman's hand shook as she held the phone to her ear. 'Does anyone else know yet?'

'Harrington and Lawton. Not all of it, but they're suspicious. Obviously she knows you were there, at the flat. So far she hasn't mentioned that nugget to anyone else.'

'Can you trust her to keep it to herself?'

'I don't know. Let's hope so.'

He hung up and Freeman threw the phone across the room. She stood up and noticed Darren standing there. He didn't speak. She wondered if Gardner would give them up to save his own skin. He should do. He didn't owe them anything. But when the police came knocking, what was she going to do? She was fucked either way. She'd already tampered with evidence. She knew she was unlikely to have a job much longer anyway, so what was another charge to go with it?

But should she save her brother or herself?

51

Lauren arrived home to find Peter waiting for her by the front door, trying to shelter from the snow under the small awning. She ran towards him and he hugged her, tightly. As she pulled back, he smiled at her, brushing her hair from her face with one hand and squeezing her hand with the other. 'Have you heard the news?' he said. 'They've arrested someone. Some drug dealer. Maybe things are going to be all right.'

'So that's it?' she asked. 'They just let you go?'

'Well, no. I'm on bail. But they haven't charged me with anything so there's a chance this will all go away.'

'Maybe,' she said and unlocked the door. He followed her inside towards the living room. She wondered whether to tell him about Jen. About the package she'd taken from her. In her heart she thought she could trust him but something was nagging at her. That maybe she should wait until she'd seen what it was.

'Lauren?'

'Could you get me a drink?' she said, forcing a smile.

'Sure,' he said and walked away towards the kitchen.

Lauren went into the bedroom and tore the package open, throwing the envelope onto the floor. It was a pen drive. She opened her laptop, pushing the USB stick in, tapping her fingers, willing it to load. She could hear Peter moving around in the kitchen, ice clanking in glasses. She knew she'd tell him about it eventually, whatever it was. She loved him, trusted him. She just needed to see whatever it was alone first. Prepare herself.

The files loaded and Lauren clicked on the first. She gasped and looked up to the door. 'Oh my God,' she muttered. She clicked on the next one, which was just as bad as the first. She felt sick and looked away. She doubted she needed to look at any more. She got the picture.

'What're you doing in here?' Peter said, standing in the doorway, two glasses in his hand.

Lauren slammed the laptop closed and stood up, kicking the envelope under the bed. 'Just checking my emails,' she said. She took a glass from him and walked back to the living room. Her hand shook and she took a swig, hoping it would help.

She sat down on the settee and Peter moved close. He put his glass down and slid his fingers through her hair, his hand resting on her neck. 'It's going to be all right, you know. We'll get through this,' he said.

Lauren tried to smile but it didn't quite work. She didn't believe him. She turned away from him, trying not to cry.

'What's the matter?' he asked.

'Nothing,' she said. He shifted position, forcing her to look at him. She wanted to say something, she truly did. Wanted to believe that she could talk to him about anything. But she couldn't. Not about this. Not after what she'd just seen. 'I don't feel too good,' she said. 'I haven't been sleeping. I think I just want to go to bed.'

'Okay,' he said and pulled her up. 'We can do that.'

'No,' she said. 'I want to be by myself.'

Peter frowned at her. 'What's happened, Lauren?'

'Nothing. I just want to be alone. To sleep.' She let go of his hand and looked at the floor.

'I'll see you tomorrow, then.'

He started to leave and she called him back. He turned, hopeful. 'Did the police tell you they'd found the photos of me?'

Peter looked at his shoes. 'Yes,' he said.

'How come they found them when you couldn't?'

Peter shook his head. 'I'm sorry, Lauren,' he said, looking up at her. 'I never went to look for them.' Lauren opened her mouth to speak, angry that he'd lied to her, wondering what else he'd lied about. 'How could I? What would it have looked like if the police had found me sniffing around his flat the morning after he died?'

'You told me you would,' she said.

'I know. And I'm sorry.'

'Just go,' she said. He almost spoke again but instead turned and walked away. She watched him leave and tried not to cry. How could he have lied to her like that? He was the one person she'd thought she could rely on and now he'd proved himself to be a liar too. Why couldn't she just find someone who would be honest with her? Maybe she never would. Maybe being Walter James's daughter meant she would spend the rest of her life with people just pretending to like her – love her, even.

Lauren wiped her face. She needed to speak to her dad. But first she needed another drink.

She made her way into the kitchen and poured herself another glass of vodka, not bothering to mix it with anything to water it down. She necked it and poured a second, feeling the heat as it went down her throat.

She went through to the living room, carrying the bottle, and called her dad.

'Lauren?' he said. 'What's the matter? I'm in the middle of something.'

'I need you to come over,' she said, trying to make her voice sound strong. Trying not to let him hear the fear, the anger, she was feeling.

'It'll have to wait.'

'No,' she said. 'It's about Ritchie.'

She heard him sigh and mutter something to whoever he was with. 'What about him?'

'Just come over,' she said. 'Now.'

'I think you should watch your tone, Lauren,' Walter said. 'I'll come over later. When I'm ready.'

'I've got the pictures.' She waited for him to respond but he was silent. 'Dad?'

'I'm coming over.'

PART 2

52

'She's dead.'

'Okay, sir, can you tell me your name?'

'Just send someone.'

'Can you tell me what's happened?'

'I don't know. I found her. Please, just send someone.'

'What's the address, sir?'

He reeled it off.

'Okay, an ambulance is on the way.'

'It's too late. She's already dead.'

'Can you tell me what happened?'

'I don't know. I found her. I just found her.'

'Tell me what you see.'

'She's on the floor. There's blood.'

'Can you check for a pulse?'

'I did. She's gone.'

'Okay, sir. Help is on the way.'

'She's gone.'

'What's your name, sir?'

'Walter James.'

'Okay, Mr James. Can you tell me her name?'

'Lauren. My daughter. Lauren.'

The line went dead.

53

Gardner put his foot down, speeding around a corner, and then tried to control the car as it slid on the road. He could barely see out the windscreen, the snow was coming down so heavy now. He'd got the call fifteen minutes earlier and at first had misunderstood but when he'd realised what had really happened, he couldn't get there fast enough.

He'd been quite happily, or unhappily, wallowing in his own misery, thinking about Freeman and her pain-in-the-arse brother. She'd told him she'd had nothing to do with setting Healy up and he believed her. It was obvious once she'd said it and it was his own stupid fault for talking out of school and getting Freeman to go and watch the flat. He should've known better than to think anything he said in Darren's presence would be confidential.

At least it'd restored some of his faith in Freeman. Not that it mattered so much. Once all this was over it was unlikely they'd see each other again. That ship had sailed. He just hoped that he could find a way to make their mess go away and get back to the nice, simple mess of finding out who really killed Ritchie Donoghue.

And now this had happened.

Gardner pulled up outside Lauren's house. The road was already busy with other cars – the first responder, the SOCOs.

If a lot of this had been kept away from the media so far, it was unlikely to last much longer. One murder was likely to attract some attention. But two murders at the same address, in the same week? That was worthy of a whole lot more attention and no one, not even the venerable Hadley, possessed the power to stop that.

He walked quickly towards the house, noticing twitching curtains from the neighbours. He wondered if any of them had actually seen anything useful this time. As he entered the house he could hear shouting.

'Let go of me!'

Gardner got the nod from the cordon officer and walked towards the kitchen as Walter James pulled away from the officer trying to restrain him. He charged towards Gardner, his face red. Someone else grabbed hold of him and pulled him away. Gardner looked past Walter and saw the body.

Lauren James was dead. Murdered in her own home. He glanced around but couldn't see much out of place. His eyes wandered to the door, to the windows. Nothing broken except a single wine glass.

'This is your fault,' Walter said. 'You let that animal out.' Gardner turned his attention back to Walter. 'I'll have your job for this.'

'Mr James, you need to calm down.' Gardner turned and saw Atherton standing behind him and wondered who Walter was threatening. Him or his boss.

'Calm down? My daughter is dead. Where's Hadley?' Walter looked around the room but the superintendent was nowhere to be seen. 'I want you off this case. You let that bastard go, you spineless prick.' Walter pressed his face close to Atherton's, spittle settling in the corner of his mouth. Atherton looked like he wanted to tell Walter where to go but instead he stood there and took it. He really was spineless.

'Who're you talking about?' Gardner asked, trying to diffuse the situation.

Walter spun around, spit flying from his lips. 'Mark Healy.'

'How do you know about Healy?'

'I know. I know you arrested him and let him go. She called me,' he said, pointing at Lauren. 'She called me. Said she'd seen someone hanging around. Someone who'd had dealings with Ritchie. Said he was called Mark. She knew him. Must've found out he killed Ritchie so he killed her too.'

Gardner felt a jolt in his gut. Mark Healy had nothing to do with this. Despite knowing the real reason he'd been at the flat, Gardner had still checked his background thoroughly. There was nothing linking him to Donoghue or Middlesbrough. All they had on him was that he'd showed up at the flat and Gardner knew that was bullshit of Darren Freeman's making.

He looked at Walter, shaking with rage. He knew someone was giving Walter information, keeping him up to date with the case, but he'd yet to work out who it was. His first instinct was Atherton, trying to score brownie points. But James was clearly no fan of Atherton. So maybe it went higher. Hadley was the one keen to do all he could for Walter James. But would he really go as far as setting up an innocent man?

One of the SOCOs passed them and Gardner stopped him. 'Any sign of the murder weapon?'

'Looks like she hit her head on the edge of the worktop. Probably a fight that got out of hand. There's bruising around her wrists.'

Gardner moved closer to Lauren's body, careful not to contaminate anything. He looked down at her and for a moment it looked like she was just sleeping. But closer inspection revealed the bruising on her wrists and blood pooling behind her head.

He stood up, feeling a wave of sadness. Not long ago he'd been desperate for Lauren to be charged with murder, or at least for them to look at her harder. He guessed that the looking, at least, would happen now.

Someone called his name and he was grateful for the distraction. He couldn't look at her any longer. She looked like a child and he couldn't help but feel that her death was partly his fault. Deep down he knew that wasn't true, but if he hadn't kept pushing . . .

'DI Gardner?'

'Coming,' he said and walked away, towards the back of the house, passing Walter who was pacing up and down like an animal, demanding to see Hadley. Did he really believe this story about Healy? That he was responsible for Ritchie's death, and now Lauren's? It obviously wasn't true, but someone wanted it to fit. He'd thought before that maybe it was just convenient, that it took the heat off Lauren. But now she was dead. So who was still benefitting from the lie?

Gardner found the scene of crime officer in a bedroom. He held out an evidence bag and Gardner took it, turning it around to see what it was. He realised it was a small padded envelope and wondered what was so important about it. And then he saw it. The envelope was addressed to him.

54

Friday, 31 December

Gardner had managed about two hours' sleep and was now on his way back to the office. Much of the snow from the night before now lay grey and charmless in ploughed piles at the side of the roads. He couldn't get Lauren James out of his mind. She'd been a young woman, foolish, prone to bad decisions. But who wasn't? And now it looked like maybe she wasn't guilty at all. Whoever killed Ritchie Donoghue likely killed her too, maybe because of something she knew, just like Walter had said. Only whoever that person was, it wasn't Mark Healy.

He'd tried to work it out, how Walter James could be connected. He doubted James had killed his own daughter, but he *knew* something. He wasn't talking about Healy because he truly believed it. Whoever was giving James the information must've known Healy wasn't guilty and had surely let James know that too. So James was covering something up, including who'd killed Lauren. And what kind of father would do that?

Despite the early hour, as Gardner walked through to his office he could hear several conversations and people rushing around with the buzz of a case going well. He sought out Harrington who was remarkably already at work.

'What's going on?'

248

'Our lovely friends in forensics have been working through the night and they've found something to link Healy to the scene,' Harrington said.

'Which scene?' Gardner asked, knowing he wasn't going to like the answer.

'Lauren James.'

'Already?'

'They found a cigarette butt outside the front door. Hadley rushed it through. Got Healy's DNA all over it. We're bringing him in again.'

Gardner felt a chill go through him. There was no way Healy had been at that house; no way he had killed Lauren James. He was being set up and it wasn't by Darren Freeman this time.

'Is there anything else? Anything from the CCTV? Or is that all they found?' he asked, following Harrington through the office where everyone was gathering for the briefing.

'So far. Someone's checking out the CCTV but a search of Healy's place should give us something else, hopefully.'

'Who authorised that?'

'Hadley.'

'Right, people, can we get on with this? We have a lot of work to do,' Atherton said, making his way to the front of the room. 'As you'll all be aware, Lauren James was found dead last night. Post-mortem will be conducted later this morning. As of yet we don't know if we're looking at a murder or an accident. It appears Ms James was intoxicated and it's possible she slipped, knocking her head on the kitchen worktop. But, considering the events of the last few days, we could be looking at a second murder. Pathologist found bruising on Lauren's wrists and upper arm suggesting a struggle or someone trying to restrain her. We're still working the scene but evidence was found outside the house linked to Mark Healy.

He is currently being sought for further questioning at his home address.

'We did find something else interesting at Lauren's house, though. An envelope addressed to DI Gardner under Lauren's bed. No prints other than Lauren's on it and no idea what was in the envelope.'

'It looked like Lauren had opened the envelope,' Gardner said. 'Which suggests she wasn't the one sending something but maybe she intercepted whatever it was. So what we need to find out is who was sending me mail and why.'

'Unless it was Lauren and she just changed her mind,' Harrington suggested.

'That's possible,' Gardner said.

'Could've been proof of who really killed Ritchie. Maybe it's what got her killed.'

'Maybe. But why would she change her mind about that? Why not just give me it in person?'

'Maybe she didn't open the envelope. Maybe whoever killed her did,' someone else said.

'But the lack of prints means we might never know,' Atherton said. 'So our priority is to find out what was in the envelope.'

Gardner, along with the rest of the team, turned as the door opened and Cartwright came in. 'Sorry,' he said and looked for a free chair. Gardner did a double take. It looked like Cartwright had had a bad night at the wrong end of someone's fist. His face was bruised, one eye blackened, his nose swollen. When he noticed Gardner staring he raised his eyebrows as if to challenge him but ended up wincing in pain.

'Glad you could join us, Cartwright,' Atherton said and Cartwright looked as surprised as Gardner felt that Atherton had admonished his golden boy rather than rushing to administer first aid.

'Sorry, sir,' Cartwright said.

Gardner kept an eye on Cartwright and wondered who'd been the lucky person to get to punch him repeatedly. And then Hadley made an appearance to inform the team that Mark Healy had been apprehended and daydreams of punching Cartwright evaporated as Gardner started to feel a little ill. The feeling worsened when Hadley personally thanked Gardner and Lawton for having the foresight to keep tabs on Donoghue's flat. 'We wouldn't have got him otherwise,' Hadley said with a fake smile, before leaving them to it. Lawton walked away without meeting Gardner's eye.

Gardner left the incident room, about to head to the canteen, when he heard the commotion behind him.

'Get the fuck off me!'

Gardner turned to the voice at the end of the hall and saw Mark Healy being led inside by uniformed officers. He turned back as more voices echoed down the hall. Walter James pushed his way through, past Atherton, shoving him aside to get to Healy. Though the older man was more than a head shorter than Healy he ran at him, knocking him into the wall.

Gardner could hear Walter's voice but couldn't make out the words he was saying to the man who'd allegedly killed his daughter. At first everyone stood back but after Walter had got a few jabs in, Cartwright stepped in and tried to pull him away. Walter spun around, fists clenched. 'Don't you fucking dare,' he said and raised a fist to Cartwright. Finally he let his hands drop and looked around at the gathered crowd. His eyes focused on Atherton. 'You'd better do your job this time,' he said and walked away.

The officer who'd brought Healy in pushed him along the corridor to one of the interview rooms. Gardner turned and saw Cartwright lurking by the door to the interview room, his face looking even worse in the natural light of the corridor.

'DC Cartwright. Are we ready?'

Gardner turned and saw Hadley coming towards them. He slapped Gardner's shoulder as he approached. 'I hope you don't mind, Michael, but I've asked Craig to conduct the interview. Thought I'd sit in for moral support.'

Gardner realised that DCI Atherton was lurking behind Hadley and thought, *Of course, where there's one arsehole there's another.* Atherton glanced at Gardner before aiming his eyes at the floor. He didn't say a word.

'Let's get on with it, shall we?' Hadley said and led Cartwright into the room. A few seconds later Harrington emerged and Gardner just shook his head at him before walking away.

He knew Hadley was mates with Walter James so of course Hadley would be a part of this. And Gardner knew he had nowhere to turn. He could go above Hadley's head but for all he knew they were all part of the same weird handshake, rolled-up trouser leg club and the only person who'd burn for this would be him.

He saw Lawton coming in and shouted her. She turned to him and said, 'Morning,' but without the usual smile. Gardner walked over to her and led her into the stairwell. He waited for it to clear before speaking.

'I need you to do something for me,' he said and she rolled her eyes, going to walk away. 'Wait,' he said. 'I'm sorry about yesterday. I should've trusted you enough to tell you everything. And I will. But for now I just need your help.'

'What do you need?' she said.

'We both know this Healy thing is bullshit. It was a mistake, but now it's got out of hand and they're setting him up,' he said, pointing towards the interview room. 'Walter James has something to do with this. With all of it. I know it. And they're covering it up. I need you to start looking at James again. We need to go over everything – his alibis, the evidence, everything. I want to know everything he's done, everything he's said, everyone he's seen. Go back as far as you can. He's up to his neck in this and we're going to find out how.'

'But—'

'I need you to do this. They're watching me. They know I'm suspicious of him.'

Lawton sighed. 'How do you know it's him? I mean, I know you don't like him . . .'

'That's got nothing to do with it.'

Lawton looked at him like he was a five-year-old. And she was right. There was a part of him that wanted to nail Walter James just on the basis of him being Walter James. But it was more than that. The man was hiding something. He knew it.

'Look, please just do this for me. Come to mine later and we can see what's what. And I promise I'll tell you everything.'

'I don't know if I can,' Lawton said. 'Me and Lee have plans, I don't know if I can—'

'Please, Dawn.' He stopped talking as a woman in a too-big suit came up the stairs, staring at them. He realised he was standing very close to Lawton and knew what the woman would be thinking. He waited for her to go up the next flight of stairs, listening for a door slamming shut.

'Will you help me?' he asked and Lawton nodded. 'Thank you. And one more thing: I need you to keep quiet about Freeman being at Donoghue's flat.' Lawton looked like she was going to tell him to go fuck himself and he wouldn't blame her if she did. 'Please. I can't explain it right now but you have to trust me. I'm trying to do what's right and I need your help.'

Lawton walked away and left him standing alone in the stairwell. He hoped that her silence was a yes and that her fishing wouldn't get her dragged into it too far, that she wouldn't be punished for being on his side. But more than anything he wanted to get to Walter James. If James had something to do with Lauren's death then he would do everything he possibly could to make sure that happened.

55

Freeman sat waiting in the stuffy office, her foot tapping beneath the desk. Maybe it was just in comparison to the freezing temperature outside or maybe it was panic making her sweat; either way it was far too hot in here. Every voice she heard outside the room made her swivel around, wondering if this was it. It was DCI Routledge who'd called her in, before she could go to him first, but she knew it wasn't just going to be the two of them in this meeting. The stupid decisions she'd made over the last few days were coming back to bite her. It wasn't a formal disciplinary yet – they'd have to tell her if it was. Give her more than a couple of hours' notice. But it wasn't going to be a friendly chat either.

The door opened and she found herself getting to her feet. She'd never been one to bow to authority or to adhere to formal protocols – not unless it was absolutely necessary – but it seemed like now wasn't the best time to be herself. Routledge nodded at her as he came around the desk, his face giving nothing away. He was followed by Superintendent Clarkson, a woman Freeman admired from a distance but close up, in the same room, wasn't so happy about.

Clarkson was a small woman, not much taller than Freeman, but could make all of the men under her command shake with fear once she got started. She was not a woman to be messed with and was the last person Freeman wanted to try and explain all of this to.

'Take a seat, Detective Freeman,' Clarkson said and made herself comfortable in the chair opposite. She looked over her shoulder at Routledge who lowered himself into a seat too.

Freeman sat down and tried to control her breathing. She'd planned what she would say on the drive over but her mind was now blank. All she could think was, *I'm fucked.*

'I think you know why we're all here,' Clarkson said, looking at Freeman over her glasses, making Freeman feel about ten years old. 'We had a complaint from the proprietor of a nightclub called Slinky's. He seems to think you tampered with his security system. I was hoping you could clear things up for me.'

'I *was* at the club,' she said and saw Routledge's eyes close slowly. 'But I didn't tamper with anything. There was nothing on the tapes for the days I was looking at and the system appeared not to be working. As far as I could tell, anyway. I'm not an expert.'

'Can you tell me *why* you were at the club? As far as I can tell it wasn't relating to any ongoing investigations. And Routledge tells me you're on annual leave, too,' Clarkson said.

'I went there for personal reasons. I misled the woman at the club, told her it was regarding an investigation into an assault.'

'And would you care to share with us the real reason for your visit to the club?'

'I was looking for someone. Somebody claimed they'd seen my brother, Darren, there. I haven't seen him for years. As far as me and my family were aware my brother died five years ago. But someone thought they'd seen him. I brushed it off at first but I was curious. I couldn't just let it go, not if there was a chance it was him. So I went there to look at the CCTV footage and I lied to get access. But I didn't think it would cause any problems. I mean, I didn't *do* anything that would cause problems. I know it was wrong and it looks dodgy but—'

'It's more than dodgy, Detective Freeman,' Clarkson said. 'Your actions have impacted on a murder investigation. We've had Cleveland police onto us. That footage could've been used as an alibi.'

'I know,' Freeman said. 'I've spoken to DI Gardner over there. I explained the situation to him. He was aware, as I'm sure you are, that the footage could be restored if necessary – if there ever was any, I mean – but he told me it wouldn't be required. That they'd found other evidence placing the suspect in Middlesbrough later on.' She stopped and wondered if she'd said too much.

'Yes, well,' Clarkson said. 'I've been informed that they now have someone else in custody. But the fact remains your actions have been extremely questionable.' She looked down at the notes she'd been taking. 'Let's go back to your reasons for being at the club.'

Freeman came out of the building, into the bitter air, and thought she was going to hurl. Clarkson had grilled her for another hour and she'd felt herself unravelling. She didn't know how much Gardner had told them. Didn't know how much Clarkson really knew. She'd told them about Darren, that he was alive. There was no way around that. Sooner or later they'd find evidence he was back so it was better coming from her. She'd told them she'd found her brother staying at her parents' house when she'd gone to water the plants the night after she'd been at the club. It wasn't the greatest lie ever told. She just hoped that Clarkson believed it. She wasn't sure *she* would've. She'd told lie after lie, digging herself in deeper and deeper. And for what?

She walked to her car, her hands shaking as she tried to open the door. As soon as she got inside and slammed the door the tears came. Thankfully the windows were steamed up so no one passing by could see her. Could see the mess she was, that she'd become.

She knew it was over. Clarkson would keep looking at her. Healy would keep talking. Gardner would have to break.

Freeman wiped her face with her sleeve, her breathing slowing down. Maybe this was for the best. Maybe she just needed to walk away from all this. Maybe she could do a Darren and just disappear.

As she sat there, leaning back against the headrest, she wondered if she could do that. If she'd be brave enough to just leave. It's not like she had much to stay for anyway. She closed her eyes, calm coming over her as she fantasised about living in the middle of nowhere, where no one knew her, no one bothered her.

And then her phone started to ring. She reluctantly opened her eyes and saw it was Gardner. And she knew she had to make her choice.

56

Gardner hung up. He'd tried calling Freeman three times now and she still wasn't answering. He wanted to know what she'd told her boss, to try and at least keep their stories straight. Part of him wanted her to own up to everything but he wondered if it was because it was the right thing to do or just so that he could have a chance of getting to Walter James. Maybe it was the same thing. Or maybe Lawton was right and he was barking up the wrong tree purely because he disliked the tree.

But even if James was innocent, there was someone else out there who wasn't. And they were going free while Mark Healy took the blame. Whatever Healy might've been, he wasn't a killer. At least not in this instance. And that gnawed away at Gardner. Yes, it was likely there was something Healy should've been locked up for but that wasn't how it worked. So how could he prove Healy's innocence without taking down Freeman, and himself, too?

He slid his phone back into his pocket and drove away from the station. He'd left Lawton to continue searching for anything on Walter James under the pretence of gathering evidence on Healy. Yes, she was chasing up CCTV from the area, trying to ascertain whether Healy had been in the vicinity of Lauren's house the night before, but she was also looking at James's movements too. So far they'd found footage of Healy getting the last train just after 11 p.m., which left plenty of time for him to have killed Lauren – in theory at least. If only Healy hadn't been so stupid as to hang around in Middlesbrough – hoping to find Darren, Gardner assumed – then maybe this would stop. If he'd got the train back earlier he wouldn't be facing a second murder charge.

Gardner drove towards Lauren James's house but not to the crime scene itself. He had something else on his mind. He'd already called her neighbour, Ann Earnshaw, to make sure they were home and now he hoped to get some answers. Mrs Earnshaw said she hadn't seen anything the night before, but was shaken by the second murder to take place across the street in a week. She had agreed to let Gardner speak to her daughter and her friend again as long as she could be present.

He pulled up, noticing the police tape flapping in the wind across the road. The post-mortem results had come back and although the pathologist couldn't say conclusively whether Lauren was murdered, she could say that it was the head injury that killed her. Whether she was pushed during a struggle or just slipped was not clear. But Gardner found it highly unlikely that it'd been an accident.

A net curtain twitched as Gardner got out of the car and went towards the neighbour's house. Mrs Earnshaw opened the door before he'd even knocked and he walked through to the living room where he found the teenage girls sitting on the settee, Kirsty hunched forward, Samantha more relaxed, slumped into the corner.

'Can I get you a drink? Tea? Coffee?' Mrs Earnshaw asked, kneading her hands together in the doorway.

'No, thanks,' Gardner said. The woman indicated he should sit and he took the chair opposite the girls. 'I just wanted to go over again what you saw on the night of Richard Donoghue's murder.'

Samantha's eyes rolled. 'We already told you what we saw.'

'I know,' Gardner said. 'But we just need to make sure. And I also wanted to ask about last night, if you saw or heard anything. You said you saw a tall, skinny man in the alley, coming out of Lauren James's gate, the night Ritchie died. Correct?' The girls both nodded. 'And when he noticed you there he got into the car. A black BMW.' More nods. 'But you didn't notice anything else. Not a licence plate or what the man was wearing?'

'No,' Kirsty said. 'It was dark.'

'And had you been drinking?' He saw the girl swallow. 'It doesn't matter to me if you had. I don't care about that. Who doesn't drink when they're seventeen? I just need to know how certain you both are about what you saw.'

Kirsty looked at her mother and then shook her head. 'No. We weren't drinking.'

Gardner knew she was lying. Her testimony would never hold up in court. 'Okay. So what about this man?' he said and showed them a photo of Walter James.

'No,' Kirsty said. 'The man we saw was tall and skinny.'

Samantha looked too and a smile spread across her face. 'That's whatshisname. The MP bloke. Did he kill someone?' She had hold of her phone and Gardner wondered how long it would be until Facebook was buzzing with rumours of Walter's involvement.

Gardner took the photo back. 'He's Lauren's dad. We're just trying to establish the facts.' He took out another photo. 'What about him? He fits your description.'

Kirsty looked at the photo of Guy James and Gardner was sure she blushed. 'Do you know him?'

'Guy,' she said. 'I don't really know him. I've seen him here before. He gave me—' She stopped and glanced at her mother again. 'He's talked to me before. It wasn't him. I'd recognise him.' The other girl nodded her agreement.

'All right. What about him?' Gardner showed them the picture of Peter. He knew they'd already been through this, seen the pictures before. But he hadn't seen their faces when they'd done it. He needed to see for himself.

Kirsty frowned at the photo. 'I don't know. Maybe.' She shrugged and handed the photo back. 'It was dark. All I know is that he was tall and skinny. Could've been anyone. But he was there last night.'

'*He* was?' Gardner said, pointing to Peter. Kirsty nodded. 'What time was that?'

'I'm not sure,' Kirsty said. 'Early, I think, like half seven or something. I saw him waiting outside for her. When she came home she let him in.'

'Did you see him leave?'

'No,' she said. 'But I saw someone else. I saw some girl. And then I saw her dad. Then I saw all the police.'

'A girl?'

'Yeah. Youngish, blond hair.'

'Did she go inside?'

'No. Just knocked and left, not long after that one left,' Kirsty said, pointing to the photo of Peter.

Could it have been Jen Worrall? Why would she be at Lauren's? Gardner tried to focus on one thing at a time and pulled out his final photo, the one of Healy. 'What about him? Have you seen him before?'

Both girls leaned over, stared for a moment and then shook their heads. 'I don't think so. But it was dark,' Kirsty said.

Gardner sighed. He knew it was a long shot. Knew that they were never going to be able to rule Healy out completely or suddenly change their minds and say the man they saw was a short, fat arsehole. But there had to be something. With whoever was pulling the strings making sure the evidence was stacking up against Healy in Lauren's murder, he knew he'd have to focus on Ritchie's death. So far Hadley was quite willing to overlook the fact that there was nothing linking Healy to the first murder at all. But maybe that's where he'd find the truth while everyone else was looking the other way. He thought about the theory they'd had in the beginning that there'd been two people involved. Two weapons *were* used, after all. He'd assumed if two people were involved it had been Lauren and, most likely, Peter. But would Peter really kill Lauren to keep her quiet? He didn't see it. He needed to know if Lauren had sent that text to Ritchie or not because if she hadn't, then maybe she had had nothing to do with his death. But if there had been two weapons, two killers, and one wasn't Lauren, then who? Maybe the man from the alley hadn't been alone in that car.

'Was it possible there was someone else in the car that first night?' he asked.

'Maybe,' Kirsty said. 'I didn't see anyone but—'

'It was dark,' Gardner said, finishing her sentence. He wasn't going to get any more answers here.

Gardner headed back to the station. He needed to find something else before Walter James and his friends managed to plant more evidence linking Healy to the case. But what? Walter apparently found Lauren. He was the one who'd called it in. Her phone records showed she'd called him almost two hours earlier and he claimed that she'd asked him to come and see her. Which is just what he did, only she was dead when he got there. According to him.

So it was back to Peter Hinde.

'Take a seat,' Gardner said and watched as the man lowered himself into a chair, the poise long gone, replaced with a red-eyed mess.

'Can you tell us where you were last night, Mr Hinde?'

Peter swallowed a few times and wiped his face, working himself up to speak. When he did his voice was croaky and raw. 'After I was released, I went to see Lauren,' he said, and then his voice broke again.

'What time was that?'

'Around seven thirty, I think. I went round but she wasn't there. I waited. She came home a few minutes later.'

'All right,' Gardner said. 'What time did you leave?'

'I don't know. A little before eight, maybe.'

'So you'd waited outside for her but then didn't stay. Why not?'

Peter sighed. 'She was tired,' he said. 'We went in. She asked me to make her a drink. We started talking and then she suddenly said she was tired. She wanted to be alone.'

'Was she upset about something?'

Peter paused. 'No, well, maybe. I told her about the man that'd been arrested, that maybe things were going to be all right.'

'Which man?'

Peter looked up. 'The man you arrested in connection with Ritchie's murder.'

'Who told you about that?' Gardner asked.

'Her father.'

'And did you recognise this man's name when Walter told you?'

'No, why would I?'

'Did Lauren say anything that gave you the impression she knew him?'

'I don't know,' Peter said. 'She didn't say much, she seemed distracted.'

'About what?' Peter looked at the desk in front of him for a long time. 'Mr Hinde?'

'We argued,' Peter said, his voice wavering. 'She was upset about those photographs. She'd asked me to find them and I didn't.' He finally looked up. 'That was the last thing we did. Had a fight about those fucking photos.'

Gardner felt a twinge of sympathy for the man sitting across from him. There was nothing proving that he was innocent; in fact, of everyone involved he seemed to have the most stacked against him. And yet. Gardner couldn't quite believe Peter had killed Lauren. Ritchie? Quite possibly. But Lauren? And how would that fit with Walter James's cover-up? He could see James wanting to help Hinde out if he'd killed Ritchie, although he hadn't gone to great lengths to do that so far. But why cover for his daughter's murderer? What would he get from that?

'Lauren asked you to find the photographs?' Gardner said and Peter nodded. 'From where?'

'Ritchie's flat,' he said.

'Did you go there? Did you try?' Gardner said, thinking about the other man they'd seen on the CCTV on Ritchie's street that night.

'No. How could I?'

'When did she ask you to go?'

'The morning she found his body,' Peter said. 'After she'd called the police she called me. She was desperate. And I let her down.'

57

Gardner drove back to the station having spoken to Peter Hinde's neighbour. He claimed to have seen Peter return home the night before, just after 8 p.m. He knew this because the TV show he was watching had just started. If he was correct, it would fit with Peter's account and, more importantly, would rule him out of killing Lauren, since she'd made her final call to her dad just after that.

Gardner went inside, squeezing his hands to get some feeling back into them. He jogged up the stairs and almost ran into Cartwright.

'Did you hear they got back a hit on the fibres found on Lauren's jumper?' Cartwright asked.

'No,' Gardner said.

'Matched a jumper found in Healy's flat. Hadley's charged him.'

'What? When?'

'About half an hour ago.'

Cartwright walked away and Gardner leaned against the wall. How had that happened? The cigarette butt was one thing. Healy probably lit up as soon as he left the station yesterday. All it took was for Walter or one of his cronies to pick it up, ready for planting when the time was right. But fibres from the jumper were on Lauren's clothes. Gardner's

266

mind raced. Someone had to have planted it in Healy's flat later. But whoever it was had been at Lauren's house. Had probably been the one to kill her. Who would've had the fore-sight and opportunity to do that?

Gardner went into the toilets and leaned against the sinks. This whole thing was out of control. Lauren was dead. Healy was being framed. And it was all his fault. He ran the tap, gulping water down from shaking hands. How had he let it go this far?

After checking in with Lawton, Gardner made another house call. There was something not right with Ms Worrall, he just hadn't worked out what it was. The possibility that she'd been at Lauren's house the night before was just one more thing that bothered him. Jen opened the door and her body language changed from hesitant to hostile.

'Can I have a word?' Gardner asked and she paused before opening the door wider to let him in. Her home wasn't what he'd expected. The flat was above a takeaway and spartan. Not in a controlled, minimalist way, more of a 'I haven't got a penny to my name' sort of way. He supposed that happened when you were an intern.

She led him through to the open-plan living room–kitchen and he noticed a bed in the corner. Clearly it was the bedroom too. She pointed to a dining-room chair and he took a seat. Jen pulled up the chair on the other side of the table.

'What were you doing at Lauren James's house last night?' he asked.

For a moment he thought she was going to deny it but her shoulders dropped slightly and she sighed. 'I saw Lauren yesterday. She came to the office.'

'To see you?'

'No, she was looking for Peter but he wasn't there.'

'So . . . she came to the office. Why did you go to her house later?'

Jen looked away and went quiet. Gardner didn't want to push her but he was sick of the lying. He stood up and wandered the few feet to the kitchen area. 'If you know something, you need to tell me,' he said and looked up at a small blackboard with what appeared to be a shopping list on it. He stopped and looked carefully. Something was familiar.

The writing.

He turned back to Jen. 'What were you sending to me?'

Jen shook her head but then her face changed and she actually looked frightened, actually looked like the twenty-two-year-old girl she was underneath the bluster.

'We found an envelope at Lauren's, addressed to me,' Gardner said. 'She took it from you, didn't she? That's why you went there.'

Jen nodded.

'So what was in it?'

'A pen drive.'

'Containing what?' Gardner knew there'd been no pen drives in the evidence collected from the house.

'Photographs.'

'Of what? Lauren?'

'No,' Jen said. 'These were pictures of Walter James.'

58

Gardner's head was spinning and he tried to think it through. Was this the answer to all of it? That this had nothing to do with Lauren. It had never been about her, it was about Walter James.

'Start from the beginning,' he said to Jen. 'What were the pictures of?'

'What do you mean?'

'I mean, what was in the photographs? Walter, obviously, but doing what, with who, where?'

'I don't know,' she said.

'Come on, Jen. You saw them. You knew enough about them to think I should see them. So what was it?'

'Just sex stuff. I don't know. Things he shouldn't have been doing. Things that could've got him into trouble. Could've ruined him.'

'So where did they come from? Who took them?' Jen's eyes filled up. 'Ritchie? He was involved, right? You were, what, working together to screw James over?'

'It wasn't like that.'

'Peter Hinde told us you were gay and you denied it. I don't care either way but I know you weren't seeing Ritchie. So let me tell you what I think is going on. I think you knew what Ritchie was up to and you were letting it happen. Walter James is a wanker, so I'd understand if you and Ritchie were in cahoots to bring him down. All I want to do is find out who killed Ritchie. And Lauren. So you need to tell me everything.'

Jen looked at him, tears in her eyes. 'He's a prick,' she said. 'But I didn't want things to end up like this. I just wanted to get back at him.'

'At Walter? Why?'

'Because he's a fucking pervert,' she said. 'Hands like a bloody octopus.'

'He assaulted you?'

She nodded. 'He came onto me when I first started. That's why I told him I was gay. I don't know why I thought that'd make a difference. But I could see how he was with other women too, other girls. He's so full of himself that he thinks he'll get away with it.'

'So you were blackmailing him.'

'No,' she said, sighing. 'I started overhearing things. Seeing things. I thought if I collected enough evidence I could do something. But I knew the police would bury it. I've seen how your lot are with him. So I was going to send it to the papers or something. But not until I found a new job. And then Ritchie caught me. I'd followed him and Lauren one night, thinking I could get something on her that'd embarrass Walter too. I knew she was into drugs and stuff. Ritchie saw me, and he was pissed off that I was following them. But when I told him what I was doing he loved it. He said he wanted in, except he wanted to make money. He wouldn't take no for an answer, he threatened me, so in the end I agreed to sell the stuff to him. I could use the money,' she said, looking around at the dump she called home. 'So we made a deal. He was going to pay me for the photos and stuff and I was going to leave my job. But then he was killed before we did it.'

'So Ritchie didn't have the photos when he died?'

'I'd sent one to him to prove they were worth the money. But that was it.'

That'd explain why Ritchie's phone was missing. 'Why didn't you come forward sooner? After Ritchie was killed?'

'Because I didn't think the police would do anything. But then I realised how much you hate him and I thought that maybe *you* would. I was going to send the drive to you but Lauren took it. I guess she saw your name and panicked.'

'But why?' Gardner asked. 'What would she think you were sending?'

'I don't know. We don't exactly get along. Maybe she thought it was something about her.'

Gardner sat back wondering what had happened last night. Had Lauren called her dad to tell him what she'd seen? Was that the reason Walter went over there last night? There certainly hadn't been a pen drive recovered from the scene. Walter must've taken it.

'Do you still have copies?' Gardner asked.

'No,' Jen said. 'I copied them onto the drive to give to Ritchie and then I deleted everything.'

'From your laptop? We can maybe restore them.'

'I don't have it,' she said. 'I gave it to my friend Joe after I deleted the pictures. I thought if I got rid of it no one would be able to trace them back to me.'

Gardner sighed. 'You think you can get it back?'

'I'll try,' she said. 'I never should've started this. I'm really sorry.'

Gardner stood up. 'Don't be,' he said. Because now he had Walter James's motive for murder.

59

Gardner couldn't make Jen Worrall any promises that there'd be no charges against her, she'd withheld a lot of evidence, but he'd certainly try his best to prevent it. As far as he was concerned, Jen was just another of Walter's victims. He'd tried to persuade her to make a formal statement but she was reluctant, afraid of what Walter James would do, so he'd driven her to her parents' house in Hartlepool and told her that she should probably start looking for another job.

And now he was escorting Walter James into an interview room and trying not to smile too much. Mark Healy might've been charged with the murder but it wasn't over yet.

'I hope this is important, Mr Gardner,' Walter said as he sauntered into the room. 'I have things I need to be doing.'

'I think your campaign can wait.'

'I wasn't talking about the campaign. My daughter has just been murdered,' he said.

'And I'm sorry for your loss,' Gardner said, a feeling of shame coming over him.

'Just get on with whatever farce you feel the need to play out and let me get back to my family.'

Gardner sat down across from Walter, his pity evaporating with every sharp word Walter said. All along he'd been thinking that James was blocking the investigation to help Lauren when in fact it was all about him. As far as Gardner could tell, James had cared very little for his daughter. 'Are you sure you don't want your solicitor present?'

'Quite sure,' Walter said.

'Fair enough. I wanted to ask you about some photographs.'

Walter rolled his eyes. 'I'm aware of the photographs of my daughter. And I'd appreciate it if you dropped it, considering the circumstances. I don't want Lauren's memory besmirched by the filth that piece of shit made of her.'

'That's fair enough. But I wasn't talking about the pictures of Lauren. I was talking about the pictures of you.'

Walter froze for a second, his eyes narrowing. 'What're you talking about?'

'It's come to our attention that some images of you have been circulating. Images showing you involved in activities that might not sit well with voters.'

Walter's face had turned a ripe shade of beetroot. 'I think you should be careful what you say.'

'I just want to know if you're aware of these images.'

'How could I be aware of something that doesn't exist?'

'So you haven't seen them, then? No one's been blackmailing you?' Walter looked like he might blow now and Gardner was revelling in it.

'I'd like to know where you got this nonsense from. Have you actually seen these images?'

'I've been made aware of their existence.'

'So no, then. I think perhaps you should try looking for real evidence instead of grasping at straws. Who told you about these photos?'

'I'm not able to share that information with you, Mr James—'

'Because it's bullshit. You think dragging me in here, making up some twaddle about pictures of me with prostitutes will—'

'Who said anything about prostitutes?'

Walter laughed. 'You know what I mean. You said they were images of activities that could upset voters. I was making a point.'

'Which is?'

'Which is, you'll be lucky to have a job by the end of the day. I have connections in this department.'

'And don't I know it. Who told you about Mark Healy?'

'Excuse me?'

'Mark Healy. You seemed to know a lot about him when I saw you at Lauren's. How did you know he was a suspect? How did you know where he'd been arrested?'

'I do a lot for you and your colleagues. A little quid pro quo isn't too much to ask.'

'It is when it concerns a murder investigation. I want to know where your information is coming from,' Gardner said.

Walter stood up and walked to the door. 'I think you should watch yourself, Gardner. I'll find out where this slander you're clinging to came from and I'll deal with it.'

'Are you threatening a witness?'

'They're not a witness to anything. They're just some little shit trying to bring me down and when I find them they'll wish they'd never been born.' He turned and walked out. Gardner was about to let him go. He'd got what he wanted. He knew the photographs were real and Walter was shaken. But he wanted to keep pulling at loose threads before they were fixed. He caught up with the other man.

'What about that woman you were talking to the night of Ritchie's murder?'

Walter turned around in the empty corridor. He stared for a moment before making his way back to Gardner. 'What about her?'

'I keep trying to contact her but that number appears to be no longer in use. What was her name again?'

Walter's eye twitched. 'I don't recall.'

'See, I don't think you talked to a woman at all. No one from the pub that night remembers seeing you with a woman.'

'Of course they wouldn't. I made damn sure no one saw me.'

'Seems odd, though. That some woman who no one else saw, whose name you don't recall, suddenly gets rid of her phone just after giving you her number. I know we all do things we regret when we're drunk but she could just not answer your calls.'

Walter came right up to Gardner's face, his breath hot on his cheek. 'You are pushing it, DI Gardner. Now, I suggest you stop harassing me and do the job you're paid to do. Mark Healy killed Donoghue and he killed my daughter.'

'Healy hasn't been charged with Ritchie's murder. And there's no evidence to suggest that he did it.'

'He killed my daughter, though,' Walter said. 'So why don't you run along and do something useful to make sure that bastard rots in hell.'

'Oh, I think you've already got that covered,' Gardner said.

'I'd start looking for another job if I were you,' Walter said and walked away. Gardner waited until he'd left before moving. He knew he was onto him and he was going to show his hand sooner or later. Gardner turned to head back to his office and saw Cartwright lurking in the doorway.

'What was that about?' Cartwright asked.

'Nothing that concerns you,' Gardner said and left him standing there.

60

Gardner drove towards Guy James's house and wondered how best to approach the subject. He knew father and son were hardly close but families have a habit of sticking together. But if it was a choice between Lauren or Walter, Gardner wondered if Guy would pick sides and start talking.

He knew he couldn't do any of it on the record, not without Walter and his mates finding out, so anything he discovered was unlikely to stick. But if it got him somewhere further, some evidence that even Hadley couldn't ignore, then it'd be worth it. Of course it could all backfire. Guy might close ranks around Walter and Gardner would be out on his ear. But he was willing to take that risk. Someone had to stand up and do what was right.

Guy opened the door wearing a onesie and holding a can of lager in one hand. When he saw Gardner he sighed and walked away. Gardner followed him inside and the aroma of marijuana hit him like a brick wall. If Guy was concerned, he wasn't showing it.

Gardner sat down amongst the pizza boxes and Xbox controllers. On the floor there was debris from spent Christmas crackers. Guy slumped into a leather armchair and took a swig from his can.

'Are you here to accuse me of killing Lauren?' Guy said, his voice without the usual swagger.

'No,' Gardner said. 'We've already checked your alibi.' Guy nodded and stared into the middle distance. 'I'm sorry for your loss,' he added. 'I truly am.'

'My dad said someone had been arrested,' Guy said. 'Same bloke what did Ritchie.'

'Nothing's been proven yet,' Gardner said, despite Healy being charged for Lauren's murder. As far as Gardner was concerned, nothing *had* been proven. 'I came because I wanted to ask about your dad.'

Guy's lip curled at the mention of Walter. 'What about him?'

Gardner looked at Guy's face. The black eye he'd sported previously was almost gone but there was still a little scab above his eyebrow. 'Who did that to you?'

Guy touched his face and scowled. 'Who d'you think?'

'Your dad?'

'Wanker,' Guy said. 'Reckons he's not bothered about the car, says he doesn't want things to go any further with the police and that and then he does this.' He dropped his hand and stared at Gardner. 'He's a pussy, though. Can't punch to save his life.'

Gardner nodded, feeling sorry for Guy, feeling worse for using it as a way to get Guy on his side. 'It's come to our attention that there were some photographs circulating of him. That Ritchie was going to blackmail him.'

Guy looked up at this. 'What photos?'

Gardner shrugged. 'The kind you wouldn't want leaked. Especially if you're running a political campaign.' Guy almost smiled but caught himself. 'Were you aware of it? Did your dad mention anything?'

'No,' Guy said. 'But he wouldn't tell me about that. Wouldn't get no sympathy.'

'Were you aware of any activities that your dad was involved in, things that he wouldn't want getting out?'

'Shagging about, you mean? He's always done that. I didn't know it was a secret.'

Gardner smiled and thought maybe he could get something from Guy after all.

'Guy,' Gardner said, sitting forward. 'We thought that Ritchie was killed because of photos he took of Lauren. But I don't think his death was anything to do with her. I think it was all about your dad.'

Guy frowned and Gardner thought that for the first time he was actually paying attention. 'What d'ya mean? My dad killed him?'

'We don't know that,' Gardner said, glad he didn't have to spell it out himself. 'Maybe your dad didn't actually do anything himself. But I think he was involved. I think he was aware—'

'Guy?'

Gardner heard the voice and panic swept through him. He stood up as Walter James entered the room. He took one look at Gardner and his face twisted.

'What the hell are you doing here?' Walter said, turning from Gardner to Guy. 'What's he doing here?' Gardner felt his stomach drop and looked at Guy.

'He was just asking about Loz,' Guy said. 'What do you want?'

'You're supposed to be coming with me to sort the funeral. You said you wanted to,' Walter said.

'Yeah, I do.' Guy looked at Gardner.

Gardner took the hint and fastened his coat. 'Thanks for your time,' he said. 'Sorry to bother you.'

Gardner walked past Walter who made no attempt to

move out of the way. Gardner nodded at him and as he left he heard Walter telling Guy to get out of his ridiculous playsuit and start behaving like a member of the James family.

61

Freeman sat by the window watching the world go by, trying not to think about how much she'd fucked up. Darren was sitting on the settee, quiet for the first time since she'd got home. Part of her was relieved that she didn't have to listen to his excuses any more. The other half wished for something to distract her from her own thoughts. She noticed how quiet the streets were. The local kids who'd been out on new bikes on Christmas Day had obviously lost interest already. Or maybe it was just too cold. It looked like it might snow.

She got up to find something to drink and Darren took it as an invitation to speak. 'You think they're going to let him go?' he asked and she stopped in front of him. 'Healy, I mean.'

Freeman rolled her eyes. As if she would be thinking about anyone else. 'I don't know,' she said. 'Let's hope so.'

'You *want* him out?' Darren said, sitting forward, suddenly animated. 'He knows I set him up. He'll tell everyone what happened, that we were involved.'

'You don't think he's already done that?'

'But if he's out—'

'If he's out, he'll come after you. Us. I know. But it's not right. It's not the right thing to do.'

'The right thing?'

'Yeah. I know that's an alien concept to you. To this whole family. But it does exist, Darren. And it might not be what's best for you, but tough. That's how life is.'

'Right, 'cause you're always looking out for what's best for me. Is that what you tell yourself? You got me put away 'cause it was the best thing for me. Being inside with all those fucking psychos was the best thing for me. Making Mam and Dad have to go there and see me like that. That was best for them. Why don't you get off your high horse? I know I fucked up. I know that. I always do. But nothing good is going to happen by letting him out. He might not have killed that guy down there but he's done some pretty shitty things and he deserves to be inside. He deserves it more than I ever did.'

'You don't get to decide that,' Freeman said.

'But you do?'

'I'm not saying that.'

'If Healy gets out, he'll probably kill me. Or maybe I'll just go back to prison. And what about you? What happens to coppers that fuck up?'

'They go to prison. Just like everyone else,' she sighed.

'Great. Maybe Mam and Dad can come and visit us both. Maybe we can even share a cell.'

'Stop it,' Freeman said.

'What? That doesn't fit with your ideal little world? Well maybe you should think about it some more, whether you want to do what's best for us, or for him.' Darren stomped off to the bedroom and slammed the door. Freeman's heart was racing. She wanted to go after him, to tell him to stop being a child, stop being so selfish. But she couldn't. She was too tired to fight any more. She was scared she'd say something she regretted. And she was terrified because part of her believed what he was saying.

The knock at the door startled her. She wiped her face, thinking it would be Gardner. At least he would talk some sense into her, wouldn't let her go down a road she couldn't get back from. Not again.

She opened the door and stopped. It wasn't Gardner. She almost slammed the door in his face, afraid of what would happen.

'Detective Freeman,' he said. 'I think we should have a chat.'

62

Gardner drove home, past boarded-up houses with the occasional inhabited one nestled between them, the residents hanging on just in case the council changed their mind about knocking the whole estate down. Lights from the few occupied houses lit the green in the front where some optimist had tried to build a snowman and some joker had moved the carrot from its face further down, making it a penis. Gardner almost laughed as he stopped at the lights and thought he needed to get some sleep. So much for New Year's with Freeman.

He wasn't really any further forward. He was pretty sure he could get something out of Guy James if he could get him alone. But Walter knew he was on to him and would try to stop anything he did. He knew he was on the right track. Walter James was balls-deep in this. He just didn't know how. He'd previously doubted that Walter could've killed anyone himself, least of all his own daughter. But the conversation that afternoon had changed things. He'd always known the man was an arsehole. Arrogant and manipulative. But maybe it was more than that. He was starting to get the feeling he was dealing with an actual psycho. The only problem was the evidence didn't stack up. Walter was at home when the witnesses saw the man in the alley. But that didn't totally discount him from being the killer. All it meant was someone else was there too. Probably someone supposed to clean up his mess. That would fit with Walter's high and mighty act.

Gardner pulled into the car park and sat in the car, thinking. He'd finally remembered to check where the text to Ritchie from Lauren's phone had been sent from, and it wasn't the club she'd been at. So Lauren hadn't invited Ritchie over that night at all. Not that anyone else seemed to care. They had their man. But what if Walter James had sent the text? He tried to go over the timeline. Obviously James had claimed to be at the office from around eleven thirty until one thirty but what if that wasn't true? What if he had left the office at the back, just as Gardner had considered days ago?

Realising in the chaos of the whole Healy thing he'd forgotten to put the request in for the information on where James's calls were made from that night, he called the office, catching Lawton, and asked her to find out.

If Walter killed Ritchie and got someone to come and tidy up after him, who would he trust? Not Guy. Had to be Peter. Which was why he hadn't bothered going to see him again. He doubted Peter would give him anything he could use. Peter might've been in love with Lauren but maybe there was still some loyalty to James.

Gardner opened the car door and then stopped. Even if Peter Hinde was guilty, he wasn't the one giving Walter information about the investigation. He wasn't planting evidence. There was someone inside helping him too. But who?

He needed some solid evidence, something no one could refute, before he could take it any further. But who was he going to take it to if it was Atherton or Hadley working with Walter James? He needed to tread carefully.

He jogged up the stairs to his flat. As he opened the door he heard voices. He stopped, key in hand, listening. It was a woman. Freeman? What the hell was she doing here?

Gardner walked into the living room and saw Freeman sitting at the table, leaning on her elbows. She looked up as he walked in but didn't speak. Gardner's eyes shifted to the man across from her and he felt a twist in his gut.

'What're you doing in my flat?' Gardner said and Walter James sat back, pulling out another chair.

'Why don't you join us? I think it's time the three of us had a little chat,' Walter said. 'Nicola and I have already caught up.'

Gardner looked back to Freeman. 'You all right?'

She nodded.

'Sit down,' Walter said.

Gardner ignored the chair Walter had pulled out for him and chose to sit beside Freeman instead. He waited for Walter to speak.

'I think you've been a bit naughty, DI Gardner,' Walter said. 'As you pointed out earlier, I *have* been getting information about the case. And I know that you've been keeping some secrets of your own. Withholding evidence, if you like. Very naughty indeed.'

Gardner could feel sweat pooling at the base of his spine. He felt Freeman shift beside him but kept as still as possible, not wanting Walter to know he was rattled.

'When Mark Healy was questioned, he claimed he'd been set up. And why wouldn't he? Don't they all say that? Except Mr Healy claimed that he was being set up by Darren Freeman. Someone who'd apparently been dead for five years. What a silly boy. Pinning it on a dead man. Except he then mentioned a club that this ghost had been haunting of late. And wouldn't you know it, it was the same club my son was at the night of the murder. The same club whose CCTV had been interfered with by someone else called Freeman.' He turned his attention to Freeman for a moment but she ignored him, keeping her eyes on the table. 'So that made some ears prick up.'

'I think we've established that DS Freeman went to the club and looked at the footage. Or attempted to, at least,' Gardner said. 'That's all on record.'

'Ah. But *you* made no attempt at retrieving any of the footage, nor did you disclose your relationship with DS Freeman.'

'As far as we knew there wasn't any footage to find. DS Freeman stated that the CCTV system hadn't been working when she accessed it. Why would I dispute that?'

'Because she'd been covering up for her brother. *That* wasn't in the official report to begin with, was it? Nor was your relationship.'

'What relationship? We worked together once, a few weeks ago.'

Walter smiled and handed Gardner a picture. 'Looks like I'm not the only one being photographed,' he said.

Gardner looked at the image of Freeman and Darren leaving his flat the day before. Another of him and Darren entering the flat the day the investigation began. His stomach tightened. James had been watching him all along.

'Now, I could maybe understand wanting to save a friend from professional embarrassment, but when Mark Healy was claiming to have been set up by Darren Freeman, a man who was apparently dead, at what point did you tell your superiors about your relationship with DS Freeman and the fact that both her and her apparently dead brother were guests at your home?'

'What do you want?'

'I want to know why an officer involved in this investigation is withholding information and, quite possibly, setting up an innocent man not only to help out a friend but also to help himself because he can't do his job properly and find the real killer.'

'This is bullshit,' Gardner said, almost laughing. 'I don't *want* Healy to go down for this. I didn't set Healy up. You did that. You planted evidence. The only person who gains from Healy taking the fall is you.'

'I didn't lead Mr Healy to Ritchie Donoghue's flat. I didn't arrest him.'

'And neither did I.'

Walter took out another photo. One of Freeman sitting outside Donoghue's flat the day Healy was picked up.

'It doesn't look good for you, does it? See, I don't much care what happens to Mark Healy. He's completely insignificant to me. But if the truth comes out, it's not going to be me that people are looking at, is it? So, I think it's time we talked like grown-ups and made a deal. Don't you?'

'Fuck you. You'd rather let Healy go down for this than find the person who really killed your daughter? That sounds to me like you're covering your own back. And I'm going to make sure everyone knows it.'

'Whatever it is you think you know, it doesn't matter. Either it's you two or Healy that's screwed. And I don't really care which it is. I'm just giving you a chance out of professional courtesy.'

'Bullshit. You *need* Healy to go down for this. There's only so much your little buddies can do. You killed Donoghue because he was blackmailing you. You killed him and then maybe because you'd been stupid enough to do it in your daughter's garden, you called someone to clear things up. But Lauren found out, didn't she? She found out about the photos and realised it was you. So you killed her too, to keep her quiet. But by this point Healy was already involved so your little rat planted evidence linking him to Lauren. Made it all nice and neat.'

'I didn't kill my daughter,' Walter said.

'No? So who did? Because it sure as hell wasn't Mark Healy. Why are you so keen to let this go if you didn't kill her?'

'You need to stop talking,' Walter said.

'Or what? You'll go to Hadley and tell him Mark Healy's innocent? Go ahead. It'll make my life easier.'

'What about hers?' Walter said. 'What about her brother?' Walter stood up and leaned across the table, face close to Gardner. 'You cared about her enough to let things get this far. I think you'll do what's right.' He walked to the door and then turned back to face them. 'Think about it. We can all walk away from this happy. It's up to you.'

63

'How the hell did he get to you?' Gardner asked when the door had closed.

Freeman moved from the table and walked over to the window. This wasn't how she'd imagined spending New Year's Eve with him. She looked down at the street, waiting for Walter to get into his car before answering. Someone was letting off fireworks already. 'Someone followed us. When me and Darren left here yesterday, someone was following us.'

'Who? Him?'

'No,' she said. 'I don't know. I didn't see them. I clocked a car halfway home. Didn't see who was driving.'

'Licence plate?'

She shook her head. 'I had more on my mind at that point.' She slumped down onto the settee. 'You know he's right, don't you?'

'About what?'

'Everything. If Healy walks away from this we're both in the shit. Me especially.'

'Come on, Freeman. He's grasping at straws. He knows I'm on to him and he's trying to keep his head above water. That's it.'

'That's it? He knows about me and Darren. He's got proof that we were here, that I was at Donoghue's flat. The only person involved in all this with any real connection to Healy is my brother and if anyone from your team decides they want to start investigating this thing properly, that connection isn't going to be hard to find. Put that together with us staying here with you and I'd say you have yourself a conspiracy. And they might not be able to prove which one of us led Healy to that flat, but that won't matter. We're the only ones who'd gain from setting Healy up.'

'I don't think they can prove Darren led Healy to the flat. I checked the phone box he called from and there are no cameras that close, nothing to show who made that call. And besides, there *is* someone else who gains from setting Healy up. The person who actually killed Donoghue – Walter.'

'But what proof do you have? Nothing.'

'Not yet.'

'Exactly. And he knows that. And if you don't back off and leave this alone he's going to show his hand first and you won't get a chance to find anything on him. You'll be out.'

'So you just want me to sit back and watch him get away with murder?'

'I don't like it any more than you do. But I need to do what's right for me and Darren. I can't let him go back to prison. I can't be responsible for that. Not again.'

'Well, maybe Darren should've thought about prison before he started fucking up my investigation.'

'So you're willing to throw him to the lions. What about me? What about you? You're in this too.'

'Because I was trying to help you.'

'So what's changed? Help me now. Do what he wants. Drop it.'

'I can't do that.'

'Why not? Healy's a vicious bastard. He deserves to be in prison.'

'Not for this.'

'What difference does it make?'

'What're you talking about? Can you actually hear yourself? You want to set him up? You want James to walk away just to please yourself? Lauren James is dead because of us. It's not just about Healy and his fucking civil liberties. It's about justice for her. I pushed and pushed at her and she wasn't even guilty. If I was going to drop it, it should've been then.' He shook his head. 'No. I can't. We caused this so we're not going to do what he says. Not going to do what suits you and Darren.'

Freeman stood up, shoving Gardner. 'Fuck you. Nothing about this is about suiting myself. He wants me to transfer here. He knows *everything* that's gone on and wants me to transfer down here where I can be his little puppet and I can't say no. So which part of this do you think is most pleasing for me?' She turned away, not wanting him to see she was on the verge of tears. 'I told them I found Darren but I've lied about everything else. He can prove we were here, that you knew all along. He can prove I was at that flat. It'll all come out unless we agree to do what he says. He can stop all of it.'

'How?'

'However he usually does all this shit. Has people he pays off to make things disappear.' She sat down again, the fight leaving her. 'He can make all this go away.'

'But at what price? You'd really prefer to be his performing monkey?'

'What I'd prefer is that none of this ever happened. But I guess that's not an option. So from the choices I do have – lose my job and probably go to prison along with my brother, or work for James . . .' She shrugged.

'He killed his own daughter. How can I let that go?'

Freeman looked at him, saw the fire in his eyes. 'You really think he killed her?'

'She had the photos of him. He was desperate not to let them get out. Not only would it destroy his career, it'd go a long way to proving he killed Ritchie.'

'But do you *really* think he killed Lauren?'

'Who else would've done it? She might've been his daughter but she was in his way. She was probably going to go to the police. For all the good that would've done her.' He sighed. 'He might put on this show about being a family man. He might shower his kids with money and gifts, but he doesn't give a shit about them. This man is not normal. He's not like you and me. He *knew* Lauren had nothing to do with Ritchie's death and he stood by and let her take the blame. If Healy hadn't got mixed up in this, Walter James would've happily let Lauren go down for it. I can't let him get away with this,' Gardner said. 'I can't.'

'And we won't. We'll find a way to get to him somehow. Somewhere down the line.'

'When? Once you've paid your debts?'

'I'll think of something,' she said. 'Please. Just let it go. Please. For me. For Darren.'

Gardner looked her in the eye. She knew it was a lot to ask but it wasn't all for her. He'd get to walk away with a clean sheet too, if not a clear conscience.

'I can't do it,' he said.

'Please. I'm begging you. I've tried to make this right but I can't. I came clean about Darren. There's nothing else I can do. We don't know how long he's been watching you. What else he has.' She sighed and put her hand on his. 'I'm sorry I got you into this but I can't see another way out. And you have to know Lauren's death is not on you.' He shook his head. 'It's not. But if Healy walks, we're all fucked. So I'm begging you. Please.'

'I don't really give a shit about Mark Healy. The principle, yes, but . . . But I can't bear to see a man walk free who I know is guilty. Who has the gall to virtually admit as much but still want me to turn a blind eye.'

'Please,' she said again.

Gardner closed his eyes. She could see him weakening and it killed her but she couldn't let it go on. 'Fine,' he said. 'You win.'

'No,' she said. 'He wins.'

64

Saturday, 1 January

Gardner had dragged himself into work despite having had no sleep at all the night before. For once it wasn't the fireworks or the booze that'd kept him up, it was the thought of what he'd agreed to. That he was going to lie down and let Walter James win. He'd made a promise to Freeman that he'd drop it and let Healy take the blame so they could all live happily ever after, but it stuck in his craw.

He'd wondered what would happen if he did play along with James's little game. How would the CPS even take the case on? Surely there wasn't enough evidence to make it likely Healy would be found guilty, not of Ritchie's murder. They had no links between Healy and Donoghue, nothing but Walter's claim that Lauren had ID'd him before she died. They had no physical evidence linking him to the original crime scene, and other than him showing up at Donoghue's flat in the days after the murder, they had no motive whatsoever. That Healy could possibly have been the mystery man in the alley wasn't enough. As Peter had said, 'tall and skinny' could've been anyone. And of course they had the evidence from Peter's car. There was nothing linking Healy to that either. The evidence linking him to Lauren's death was stronger – the cigarette butt, the fibres on the jumper found in his flat. But that was it. Where was the motive? How likely was it that this was even going to go anywhere?

And yet. The magistrate had denied him bail. Maybe Walter James had more connections than they thought.

Gardner looked around the room as Hadley wittered on about the good work done by the whole team. He was surprised to see so many people there on New Year's Day. By the looks of them, many were suffering.

He turned his attention back to Hadley as he was finishing up and thought he saw him wink at Cartwright, who was leaning against a desk, a smug look on his face, despite the bruises on his face yellowing around the edges. Gardner felt sick to his stomach. Cartwright would probably come out of this with a promotion. That's what you get for toeing the line. Gardner was about to excuse himself when Hadley mentioned his name, singling him out for steering the team to a brilliant result. Gardner felt all eyes on him and wondered if everyone else could smell the bullshit as strongly as he could. He didn't want praise. He didn't want any part of it.

His eyes went around the room and found Atherton lurking at the back. His usual self-satisfied stance – back straight, hands behind back – wasn't there today. Instead he stood with his arms crossed, his eyes downcast.

'And I know Mr James would like me to pass on his deepest thanks for treating this matter with sensitivity and respect, and dealing with this difficult time for him and his family in such a professional manner,' Hadley continued.

Gardner kept his eyes on Atherton. Something wasn't right. It wasn't just that Hadley had taken over his role as Suck-up-in-Chief. Every time Hadley mentioned James's name or the 'outstanding result', Atherton pulled a face. Was the guilt getting to him? Or was Atherton actually showing some backbone? Did he believe it was all crap too?

'Thank you, ladies and gents. Now let's get back to what we do best,' Hadley said and the group dispersed. Gardner started following them out when Hadley called to him. 'A word, please,' he said.

Gardner held back. He watched Atherton head for the exit and saw him nod in his direction before leaving him with Hadley. 'What can I do for you, sir?' Gardner said.

'I understand you brought Walter James in yesterday. Asked him some rather personal questions.'

'Some new evidence had come to light.'

'About what? We've got our perpetrator.'

'Maybe.'

'Maybe? You think Mark Healy isn't our killer? You think the scientific evidence linking him to the murder of Ms James is incorrect?'

Gardner bit his tongue. He'd promised Freeman he'd drop it. Besides, if he was going to bring any of this up, it wouldn't be with Hadley.

'Fortunately Mr James isn't filing an official complaint regarding your harassment of him. He understands the frustrations that go with the job. But now that this is over I'm telling you to keep away from him. Any further dealings with him about the case will go through someone else. Do you understand? I don't want you anywhere near him.'

He's the one turning up to my flat, Gardner thought, but he nodded at Hadley. 'Anything else, sir?'

'No,' Hadley said, and Gardner left him to it. He went downstairs and stopped in front of Atherton's office. He was about to knock but something stopped him. Even if Atherton hadn't spent the last few years trying to get in with James, would he really believe Gardner when he told him something was wrong with the case? Atherton had never liked him.

Gardner kept on walking. He'd promised Freeman and Hadley he'd leave Walter James alone. But what harm would it do asking other people a few more questions about the case? Jen still hadn't got the laptop to him, claiming her friend had gone away over New Year, so a few quiet enquiries would have to tide him over until then.

He collared Lawton in the corridor. 'Did you get anywhere with the information on James's phone?'

She shook her head. 'Hadley's keeping tabs on all requests regarding the case. I couldn't get it. Sorry.'

'Shit,' he muttered. 'Okay, thanks anyway.'

He left her to it and got into his car, calling Mrs Earnshaw to check if Kirsty was home. He made sure he had some new photos to show the girl. Nothing wrong with just double checking.

Tell Me Lies

65

Freeman found Walter James at the back of the cafe, in the corner, just where he said he'd be. It was remarkably busy for New Year's Day and Freeman wondered if all of the people there digging into fry-ups were trying to combat the inevitable hangovers or if they just had nowhere else to go. No one even blinked as she made her way through to the back without ordering. She wondered how Walter had found the place. He'd obviously chosen to meet in Blyth where he'd be less likely to be recognised, but it didn't look like the kind of place he'd usually set foot in. Still, at least there were enough people around to put her off trying to discreetly murder him. Something she'd thought of, even if he hadn't.

He stood up as she approached and she rolled her eyes at his faux chivalry. 'Happy New Year, Detective. So glad you called,' he said and took his seat again. She didn't want to sit, didn't want to play nice. She hadn't wanted to meet at all. She'd called and said, 'Fine' to his deal but that wasn't enough for him. He wanted to discuss things. So here they were.

She sat and waited for him to speak but he just stared, smug grin bubbling under the surface. 'What do you want?' she asked, eventually.

'I want to know we're on the same page,' he said.

'I already told you we were. You win.'

'And what about Gardner? Does he feel the same way?'

'He's dropping it,' she said. She knew it pained Gardner to do it but he'd promised he would. And it wasn't like she was doing this because she wanted to. What other choice did she have?

'Are you sure?' Walter asked. 'He seemed reluctant yesterday.'

'No shit. You want him to send an innocent man down. You want him to let you walk away from murder.'

Walter either didn't hear her or just didn't care. Instead he sipped his coffee and studied her. 'I think we're alike, you and me. Self-preservation. That's what got you here, isn't it?'

Freeman wondered how much of that was true. Yes, she'd originally got into all this because of Darren and her guilt about the past. But what about now? Was she making a deal with the devil just to prevent Darren from going back to prison? Or was it more selfish than that? If she wasn't at risk herself, would she still be sitting here?

'I'll start putting things in motion for your transfer. Superintendent Hadley's keen to add you to his team. You've an excellent record, aside from these past few days.'

'What about Blyth? I'm on the verge of a disciplinary.'

'I wouldn't worry about that. Let your superiors know of your intentions to move, for personal reasons. You already have a place in Middlesbrough; the rest doesn't matter. I'm sure they won't put up a fight.'

Freeman felt a pressure bearing down on her. James was probably right that no one would make a fuss. She was a solid detective, did her job well and all that, but she had no real ambition to move on up the ladder, wasn't the media-friendly type. No one would care about her leaving, they'd just ship someone else in who could do the job equally well. And the disciplinary? If they could get away with brushing it under the carpet, so be it. The less paperwork the better. She could be someone else's little problem.

She knew once the ball was rolling she'd be out of Blyth in a month, tops, and that bothered her more than she cared to admit. She'd spent her whole life in Blyth. Spent most of it complaining about Blyth, but still. It was home. It was what she knew. She could be herself, get on with her job without too much interference. What would happen now? She'd be Walter James's little performing monkey. She knew she would never last. She'd do it, for now, to make sure Darren and Gardner were all right. And then she'd walk away.

'What about Healy?' she asked. 'He's going to keep talking. Someone's going to put it all together, sooner or later.'

'I wouldn't worry about him.'

'But if he talks—'

'Don't worry. I'll take care of it,' he said.

66

Just like the last time, Kirsty's mum opened the door before Gardner had knocked. She had oven gloves slung over her shoulder and Gardner could smell something cooking. He noticed the table in the next room was set with fancy decorations and wondered if coming had been a good idea. Just because he had nothing better to do on New Year's Day didn't mean he should barge in on the rest of the world.

He showed Kirsty a new photo. 'Have you seen him before?' he asked, careful not to suggest anything that could influence her response.

Kirsty sighed. She was probably as sick of this as he was. 'No,' she said. 'I don't think so.'

Gardner put the picture of Hadley on the seat beside him. He'd tried to crop the picture as much as possible so there was no uniform, no way to identify him as a police officer. He knew it was unlikely he'd get anything from the girl but he had to check. Whoever was giving Walter information was also planting evidence. And that had to be someone on the team. And whoever it was, it was possible, if they'd been at Lauren's house on the night of Ritchie's murder, that Kirsty might've seen them. She'd been unable to give much information so far but maybe all she needed was to see the face in front of her. The right face.

'What about him?' he said, holding a picture of Atherton. She shook her head again and Gardner realised it couldn't have been Atherton. His ridiculous moustache would've stood out a mile. 'Okay, what about him?'

Kirsty sighed and stared at the picture and then something dawned. She sat up straight. 'Yeah. That's him,' she said.

Gardner felt a fizz of energy, although he knew it was unlikely this testimony would stand up in court. All he wanted from his visit was a clue as to who had been there that night, who had been mopping up after Walter James from the start.

'This is who you saw in the alley?'

Kirsty squinted at the photo and pulled a face. 'Maybe,' she said.

'Maybe? I thought you said it was.'

'No, I mean it was him from the other day.'

'Which day?' Gardner felt his high dropping. She must've recognised him from the investigation.

'The day Lauren was killed,' Kirsty said.

Gardner tried to picture the scene. Had he been there? He was usually hanging around like a bad smell but no, not that night. He was sure of it.

'Do you mean when we showed up? After Mr James called the police?'

'No. I saw him before. He went into her house. I thought it was her boyfriend again at first but it wasn't. I remember thinking she had them queuing up. It was him. Definitely.'

Gardner's heart was racing. It was all making sense. 'Okay, Kirsty, this is important so I need you to think carefully. Did he let himself in? Or did someone open the door to him?'

'Someone opened the door.'

'Was it Lauren?'

Kirsty frowned and looked at the floor. 'I'm not sure,' she said. 'Someone let him in. But I didn't see who.'

'Do you remember what time it was? After her dad showed up?'

Kirsty pulled a face. 'Maybe. I don't know for definite.'

Gardner stood up. He noticed Mrs Earnshaw lurking in the doorway. 'I'm going to need you to make a statement,' he said. 'I'll be back, though.' He raced out of the house and headed to the station.

He found Lawton on the phone, and nodded for her to come and join him. She finished her call and followed him. Gardner found an empty room and pulled her inside.

'What's going on?' she asked.

'I know who's been helping Walter James, who it was in the alley that night.'

Lawton looked at him with wide eyes. 'Who?'

'Cartwright,' he said.

67

Gardner asked Lawton to start looking at the CCTV from the night of Ritchie's murder again, and this time to include anything near Cartwright's address. See if Cartwright was out and about that night. He went into the office and tried to block out the noise coming from ringing phones, conversations between colleagues, and the odd clink of spoons in mugs. He'd already known Cartwright was pandering to Walter at every juncture. Cartwright was straight up the arse of anyone who could give him a leg-up on his climb to the top. But how had Gardner not seen just how much he was really doing?

Gardner had assumed that Atherton or Hadley was running the show and Cartwright was just taking orders, doing what good little boys do. It was clear Walter James was getting special treatment. And that was certainly coming from on high. Cartwright didn't have the sway to let him get away with the things he was doing. But it was Cartwright who was making things fit. The question was, did Hadley know?

Gardner knew that the forensic evidence linking Healy to Lauren's murder had been planted, so Cartwright wasn't averse to seriously stepping over the line. Atherton and Hadley were power-hungry and not disinclined to a bit of quid pro quo, as Walter had put it. But were they willing to actually break the law? Did they know the extent of what was happening with Healy or were they just happy to accept the facts as they saw them without looking any deeper?

Gardner knew that Walter James had a history of involvement in dodgy dealings, in questionable business transactions and occasionally incidents involving violence. Lawton herself had once been first on the scene at a stabbing in a pub where the victim claimed James had been responsible, not directly but possibly had paid someone else to do it. In the end James had never even been questioned. Nothing had ever got near to sticking to him. The only time he'd even been questioned seriously was in a fraud case, which had been quickly dropped and Walter exonerated. The rest was all rumour and hearsay. But Gardner could remember some of those rumours.

Lawton was busy searching through CCTV so he started digging himself, looking for any reports that'd been linked to Walter James, however tangentially. He wasn't concerned with the cases themselves, not with the events or who was eventually convicted. What he wanted to know was which officers had been assigned. And an hour later he'd learned that DC Cartwright had been involved in several in the last two years. He knew Cartwright had a knack of talking Atherton into letting him do just about whatever he wanted. Gardner had always assumed that it'd been Atherton who'd wanted him in; he was, after all, his golden boy. But what if it wasn't Atherton pulling the strings? Was Cartwright covering for Walter James off his own bat?

He went to Lawton. 'Anything?' he said before he'd even reached her desk. Lawton nodded and showed him some screen grabs.

'The camera closest to Lauren's house, the one we saw Guy James on, I got this.' She showed him an image of a man walking at 1.40 a.m., the night of Donoghue's death. The image wasn't spectacular but there was something familiar about it.

'I'm not sure it means anything. Whoever it is wasn't necessarily going to Lauren's from there. He could've turned off this street and gone anywhere.'

'Just see if you can find anything else from the nights of both murders. Near Lauren's and near Walter James's office. If Cartwright was there, he must've returned Peter's car to the office,' he said.

Lawton looked worried. For some reason she had the idea that the police were the good guys all the time. She was idealistic. But between him and Cartwright her bubble was about to burst. 'By the way, Atherton wants to see you,' she said.

'What for?' Lawton looked away. 'Have you been talking to him?'

'I needed to say something. About Healy,' she said.

'What about Healy?'

'Just that I didn't think it was right. I haven't said anything else but I can tell he agrees. You should talk to him about this.' She pointed at the figure on the screen.

'About Cartwright? He's his little pet. If I go to Atherton about this it'll be over before we even find anything.'

Lawton shrugged. 'He wants to see you, anyway,' she said and pulled her coat on. As she did her sleeves rode up and Gardner noticed bruises.

'What happened?' he asked and she pulled her sleeves down.

'Nothing,' she said.

'Dawn,' he said but she didn't turn back.

'Just speak to Atherton.'

68

Gardner made his way to Atherton's office, angry with Lawton for going to the boss behind his back. But then he'd been hiding things from her throughout the investigation so who was he to talk? And maybe she was right. He'd seen how Atherton had reacted this morning in the briefing. Maybe her going to him first would make things easier. If it wasn't only *him* having doubts, then maybe Atherton would have to act. But how was he going to react to what Gardner had to tell him? It was one thing to say he thought they had the wrong man, but quite another to say he suspected Walter James was involved. And now he had to bring Cartwright into it too. Was Atherton even going to believe him, never mind do something about it?

He knocked on Atherton's door and got the usual 'Enter'. He went inside and closed the door behind him. Whichever way this went, it wasn't something he wanted the rest of the station listening in to.

'DI Gardner. Take a seat,' Atherton said and took his usual position by the window. Gardner wondered if the man ever used the chair on his side of the desk. 'Your girl, Lawton, came to me earlier. Has some doubts about the investigation. Are you aware of that?'

'Yes, sir,' Gardner said.

'And?'

'And I think she's right.'

Atherton raised an eyebrow. 'You don't think we should've charged Mark Healy, despite the evidence?'

'No, I don't. The evidence we have on Healy isn't that much stronger than what we had on Lauren James or Peter Hinde. The only difference is, no one cares enough about Healy to make a fuss about charging him.'

'So you think Ms James was guilty. And her death was what? Revenge?'

'No,' Gardner said. 'I don't think she was guilty. I admit I did for a while but not any more. I think the same person that killed Donoghue killed her too.'

'And who do you think this person is?'

'Walter James,' Gardner said and watched Atherton's face carefully. He wondered if he should continue with what he knew, or thought he knew. Whether Atherton would back him or if he'd be making things worse than they already were.

Atherton sighed and finally, possibly for the first time in his career, took a seat in front of Gardner. 'You realise that by going down this path you'll be risking your career? Walter James has a lot of sway with this department.'

'Even if people find out he's a murderer?' Gardner said.

'*If* people find out. James has money and powerful allies. Things that go a long way these days.'

'You're not disagreeing with me, though.'

Atherton rubbed his hand over his face, smoothing down his moustache. 'What do you have on him?'

Gardner wondered if this was a set-up, if Walter James had sent Atherton in to find out what Gardner had, if he was still looking into him. But he didn't have much choice other than to confide in Atherton. He couldn't do this by himself. He needed the information on James and maybe Atherton could help him. He'd seen the way Atherton had reacted to Walter James's humiliation of him at Lauren's house. He'd just taken it, but maybe not quite as easily as they'd all thought. Maybe he had a bit more spine than he was given credit for. 'Not a great deal, not so far. But I haven't joined up all the dots yet. I need to find out where James made his late-night call from. Lawton tried to get the information but Hadley blocked it. I don't think he was at his office, I think he was at Lauren's. I think he went there, that he texted Ritchie and then called someone to come and help him once he'd killed him. Our eyewitnesses saw a man in the alley behind Lauren's house.'

'A man that didn't match James's description.'

'Right. I think James had gone by then. Whoever was in the alley was sent to tidy up. James left before our witnesses showed up. He was tucked up in bed at the time we were looking for someone.'

'Why would he involve someone else?'

'Because someone had to clean things up. Walter James couldn't be seen doing that, someone would recognise him. But at the second murder, James was the one to call it in. He had a reason to be there.'

'You can't really believe he'd kill his own daughter.'

'I think he'd do whatever was necessary,' Gardner said.

Atherton looked horrified. 'Why?'

'Because she knew he killed Donoghue. She had something that proved his motive. Some photographs and tapes that he didn't want getting out.'

'And you have these photographs?'

'Not yet. I'm working on it. Jen Worrall had them in her possession, had planned sending them to me.'

'The envelope from the house,' Atherton said.

'Right. She deleted the copies from her hard drive and passed the laptop to a friend to cover her tracks. She's trying to get it back.'

Atherton stood again and turned his back to Gardner, who wondered if he'd shared too much. 'We need to tread carefully,' Atherton said after a few moments. 'And we need to find out who this second man is.'

Gardner tried to weigh up his options, figure out whether he should spill to Atherton. He sighed and decided, what the hell, he'd come this far. 'I think I know who it is,' he said, and Atherton turned back and raised another eyebrow. 'Craig Cartwright.'

69

Freeman threw her keys onto the table and Darren looked up from the settee. She could see he was trying to judge her mood, just like they used to do with Mam when they were kids. God, she hated the thought that she was turning into her mother.

'It's done,' she said and sat down beside him, shoving his feet over to make some room.

Darren frowned at her. She'd told him about the deal the night before. He'd been there when Walter James arrived, introducing himself as if he were canvassing for votes. Prick. She'd told Darren she had to go back to Middlesbrough and he'd wanted to go with her but she'd said he'd done enough damage already and should stay put. She'd regretted it on the drive down to Middlesbrough but hadn't called to apologise. That would've been too weird for both of them. Apologies were inferred in their family. Just like saying 'I love you'. No one wanted to freak anyone else out with overt displays of emotion.

'So you're going to, like, move to Middlesbrough?' Darren said.

'Looks like,' she said.

'Are you going to live with Gardner?'

She pulled a face. 'No. Why would I do that? There're other houses in Middlesbrough.'

'Yeah, I know, I was just . . .' He stared at the TV for a minute. 'Are you all right with it?'

'Am I all right?' Freeman said. 'Of course I'm not fucking all right. I'm going to spend the rest of my working life doing favours for that piece of shit. I'm going to have to leave Blyth. I'm going to have to move house, which is a total pain in the arse.'

'I thought you didn't like Blyth. Or this place?' he said.

'I don't,' she said. 'But that's not the point. Why do you think I haven't moved before now? Moving is a nightmare. Getting a new job is a nightmare.'

'But you've got a job. He's sorting it, right?'

Freeman jumped up. 'You don't get it, do you?'

'I do get it. It sucks. It sucks and it's my fault. But you didn't have to agree to it. You could've told him to piss off.'

'Oh, sure. And then we'll all go to prison. That'd be better.'

'Come on, Nicky. I would've owned up to it if you'd let me. They know I'm alive. How long's it gonna be before they work out what happened? For all you know this guy will screw you over anyway. I was the one who told Healy to go there. I would've told them that. I still will.'

'It's too late, Darren. Sending Healy to that flat is just a part of it. I broke the law for you. I wiped those tapes. I lied to my boss. Gardner's been covering our arses too. This isn't just about you any more. Why can't you get that through your thick skull?'

She walked away, going into the bathroom and slamming the door. She slid down onto the floor and dug her nails into her palms. Why had she let it get so out of hand? Everything she touched turned to shit. She might as well work for James. She wasn't helping anyone else.

The gentle tap at the door made her want to cry. 'Go away,' she said. He knocked again and tried the door but she kept her back pressed against it.

'I'm sorry, Nic,' Darren said. 'I really am.'

She closed her eyes and then moved away from the door. Darren came in and sat beside her on the tiled floor. She could see the tumbleweeds of dust behind the toilet and thought, *I'm going to have to clean up before I leave.*

'What're you going to do?' she asked him and he shrugged. 'Please tell me you're not going to go back to Newcastle. To *her.*'

Darren shook his head. 'I don't know.'

'Darren . . .'

'I know,' he said, sighing. 'She's not always like that, though. We've been together for a while. She helped me get better.'

Freeman almost started arguing, wanting to know how the lying little cow had helped. How someone capable of stealing money for coke and letting you take the fall for it was really helping. But Darren's face made her stop. He clearly had feelings for the girl, whether she deserved them or not.

'I guess we're over,' he said. 'But I have to tell her to her face. I'll have to get my stuff.'

'What about the guys from the club? They'll still be looking for their money,' Freeman said.

'Yeah,' Darren said. They sat in silence for a few minutes and Freeman rested her head on his shoulder.

'You could come and stay with me, at my new place. Just 'til you figure things out,' she said.

'Cool.'

'I suppose we should let Mam and Dad know you're back too.'

'Yeah,' he said. 'You know she'll freak out about me living with you, right?'

'I know,' Freeman said and tried not to smile. 'She's already going to be pissed off that I didn't show up for dinner.'

70

Gardner waited for Atherton to smile and show his hand, letting him know he'd just made a terrible mistake by confiding in him. Or to blow up and berate him for accusing his golden boy. But Atherton just stood there, his face losing colour by the second.

'Cartwright?' he said.

'Yes, sir.'

'I knew he was close to James. Wanted to be in his inner circle. But this . . . ?'

'Pardon me for saying, sir, but you've been known to rub shoulders with him too.'

Atherton waved a hand, dismissing him. 'Trying to get brownie points. I'm not the kind of officer Walter James really favours. There's nothing I could offer him that he doesn't already have.'

Gardner noted the resignation in his voice. 'But Cartwright? What's he got to offer?'

'I don't know. Blind loyalty? Craig's ambitious. I tried to take him under my wing but it appears my wings weren't big enough.'

'What about Hadley? Is he . . . ?'

Atherton looked nervous. 'Hadley and James have things to offer each other and Hadley will go to great lengths to make sure his chum isn't tarnished by any of the many brushes he comes up against. But this? I don't believe he'd be in on this. Not knowingly. And Cartwright? You really think he's involved as deeply as you said?'

'He fits the description of the man in the alley that night. He was there the night Lauren died. The neighbour saw Cartwright go into her house.'

'And she's sure of that?'

'I think so. She ID'd him from a photo without prompt.'

'So you think Walter James killed his own daughter and had Cartwright come and clean things up for him?'

'That's my belief, yes. Only the witness can't remember whether she saw Cartwright at Lauren's before or after James arrived.'

'Meaning?'

'Well, she didn't see who let Cartwright in so it's possible James got there earlier than he claimed. Because as deep as I think Cartwright is in this, I can't see him killing James's daughter on demand. I think Walter went over there, fought with Lauren over the photos and things got out of hand. Then he called Cartwright up for help, same as with Donoghue's murder.'

Atherton sighed. 'What else?'

'Lawton's looking for more CCTV footage. We're trying to trace his footsteps both nights.'

'All right. I want to speak to him. Find him.'

'No,' Gardner said and received a warning look. 'We don't have enough yet, just the word of a teenager who might well have been drunk at one of the scenes. All we'll do is alert Cartwright and James that we're on to them. Let's wait and see what Lawton comes up with. Can you authorise getting Cartwright's phone records? And the cell site data from James's phone?'

Atherton nodded. 'Leave it with me.'

Gardner nodded back and left Atherton alone, hoping he wasn't about to blow the whole thing.

71

Freeman drove towards her parents', her mind somewhere else completely. She rarely went to their house these days but it was automatic, finding her way there; a muscle memory buried deep. Darren sat beside her, shuffling in his seat, no doubt trying to think of a good opening line for when their mam opened the door. Or maybe just a good excuse not to go.

Freeman had decided that it needed to be done now, while they were both still free, before she'd have to say, 'Look, Mam, we're in a bit of trouble.' At least now maybe her mam would just be happy Darren was back. And maybe by her bringing him there some of that happiness would bounce back onto her. She wasn't sure how pleased they'd be that no sooner was he back then he was planning to leave again, to go and live in Middlesbrough with the enemy.

As Freeman pulled up outside her parents' house she felt dread sweeping over her. What *were* they going to say? Mam and Dad might be overwhelmed by happiness to start with but sooner or later the questions would start. And most of that was on Darren. But they'd want to know why he chose to go to Freeman first instead of them. They'd want to know how long he'd been back and why she hadn't told them sooner. Some way or another she'd be to blame for something. That was par for the course.

She looked at Darren who was staring at the old house with something akin to wonder. How was he feeling about this? He'd chosen to walk away from it all – had he regretted that? Or was he just regretting coming back?

'Shall we?' she asked.

They walked slowly up the drive and Freeman noticed the wreath on the door that'd been in use for as long as she could remember. It'd seen better days but her mam refused to throw it away. She couldn't remember if it had been made by one of them at school or if it was shop tat. Either way it was probably going to outlive them all.

She hoped neither her mam nor dad were looking out the window. She didn't want them keeling over before she and Darren'd even got inside. Darren stopped halfway up the drive, Freeman only noticing when she was at the door. She started to go back to him.

'Maybe you should go first,' he said. 'Sort of, like, warn them or something. Or prepare them.'

She got hold of his jacket and pulled him to the door. 'It's not *Surprise Surprise*. Let's just get it over with.' She knocked and remembered knocking on the doors of every house in the street, running away before the neighbours answered. Her and Darren leaving Mark lagging behind, having to explain himself. Darren might've been the youngest, and she might've been the only girl, but it was Mark who was always left out of their games, always left behind. She looked at Darren. He hadn't changed much from being that kid and she was happy he was there. She didn't want him to leave again, couldn't take it again. If the shit hit the fan she knew that she'd take the blame. If necessary, she'd tell them she was the one who'd set Healy up. They'd just got Darren back; there was no way she could let him go again. No matter what it took.

Freeman took hold of Darren's hand, squeezing it as she heard the key turning in the lock, someone muttering behind the door. Darren looked at her as if she were mental and pulled away like she had fleas. She tried not to laugh at his puzzled and disgusted face.

And then the door opened and her mam was standing there, tea towel in chapped hands. She looked at Freeman first. Surprised to see her, almost giving her a smile before catching herself. And then she saw Darren and for a split second she looked like she couldn't quite place him, like she was trying to remember his name. And then the colour drained from her face. Her hands came up to her mouth, shaking, in slow motion.

'Hi, Mam,' Darren said and Lorraine Freeman let out a sound like a wounded animal.

Freeman stepped onto the doorstep, taking her mam's arm, trying to lead her inside. She had no idea how to handle this but the one thing she did know was that her mam wouldn't want to do this in public. Darren was just standing there, hands in pockets. As Freeman tried to get her inside she pulled away, reaching out to her youngest son, touching his face.

Freeman stepped away. Maybe she didn't need to think of anything to say yet.

'Jesus flipping Christ.'

Freeman turned and saw her dad standing there, staring at Darren too, a grin forming on his whiskered face. 'Hi, Dad,' she said and he acknowledged her with a brief pat on the shoulder before stepping forward and putting Darren in a headlock, rubbing his hair like he was a child.

'Behave, Dad,' Darren said, trying to pull away. Freeman, Darren and their dad stood, smiling at each other, and then looked to their mam. But she wasn't smiling with them. Tears ran down her face, her chin quivering. 'Mam,' Darren said, reaching out for her. But she turned away and ran down the hall, through the kitchen and out the back door. The three of them stood there, silent, the sound of a car going past outside.

After a few moments in which no one moved, Freeman sighed. 'I'll go then, shall I?' Neither Darren nor her dad said anything so she followed her mam outside. She found her at the end of the garden, sitting on the old wooden bench beneath the apple tree.

'You all right?' Freeman asked, knowing it was a fairly stupid question.

Her mam wiped her face with one of the many hankies she had stuffed up the sleeve of her cardigan. 'How long have you known?'

'A couple of days,' she said. She was going to add 'give or take' but decided to leave it. Lorraine looked like she'd been slapped.

'Days?' she said.

'I'm sorry we didn't come sooner. Things were . . . difficult.'

'Difficult?' Lorraine said. 'Difficult! Difficult is going to visit your son in prison. It's seeing him drink himself into oblivion and listening to him tell you he wishes he was dead. It's thinking your boy is dead for five years.' She stood up and slapped Freeman across the face. The cold air made it sting more than it should've. Or maybe it was just because it came from her. Or because, at that moment, Freeman felt she was right to do it. Freeman held back her tears. She didn't have the right to cry.

'I'm sorry,' she said.

Her mam turned her back to her but Freeman could see her shoulders shaking. She didn't know what to say any more. She could hear a helicopter somewhere in the distance. Probably the police looking for some little bastard. Maybe some little bastard like Darren. She was about to turn and go back to the house, get Darren or her dad to come out and try their luck. But she stopped. She needed to stick it out. Needed to do what she should've done years ago.

She moved forward, stepping in front of her mam. Lorraine sniffed, tried not to look quite so pitiful in front of her. But that was the problem with this family. No one let anybody in.

'I'm sorry,' Freeman said again. 'For everything.' She hugged her mam, pulling her head towards her, resting it on her shoulder. She could feel Lorraine's body, tense and cold, but after a while she softened. Let herself be looked after.

Eventually Lorraine pulled away.

When Freeman had managed to coax her mam back inside, her dad and Darren looked like they'd caught up already, as if the last five years had never happened. Darren was trying to look interested as their dad went on about the bowls club and how their next-door neighbour was at war with *his* neighbour over putting up a fence. But as soon as Freeman and Lorraine came through the door, the chit-chat died down and the house took on another awkward atmosphere.

Lorraine was staring at Darren, her face still splotchy with tears and anger. Freeman tried to think of something to say but her dad beat her to it.

'Why don't you come and get your present from Mark and the family, Nic?' he said and led Freeman out of the kitchen, closing the door behind him. He put his hand on her cheek and rested his head on hers. 'She'll come around,' he said.

From the living room, despite her dad watching *Dad's Army* at high volume, she could still hear her mam's voice. She couldn't hear exactly what was being said but at least she was talking. Every now and then she caught her dad trying to listen in too but once he'd noticed her noticing he'd feign innocence and force a laugh out towards the TV before shaking the tin of Quality Street at her.

A couple of hours later, Darren and their mam emerged. She was no longer red faced and had the clipped tone Freeman had grown up hearing. 'So,' Lorraine said. 'There're plenty of leftovers since none of you bothered to let me know if you were coming or not. It'll be about forty minutes so one of you can get off your bum and help me lay the table.'

Freeman watched her mam walk away, trying not to smile, trying to keep up the pretence of being Lorraine Freeman. And for the first time in a long time she felt happy. Actual, proper happiness. She just tried not to think about how long it'd last.

72

Monday, 3 January

Gardner had spent the weekend unable to settle. He'd tried staying at home but knew he needed to keep at it so had spent most of his time at the office going over and over all the evidence, searching desperately for anything that pointed to Walter and Cartwright.

Atherton had pulled a lot of strings and by mid-morning had hold of Cartwright's phone records. For someone so close to James, there had been very little contact between them. None, in fact. There had to be another phone and Gardner would put money on what the number would be. Walter James's mystery woman from the pub was likely to be none other than Craig Cartwright. The fact that the call had been made nowhere near his office either made it clear James had been lying to them from the start. But they were going to have to dig a lot deeper to find a link between Cartwright and that phone. In the meantime they had his landline records, which again had no calls from Walter James himself. What they did show was a call an hour and a half before Walter called 999 to report Lauren's death. The call lasted just over a minute and they'd traced it back to a phone box in the town centre, opposite a Tesco Express who had kindly provided them with CCTV footage showing Walter James using the phone at that time.

They were in business.

* * *

Atherton led Cartwright down the corridor and Cartwright made a joke about some bullshit or other that Atherton pretended to laugh at. But once Cartwright saw Gardner waiting there the grin disappeared. Atherton indicated for Cartwright to go into the interview room and he frowned but did as he was told.

'What's up?' Cartwright asked as they closed the door behind them.

'Take a seat, Craig,' Atherton said and Cartwright pulled out a chair, his face changing as Gardner and Atherton took their places across from him.

'What's going on?' he asked.

'We've been looking over some of the evidence in the Donoghue and James cases,' Gardner said.

'Why? We've got our guy.'

'Well,' Gardner said. 'We've got *a* guy.'

'You're friends with Walter James, aren't you, Cartwright?' Atherton said and Cartwright lost a little colour from his cheeks.

'I wouldn't say that, sir.'

'Oh. Perhaps I got the wrong end of the stick. I thought I'd seen you at a number of his functions.'

'Networking. Doesn't make us friends.'

'You've been very good to him throughout his ordeal this last week or so, though.'

'Because of his support of the department. You know as well as I do, sir, that Superintendent Hadley doesn't want to rock the boat.'

'Very true. Which is why we're keeping this to ourselves for now.'

'Keeping what to ourselves?' Cartwright asked, hands knotted in front of him.

'We suspect Walter James was involved in the murders of Ritchie Donoghue and Lauren James,' Gardner said.

Cartwright licked his lips and looked back at Atherton, maybe hoping his old mucker would start laughing and tell him he'd been had. 'Why would you think that?'

'Certain evidence has come to light,' Gardner said, 'that places suspicion on Mr James on the nights of both incidents.'

'What sort of evidence? You think he killed them?'

Gardner shrugged. 'That remains to be seen.'

Gardner could almost see Cartwright's arse cheeks clench. 'What about Healy?' Cartwright asked.

'That's still a possibility. We're not ruling out someone else assisting Mr James.'

'Who?'

Gardner allowed himself the briefest of smiles and watched Cartwright squirm. The little shit didn't know if they were on to him or not and he was panicking.

'Walter James made a call the night of Ritchie's murder. He claimed it was to a woman he met in the pub but we've been unable to trace her and the phone's no longer in use. We think it's likely that whoever that phone belonged to was his accomplice,' Gardner said.

'Why?' Cartwright asked. 'Have you found the phone?'

'Not yet,' Atherton said. 'But there's something else. The night of Lauren's death, Walter made another call.' Cartwright shuffled in his seat, his jaw muscles working overtime. 'We have CCTV images of him going into a phone box and making a call that lasted about a minute. Nothing wrong with that, although you do wonder why a man like James would go to a call box. He's got a mobile. He was close to his office; he could've used the phone there.'

Gardner and Atherton said nothing for a while, waiting for

Cartwright to let that sink in. He'd know that they'd have already traced the call, know what was coming.

'Yeah, he called me. Asking about the case. Wanted to know why Healy had been released.'

'And what did you tell him?' Atherton asked.

'Nothing. Just said it was procedure. We didn't have enough to hold him.'

'Okay,' Gardner said and looked at Atherton. They'd discussed it beforehand, decided not to show Cartwright everything just yet. Wait it out, see how he reacted. They all sat in silence for a minute or so, the muffled sounds of life going on at the other side of the door. Cartwright was the first to break.

'Am I being accused of something here?' he asked, trying to force a laugh.

'We just want to know about James,' Gardner said. 'You're pretty cosy with him.'

'We're all cosy with him,' Cartwright said, pointedly looking at Atherton.

'I'm not,' Gardner said. 'I wouldn't piss on him if he was on fire.'

'And that's what this boils down to, isn't it? You don't like him, or me, so you're on a witch-hunt. And you're just going to sit there and let it happen?' he said to Atherton.

'Watch yourself, Cartwright,' Atherton said.

'We've got the man who did this in custody. No one else seems to have a problem except him,' he said, jabbing his finger at Gardner. 'And I can't believe you're listening to him over me.'

'I don't listen to anyone,' Atherton said. 'I'm quite capable of forming my own decisions.'

'So you really think I'm involved in all this? You're taking his word over mine? It's not the first time he's fucked over another copper, is it? You should watch your back, sir, or who knows, maybe he'll be accusing you next.'

'That's enough,' Atherton said. 'No one's accused you of anything. Yet.'

Cartwright looked at Atherton like a child who's been told off. Atherton had always let him do whatever he wanted, given him a long leash, and now he was hanging himself with it.

'I don't think Mr James had anything to do with this. And all I've done is my job. I kept him happy, just like Hadley told me to. Doesn't make me guilty of anything. You got any proof other than this phone call? No. Because there's nothing to prove.'

'You're getting kind of excited there, Cartwright,' Gardner said.

'No shit. You're accusing me of being involved in two murders.'

'Who said that? It's Walter James we're interested in.'

Cartwright shook his head. 'Have you spoken to him? Has he said anything?'

'About what?'

'About me.'

'Why would he?'

Gardner listened to Cartwright's heavy breath and knew that he'd been right. Cartwright was in up to his neck. They just needed a little more time to prove it.

'I think that'll do,' Atherton said and nodded to the door. Cartwright stood up and shoved the chair back towards the table, glaring at Gardner as he left.

'So, what now?' Gardner asked. 'Should I bring James in, see if we can rattle him too?'

'Not yet,' Atherton said. 'I want to speak to Mark Healy first.'

Gardner felt his body tense up. 'What for?'

'Because I want to know his part in this. If he's been set up to cover for Walter James I want to know how and why. He must've had some link to either Donoghue or James to start with and I want to know what that link is.' Atherton stood up, folding his glasses and sliding them into his pocket. 'And another thing. Darren Freeman.'

Any good feeling Gardner had had in toying with Cartwright evaporated. Maybe he should've left things alone.

'It might be worth bringing him in. See what he knows about all this. See if your friend DS Freeman has tracked him down.' He slapped Gardner on the shoulder. 'We'll catch them,' he said and left the room, leaving Gardner wondering just who it was that would get caught.

73

Freeman watched Gardner walk across the car park, shoulders hunched in a pointless attempt to keep the rain at bay. She wasn't sure why she'd come, why she'd decided to tell him in person. Maybe because she needed him to tell her things were going to be all right. That everything was going to work out and that coming to Middlesbrough was going to be the best thing she ever did. She knew it'd all be bullshit, but she still wanted to hear it.

He climbed into the car, shaking some of the rain from his face. 'I can't stay too long. I'm in the middle of something. But Atherton's talking about bringing Darren in.'

'Yeah, well, we both knew that was bound to happen,' she said. 'He knows the story we're telling so as long as James keeps his end of the bargain we might be okay.' She sighed. 'I just wanted to let you know that the transfer's going through. I should be in Middlesbrough in a few weeks.'

'That's good.'

'Is it?'

'Come on, Freeman. Walter James is full of shit. He might be able to pull strings and get you here but you're not going to be doing favours for him. He's never going to reveal what he knows about you and Darren because it'd mean opening a can of worms that he won't want to let out.'

'Maybe,' she said. 'But it's always going to be hanging over me.'

'Don't worry about James,' he said before his phone started ringing. 'Excuse me.'

Freeman half listened to Gardner's conversation, sitting looking out over the car park at people coming in and out of the building. *These are the people I'll be working with*, she thought, and wondered how many were arseholes. How many were on the take, how many were in Walter James's pocket. At least Gardner would have her back.

'When did it happen?' Gardner said, his voice tense. She tried to hear what was being said on the other end but couldn't hear over the sound of the rain. 'It was James, I know it. Shit,' he said, slamming his fist against the dashboard.

Freeman listened to him. Whatever had happened had pissed him off. And whatever had happened had to do with Walter James. Gardner hung up and turned his head away, staring out of the window. 'What's going on?' she asked.

'Mark Healy's dead.'

Freeman looked at the back of Gardner's head, the words sinking in. She could feel the world closing in on her.

'Another prisoner attacked him last night,' he said, finally facing her.

'Why?'

Gardner pressed his fingers to his eyes. 'I think they wanted him out of the picture so he couldn't talk any more. They're trying to end it.'

'Who?'

'Walter James and Craig Cartwright. One of my DCs. We think he was involved somehow. Helping James.'

Freeman felt a wave come over her; she thought she was going to be sick. 'So you're still investigating?'

'Come on, Freeman, that's not the point right now, is it? A man is dead.'

'I know that! But you promised to leave it. I made a deal with him on the basis that you were dropping it. You think he's just going to sit back and let this go now? He's going to tell them what I did. He's going to tell them we set Healy up. Fuck, he can probably even make it look like I got Healy killed for all I know.' She could feel her breath coming too fast, too shallow. Her lungs were burning.

'That's not going to happen,' Gardner said. 'I'm building a case against him.'

'After you promised you'd drop it! Why didn't you just let it go?' She could feel her pulse in her neck, knew she was out of line but couldn't stop. 'If you'd left things alone Healy wouldn't be dead right now. Lauren James might not be on you but Mark Healy sure the fuck is.'

Gardner looked at her and she knew what he was thinking. What she was thinking too. That it was bullshit. That this was on her, not him.

'Go home,' he said.

She watched him get out of the car, grateful at least that he hadn't been truthful about whose fault it was, and wondered when it was going to stop. She was the one who'd caused Healy to be tangled up in this. She was the one who'd fucked up from the start, deleting those files – not Gardner, not Darren. Maybe she'd been wrong to agree to James's terms, but she'd been scared. Now she'd seen just how far James would go, though, now she was really frightened.

74

Gardner spent the next few hours trying to put Freeman out of his mind. He knew he'd been wrong to go behind her back but it had to be done and if she couldn't agree with that then so be it. But her accusation about Healy's death being on him? He knew she was lashing out, knew that she blamed herself. Still, maybe he *was* partly to blame. He'd wanted to keep searching, not just to get to Walter James, but to prevent an innocent man going to prison. And now that man was dead. If he hadn't pushed Walter James, hadn't taunted him, maybe Healy would still be alive. But if he'd never agreed to help Freeman and her brother, Healy would never have got caught up in James's games. He couldn't get away from that. If he'd just done what was right from the start.

Between him, Atherton and Lawton, they'd searched through most of the prisoners' records, trying to find any link between one of them and Walter James. It'd been a long day and his eyes were starting to blur. But he knew it was in there somewhere.

The prison knew who'd actually killed Healy. A man named Alan May. That was simple. Although he wasn't talking about why he'd done it. It wasn't the first incident he'd been involved in so no one was looking too hard at a motive. No one but them. But so far they hadn't found any links. It had been suggested that it'd been random. Just another violent incident in prison. But Gardner knew there was nothing random about it.

'Keep looking,' Gardner said to Lawton and grabbed his coat. He wasn't sure where he was going, just knew he needed to get out for a while and maybe driving around would help him think. What they had so far didn't prove anything. They could link Cartwright and Walter but only that they'd been talking, that Cartwright had passed on information. That was it. The CCTV footage they had from the areas close to Lauren's house and Walter's office wasn't clear enough to prove it was Cartwright. He'd been clever enough to cover most of his face and a man walking about with a hat pulled down low and a scarf over his face in December wasn't suspicious. And then something clicked. The man who'd been on Ritchie's street, before and after Guy James showed up. It was the same man, the same clothes, he'd swear to it. He called Lawton and asked her to check. Although, unless they could prove that man was Cartwright, they still had little. Just one man in three areas of interest.

Gardner found himself driving towards Cartwright's flat. He didn't know what he thought he would do there but he pulled up across the street and turned the engine off. What was he missing? He sat for a while looking around the street and then he noticed the pizza shop he was parked in front of. He could see security cameras above the counter.

He pulled out his phone and called Lawton again. 'Did we check the cameras from the pizza shop across the street from Cartwright's flat? Princess Pizza?'

'I don't think so,' she said. 'I don't remember seeing them on the list of registered CCTV.'

'Maybe it's time we did, then,' he said and hung up.

'Can I help?' the man in the takeaway asked, putting his newspaper down as Gardner went in. They were hardly rushed off their feet.

Gardner showed his ID and the man recoiled a little. 'Your cameras,' Gardner said, nodding above him. 'Are they working or for show?'

The man scratched his head. 'Working,' he said. 'We haven't had them very long, haven't got around to registering.'

'Do they point out on to the street?'

The man looked up as if he'd never thought about it before. 'I don't know,' he said. 'Hang on.' He disappeared out the back and another, older man, appeared.

'We've had our windows put through many times. Always trouble out there,' he said and let Gardner behind the counter, beckoning for him to follow.

75

Tuesday, 4 January

'What was the phone call to Cartwright about?' Atherton asked but Walter just continued with his tirade of abuse, clinging desperately to what little dignity he had left. All he'd done so far was rant and rave and demand that Superintendent Hadley be summoned immediately. But when he realised that wasn't happening he turned his attention to Atherton.

'What gives you the right to bring me in here like this? You're nothing, Atherton. Pathetic. An arse-kissing nobody who wants power but doesn't have the balls to follow through and grab it.'

Harry Warren looked slightly uncomfortable at his client's outburst but kept his mouth shut. James had already made it abundantly clear that he was in control of the situation. Having Harry there was merely a formality for him. But as it was the first time he'd even considered having a solicitor present, Gardner took it that James was rattled.

Gardner watched Atherton take the accusation, his face barely changing, despite the fact that what James was saying was pretty true. Gardner's perception of Atherton had changed somewhat over the last couple of days, but it didn't wipe away the memory of his superior's struggle to get to the top.

'And you,' Walter said, turning his ire on Gardner. 'Why don't you tell us about your friend Freeman. See if you still have the moral high ground then.'

Gardner felt his pulse quicken but kept his mouth closed. He could see Atherton's eyes flash his way at the mention of Freeman's name but he was smart enough not to let Walter know he was the slightest bit curious.

'We just want to know about Cartwright,' Atherton said.

'What about him?' Walter asked.

'You called him the night Lauren was killed. What did you talk about? And why did you go to a phone box instead of using your own phone?'

'My battery had died.'

'Okay. So what was so important to discuss that you had to find the nearest phone?'

'We talked about the case. He'd been giving me information.'

'About Mark Healy?'

'About the case in general. About how you let a known killer go,' he said.

'So Cartwright was just updating you. He do that a lot? Favours for you?'

'Not really.'

'And yet you called him.'

'Because I could trust him to give me the information I wanted. He has no qualms about opening his mouth.'

'Were you aware Mark Healy was killed in prison?' Gardner asked.

'Yes.'

'How do you feel about that?'

'I don't really have any feelings about it. Not my problem.' Walter stared at Gardner without blinking. 'Next question.'

'We've got evidence that Cartwright was out the night Ritchie Donoghue was killed. And we also have a witness who said he was at Lauren's house the night she died. Was he there to clean things up for you? Maybe plant a bit of evidence? It does make me wonder what he's trying so hard to cover up.'

'I'd like a moment with my client,' Harry said, looking like he was about to burst if James didn't start letting him speak.

Gardner and Atherton got up and as they left, Gardner noticed Walter's nails digging into the wooden desk in front of him until his knuckles went white.

Gardner got the nod from Harry and they went back into the room. Walter sat silently with his hands resting on the desk for a long time and Gardner was about to call it. Walter was messing with them. Wasting their time. He knew as well as Gardner did that they had nothing on him. Not really. Apart from the fact he'd lied about being at Lauren's that night, about calling Cartwright, probably while he stood over Ritchie's body. But they were keeping that to themselves for now, waiting to see what he'd give them on Cartwright. After a few minutes it seemed that he wasn't going to give them anything.

And then Walter looked up.

'I asked Craig Cartwright to go to her house that night,' he said.

'Which night? The night Lauren was killed?'

'No,' he said, shaking his head violently. 'The night Ritchie was murdered. I asked Cartwright to go there. To talk to him. I thought it'd be better coming from a police officer. I thought Ritchie might pay attention.'

'But?'

'Things must've got out of hand. He said Ritchie lashed out.' Walter took a moment, steadying himself, and Gardner held back the desire to roll his eyes. 'Cartwright has a temper. I should've known better than to leave them together.'

'So you're saying you weren't there?'

'No.'

'And you believe Cartwright killed Ritchie,' Gardner asked, again not believing that Cartwright would go that far. No matter what he thought he was going to get in return for helping James, even Cartwright couldn't be as stupid as to commit murder.

'Who else would've killed him?' Walter said.

'So why didn't you come forward earlier?'

Walter looked at his solicitor. 'I was afraid. For my family.'

'Cartwright threatened you?' Gardner said.

'Yes.'

Gardner looked to Atherton. They both knew it was bullshit. But they needed to listen to his whole story in order to find any nuggets of truth. Something they could put to Cartwright.

'So what happened with Lauren?'

'I was wavering,' Walter said. 'Cartwright knew it. And maybe if you hadn't been looking so hard at Lauren I wouldn't have done anything. But . . . I couldn't bear the idea of my Lauren being punished for something she didn't do. So I told her what'd happened. We were going to go to the police, together. And he . . . He killed my little girl.'

'Why didn't you come forward after Lauren's murder?' Atherton asked.

'Because I was *afraid*,' Walter said. 'I was afraid of what he'd do to the rest of my family.'

'Okay,' Gardner said. 'So you asked Cartwright to go and talk to Ritchie. When did you ask him?'

'That night. I'd come out of the pub with Peter. I went to the office and I got Lauren's message. She was scared. I was worried about her. I was going to talk to Ritchie myself but I thought it'd be better coming from Cartwright. I thought Ritchie would back off if he thought the police would do something.'

'Why Cartwright?' Gardner asked.

'I knew him from various events, knew he was someone willing to go the extra mile. He's ambitious. I also knew he was someone who could look after himself. I thought he'd be able to stand up to Donoghue.'

'So you were at the office when you called Cartwright?' Atherton asked.

'Yes.'

'And what time would that've been? Because we can't find any calls to Cartwright's landline or mobile that night.'

Walter sighed. 'It was another phone.'

'The phone you claimed belonged to a woman you met in the pub?' Gardner said.

'Yes,' Walter said.

'And why did you use that phone?'

'That's the number he gave to me.'

'But you have his landline. You called him on that the night Lauren died.'

'I got that later. He got rid of that mobile after he'd killed Ritchie.'

'All right. So you called Cartwright after one in the morning and asked him to go and talk to Ritchie. Why did he go to Lauren's house? How did he know he was there?'

'I told him.'

'And how did you know?'

'I . . . Lauren had said he was hanging about. Wouldn't leave her be. I assumed he'd still be there.'

'Okay, so you called Cartwright and told him to go to Lauren's. Then what?'

'And then nothing. I went home to bed. I went in to work the next day and got a call telling me what'd happened.'

'But you said nothing,' Gardner said.

'I told you. He threatened me. My family.'

'When? When did you see him again?'

'When he came to the office. You were there. You saw him. Why do you think he showed up at my office by himself? Why he was so keen to escort me to the station alone?'

Gardner looked to Atherton, letting him take over. 'What happened the night of Lauren's murder? Mark Healy had already been arrested and released. Presumably Cartwright told you about him.'

'Yes,' Walter said. 'He told me they'd got someone, that things would be fine if I kept my mouth shut.'

'But you didn't. Why not? You said you were scared for your safety, the safety of your family. Why did you choose *then* to do something?'

'Because I couldn't sit back and let an innocent man take the blame.'

'So how did Cartwright become aware of your moral quandary? Why did you call him?'

'I'd spoken with Lauren and she convinced me to come forward. That it was the right thing to do. That we'd do it together.'

'So why call Cartwright? Why tell him?'

'I wanted him to know I wasn't afraid any more.' Walter wiped his nose, patted his eyes with the folded handkerchief.

'How did he get Peter Hinde's car?' Gardner asked.

'What?' Walter said, whipping his head around to look at him.

'The car. Whoever killed Ritchie Donoghue was with him in the car beforehand. How did Cartwright get the car from the office, and why bother?'

There was a knock at the door and they all looked up. Lawton stuck her head around the door and nodded for Gardner. 'You need to see this,' she said.

76

Gardner came out of the room with Atherton, knowing James was lying through his teeth. He was already at Lauren's when he called Cartwright. He'd already killed Ritchie by that point, Gardner just knew it. But he guessed some of the stuff James had said about Cartwright was true; the little favours, for example.

They followed Lawton to the office where she had finished going through all the footage from the pizza shop opposite Cartwright's and it'd shown them a lot. They had proof of Cartwright leaving his flat at 1.15 a.m. the night Donoghue was killed, returning just over two hours later. The footage from cameras close to Walter's office showed the same man, in the same clothes, though his face was concealed, on foot at 2.05 a.m., presumably after returning Peter Hinde's car. Strangely there was nothing showing him collecting the car.

But more importantly it showed Cartwright going out the night Lauren died, and returning home half an hour before Walter James called 999 to report the murder of his daughter.

'There's more,' Lawton said and showed them more footage. 'About half an hour after Cartwright returned home the night Lauren was murdered, a car pulls up outside his flat. Car's registered to a woman called Janine Smiley.'

'Who's she?' Gardner asked and Lawton shrugged.

'The images show Cartwright getting in, holding a paper bag. They left and ANPR shows they went to Newcastle. I've traced them to the street Healy lived at. Then she dropped him off back home again almost two and a half hours later where a man appears to be waiting for him. A man Cartwright doesn't seem pleased to see.' Lawton pressed play on the tape. The man charged at Cartwright, pushing him into the wall. Cartwright held up his hands and calmed the man before leading him into his flat. The man emerged twenty minutes later. In the morning, Cartwright had appeared with a smashed-up face.

The man in the image had a hood pulled up, his face unseen. But Gardner would bet the world that it was Walter James. So what had Cartwright done to piss him off so much?

'That's interesting,' Atherton said. 'Doesn't look like Walter James is as scared of Cartwright as he claims.'

'No, he doesn't,' Gardner said, only half listening. He leaned over Lawton and found the screen grabs of Cartwright leaving and coming back the night of Lauren's murder. 'Look at the times,' he said. 'Cartwright left home just after Walter called at eight fifteen. Walter claimed he didn't go over there until much later, which was confirmed on the CCTV opposite his office, which showed him leaving just after nine thirty. Kirsty couldn't remember who got there when, but this proves Cartwright went out to go over there long before Walter arrived. And he returned home half an hour before Walter James called 999 to report the murder of his daughter.'

'So, Walter killed her as soon as he got there and then called the police. It's not implausible,' Atherton said.

'No, it's not. But if Walter killed Lauren, Cartwright would've had to have been there at the time, *or* have come back later to plant the evidence. But he didn't. He had to have left the cigarette butt there before Walter arrived. And the jumper found at Healy's? The fibres were *on* Lauren. It was *worn* by the killer and then taken to Healy's flat. Walter didn't show up at Cartwright's until *after* Cartwright had returned from Newcastle. The only way he had the jumper was because he was wearing it when he killed her.'

77

Gardner slid a picture from the CCTV towards Walter. 'Is this you? This is a few hours after Lauren died.' The image showed the man shoving Cartwright against the wall outside his flat. 'What happened, Walter?'

Walter closed his eyes and pressed his lips together. 'He killed Lauren,' Walter said. 'He killed her and I wanted to hurt him.'

'So Cartwright killed Lauren to keep her quiet and he framed Mark Healy,' Atherton said, trying to get Walter talking some more. Cartwright had been arrested and Gardner had already asked the lab to check if they could find a match between clothes found in Cartwright's place and the fibres from the jumper found at Healy's.

'How did Healy get involved?' Atherton said and Gardner felt his stomach tighten. Of course Atherton was going to ask the question sooner or later. Gardner looked Walter in the eye and wondered if this was where they both came tumbling down.

'I don't know,' Walter said. 'Perhaps you should ask DI Gardner. It was one of his team who arrested him.'

Gardner and Atherton left the interview room and found Lawton. They wanted to talk to Cartwright again in the light of the new evidence and thought she might like to sit in, considering she'd been the one to find it.

'So, do you believe him?' Atherton asked, nodding back at the room Walter sat in. 'That Cartwright killed Ritchie too? That it just got out of hand?'

Gardner shook his head. 'Something's not right. There's no way Walter James is afraid of Cartwright. He might be a nasty little bastard but he's got no power. James has half the department under his thumb. He's still lying. He's still claiming he was never at Lauren's.'

'But Cartwright killed Lauren. We agree on that. And what reason would he have unless she knew something and he didn't want it getting out?'

Gardner wondered how much he should continue to push. Walter could've spilled the beans on Healy but he didn't. He'd hinted at it but hadn't actually talked. Why not? Because Walter still had plenty to play for. So far most of the evidence pointed to Cartwright and he knew it. He could play along with being the one who led Cartwright to Ritchie, to Lauren, but he was the victim. A scared old man. But Gardner couldn't let it go.

'He has to be involved somehow, more than this bullshit about asking Cartwright to talk to Ritchie. He was being blackmailed. That's what this is about. Lauren's situation had nothing to do with it. Walter wasn't going to let these photos get out, whatever it took.'

'So he asked Cartwright to go there and speak to Ritchie for him, not Lauren.'

'No. It doesn't fit. What about the car? He hasn't answered that, hasn't even tried to explain it. Cartwright wouldn't have used Peter Hinde's car.'

'Unless Walter was trying to set Hinde up. If he'd found out about him and Lauren. Told Cartwright to take his car.'

'Which would suggest premeditation. Why send Cartwright in the car if he was just going to have a quiet word? And how would he get to it? We've already seen the car driving towards Lauren's house before Cartwright even left his place. Someone else drove the car there. And we both know who that is. He's lying. We need to bring up the phone call, let him know we know he's lying. See if it shakes anything else out.'

'Talk to Cartwright first,' Atherton said and Gardner and Lawton went into the room where Cartwright was sitting. He sat up straight when they entered.

'We have two eyewitnesses who saw you in the alley behind Lauren's house the night Ritchie was killed,' Gardner said, taking a seat.

'You have two drunk kids who saw *someone*. They couldn't pick him out of a crowd.'

'We also have a witness who saw you going into Lauren's house the night she was killed. What were you doing there?'

'This the same witness who changed her tune about who was in the alley? She swore it was Peter Hinde five minutes ago.'

'We're not talking about the alley. We're talking about her seeing you enter Lauren's house that night.'

'I was never at Lauren's house that night.'

Gardner opened the folder in front of him, taking out several images from CCTV cameras. He laid them out one by one in front of Cartwright. 'That takeaway across the street from you have had a lot of trouble recently. Got themselves some CCTV cameras.' He pointed to the first picture. 'This is you coming home not long before Walter James called nine-nine-nine the night Lauren died. You know, the night he called you from a phone box.'

'So,' Cartwright said. 'What's your point?'

'Where'd you been?'

'The supermarket.'

'You don't have any shopping with you,' Gardner said, pointing at the image.

'They didn't have what I wanted.'

'What about when Ritchie died?' Gardner said and slid forward the two images of Cartwright from that night. 'Here's you leaving at one fifteen a.m. and then coming home again just after three. Late night.'

'So what? I go out at night. It's a free country,' Cartwright said and Gardner could see the sweat on his upper lip.

'Where'd you go?'

'Out. To a club.'

'Really? So who'd you go with?'

'No one.'

'That's a pity. Where'd you go? Which club?'

'I don't remember. I was out looking for pussy. Okay? That's it.'

'And did you find it? You came home alone again a couple of hours later.'

'No,' Cartwright said. 'All right? I didn't pull.'

'And you don't recall which club, which is a shame because if you did we could check your alibi, couldn't we?'

'Unless someone wiped the tapes,' Cartwright said and knocked Gardner's smile a little.

'Take a look at this, Cartwright,' Gardner said and slid a screen grab from the CCTV across the desk. 'Can you tell me what's happening in this picture?'

Cartwright glanced at the image and shrugged. 'I was obviously going out somewhere.'

'Not in your car, though. Who's Janine Smiley?'

'My girlfriend. It's her car.'

'Yes, we know that. We also know that her car was spotted

going to Newcastle late on Thursday night. Just a few hours after Lauren James was murdered.'

'So?'

'Why did you go to Newcastle so late that night, Cartwright? Another club?'

'I was just going out for the night.'

'Near Mark Healy's flat?' Cartwright said nothing. 'I think you were going to plant evidence at Mark Healy's house. Evidence linking him to Lauren James's murder.'

Cartwright frowned, looked like he was about to speak and then stopped.

'We know you were helping Walter James from the start. He asked you to go to Lauren's house the night he killed Ritchie, asked you to clear up. But something went wrong, didn't it? Those girls saw you and you panicked. You left before you could move the body.'

'No,' Cartwright said.

'And once you'd done that, you had to keep covering. Had to keep doing what he wanted. You knew if you let the truth out about Walter James, you'd be up to your neck in it too. Or didn't that bother you? Was it all just to suck up to Walter so you could climb your way to the top?'

'This is bullshit.'

'Did you know Mark Healy was dead? Of course you did. Was it you or James who organised it?'

Cartwright looked like he was going to be sick. 'I've got nothing to do with any of this. I didn't get Healy killed. I didn't even know.'

'So you're saying Walter James did it?' Gardner waited but Cartwright just sat there like a rabbit in the headlights. 'What else did James do?'

'This is all bullshit. None of this means anything. You know that. You've got nothing. It's the same with Mr James. You're determined to bring him down but you can't. Because you've got nothing. Nothing on me. Nothing on him.'

'I admire your loyalty, Cartwright,' Gardner said. 'But maybe you should rethink it a little. You really think Walter James is sticking by you? He was willing for his own daughter to take the blame for a crime she didn't commit, just to save his own skin. You think you mean more to him than she did?' Gardner stood up and went to the door. 'There's more where this comes from,' he said, holding the folder up to Cartwright. 'So you just have a think about it. Who's it going to be? You or him?'

78

Freeman pulled up outside the flat Darren had been sharing with Rachel. She didn't want to be there, didn't understand what possessions Darren could possibly have and need back that he'd risk going there for. Even though Healy was dead, Darren was still worried the club guys would come after him for the money. The police had restored the CCTV footage and no doubt Gary and Tommy would've watched it by now, keen to see what all the fuss was about. They'd know Rachel took the money, and that might make Darren guilty by association. Coming back for a few bits of tat seemed stupid.

But Freeman knew it wasn't about his belongings. It was about Rachel. And that's what worried her, even more than the club guys. She was more dangerous than they were. At least for Darren.

'You want me to go up?' Freeman asked Darren but he shook his head.

'No. I'll go.'

'All right,' she said and opened the car door.

'I can do it alone,' he said.

Freeman didn't answer, just started walking towards the flat. She heard him slam the car door and shuffle his way after her. He let them into the flat and she started picking things up, shoving them into a bin bag, not caring whether they belonged to Darren or not. She didn't want to be there any longer than necessary. And if Rachel wasn't there for him to tell her in person that she was dumped, Freeman could live with that. At least she could say they tried.

'Hey, babe.'

Freeman turned and saw Rachel emerging from the other room, barely clothed. She reached out for Darren, throwing her arms around him, all smiles until she saw Freeman and backed away.

'What's she doing here?' Rachel said, as if she weren't the person in the wrong. Freeman was about to tell her to shut it when Darren took Rachel's hand.

'She's my sister,' he said. 'She gave me a ride over here.'

Rachel eyed her up, probably wondering what she could use as a weapon this time. Darren gave Freeman a look and she broke eye contact. 'You've got five minutes,' she said and took the bin bag into the bedroom, leaving the door open to make sure he didn't say anything stupid.

'I'm really glad you're home,' Rachel said. 'I've been really scared. Healy's dead.'

'Yeah, I know,' Darren said and Freeman held her breath for a moment, wondering if he'd tell her what'd happened. Darren saying something stupid was a given. But this time he proved her wrong. 'Listen, did you get any money? Did you sell the coke?'

'Why? Healy's dead.'

'So? Those guys from the club won't care about that. They'll still want their money. We need to pay them back.'

'Yeah, well, I tried,' she said. 'But the guy I was selling to totally, like, gypped me.'

'Rach, these guys are gonna find out it was you. They'll be looking for us.'

'But you'll look after me, right?' she said in a baby voice. Freeman couldn't take any more. She went back into the living room.

'Darren, we're going,' she said.

'Where?' Rachel said. 'Can I come? I don't want to stay here by myself.'

Darren looked like he might say yes so Freeman took him by the arm and dragged him away from her. 'Tell her,' she said.

'Tell me what?'

Darren looked at his shoes. 'Rach,' he said. 'I can't stay up here. I need to leave. There's all this shit going on so I—'

'What?' Rachel said, the baby talk done with. 'You're dumping me?'

'We should just not see each other for a while. That's all.'

'But why? I can come with you. We go everywhere together, remember. I love you.'

Darren finally looked up. 'No, you don't,' he said. 'I know you were sleeping with Healy. I might be stupid, but I'm not *that* stupid. You were the only person who was there for me for a long time. And I do love you. So don't go back to the club, all right? Leave if you have to. Just . . . You can't come with me.'

'Darren,' Rachel said and tried to go after him as he left the flat. Freeman stepped in front of her and Rachel stopped. She looked down on Freeman but she still looked scared.

'Leave him alone,' Freeman said. 'Do what he said and leave, but if you ever come near my brother again, I'll arrest you.' She turned to follow Darren but then looked back at Rachel. 'In fact, if you come near him again, I'll kill you.'

79

They figured they'd let Cartwright stew for long enough so they walked back in, Gardner now carrying a laptop. They found him pacing the floor. He stopped when they entered, his face changing from worried to blasé. 'You ready to let me go yet?' he said.

'Not yet,' Atherton said. 'Sit down.' Cartwright sighed as if it were nothing more than an inconvenience. But Gardner could see the worry behind his eyes.

'See, I thought it was James. I thought *he* killed Lauren. Thought he was twisted enough to murder his own daughter. But it was you, wasn't it?' Gardner said and watched Cartwright's face drop. 'You killed her. That's why your face is like that. It wasn't part of the plan.'

'You're wrong,' he said. 'You talked to Mr James yet?'

'Yes,' Gardner said. 'Had quite a lot to say for himself.'

'Yeah? Like this is bullshit?'

'Not quite. He claims you killed Ritchie Donoghue *as well*.'

Cartwright looked like a kid who'd been kicked. 'No, he didn't,' he said and looked from Gardner to Atherton. 'You're lying.'

'No, I'm not,' Gardner said. 'Told us everything. And at this point I'm inclined to believe him.'

'You're lying.'

354

'How many phones do you have, Cartwright?'

'What?' He almost laughed but it was a desperate laugh, trying to cover up his panic. 'Two. A mobile and a landline.'

'So you don't have another mobile. An unregistered one?'

'No.'

'Huh. It's just that Walter James claimed to have called you on this other phone. Asked you to go and have a chat with Donoghue, get him to leave Lauren alone. But things got out of hand and you killed him.'

Cartwright was shaking and Gardner couldn't tell if it was through fear or anger. But it didn't matter. It was a reaction. And he could work with that.

'Claims you also killed Lauren so she wouldn't talk. A warning so *he* wouldn't talk.'

'No,' Cartwright said, his voice now like a child's. 'He wouldn't say that.'

'Why not? Because he's your friend?'

'Because it's not true!'

'Thing is, Cartwright, there's a lot of evidence that supports what he's told us. So if it's not true, like you say, you're going to have to convince us.'

Cartwright laughed. 'You remember that I'm a detective too, don't you? I know the tricks you use. You think you're going to get me to talk with this bullshit? You think you can play us off each other? Not going to work, mate.' He sat back, satisfied with himself.

'You're right,' Gardner said. 'I have been known to do that. Which is why I thought you might want to see this.' He pressed play on the laptop and the footage of Walter came on. But Gardner didn't watch the screen, he watched Cartwright's reaction. When he was satisfied that Cartwright had seen enough he stopped the video. 'So,' he said. 'Have you got anything to add?'

Cartwright was shaking properly now and this time Gardner could see the anger in his eyes. And it was that kind of anger that got people talking.

'I didn't kill him,' Cartwright said. 'I swear to fucking God, I didn't kill him. *He* called me. Told me to get there, that he had a problem, that he'd had a fight with Donoghue and things had got out of hand. Told me he was in the garden and it needed sorting. When I arrived, he'd already gone. He'd killed him and he didn't know what to do. He just left him there and expected me to fix it. Get rid of the body, the evidence. Make it all go away.'

'But?'

'I didn't want to. I checked for a pulse but it was too late. I didn't know what to do. I thought maybe I should call it in but there'd be questions. So I wiped the spade down. I didn't see anything else, no other weapons. I guess he took the rock or whatever with him. He'd left the car. Wanted me to move the body, get rid of it and the car. I went back to the alley, opened the boot, but then I couldn't do it. I was going to make an anonymous call maybe. And then those girls showed up. So I just got in the car and drove. Took it back to the office. And that was it. I went to see Mr James the next morning, tried to explain why I hadn't done what he wanted. But there were other people there. That girl, the intern. She kept hanging around. I couldn't say anything. But I never killed anyone. I swear. It was him. Not me. I didn't do anything wrong except keep my mouth shut.'

'What happened after that? After you returned the car?' Gardner asked. 'Did you go to Ritchie's?'

Cartwright considered this for a second and then nodded. 'Yeah, I walked over there. James wanted me to find something for him.'

'So he'd told you about the photos, told you what all this was about.'

'He just said there were some sensitive pictures he needed back. I went over there but I never found them. Just the stuff on Lauren but I left those. He didn't mention those pictures.'

'Okay, what about Lauren? We have evidence placing you at the scene before she died. Walter James called you before that. Did he tell you to go there too?'

'Yes,' Cartwright said, his voice wavering. 'He said she knew it was him. Somehow she'd got the photos. That was what all this was about. Fucking photos. He killed Ritchie over them and then when Lauren found out he told me to get them back.'

'That was it? Just get them back?'

'Yes. He said he was going there later on. But he told me to go and get the pictures before it was too late.'

'So what did you do?'

'I went there and got them back.'

'That's it?'

'Yes.'

'She was alive when you left?'

'Yes. He must've killed her. They must've had a fight or something.'

'So who planted the evidence linking Healy to the scene? Walter?'

Cartwright's eyes darted around. He was lying and trying to think of a way out of it. Gardner had believed him until this point. But they knew he'd killed Lauren so was the rest of it a lie? 'I don't know. I suppose he must've.'

'How would he do that?'

'I don't know! How does he do anything?'

Gardner sighed. Why was Cartwright bothering? He must know what they'd have, what they'd find. He was already in it up to his neck.

'We've searched your flat, Cartwright.'

Cartwright looked ill but he shrugged anyway. 'So?'

'We found the same fibres on your jacket as we found on Lauren. So unless you were tussling with Healy too,' he shrugged, 'I think there's only one explanation.'

'No.'

'We have evidence you went up to Newcastle after Lauren was killed. That you went to Healy's flat. *You* planted the evidence. After *you* killed her.'

Cartwright looked like he might cry. 'No. He made me go back there. He told me what'd happened and told me to make it look like Healy had done it.'

'How did he think you'd do that?'

'He saw me pick up the cigarette butt from outside the station.'

'So you were already planning to set him up?'

'No,' Cartwright said. 'He told me to do it. He told me to do all of it.'

'Walter was the one to call nine-nine-nine from Lauren's. That was half an hour after you got home. You never went back there. You didn't leave your flat again until your girl-friend showed up to take you to Newcastle. You went to Lauren's, killed her, and left. Walter arrived after you'd gone and you'd already set things up to look like Healy was guilty.'

Cartwright was sweating. He looked like a caged animal. 'I don't know,' Gardner said. 'Maybe he knew what you were going to do. Maybe he planned that too. It seems like he's really good at manipulating you, Cartwright.'

Cartwright bowed his head and it took a moment for Gardner to realise the man was crying. He chanced a look at Atherton. Maybe they were getting somewhere. He was desperate for Cartwright to tell them more, to give them something that could bring Walter James down too, because what they had so far wasn't enough. Not as far as getting James was concerned.

'It was an accident,' Cartwright said, his voice quiet and trembling. Atherton went to speak but Gardner held up his hand. 'I didn't want to hurt her. I felt sorry for her. But she was drunk. She was staggering about, screaming at me. All I wanted was the pen drive. That's what he told me – just get the evidence.' Cartwright looked up, his eyes red. 'He said if I didn't get it we'd both be screwed. He said do whatever it takes. But I didn't want to hurt her. It was an accident.'

'Why was he desperate to get the photos back? So there were a few photos of him up to no good. Why do all of this?' Atherton said.

'It wasn't a few photos. It was hundreds. It was video. Stuff that could ruin him.'

'What sort of stuff?' Gardner asked.

'I don't know. I swear. I just know he didn't want it getting out.'

'You didn't look? You weren't curious about what could possibly be worth all this?'

'No,' Cartwright said. 'I trusted him.'

They all went quiet and for once Gardner almost felt pity for Cartwright. Almost. He was a piece of shit. No one had forced him to do any of this – not even Walter James. He could've said no. Could've walked away. Could've spoken up a long time ago. But he hadn't. He'd let James charm him into thinking he was worth something.

'I can prove it was him,' Cartwright said. 'I can prove he killed Ritchie.'

'How's that then?' Atherton said.

'The phone. Ritchie's phone. Walter tried to delete the photo off it but you can get it back, right? I can tell you where he dumped it. He told me. Asked if you were likely to find it.'

Gardner kept his face neutral. Cartwright was panicking and maybe he was going to give them everything.

80

Gardner and Atherton waited for Walter James to be brought up to the interview room. Cartwright had been charged with Lauren's murder and as things stood it was looking like he could be charged with Ritchie's too. But despite the clear link to Walter James, and despite the fact that Cartwright had no reason to be there without James's involvement, Hadley was still resisting charging his mate too.

Cartwright had been telling the truth about Ritchie's phone. A team had retrieved it from where Walter had dumped it, but it'd been wiped and smashed. There was no chance of getting prints from it but they were working on restoring the photo that was allegedly on there. The photo that would prove Ritchie'd had something on Walter, something that would give Walter motive for murder. But in the meantime, Gardner had something else to put to James. Something even Hadley couldn't argue with.

'Take a seat, Mr James,' Atherton said and Walter sunk into the chair.

'Has he been charged?' Walter asked.

'We're just tying up some loose ends,' Gardner said, ignoring the question.

Walter sighed. 'I've told you everything I know.'

'Not quite everything. See, I might've believed your story

if it hadn't been for a couple of little details,' Gardner said. 'As much as I believe a lot of things you've told us about Cartwright, a lot of things the evidence backs up, there's something bothering me. Want to know what it is?' Walter didn't respond but Gardner could see some of his old spirit fighting to get out. 'I don't believe for one second that someone like you would be afraid of someone like Craig Cartwright.'

'I don't think you're in any position to speculate on Mr James's state of mind,' Harry said.

'He's a killer,' Walter said. 'You said yourself you have evidence of that.'

'That may be so. But I don't think you're afraid of him. Afraid of what he knows about you, maybe. But not of him. And not for your family. A son you despise, a wife you cheat on repeatedly. Lauren, I maybe could've accepted, but then you let her down, didn't you? You were the one who sent him over there that night. You were willing to sacrifice her to keep yourself out of it.'

'Enough, Detective. Mr James has been through enough without you implying he could've prevented his daughter's death,' Harry said.

'You said you called Cartwright from your office the night Ritchie was murdered. But that's not true either, is it? We have cell site data showing you were nowhere near your office when you made that call. You were at Lauren's. You were the one who lured Ritchie Donoghue there in the first place. And maybe to start with it *was* about Lauren, maybe you thought you'd warn him off. But he didn't like people disrespecting him any more than you do and he showed his hand. Told you he had something on you, showed you proof of it on his phone. And you lost control. You were the one who got him there and then you killed him. And then you got Cartwright to come and clear up. Except he messed up. He has a habit of doing that.'

Walter swallowed and his eye twitched. 'That's ridiculous.'

'But you *were* there,' Gardner said. Walter cleared his throat and looked to his solicitor. 'How else do you explain it? How else did Cartwright get Peter's car?'

'All right,' he said, almost inaudibly. 'I did go there.' His solicitor coughed and Walter waved him away. Arrogant to the end. Always knowing better. 'I did go there. I went for Lauren. She was out when I got there but I knew this thing with Ritchie was out of control so I decided to do something about it. I saw Lauren's phone and I sent a message to him, asking him to come over. Then I asked Cartwright to come and talk to him and then I left. What happened after that, I don't know exactly. All I know is that I regret it. If I hadn't interfered, none of this would've happened. Lauren wouldn't be—' He stopped and closed his eyes as if it were all too much. But Gardner saw right through him.

'So you lied? From the very start? And if Cartwright was to blame, as you insist, if you'd come forward straight away, you *could've* prevented Lauren from being killed.'

'That was not something I wanted to happen,' Walter said and took a gulp of water. Gardner waited for him to speak again but when he was silent, Gardner continued. He wasn't done yet.

'There's something else I wanted to ask you,' he said and watched Walter closely. 'You said you texted Ritchie and then called Cartwright to come and talk to him. But the call to Cartwright was quite some time *after* the text. Quite some time after Ritchie might have got there.'

'So?' Walter said. 'I didn't think of it until later. I'd originally planned to talk to him myself but later decided it would be better coming from a police officer.'

'So was Ritchie already there when you called Cartwright?'

Walter paused, maybe weighing up his options. Gardner could see a little sweat on his upper lip now. 'I don't remember.'

'Because what I don't understand is why you'd leave the car there. Why not drive it back to the office yourself?'

'I'd had a drink. I realised that I shouldn't have been driving, so I left the car and walked back. Thought I'd pick it up the next day,' Walter said and Gardner noticed Harry nod.

'So why go back to the office? Why not just walk home?'

'I needed to pick things up from the office. I told you that before.'

'Why didn't you get a taxi back?' Atherton said.

'I wanted to walk,' Walter said, raising his voice. 'I don't know what you think you're doing, Detective,' he said, staring at Gardner. 'I've told you what I know. I've apologised for any mistakes I made. But all this,' he said, waving at the notes on the table, 'proves nothing. Cartwright killed Ritchie just like he killed Lauren. I don't know what else you want.'

'Cartwright told us where you dumped Ritchie's phone,' Gardner said and watched Walter for a reaction. He didn't give any. 'We're currently retrieving the data. What do you think we'll find?'

'I have no idea,' Walter said, sighing.

'You don't think there'll be anything relating to you on there?'

'I would doubt it,' he said and sat back in his chair. He glanced at his solicitor.

'Was there anything else, Detectives?' he asked and Atherton shook his head.

Gardner and Atherton stood in Hadley's office and argued until they were blue in the face but Hadley refused to budge.

'We're not charging him with Donoghue's murder until we have something solid. You know as well as I do he'll have the best legal team money can buy and we have *nothing* that proves he killed anyone. These pictures you claim to be motive, where are they? You have nothing. Charge him and he stops talking. And the CPS will laugh in your face if you take what little you have to them.'

'We might not be able to say which one of them actually killed him, but we know there were two weapons. We know they were both there. We can go with joint enterprise if nothing else.'

Hadley shook his head. 'That just weakens the case.'

'He's lied through his teeth all along.'

'That's not unusual. Most people do when they're tied up in something like this. They tell one lie, dig themselves a hole they can't get out of. Doesn't mean they're guilty.'

Gardner thought he was going to blow. Why was he still trying to help Walter James? 'What about conspiracy to murder?'

'Or perverting the course of justice, concealing evidence, at the very least,' Atherton said.

'Conspiracy is difficult to prove,' Hadley said. 'There's nothing to show he planned Donoghue's murder.'

'What about the text? What about bringing Cartwright in?'

'Doesn't mean he wanted him dead,' Hadley said. 'Walter claims he only asked Cartwright to talk to Donoghue.'

Gardner wanted to keep going, wanted to tell Hadley he was either a gutless idiot or else he was as corrupt as Walter James. Instead he bit his tongue and left the room.

He went outside and paced up and down, wanting to punch something or someone. He thought about going and buying some cigarettes but his wallet was upstairs and he doubted it would help anyway. He stopped moving and leaned against the cold brick wall. What *was* he doing? Maybe he should've known James was untouchable. It didn't matter what they found, how much they argued. He was fucking invincible. He should've listened to Freeman and let it go. If he had, maybe Mark Healy would still be alive.

He looked up as the doors opened and saw James and his smug solicitor leaving the building. Walter looked across at him and then said something to Harry before coming over. Gardner's stomach tightened.

'Concealing evidence?' Walter said with a smile. 'That's it?'

Gardner wondered if Hadley had been talking already or if it was just his solicitor's best guess at what they'd throw at him. Either way, James knew he was going to walk.

He turned and added, over his shoulder, 'And you know what they say about people in glass houses, Detective. You've been warned once.'

366

81

Wednesday, 5 January

Gardner rang the doorbell again and stood back, looking for movement in the house. Eventually a light came on and the door opened.

'Mrs Worrall?' he said and Jen's mum nodded. He showed her his ID. 'Is Jen home?'

'Yes,' she said and let him in. She turned to shout to Jen but she'd already appeared in the hallway, holding the laptop out to him.

Gardner took it and she said, 'You think you can restore everything?'

'I hope so,' he said.

Gardner took the laptop back to the station, making sure it was in the hands of someone he trusted. Ziggy Morrison was the best computer guy he knew and, something that always made Gardner wonder why he was working for the police, was also anti-authority. If there was anyone who was less likely to be on James's payroll than Ziggy, he'd yet to find him.

Happy that the evidence was safe, Gardner headed out to try and drum up some more support. He knew he was on dangerous ground and James's little warning outside the station had rattled him. But he'd come this far. He needed to see it through.

367

He knocked on the door and it took a while before Peter Hinde answered. When he finally did, he took one look at Gardner and sighed. He looked like all the life had drained from him some time ago. He was like a ghost.

'Peter,' Gardner said. 'You mind if I come in?'

Peter shook his head and let him in. The house was dark and cold. He followed him through to the living room and saw a duvet thrown on the end of the settee, and a lot of bottles scattered across the coffee table. The place had a stale smell.

Gardner switched on a light and Peter flinched. 'Sorry,' he said and Peter just waved him away, sitting down on the edge of the settee, head in hands. Gardner wouldn't be surprised if he was suffering from a major hangover.

'We've charged Craig Cartwright with Lauren's murder,' Gardner said and Peter barely looked up. 'He said it was an accident.'

'An accident?' Peter said, some life coming back to his voice. 'Why was he even there? Why was—' He stopped. 'I don't understand. What did he even have to do with her?'

'Cartwright had nothing to do with her. Or Ritchie. He was acting on behalf of someone else. Your boss.'

Peter looked confused. 'What are you talking about? You think Walter did this? He loved Lauren.'

Gardner wasn't sure of that any more. He thought the only person Walter was capable of loving was himself. 'I don't know if he told Cartwright to kill Lauren, but he sent him over there.' He let that sink in and Peter's chin trembled. 'I'm sorry,' he said. 'I know you cared for her.'

'I loved her.' Peter stood up and walked to the window. 'How do you even know this?' he said, turning back. 'That Walter had something to do with it?'

'We have evidence he called Cartwright that night, shortly after Lauren called him. She told him she had something, some photos of him. Photos that I believe are the reason Ritchie was murdered. She didn't tell you about them?'

'No,' he said. 'What kind of photos?'

'I'm not sure yet. But something bad enough to kill for.' Peter shook his head again, trying to process what Gardner was telling him. 'Were you aware of any activities he was involved in that he wouldn't want getting out?'

Peter almost laughed. 'He was cheating on his wife. He'd cheated on all of them. But I'm not sure that was a secret.'

'Nothing else? You're as close to him as anyone. You weren't aware of anything else?' Gardner waited but Peter just stood shaking his head. 'Let me be clear here. This is a man who sent someone to hurt his own daughter, so if you're protecting him—'

'I'm not protecting anyone,' Peter said. 'I don't know anything about any photos. Where did they come from? You must have some idea if you're aware of their existence.'

'Jen Worrall,' he said and Peter looked shocked. 'She'd been filming him, collecting evidence.'

'What for?'

'He'd been sexually harassing her. I guess she wanted revenge. But then Ritchie Donoghue got wind of it and wanted in, wanted to blackmail him. That's what this is about. So there's something more than cheating on his wife in those pictures. Jen hasn't exactly been forthcoming about the precise nature of the photos. She'd deleted them but we're working on restoring them. But in the event that doesn't happen, I could really do with some help. So if you're aware of anything that could help prove what he's been up to, I'd really like to know.'

Peter sat down and looked like he needed another drink. 'I can't get my head around all this,' he said and put his head in his hands.

Gardner knew he wouldn't get any more from him now, if he knew anything at all. It was doubtful that Walter James kept *all* his dirty secrets from Hinde, but maybe this one had been something he'd kept to himself. He stood up but Peter didn't move. 'Call me if you think of anything. This could be the best chance at getting him to pay for what he's done.'

82

Gardner took the coffee from Atherton who sat down across from him in the deserted canteen. He never thought he'd see the day when he and Atherton were drinking together. They sat in silence for a while, both processing what had happened. That Craig Cartwright had been doing these things under their noses for so long. They'd found a lot of cash in Cartwright's flat, presumably from Walter, payment for various jobs. He hoped both Cartwright and James thought it had been worth it.

'Word has it, Walter James has been talking to George Harper,' Atherton said, and Gardner felt his heart sink. Harper was a brilliant, and expensive, defence barrister who'd managed to win dozens of high-profile cases. He was a man who seemed to relish the game more than anything. He was perfect for Walter James.

'He must be getting worried,' Gardner said, knowing it meant little. They still hadn't restored the photos from Ritchie's phone or Jen's laptop and Hadley was still reluctant to press charges. 'You think he could get off?' Gardner asked.

Atherton shrugged. 'I sincerely hope not. If he does, I'm sure he'll find a way to punish us all.'

They sat in silence for a while, sipping coffee and contemplating the possibility of James going scot-free. As much as

Atherton was probably crapping himself at the thought of what James would do to him for daring to stand up to him, Gardner knew it would be worse for him. And Freeman. He had to pray it never came to that.

'So,' Atherton said, drawing out the word until a uniformed PC had passed them and left the room. 'I spoke to Darren Freeman this morning.'

Gardner nodded as if it were news but Freeman had already called to let him know her brother had been summoned.

'Unsurprisingly he confirmed his sister's story about her finding him at their parents' house. Said he'd been back in Newcastle for a while, had indeed been hanging around that club. But he claimed to know nothing about Mark Healy.'

'He denied knowing him?' Gardner asked.

'No. He said he knew him. In fact, he admitted to having had a dispute with the man. But he claims he never lured him to Donoghue's flat. Claims he'd never heard of Donoghue. And we certainly can't find any links between them. Bar one. So, are you going to tell me about you and DS Freeman or do I need to start another investigation?'

Gardner felt a wave come over him. At once feeling the pressure of what he'd done and wondering how he was going to get out of it and, at the same time, the relief that the question had finally come. He knew that Cartwright and Walter would start talking if they had nothing to else to play for. If they were going down they'd make sure he did too.

He looked Atherton in the eye. 'DS Freeman and I have, or had, been . . .'

'You're in a relationship?'

'No,' Gardner said. 'I wouldn't say that. It was maybe heading that way.' Gardner stopped. Atherton was the last person he thought he'd be talking to about this. 'I'd invited her over for New Year. And then all this kicked off. Clearly I wasn't toeing the line so James had someone watching me. I saw cars outside my flat; I was followed. I don't know what he thought I was going to do, but . . .' He sighed. He was trying to stay as close to the truth as possible without getting them all sent to prison.

'When the stuff came up about Slinky's nightclub, I heard Freeman's name and found out what was going on. I know I should've passed it on to someone else, or at least declared my interest, but I didn't. I wanted to hear it from her first. She told me she was looking for her brother but the tapes weren't working. She swears that's true and I believe her. You've checked the restored footage and there's nothing on there that she'd want to cover up.'

'Except the fact her brother was at that club. That he *is* alive.'

'She wasn't covering that up. No one was. At that point she didn't even *know* he was alive. When she went to the club she couldn't find anything on the tapes. I don't know what happened with them; maybe she did delete them by accident. But she had no reason to want to hide anything. She wanted to find him. And when she did find Darren later he told her he'd been threatened by Mark Healy and she was trying to keep him safe. She came to me for help and Walter James saw us. Between him and Cartwright they managed to find out what was going on and I believe they led Healy to Ritchie's flat. They knew I couldn't say anything because it would look like Freeman had set him up.

'James came to me to make a deal. Let Healy take the fall and he'd make any links between Freeman and the case disappear, as well as the fact I never declared what I knew about it all. I know I should've come forward sooner but I wasn't sure who I could trust. I kept trying to find a way to make it right. You know that. That's all I've been trying to do here.'

Atherton rubbed his moustache. 'That the truth?'

'Yes.'

The DCI stared towards the door for a long time, possibly enjoying making Gardner sweat. 'I can't promise it won't go any further. It's possible Cartwright and James will talk. Although it's your word against theirs.'

And that was what Gardner was banking on. That no one would believe them. Cartwright's word was basically worth nothing any more. But James's? That was trickier. Whether he walked or not, he still had something on them.

'Go home, Gardner,' Atherton said, pushing himself to his feet.

Gardner watched him walk away and wondered if that was it. Game over.

83

Thursday, 6 January

Gardner tried Freeman for the third time but she wasn't picking up. Part of him was relieved. He knew he needed to apologise but wasn't sure how she'd take it. He wasn't quite willing to admit defeat. There was still a small chance they could get Walter James, if only they could restore the photos. But deep down he knew it was over. James had too many powerful people on his side. He was lucky that James enjoyed power games so much, or else he would've pointed the finger at him and Freeman by now, showing Hadley and Atherton proof that Gardner had known Darren was alive long before he claimed. That Freeman had been outside Donoghue's flat that day.

He hung up as the news came on and Hadley's face filled the screen. Gardner turned up the volume and sat back to hear what the superintendent had to say.

'In connection with the murder of Lauren James, I can confirm that a man has now been charged and is in police custody. In response to previous reports in the media I can confirm that this man is a serving police officer. At this time I cannot divulge any further information but I will say this: no one is above the law. We have zero tolerance for criminal behaviour and underhanded dealings in this department. Trust me when I say anyone involved in illegal activities will be weeded out. This force is made up of honest, hardworking men and women who protect our community every day. Their reputations should not be tarnished because of one incident. Thank you.'

Hadley turned away and the reporters shouted questions. Walter James's name was bandied about but nothing was confirmed or denied.

Gardner turned the TV off. It was all he could do not to vomit. He didn't know how much Hadley knew, how much he'd sanctioned, but he knew one thing: Hadley knew Walter James was dirty. His palms had been greased enough that he was a little dirty too but Gardner knew it was unlikely he'd ever get the chance to prove it.

He stood up and went into the kitchen, returning when he heard the phone ring. He expected it to be Freeman, furious at the outcome. When he answered he was surprised to hear someone else.

Gardner arrived at Peter Hinde's house and was surprised to see him dressed and looking a lot more like his former self. He ushered Gardner into the living room and Gardner was even more surprised to see Jen Worrall sitting there.

'Take a seat,' Peter said and sat down beside Jen. The bottles had gone.

'What's going on?' Gardner asked and Jen looked to Peter.

'After our talk the other day I called Jen. I told her what you'd told me, about Walter. About Lauren.' Peter took a moment. 'I asked her what she knew and she told me about the photos, about what they showed. Made me sick. Made me realise I don't know a thing about Walter James.'

'What was in the photos, Jen?' Gardner asked, but before she could respond his phone rang. 'Hang on,' he said. He listened to Ziggy tell him he'd managed to restore the footage from the laptop and phone and felt his heart race. 'And?' he said, looking at Jen while Ziggy spoke.

'Serious shit, man,' Ziggy said. 'Walter James engaging in various sex acts. On several occasions with a clearly underage girl. You want me to pass this on to anyone?'

'No,' Gardner said. 'I'll be there shortly. Don't speak to anyone and don't let the laptop out of your sight.'

He looked at Jen who was crying now, unable to look at him. 'You knew what was happening and you let it go? For what? To make some money?'

'Detective Gardner,' Peter said. 'Please. It's not her fault.'

'She knew what he was doing and said nothing. How is that not her fault?'

'I'm sorry,' Jen said, unable to speak properly through her tears.

'Sorry?' Gardner said. 'I don't think sorry cuts it. How long had it been going on? How many have there been?'

'I don't know,' she said.

'How did you even get them?'

'I set up a camera in his office,' she said. 'I was never there at the time.'

'He did this stuff at work?'

'He doesn't care,' Jen said. 'He's so fucking arrogant. So sure of himself. He knows no one will stand up to him. No one will stop him. That's why I didn't say anything. I didn't think anyone would do anything.'

'*I* would've done something.'

'I was going to tell eventually. I was. And then Ritchie got involved. Nothing like that, nothing with the young girls, had happened before he got involved. I swear. It was other stuff. Prostitutes, but not young girls like that. But I knew I'd have to do something. I was going to send it to the papers, anonymously, just embarrass him. And then Ritchie found out and he made me keep going. When we got this stuff he said it was enough. I guess he was going to blackmail him.'

'This was what was on Ritchie's phone?'

She nodded. 'Just one picture. He was supposed to pay me,' she said, her face flushing. 'I just gave him that one picture to prove it was worth it.' She started crying again.

Gardner sighed. 'Why didn't you tell me this before, when you told me about the photos?'

Jen shook her head and wiped her face. 'I was scared,' she said. 'It had crossed my mind that maybe Mr James killed Ritchie, because of these. I didn't want him finding out they'd come from me.' She looked at Peter. 'It's my fault she's dead, isn't it?'

Peter said nothing and Jen's face crumpled. Gardner ran a hand through his hair. He could understand Jen being scared. She was a kid who'd dug herself in way too deep. He could even understand that she might think no one would believe her accusations, if that's all they were. But she'd had proof. Real evidence. And yet . . . He knew as well as anyone that in the wrong hands, evidence could be manipulated.

'I'll need a statement. From both of you.'

Peter nodded and said, 'There's something else too.'

84

Gardner watched as James was led into the interview room once again, the look of disdain still there. If it had been in different circumstances, Gardner might've felt Christmas had come late, with all he had to put to Walter. But in the end there was nothing to be happy about – three people dead and many abused girls, mostly underage. Any pleasure he might've got from bringing James down was diluted by those facts.

'We managed to get the photo from Ritchie Donoghue's phone,' Gardner said. 'Can you guess what it was?' Walter said nothing, just blinked, slowly. 'Course you can. He showed it to you, didn't he? In the car, just before you killed him.'

'Detective,' Harry interrupted, but Gardner ignored him and slid the photo across the table. The solicitor slipped his glasses on but Walter didn't move. Didn't need to. He just stared at Gardner, face impassive. Harry licked his lips and took his glasses off. 'I'd like a moment with my client,' he said.

Gardner stood to leave, stopping by the door. 'You can keep that one,' he said, nodding at the photo. 'We've got plenty more. In fact we've got everything. They're *safe* with us.' He watched Walter's face change and he knew he'd been understood. He left the room, and knowing they'd probably be a while, went to find Atherton.

'So?' Atherton said when he saw Gardner.

'He knows he's fucked,' Gardner said. 'They're in there probably trying to find a way out of it but I'd say this time he's on his own. Hadley's going to have to move on this, right? He can't brush this one under the carpet, even if he's not willing to link it to the murders.'

'I've spoken to him. I think he's panicking about his close relationship with a man who'd sleep with underage girls, how he's going to spin it. I'd say being charged with perverting the course of justice is the least of James's concerns right now.' He stood up and came around the desk to Gardner. 'Good work,' he said, slapping him on the back.

Gardner left him to it and headed back to the interview room to see if Walter wanted to talk yet, because he certainly did. Maybe he shouldn't have antagonised him, not after everything that'd happened, but Gardner felt like he might just have the upper hand for once.

After Jen Worrall had told Peter Hinde about the photos of Walter, Peter had known there'd be other things to use against his, now former, boss. He knew James had a safe at home, under the floor in the garage. He didn't know what was in there but James had referred to it before. Peter had gone to the house and spoken to Walter's wife, who'd given him access, thinking Peter was still looking out for her husband. If he'd shown her the photos he probably wouldn't have had to lie.

In the end there was nothing in there that could bring Walter down, nothing but a rather large pile of money and some more photographs. Peter had handed the photos over, thinking Gardner might want to see them as they were photos of him. And Freeman and Darren.

Gardner wondered if they were the only copies. Possibly, as they were in a safe. But regardless, he had already told most of the truth to Atherton. The photos were just something for Walter to cling to. And now he had nothing and he knew it. It was likely that he'd be charged with Donoghue's murder any day, now Hadley knew he couldn't keep protecting him.

They still didn't have proof about what had happened to Mark Healy. The prison was still insisting it was a dispute between inmates, nothing more. But it'd been Lawton who'd found the link. They'd spent hours searching for a connection between James or Cartwright and the prisoners when they should've been looking at the staff. Lawton found one prison officer, Jeff Owen, who was friends with James, and who had been investigated once before. But as the prisoner, Alan May, wasn't admitting to anything, they couldn't prove a thing. Owen was probably giving May all kinds of favours for being his little helper, and with a life sentence, May was more likely to keep taking the bonuses than to grass anyone up.

Gardner headed back to the interview room, pleased with the result, but not complacent. Even though the photos of Walter had been submitted as evidence, Gardner wondered who else was on Walter James's payroll, how far his reach stretched, whether anyone would still be willing to do him little favours or if the current situation meant people would be distancing themselves as much as possible. He wondered how likely it was that all the evidence would remain where it was supposed to. He'd taken some insurance just in case.

Walter James was done.

85

Four Weeks Later

Freeman carried another box up the stairs, dumping it in the
hallway, noticing Darren was taking another break on the
settee. She opened the box and finding a pair of Converse,
threw one in her brother's direction.

'Oi!' he said, batting the shoe away.

'Get off your arse and help,' she said and Darren huffed
before pushing past her, back out to the car.

Freeman went to the window and looked out at the sea
view, watching a few brave seagulls circle around above the
crashing waves. It made her cold just looking at it. She hadn't
found a place in Middlesbrough; she'd gone out to the coast
to Redcar instead. If she had to be on Teesside at least a sea
view would ease the change. And a two-bedroom flat above
an empty shop was within her budget. Even if having a spare
room gave Darren the idea that his stay would be more than a
brief transitional period. To be honest she didn't mind that
much. She couldn't really leave him at their parents', not with
their mam treating him like a child and bowing to his every
whim. Even Darren had got sick of it after a few days. Not to
mention their dad.

'Where's this going?' Darren said and she turned and
looked at the rocking chair he was carrying.

'Bedroom,' she said.

'Mine or yours?'

'Mine,' she said and added, 'You don't have a bedroom,' as he disappeared. She turned back to the view. Maybe this wouldn't be as bad as she thought. When she'd seen the news of Walter James's arrest, a part of her felt relieved, another still worried that the case was going to come back and bite her. She hadn't shared anything that'd gone on with her parents but had eventually told them she was transferring to Middlesbrough. Her mam had taken it as a personal affront. Freeman had let Darren tell her he was going too.

She hadn't really spoken to Gardner. But after ignoring so many calls she'd finally given in and answered one. He'd let her know he'd told Atherton most of it, and asked if she was still coming. She'd answered everything with one-syllable responses and eventually he'd taken the hint.

She felt bad about it. He'd been trying to do the right thing. And to be fair, none of this would've happened if she hadn't deleted those files, if she hadn't dragged Gardner into it in the first place. But she wished he hadn't gone behind her back.

Freeman jumped as Darren came up behind her, prodding her in the back with another box. 'Are you going to help or just stand there?' he said, joining her at the window.

'How much more is there?'

'Couple of boxes,' he said.

She nodded and kept her eyes on the sea. It wasn't the greatest view. It was partially blocked by another building and it wasn't exactly a picture-perfect beach. But it was soothing. If the window was open she could even hear the waves. She'd deliberately taken the smaller bedroom because of that. She got the feeling she might need it.

'You remember when we came here on holiday?' Darren said. 'We stayed on that crappy caravan site where the kids in the one next to us were always sitting outside picking their noses.'

Freeman smiled at the memory. She hadn't thought about that holiday in years. 'Yeah, one of them kept telling us his mam shaved their heads because they had nits.'

'Not exactly a dream holiday. But it was a laugh.'

'Remember when Mark asked us to bury him in the sand and then started crying when we ran off and left him?'

Darren started giggling. 'And then mam went mad at him for being late back and his fish fingers were all burnt. She went mental.'

Freeman laughed too until her laughter turned into tears. She turned away from Darren. 'I'll go and get the last of it,' she said.

'It'll be all right, won't it?' Darren asked.

Freeman pressed her lips together, trying to compose herself before turning back to him. When she did she smiled. 'Yeah, it'll be fine.'

Darren nodded and she went down the stairs for the last of her stuff. *Just keep telling yourself that,* she thought. *Everything will be fine.*

86

Gardner walked up the stairs carrying a plant that already looked half dead. He knocked on the door and she opened it, covered in paint and looking flustered.

'Oh,' she said.

'Hope I'm not interrupting.'

Freeman paused before shaking her head. She stepped back and let him in. 'Mind the walls. Wet paint,' she said, wiggling her fingers. She bent over and found a cloth to wipe her hands. 'How did you know where to find me?'

'Darren. He answered your phone,' Gardner said.

Freeman looked over her shoulder and Gardner noticed Darren lurking by the bedroom door, remarkably free of paint splodges. He saw Freeman give her brother a dirty look and he wondered if he'd done the right thing by coming.

'Here,' he said, handing the plant over to her. 'It's a peace lily.'

'Clever,' she said, putting it down on the kitchen worktop. The smaller package balanced on the soil slid off onto the counter but she ignored it.

Gardner cleared his throat and glanced around the flat. It was nicer than his place, even with all the boxes and decorating gear littered around. 'Nice flat,' he said.

'Thanks.'

Gardner looked to Darren, hoping he'd suddenly developed conversational skills that could help him out. But he just stood there looking as uncomfortable as Gardner felt.

'I think I'll go and get some fresh air,' Darren said and waved to Freeman as he left. Gardner rolled his eyes. He wanted Darren to talk, not leave.

'So,' Gardner said when it was just the two of them. 'I'm looking forward to Monday. It'll be great having you there. Save me from the dual horrors of Harrington and Murphy. At least there'll be someone normal on the team.'

'Can we not?' Freeman said and sighed. 'Thanks for the housewarming gift but . . . I think we should just stop whatever this is.'

'I don't—' Gardner started.

'You're going to be my boss.'

Gardner looked at the floor. 'I know that. I'm not here to try and . . . I just wanted to know things are all right between us. That we're friends.'

'Are we?' she said. 'We worked together once. We maybe almost went out. And then you lied to me. So no, I don't think we're friends.'

'I didn't lie to you.'

'You told me you were going to drop it. I made a deal with that wanker and you just ploughed on with your vendetta, regardless of what happened to me or Darren.'

'I was doing my job. Walter James killed a man. Two if you count Healy. He allowed his daughter to be killed. He's a paedophile. How could I let him walk away from that? You really think I should've just let it go?'

'No,' she said, sighing. 'Maybe you're right. Maybe we *both* should've gone after him.'

'So what's the problem?' Gardner asked. 'It worked out, didn't it?'

'So far. But what if that changes?'

'No one's going to believe Walter James or Craig Cartwright. No one. Hadley's washed his hands of them.'

'But we still have to work together and I don't know if I can trust you. And I'm pretty sure you don't trust me. You thought I'd set Healy up.'

'But—'

'Look, I know you did it for the right reasons. I get that. I do. But in the end I don't know that I can trust you.'

Gardner stepped forward but she moved away. 'You can trust me,' he said.

'Well, we'll see, won't we?' she said.

'Nicola . . .'

Gardner stopped talking as Darren came back in. 'Should I, like, go again?' he said.

'No,' Gardner and Freeman said at the same time.

'Okay,' Darren said and sloped off into one of the bedrooms.

'You *can* trust me,' Gardner said again before turning to leave. He stopped by the front door, hoping that she'd come after him. As he opened the door she appeared in the hallway and he paused, his hand on the door.

Freeman stood there as if she was going to say something, her eyes filled with sadness. Her mouth opened slightly but then she bent down and picked up her paintbrush.

'I'll see you on Monday then,' Gardner said and closed the door behind him.

Freeman felt bad for not accepting the apology but she was still pissed off. Maybe in time it would seem less important but at the moment it was everything.

She looked at the peace lily he'd brought which she'd dumped in the kitchen. As gestures went it was kind of cool. She picked it up, wondering if it needed watering, wondering how long she'd be able to keep it alive, and noticed the smaller package.

She picked it up and unwrapped it. Inside was a USB stick wrapped in a note. She took it to the table and dug out her laptop from under a pile of discarded bubble wrap. She plugged it in and read the note while she waited for it to wake up.

Freeman,
  Thought this might be safer with you. If it comes to it, do what you want with it. It's your call.
  Gardner

Freeman frowned and looked up as the images started to appear on her screen. She winced as she caught sight of the first photo of Walter James and closed the laptop. She'd seen enough to get the picture.

She smiled. A peace lily was just the beginning.

ACKNOWLEDGMENTS

Thanks to everyone who helped make this book happen, especially:

The brilliant team at Hodder and Mulholland, in particular my fantastic editor Ruth Tross, publicist Becca Mundy, and copy editor Amber Burlinson.

My agent, Stan.

Jen Worrall for letting me name a character after her via the Authors for Philippines online auction (and thanks to Stephen Morris for the bid).

My family – Mam, Dad, Donna, Jonathan, Christine and Maria.

Cotton and Abbey for taking me for walks to clear my head.

And Stephen, as always, for keeping me sane and putting up with everything that goes with getting ideas from brain to book.

Also by Rebecca Muddiman

GONE

Troubled teenager Emma Thorley vanished
without a trace eleven years ago.

But now a body has been found...

As news of the discovery travels, the past comes
back to haunt all those involved, from the
police to Emma's friends and enemies.

Because some secrets cannot be buried for ever...
and some dangers never go away.

Available in paperback and ebook now.

MULHOLLAND
BOOKS
HODDER